# Father Figure

# Contents

Amalia's arm grazed the wall when stumbling from the kitchen into the dark mudroom. Dingy white paint chips rained to the floor and clung to her favorite new red blouse while passing through the dilapidated archway. She cradled her elbow, flicked off the last few flakes of her mother's venom, and firmly held her ground. "It's not fair. You let Greg hang out with his friends all the time."

"Leave your brother out of this conversation. Your responsibility belongs first to this family and then to the hardware store. Who said anything about friends? Now get yourself off to practice." Janet's one good eye stubbornly left behind after diabetes stole the vision in her other glared while Amalia reluctantly marched toward the back door. "You're a spiteful little child."

"I'm taking out the trash, Momma." Her voice carried the defeat of a soul unable to find the words or summon the strength to defend herself anymore. As she leaned over, the scoop neck on Amalia's blouse revealed the slightest hint of cleavage between her ample breasts.

"Stop right now. What are you wearing?" Janet's tone lingered thick over such insubordination. A special brand of disdain had been developed by watching her daddy preach to his Southern Baptist congregation for nearly forty years before he anxiously married her off to Amalia's father.

"It's just a pretty shirt I found at a yard sale. I'm not showing too much skin." Amalia dropped the trash bag on the mudroom's gray linoleum and recalled the similar, previous lectures. She refused to turn around to face the woman. "I'm not a child anymore, Momma."

Janet stampeded through the kitchen and kicked the garbage into the far corner. Though the vinyl flooring had peeled away from the walls as the house settled, it was still not one of the more noticeable improvements desperately needed in their home. "It's lesson time, girl."

Amalia yelped and dashed to safety after a cast iron frying pan full of hot grease collided with bare skin on the back of her arm. "No, Momma, please..." She dropped to her knees, scooted across the mudroom floor, and cowered behind the pantry door to protect herself from any further blows. An acrid burnt plastic odor from a fiery singe on the linoleum beneath her wafted through the air as she shuddered in pain. The nerves in her forearm and elbow convulsed when the wound began to blister from the impact of her mother's lesson.

"Someday you'll learn how to behave yourself." Janet grudgingly placed the frying pan on the washing machine and lifted Amalia by the curls of her hair. She tightly squeezed her daughter's breasts while trying to raise the blouse over Amalia's head. "I don't know where you got these girls from. You're hoping to entice all the boys to put their dirty little hands where they don't belong."

Amalia pushed away her mother's sticky fingers willing to risk more punishment if she kept them off her trembling body. The putrid smell of Janet's three-day-old sweat and decaying teeth littered the air between their lips. "Leave it. I've got a bra on underneath to keep them strapped down. I know the rules."

Amalia's breasts had begun to develop when she turned eleven years old. By thirteen, a custom-size bra was bought to contain them. Dresses were never allowed given the attention they'd drawn to her body's hourglass shape. Though Janet's words were enough of a rebuke, reduction surgery was still threatened should Amalia's breasts grow any larger.

"I pray every night for them to stop getting bigger and for God to teach you some morals. It's like you're rubbing my great Aunt Tilly's rose garden's Miracle Grow on those dirty pillows. Tramps like you get themselves into some mighty trouble when they don't protect their bodies." Janet stomped back to the kitchen with the now-emptied frying pan and quickly snapped her fingers. "Cover yourself up or forget about going away to college this summer."

"Yes, Momma." Amalia heaved herself from the floor with the help of the door handle and collected the remains of her veiled dignity.

"And put out the trash already. It smells like a sewer in here," snickered Janet.

Fighting back the tears brimming on the surface of her weary eyes, Amalia sighed with relief upon noticing the frying oil hadn't ruined her blouse. In a rush to tend to her wounds while running through the living room and up the flight of stairs, Amalia crashed into her father, Peter. At sixty, he'd settled into a grandfatherly presence, contented by a quiet and ordinary life. He'd aged quickly in the Graeme household. Everyone did.

"Daddy, I'm so sorry. I was…" Amalia hugged her father, rested her head against his narrow chest, and listened to his enfeebled lungs wheeze with exertion.

Peter fell toward the wall and knocked over the family portrait they'd photographed during Greg's high school graduation. "Oh, my pet, what's wrong?" He pulled Amalia closer with one hand and adjusted the brass picture frame with the other. A thin layer of ashen skin failed to cover years of misery being married to Janet. He'd long-accepted divorce would never be permitted by the daughter of a Baptist preacher and that his life would be fraught with reproach. "Did you have another squabble with your mother?"

Amalia sniffled and concealed her burns, desperate to splash cold water on the pain. "She hates me, Daddy. Momma never loved me the way she loves Greg."

"That's not true, honey. She's tougher because you're leaving later this month." Peter brushed away a few loose curls from Amalia's face and smiled with a fatherly love that hadn't receded over the years. "What happened this time?"

A cherubic expression brightened her pale face with the hope he would understand but disappeared once she remembered begging had never helped before. "I asked if I could go to the lake today with the rest of the softball team for Brant's town fair, but Momma says I have to work at the store like I do every other day."

The population of their hometown, Brant, Mississippi, founded in 1784, hovered around five hundred inhabitants, the majority born and raised in the surrounding isolation. The Graeme family, still considered outsiders, had arrived in the mid-1800s settling about a half mile from Lake Newton—the livelihood once used to transport goods to the neighboring settlements. Over the years, as the county paved new roads to share crops more efficiently among all the nearby villages, the lake became a gathering place for the local families and visitors to enjoy each summer. Store owners had organized a bicentennial celebration for the upcoming weekend where all the citizens would barbecue ribs, hold square dancing lessons, and play various outdoor games. Amalia looked forward to it every year believing she always had the chance to find a new friend who might make the rough days pass by a little easier.

"Your momma knows best, honey. We need to be available for our customers." Every penny was important to Janet Graeme, especially with two kids attending college—they could never close the store early. Janet often reminded them how pitching in around the house or store was impossible on account of her many illnesses. Peter nudged Amalia away and kissed her cheek. "You can leave work early to meet your teammates at tomorrow's picnic. Will that make you happy?"

"It helps, but I'll be the only one not going tonight." Amalia buried her flushed cheeks into the crook of his left arm. He always smelled of Old Spice. She'd bought him the same cologne for Father's Day every year since shopping on her own.

If Peter noticed the stinging red color or the slight favor of her left arm, he either ignored it or thought she'd injured herself in a recent softball game. He adhered to an insulated belief that his wife's normal way of parenting didn't include hurting or abusing their daughter. It wasn't the first time he'd misjudged a situation. Peter once took Amalia to a movie theatre as an early birthday present telling Janet they'd stayed behind at the store to count inventory and order stock, but she found a few popcorn kernels on the floor of the family Dodge the next morning while driving to church. Janet waited until Amalia arrived home from school later that week to teach her daughter a lesson about lying. Though Amalia had only been trying to catch a schoolboy's attention by lightening the color of her hair with lemon juice, it was a vengeful wrath she'd unexpectedly invited as Janet took a pair of shearing scissors to her daughter's golden mane. The emotional scars from an abusive home life were profound, but Amalia never regretted sneaking off to watch the movie. She was proud of being a daddy's girl. He was her hero, the father she'd always treasure, the man who made it easier being the daughter of the wicked Janet Graeme.

Peter patted Amalia's back offering any chance to ease her disillusion. "I know, but tomorrow when you go to the lake, everything will be back on track. Bring some clothes to change into so you don't have to come back home in between. Do you understand what I'm saying?"

"I can't wait. I love you, Daddy." She hugged him again and raced up the stairs to change her shirt before her mother had another outburst. Amalia applied cream to her wounds, then chose a long-sleeve button-down sweater she fastened two inches above the dip in her neck. After checking the mirror and wishing a bit of foundation could hide the uneven colors, she splashed water on her face to erase the evidence of her pain. One of Janet's more ridiculous judgments echoed among Amalia's numbed thoughts. '*Only the vile women in this town wear makeup!*'

Amalia flew back down the stairs and searched for the trash bag she'd left behind, realizing it would mean another lashing if her mother had stumbled upon it first. As she rushed into the living room, her father handed her a banana and elbowed her out the front door. "I already put it in the outside bin. Get to softball practice, my pet." His voice barely audible, his expression as loud as a parade.

Amalia smiled and released an uncontrollable giggle as her countenance relaxed for the first time that morning. Although the tense nerves in her neck retreated into partial hiding, her body remained hypervigilant and always waited for the next blistery strike from her mother. She left the house flickering with excitement for the town's festivities over the weekend but frightened at what her teammates would say about her missing the lake party. No one ever declined their much sought-after invitations without hazardous repercussions.

Although she'd graduated high school two months earlier, Amalia continued playing in the county's summer tournaments to keep her pitching skills primed for college games. Risking a loss of the unexpectedly received scholarship—as it was the only reason she could afford to go away to school—was not an option. After practice, where she conveniently forgot to tell her teammates about missing the upcoming lake party, Amalia worked side-by-side with her father for a few hours and avoided any further trouble with her mother at home. Once Amalia climbed into bed that evening exhausted from an emotionally and physically grueling afternoon, she drifted asleep clutching her pillow and wished things would somehow improve the next day.

* * *

The following morning, Janet took the family's only car to the First Baptist's services leaving Amalia and Peter to trudge the two-mile distance to the center of town. Graeme Hardware Store was part of the town's original train depot when first built in the mid-nineteenth century. Shortly before World War I, the train line was rerouted to a larger city a few miles away. This prompted Brant's town council to vote in favor of converting the train depot into a lunch café and expanding the footprints of local shops hoping it would draw more income from surrounding villages. Losing the train station left Graeme Hardware Store with far fewer customers managing barely enough to keep afloat during a good year.

Peter unlocked the store and began his morning routine to review the previous day's sales and prepare the inventory. While he dragged a rolling stand filled with buckets of nails and screws to the exterior porch of the store, Amalia brewed a fresh pot of strong coffee. She retrieved a starter till from the safe under the desk and counted a hundred dollars in small bills and coins, then placed it in the cash register atop the laminate countertop. She grabbed a few dollars to buy breakfast from the local café and strolled to the front of the store. The sharp clank of the bell loosely hung by a nylon cord on the door bounced off all the metal tools and reverberated throughout the building. Amalia held the outer screen door to prevent it from slamming shut and made a mental note to convince her father to repair the hinge that afternoon.

Customers didn't appreciate buying tools from a hardware store with a broken front door.

"I'll be right back, Daddy." Amalia bounded down three short steps and traveled the building's main wooden pathway. Frustrated by the inability to meet the girls from the softball team the prior night, Amalia recoiled at how much of an encumbrance Brant had become to her over the years. She often daydreamed of leaving it all behind but remembered no one had ever escaped. She scoffed at her emotions, slid her fingers across the pathway's splintered handrails, and ignored the desire to run deep into the woods.

When she reached the entrance to the café, a familiar voice called out to her from the parking lot. It was deep, full of confidence and strength—a tone rarely heard in Brant most days. "Is that you, Amalia?"

She turned and recognized her older brother's high school best friend approaching the pathway. "Bryan, how's it going?" Amalia leaned in to hug him, keenly aware of the temperature changing in the surrounding air. "I haven't seen you in forever." As his arm curled around her back, Amalia breathed in his masculine woodsy scent, surprised by a palpable force settling inside her body. The season's harsh sun had tanned his skin a few shades darker. It looked good on him.

"I'm doing okay. How's Greg?" Bryan's cerulean blue eyes peered directly into hers and connected to her thoughts as if he sensed what was happening inside her body before she did.

"You look fantastic, B-Balls." Amalia's bashful lips curled upward as the words escaped. The three of them had played hoops every Sunday when Bryan visited the Graeme's house after church. Amalia had once thrown a basketball directly at him during a game of *H-O-R-S-E*, but the ball smacked him in his crotch. He kept repeating '*My balls are swollen*' all day—his eyes wincing, earning the name, B-Balls. "Greg comes home next week. He's still packing up his apartment."

"That's great. I can't believe it's already been four years since he left for college." Bryan stretched against the pole next to her, his bright white high-tops scraping the walkway beneath him.

Amalia scanned the full length of Bryan's body for the first time—he'd grown taller since they last swam together at Lake Newton. A few extra inches of muscles adorned his arms and chest stretching his shoulders apart wider than before. His tight-fitting Levi's made it exceedingly difficult to ignore the way the jeans selfishly hugged his thighs and butt.

As Amalia settled her elbows on the wooden handrail, the top button on her blouse pulled apart. Bryan's gaze dropped a few inches then quickly shot back up as if he didn't want her to notice him focusing on her chest. She fantasized he'd grown attracted to her in those last few seconds. A temptation to leave the button open intensified. Her fingers decided before her brain processed what was happening and refastened the loop on their own accord. "Yep, it's been a long time. You look good. Exercising has paid off."

"You, too. I mean, you look great, too. Different." Bryan's voice hesitated before he shoved both hands in his pockets. "Older. You've grown up a lot is what I meant to say. Umm, yeah, so what've you been up to?" His attention darted to a patch of grass beyond Amalia where a small pot of daffodils sat in the dirt, besieging someone to admire or care for them.

Amalia shrugged and ran her fingers through her hair. "Just finished high school in June. I visited Greg last year at college and thought it would be a potential place to escape Brant. I'm so excited they accepted me!"

Bryan leaned forward and flicked off a small bug from her arm. His fingers lingered longer than either of them had expected. "Congratulations. Brant isn't so bad, is it?"

Amalia's body flushed. Within seconds, the ant was gone, and Bryan retreated while tucking his hands back into his pockets. His cool skin had been a refreshing welcome to her body. "Yeah, it is, especially with Greg living away for so many years. Things at home are awful, but I'll be out of this pitiful place soon enough."

"You're a bit harsh, but I guess I understand wanting to get away." Bryan cocked his head as if he'd recognized something new or different. "Were your eyes always as green as emeralds? I don't remember that about you."

Amalia tossed her hair to the opposite side considering this might be his way of flirting. She wouldn't mind if it were true. She'd been waiting for the infamous first crush to finally make its way to her. "Yes, but they've gotten a deeper shade the last few years. I wish I had the whole blonde and blue thing." When Bryan smiled, his dimples drew attention to a strong jawline. Amalia blinked hard after staring at him for far too long.

"No, they're the perfect color for your complexion. They're sparkling at me." Bryan cupped his hands together to crack his knuckles and stretch his fingers. "So… are you going to the picnic at Lake Newton this afternoon?"

His voice reminded Amalia of the rich tone her clarinet made when she'd taken lessons years ago before her mother twisted one of the register keys and cracked the mouthpiece, leaving it broken beyond repair. Its echo resonated inside Amalia's body as Bryan fidgeted with his belt buckle. "Yes, Daddy told me I could leave mid-afternoon. I can't wait to smell the jasmine and take a boat ride under the bridge."

Amalia blushed with excitement that Bryan might attend the picnic with her to share a canoe on the lake. It wouldn't be a date. She wasn't allowed to go on a date until her eighteenth birthday, which wasn't for nearly two months. Bryan was also her brother's best friend. He'd laughed at her when she spilled pasta all over herself at dinner calling her a little piglet ever since she was six years old.

"I was gonna meet some friends later tonight. How about you and I meet up beforehand? Three o'clock at the magnolia tree by the statue of Old Man Newton. Wanna come?"

When a tattoo peeked from beneath the edge of Bryan's black V-neck t-shirt, Amalia suppressed a desire to thrust her hands on him. "Yes, I'd love to." She answered too quickly, but something foreign had pushed the words from her mouth without consent. What if Bryan sensed her all-too-excited tone? She tried to downplay her interest and fiddled with her shirtsleeves. "I mean, sure, that would be cool. If I get out of work in time, I'll try to meet you there."

"Definitely." Bryan leaned in with vigorous enthusiasm. "It would be great to hang out if you can make it."

The wind carried the scent of cinnamon-flavored breakfast rolls across the pathway luring Amalia's hunger to the surface. She and Bryan gazed intently at each other until Amalia's fragile mind reminded her to leave before saying anything stupid. "I should get back to the hardware store. Maybe I'll see you later." She walked up the last step and twisted toward him. "Thanks, B-Balls." A tiny snicker slipped through her shaky lips. Uncertainty lingered over the cause, either remembering Bryan crying about the ball smacking him or at herself for the sudden unabashed enthusiasm he brought to her today. Either case, she wanted to be near him again.

"Cool." Bryan stepped backward nearly tripping over the corner post. He turned around, waved goodbye, and paraded across the parking lot with a confident stride.

After Bryan's silhouette vanished, Amalia wished for the courage to call him back. She was afraid of behaving like an impulsive child when he was four years older than her, a boy who surely had much more experience than she offered. She tried to keep herself from glowing and quickly headed to the café to order breakfast. Drawing in a deep breath, Amalia imagined reasons why Bryan might be interested but also worried he was just a good family friend. What surprised her the most was a lasting impression that a few more weeks in Brant might not be such an unwelcome prison.

Chapter 2

# Brianna, June 2004

Brianna's animated, full lips raced as she linked arms with her best friend, Shanelle, and circled the northwest corner of the campus quad. They'd been on a final tour before deciding which college Brianna would attend that fall. "This place is fantastic. Did you see those locker rooms? To die for!" Her almond-shaped eyes opened wide and bright upon visualizing the first true separation from her hometown since birth. *Was it possible to be afraid of and thrilled over something at the same time?*

"Be careful!" Shanelle yanked Brianna backward before crashing into the security alert call box. "It's like you're in a trance right now."

Wisps of shoulder-length auburn locks covered Brianna's face when a few gusts of wind blew through the meandering pathways. She stopped near the entrance of a small, newly sod-laden area filled with ornate wrought iron benches and old-fashioned black lamp posts. "I belong here."

"You need to come with me to Woodland College in a couple of months. It's unreal." Shanelle adjusted the collar of her white polo and tossed dark black curls a few inches off the flawless, smooth skin on her forehead. "We'd finally escape, Bree."

Shanelle was the only person who could call her Bree. Shanelle's tone offered intimacy unlike the sarcastic high-society ladies who sniped at Brianna when she once worked as a hostess back home in

*15*

one of New York City's Upper East Side clubs. *'That's not what I ordered, Bree. Can't you people get anything right?'*

Brianna sighed while soaking in a panoramic view of the Pennsylvania landscape. Woodland's homes had an abundance of old cedar swings strung from willow trees, smelled of honeysuckle, and suggested the opportunity for true independence. "It's pretty amazing. I love *The Big Apple*, but it's time for a change. I need to get the hell away from all the clamor and crazy drama back home." Brianna had been raised in an apartment several floors above a jazz club that jammed until four o'clock every morning. Though the music was intoxicating, dealing with the constant flood of smarmy denizens and their disgusting catcalls had become tiresome over the years.

"So, what's your verdict?"

"I guess I have to choose soon, don't I?" Brianna had spoken with her mother ad nauseam all spring about selecting a college, but she kept holding off on making a final decision since revealing the truth would be too difficult.

Shanelle nodded and fixed a kink in the chain on the ruby necklace hugging the curves of Brianna's neck. She'd given it to her for Christmas the previous year and admired how it added the perfect amount of color to Brianna's heart-shaped face. "Late admission acceptances are due at noon tomorrow. You already missed all the first-round deadlines. Your mother must be freaking out that you haven't settled on a school."

Despite having a strong relationship trusting and supporting one another over the years, Brianna's mother tended to control her daughter's freedom to make her own choices. The resulting pressures of jumping into adulthood with minimal life experiences had begun to paralyze Brianna to the point of desperation and instability. It was especially arduous given no father—or any other relative—was present to offset the balance in their tiny, two-person family unit, nor were the reasons for their non-existence anything Brianna had understood. Questions frequently floated throughout her mind about her missing parent, complex personality traits, and inherent lack of confidence.

The vacuum she lived in compelled her to wonder if there were other family members like her who might have found ways to avoid depression and unearth a ray of hope that their future could be different. Brianna ultimately traced her indecisiveness and lack of comfort within her own skin to an all-consuming need to discover the identity of her father. If he'd been around, despite knowing nothing about him, she was positive her situation would be better. Fathers always protected their little girls and showered them with love.

"I told her we needed to open your family's summer house." Brianna stretched her calves lifting her legs one after the other on the nearest bench. A slight moan escaped her lips as though she'd stumbled upon a secret stash of much-desired milk chocolate hidden in the closet. It was the only dessert the coach allowed during soccer season, but when Brianna needed a piece, there was no hampering the craving. "An overnight trip since school's practically over."

"She bought it?" Shanelle reached for Brianna's leg and rubbed the overworked muscles below her knees. "Lower your waist and stretch your hamstrings."

"Yeah, she had to work late, anyway. Second quarter tax reports due to her boss on Monday." Brianna's mother earned a certain satisfaction from her job, but she'd also been working excessive overtime the last few years. *'You've got college payments. Money doesn't grow on trees!'* Brianna often used their financial limitations as an opportunity to pry further into history by questioning if there was family money or potential future inheritances. She'd been brushed off at every opportunity to learn anything of substance given the impenetrable wall her mother had built around the past. "How much time before we catch the train home?"

"Thirty minutes. At least we don't have to drive the entire day. I did that last time with the 'rents when they made it a family trip. It wrecked me." Shanelle's father, Dr. William Trudeau, a well-respected African American geneticist in one of New York City's top research facilities, and her mother, Maria Allende Trudeau, the first Latina partner in a prestigious law firm, had taken a few days off to accompany their daughter's initial college visits. Shanelle luckily escaped without them on this jaunt by kidnapping Brianna in a last-minute attempt to convince her best friend to choose the same school. A close cousin in the family had graduated the year before and paved the way for Shanelle to follow suit to Woodland College on a full scholarship.

"At least you've got that huge townhouse, and your parents leave you alone to do your own thing. Try cohabitating in a small box with a mother who's always in your business."

"She's a dog with a bone, but I know you adore her." Shanelle knelt on the grass and inched her fingers above Brianna's knee massaging the back of her thigh. "Relax, this will help."

Brianna concentrated on the pleasure and let Shanelle's hands work their magic on her sore legs. They'd run a few extra miles that morning before the campus tour started, unable to practice any other time during the trip for the final soccer championship game back home. "That feels amazing."

"I told you it would help, Bree. If you'd only let me..."

"Thanks, but we should quit dawdling." Brianna jerked her leg away and adjusted her navy blue capri pants after they'd twisted halfway around during the unexpected and almost too intimate massage. "I still need to finalize a few plans for tomorrow's prom."

Shanelle navigated the pathway toward the main intersection leaving Brianna to retie her laces and fuss over her concerns about the dance. "I can't believe you're going with that primitive ape."

"You've made your point already. Let it go."

Brianna waffled in an on-again, off-again relationship with Doug, the star player of her school's basketball team, who thought it was acceptable on their first date to complain when she wouldn't let him grope her in the dark at the movies. When he'd asked her to prom a few weeks earlier, she'd been having a difficult day with the soccer coach and unwittingly agreed to attend the dance with Doug. Though she'd contemplated canceling, it would have been harder to find another date with little notice. It was also far more intimidating to consider the tempting path of showing up with Shanelle as her plus one.

As Brianna pulled her hair into a ponytail and wrapped it with a butterfly clip at the base of her neck, Shanelle snapped a photo. "You look more relaxed and sexier with your hair loose."

Brianna ignored the compliment, eager to change the subject. "I'm glad I came to Woodland today. It's helping me make a decision." She caught up to Shanelle as they approached the end of the pathway.

"About us?" Shanelle smiled with affection in Brianna's direction, then tilted her head toward a blaring noise in the distance.

A car speeding at least twenty mph over the limit revved its engine while driving down the nearby hill. The tour guide had told them earlier it was normal for students to drag race on the outskirts of campus. Brianna, preoccupied with the car's approach, hadn't heard Shanelle's question and kept walking. "I'm sorry, what did you say?" She glanced sideways, oblivious the vehicle wasn't slowing down as it advanced to the intersection.

"Never mind. Don't get too close to the curb, Bree. That idiot isn't paying attention."

Brianna focused on the driver who was ignorant to the flashing red light less than a hundred feet away from his sleek white convertible. "He's staring like I'm dessert later tonight. What the hell?" Offended by his leer, Brianna squinted and guffawed. "What are you looking at, creepy asshole?" She lifted her arm and twisted a hand around while raising her middle finger.

"Watch out!" Shanelle stopped Brianna from entering the crosswalk. As she fell backward, Brianna temporarily lost her breath from the forceful grip.

The driver plowed through the intersection until he finally broke from his stupor turning the wheel too far to the left and skidding off the pavement onto the curb. Within seconds, his car crashed into the corner of the alumni building thirty feet from where they stood. The screeching twang of metal colliding with brick penetrated their eardrums as the whole incident unfolded.

Brianna rushed to help, but Shanelle's determined hands held her back. "No! I'm calling 911. The car could catch fire. Don't get close to it."

Within seconds, one of the campus patrol cars parked a few feet away, and a security guard dashed over to pull the driver from the wreckage. An older woman with a Middle Eastern accent and a spiky silver hairdo ran from the Alumni House veranda, gesturing and yelling in hysterics. "There's someone in the passenger seat, too. Help him!"

"We should do something," Brianna pleaded with Shanelle as the county police cruiser slammed on its brakes. Its blasting sirens pierced every cell of her body as though she were the victim being tossed around in the convertible. Brianna wiped her hands on her pants pockets and flicked off the residue from the dirty ground. "Shouldn't we?"

"They have it under control. Do you want to stick around and risk missing our train home?" Shanelle firmly held Brianna's trembling hand to allay her nerves and shock.

Brianna paced the corner while considering her options. If she stuck around, a police report would need to be filled out, but all she could add to the summary was that he'd been intently ogling her from a distance. The driver didn't hit anyone or another car, and there were other witnesses to the accident who could give all the details. If Brianna missed the last train, she'd arrive home late forced to explain to her mother the true purpose of the last two days. "I guess we can leave."

"They're already getting help, the ambulance just arrived." Shanelle linked their elbows together and rested her head against Brianna's shoulder. "Come on, there's another bus stop on the opposite side of campus."

"Thanks. I'm so glad you were here with me. I would've flipped on my own."

Shanelle hugged Brianna and kissed her cheek as they separated. "You'll always have me. Don't forget that."

\* \* \*

After taking a shuttle bus from Woodland to Pittsburgh, they boarded the long-distance Amtrak train ready for their half-day trip home to New York City. Shanelle sank into a window seat of the business class car insistent on paying for the upgrade. She'd often sprung for their excursions, enjoying luxury items, especially when she experienced them before anyone else. Life was a competition among the six siblings in the Trudeau family, and Shanelle rarely let anyone else win.

The conductor checked their tickets before traipsing through the aisle. "Thanks, ladies. Let me know if you need anything. Happy to help you out." A raunchy combination of day-old chowder and weed poured from his skin, leaving both girls wanting to retch.

Shanelle brushed him off, then rested her soothing hand on Brianna's as the train departed the station. "Are you doing any better, babe?"

"All this indecision just makes me recognize how tired I am of being alone and confused." Brianna opened her purse and checked her image in a compact mirror. Her reflection displayed an unknown figure with dysfunctional personalities haphazardly glued together in the most twisted ways. Every time she made progress in understanding something about herself, two more issues, concerns, or fears to address popped up. She eventually gave up and cast herself as merely just another lost member of society trying to conjure a hidden self-confidence without life's necessary instruction booklet. "When will it be my turn to catch a break?"

"We all worry about those things sometimes." Shanelle slid further into the seat and fiddled with the controls until the cushion's angle suited her preference. "You'll find the answers soon... but until then, I've got your back, hon."

"No doubt." Brianna reapplied lipstick and smoothed out her flushed cheeks before snuggling against Shanelle. "I turned my phone off. I don't want any interruptions while we talk."

Shanelle lifted her head a few inches away from the pillow on the seatback. "You said you made a decision about us earlier. I knew you'd come around to believing me." Shanelle spent most of her time trying to convince anyone in her immediate circle to accept that her advice was necessary and prudent. Pressuring people had always been the approach worn on the exterior of her heart like a badge of honor when she selected you as a friend. If chosen, your life was bound to improve. Brianna still hadn't been convinced of that result.

"No. I said I made *a decision*. About college." Brianna dropped her purse to the train floor and focused on the magazines tucked into the seat pocket. A *Welcome to Pittsburgh* catalog with a dog-eared upper right corner halfway through its pages caught her attention. She flipped through the magazine and found an article entitled '*Are You Ready for a New Life?*' She believed in signs. This had to be one of them. "The only problem is that escaping my mother was never an option during our negotiations about where I should attend school."

Brianna wasn't sure how to tell her mother she didn't want to stay in New York for college, which was the plan they'd originally agreed on. Besides a handful of tenants in their ancient six-story brick tenement, Brianna's mother had only ever interacted with a few accounting colleagues in her downtown office. The woman's irrational fears and helicopter parenting had prevented Brianna from ever leaving the city in the past. She'd gotten permission for a few class trips upstate to Kykuit, the Rockefeller Mansion, and on the subway to Queens with Shanelle's family for the US Open. Even then, Brianna's mother had insisted on check-in phone calls every two hours to verify nothing bad happened along the way. While Brianna loved her mother, sometimes the pressure was claustrophobic.

"Maybe she'll surprise you this time. You never know," said Shanelle.

Brianna savored the pastoral landscape as endless farms and charming small towns passed by the narrow window. An unquenchable thirst for exposure to something different obliged her to experience the rest of the world before becoming too jaded about life from a major metropolitan's perspective—always fast-paced, constantly dirty, and a sense of falling behind schedule before you even started the day. While she wasn't quite ready to move cross-country, knowing Woodland College was just two states away comforted Brianna in a way that made leaving home easier. It also happened to be where her best friend would attend school despite Shanelle being one of the more *complicated* parts of life she'd struggled to understand. "I'm worried about her being all alone."

"Your mother might want the apartment to herself to entertain *gentlemen callers*. I wonder when she last got laid." Shanelle rumbled at her words always amused by her humor and reactions to her friend's comical home life.

"Like I know. That's nasty. I don't want to think about it. Do you ask your parents that question?"

"I'm just sayin'. Has your mother ever gone out on a date? I've known you for two years and not once can I remember her going out with a man. Maybe she's also a secret—"

"Shut up. Not everyone is out-and-proud like you, Shanelle. We all haven't craved tits and vaginas since we were babies. I mean, seriously… when did you come out of the closet, two years old?"

"I told my mother in the third grade. She'd always known I'd be her smartest child."

"Because you're gay?"

"No, when they pulled me away from her the day I was born, I went right for the nurse's boobs, grabbing them as if I already knew what I was doing. My mother told my father that night— *This last kid is gonna play by a whole different set of rules.*"

Brianna punched her best friend in the leg. "You're so ridiculous. All newborns do that. You make up those stories. I bet your mother would say you're lying."

Shanelle tossed her phone across the seat. "Call her right now."

"I'm not calling your mother to ask if you grabbed the nurse's tits."

"Not that, you psycho. Call your mother. Tell her you've decided."

"About Woodland?" The timbre in Brianna's voice grew sharper. Telling her mother about losing a soccer game was tough. Explaining the 'C' on the algebra quiz after having spent hours studying together was painful. Revealing a desperate need to leave New York would mimic a disaster of epic proportions. The dust wouldn't settle for years.

"Yes, why do you keep asking me? You've made it perfectly clear you haven't decided if you want to be my girlfriend. I'll keep my cookies to myself until you want some milk to go along with them."

"Shhh, not so loud. I told you. I don't know if I'm into girls in that way. I need more time."

Shanelle shifted the seatback upright and pushed Brianna off her shoulder. "I know very few things I consider facts. I know my father would do anything for me. I know Venus was robbed in that last tournament. Serena did *not* deserve to win after that lazy performance. She got lucky." Shanelle reached for Brianna's chin and gazed directly into her eyes. "And I know you're a lesbian. A big one who wants to get all up in..." Shanelle practically screamed the last line until the rough bounce from the train shifting tracks pushed their lips a few inches closer.

Brianna stared into Shanelle's eyes lost in the richness of their color. She lifted her hand to the back of Shanelle's neck, running her fingers through her best friend's hair and breathing in her vanilla scent. "When the light hits you this way, I swear you're the most beautiful girl I've ever seen."

"You're tempting me to kiss you, Bree. I can't be the only one excited by this attraction. The glow of your skin. My quickening pulse. Your eyes have completely betrayed your thoughts. You don't want me to stop, do you?"

Only the smallest bit of attainable distance separated Brianna's lips from a pleasure she wanted to experience. "Maybe I don't."

"Then let me show you my world." Shanelle locked on to Brianna with a powerful force that had zero intention of ever letting go. One of the two girls clearly knew what she wanted.

Brianna's fingers grazed Shanelle's forearm, tantalized by the smooth curves in the nook of her elbow. "Your skin feels so soft." She traced the outline of Shanelle's muscular arm all the way to the dip between her neck and shoulder.

"I promise I'll treat you right." Shanelle nuzzled against Brianna's neck, their ears tickling one another with an unparalleled electric pulse brewing from each brush.

A loud gasp of forced air poured into the room when the train doors suddenly opened, followed by the conductor's nasally voice. "Dining car opens in ten minutes. Two doors back." He slogged through the entire space in less than ten seconds, though it was too long for Brianna who struggled to hold on to the moment.

Whatever had been building between them evaporated upon noticing the searing glare from the sourpuss across the aisle monitoring their every move. An older lady with bluish-gray hair and beady eyes filled with obvious contempt turned her head intent on chastising them. The perfectly round 'O' between her lips released a condescending huff, and her pupils burrowed deep into a bigoted space inside her head that lacked a sense of humor. Although society had become more accepting of homosexuality, teenage girls having a raucous conversation on a train about being in love would not easily be tolerated. Once you added in the bi-racial factor, it would undoubtedly be a double whammy to overcome in the future. It wasn't something Brianna had the strength to deal with at that moment.

Shanelle tore open a bag of M&Ms and selected a brown one, holding it between her fingers for the old woman's benefit. "You need some chocolate to fill that pie hole, ma'am? I'm a good shot. I could pitch this whole bag in that droopy wrinkle sack you call a face. It is people like you who—"

As Shanelle twisted her hand and readied her arm to toss the candy across the aisle, Brianna grabbed her by the wrist and whispered, "Would you stop? Seriously. You need to give me a little time to figure this out. You're my best friend, but I don't know what else I want." Humiliated over the outburst, Brianna sank further into the seat. She hated having the spotlight focused on her, afraid of everyone's judgment and cruelty.

Brianna first thought she might be attracted to girls when a boy in her seventh-grade class offered to show her his penis. It'd been some sort of flash dance that swept across the school prompting everyone to drop their pants behind closed doors. When the boy picked her as his hopefully willing partner, she told him he had a weird smell and that she'd rather spend time with his sister. It'd flown out of her mouth before she could stop it, barely having met the girl once at his birthday party the prior month. The boy shuffled away, disappointed, but didn't notice what had been dangerously surfacing inside Brianna's mind.

By high school, the anxiety over being caught staring at other girls' bodies destroyed any ability to comfortably change clothes in the locker room during PE classes. When an opportunity surfaced to join the soccer team instead of attending gym, Brianna jumped on it, keen to quarantine confusing thoughts about her sexuality. She purposely changed into her uniform behind the safety of a stall in a hallway bathroom that no one ever used, telling everyone else it was easier to get dressed on her way back from an after-school college prep course.

Soccer became a way to eliminate the curious but traitorous thoughts from her mind, allowing her a physical release to all the tension and fears stemming from someone finding out her secret. Though it'd worked the first season, the truth returned with full force when she met Shanelle at a tryout for the city's soccer club on a quest for a college scholarship. When Brianna had gone for the long-drive kick to score the winning goal of the tournament's final game, Shanelle came bounding from nowhere and shoved Brianna to the ground. Brianna's first reaction had been to fight back by chasing after Shanelle, not expecting her opponent to retaliate, but she did. The girls tumbled on the field together, igniting an intense heat inside Brianna's body as parts of her smashed into another girl in a way that teased and tortured her. When they landed inches from one another on the sidelines, Shanelle whispered before quickly jogging away, *"Damn, you're pretty hot."* Brianna laid helpless on the ground, interpreting all the emotions and physical reactions growing more desirous than ever inside her adolescent body. The moment their eyes locked, Brianna accepted her past inability to conquer the powerful magnetic force of her deepening sexual attraction to women.

Shanelle acknowledged the temporary setback on the train. "Fine, I'll stop. I just adore you too much to let you struggle. That's why Woodland will be perfect. It's the Sarah Lawrence of the Midwest. My cousin raves about the parties and the bars where we can get blitzed. With hot girls. Cool ones. Not the freaks I deal with back home."

Brianna leaned in and gripped Shanelle's neck with both hands, pulling their faces within inches again. "I know you do. Thank you for being patient with me. Can we let this go right now? Let's focus on how to explain Woodland to my mom."

"The other lesbian in denial?"

Exasperated, Brianna dropped her head against Shanelle's neck. "She's not gay. She just doesn't date."

"A nun doesn't date, Bree. Your mother's vagina reminds me of Old Faithful. It's full of hot air and steam, only hers hasn't blown in years. Ain't nothing been in there since Moses parted the seas."

"Then how was I born? And I don't think it was Moses."

"Immaculate Conception. We'll call her *Proud Mary*." Shanelle jumped up and danced in the aisle, rolling her arms in a circular motion. "*Left a good job in the city. Workin' for the man ev'ry night and day...* Oh wait, I forgot, there are no men allowed in that dusty old trap door between her legs." Shanelle's face boasted a grin the size of Texas as she fell into the plushness of the seat.

Brianna cracked up. "I'm gonna tell my mother you said that."

"You know I'm just trying to make you laugh, babe. Sometimes I'm a little too direct and harsh, I get it." A few seconds of silence passed between them as their knees gently fell against one another. "What about your father? Are you still thinking about hiring someone to investigate his identity?"

When Brianna turned six years old, the only present she begged for was to meet the mysterious parent, or, at the very least, to view a picture of him. In her dreams, someone like John Stamos would show up with a guitar crooning about how much he wanted to raise his baby girl and teach her the ways of the world. She'd imagined the perfect dad surprising her with a comforting bear hug and a believable explanation for the lengthy absence. Perhaps he'd been working in outer space or had amnesia. Maybe he'd been chasing criminals and was forced underground. No matter how crazy the reasoning, it was less painful to believe something outrageous than accept he chose to disappear from his daughter's life. Just once, she wanted to sit on his lap while he said he loved her the way all fathers do in the tear-jerker family movies that aired 24/7—and they often watched—on the *Lifetime* television network. It wasn't about replacing the amazing times she cherished with her mother but adding to them with the familiarity of a traditional and normal family like everyone else around her.

"Maybe. She's adamant about not discussing his existence or the past with me."

"Hasn't she lived anywhere else? Been in love? Were they married?" asked Shanelle.

"I don't know. My birth certificate only lists his last name."

"Which is?"

"Porter. Same as my last name."

"But that's not your mother's last name."

"No. I have no clue where the name Porter came from."

Shanelle tapped her feet on the train's carpeted floor. Her mind sometimes went into overdrive when processing potential solutions. She twitched with anticipation when an idea popped up. "Porter. As in an apartment building or hotel worker?"

"Yes." It hadn't occurred to Brianna until Shanelle brought up the meaning of the word.

"Maybe she randomly hooked up with some hotel porter, didn't know his real name, got pregnant, and named you after his broke-ass job?" Shanelle's obnoxious guffaw filled the silent space within the entire train car. "That's classic *Proud Mary*."

Brianna laughed, too. As stupid as the explanation sounded, she was scared it could be true. "You're awful. Why would I ever want to go to Woodland? I should run away from *you*."

Shanelle rolled her deep brown eyes, pausing while Brianna considered joining the dark forces of a special inner circle only they shared.

"Your mom has a story to tell, Bree. You need to ask her this weekend when you tell her you're attending Woodland. Get it all out at the same time."

Brianna sighed with heavy exhaustion. "It's time she stopped hiding my father's identity."

"Maybe you've got a brother named *Bellhop* and a sister named *Concierge*. That might be why you don't know anything. She's ashamed of getting it on with the dirty porter man in a mop closet after learning he bumped uglies on the lobby floor one lonely night with *Beret*, the hat-check girl."

"That's just wrong. You're so on my shit list right now." A well-timed shove into the side of the train improved Brianna's attitude, especially when Shanelle's shocked expression encouraged her to repeat it.

"We make a good team, don't we?" After a few moments of silence, Shanelle tapped her fingers against Brianna's thigh. "Penny for your thoughts?"

"I just have too many decisions to make."

"Of everything going on, what's most important to you right now?"

With no hesitation, Brianna responded, "To find my father and learn where I came from. I can't do anything else until I meet him. It's killing me inside to know nothing about him."

After eighteen years of having no information, it was time to pressure her mother into turning over the keys to the past. Brianna needed a game plan that would help locate both her confidence and a direction for her future. Both had been nonexistent for too long. When she stepped back to find a common denominator among everything that had paralyzed her, learning where she came from presented the ideal way to deal with her anxiety and concerns over actually living instead of blindly trudging through life.

Shanelle pondered her response. "Besides your mother, who else might have any information?"

"I could talk to Lenny. My mother once mentioned how they'd met before I was born." Lenny owned several apartments in their building and managed the jazz club on the ground level. He might offer a few clues to solve the mystery. Lenny once encouraged her to ask questions like all the skilled detectives, giving her the first set of Agatha Christie novels to cut her teeth into.

Shanelle cleared her throat. "I might have a plan to help you. Let me check on something when we get home." She grabbed a blanket from the side compartment and tossed it over them both. "But first, a nap."

Brianna stretched her legs and settled into a comfortable position, reassured in knowing Shanelle would stick by her each step of the way. In her mind, Brianna had been abandoned at birth and was afraid the unknown reason would never be solid enough to allow her the chance to feel complete. Frightening thoughts and panicked feelings about the risk of being left behind or feeling unloved by every potential man in the future disturbed her. She also lived in constant fear about making the wrong decision when selecting a college, discovering her passions, or choosing a potential career.

Finding her father offered the only hope left to prevent the emptiness that churned inside her body from controlling her thoughts and consuming her ability to survive. Brianna often questioned whether it was time to toss a white Hermès scarf around her neck and stagger into the ocean, where the vast abyss could wash away the depression and relieve all the pain.

# Chapter 3

# Amalia, August 1984

As much as Amalia tried to ignore the early morning conversation with Bryan, it was futile to fight nervous anticipation throughout the day. She incorrectly counted change for Mabel Newton, an old spinster who chastised her inability to pay proper attention to customers. When blood seeped through the small cracks in Amalia's skin from the counter's splintered edges, Amalia's father had to tell her three times to stop rapping her knuckles before she listened.

After a customer paid for his cans of wood stain and sealant, Amalia noticed it was time for the picnic. "Is it okay to leave for the lake now, Daddy?" She squeezed his hand before stepping away to find her belongings. "I locked the till in the safe and prepared the new one for Monday morning. I cleaned the coffee pot and updated the ledger with today's sales." Amalia knew her father wouldn't force her to stay but assuring him that helping run the store was equally as important needed to be conveyed. "Thank you so much for letting me go to the—"

As Amalia leaned in to kiss her father's cheek, the bell on the front door clanged. Its harsh smack against the swollen jamb interrupted her words. "Just where did your father let you go, child?"

Amalia smelled the Vicks VapoRub lathered on her mother's skin every morning to breathe more easily. The stench lingered in each corner and lurked in every crevice of their home. Janet's throat glistened like an old wet rag, drawing unnecessary attention to folds of skin wrinkled all around her neck.

"Nowhere special, Momma. I went to the store to get our lunch." Desperate fear prevented Amalia from focusing on her father's reaction. She understood it wasn't right to lie but also knew if her mother caught wind of the trip to Lake Newton, meeting Bryan that afternoon would never happen. "What brings you to the store?"

Peter shuffled toward Janet and leaned in to kiss her hello. She waved her hand to stop his approach. "This store belongs to me, Amalia. I don't need your permission. You hear that, Peter? Your daughter thinks I ought to have a reason to show up, as if this is your special little place together. What nonsense!" Janet hobbled toward the desk chair, clutching her handbag tightly against her chest. "Get me something to drink, Peter."

"Amalia didn't imply you shouldn't show up here, dear. She meant no harm in asking what made you stop by." His voice had little confidence, but he attempted to keep basic control of the conversation. He grabbed a can of soda from the refrigerator and poured some in a Styrofoam cup. "She's been an immense help today."

"I see where she gets it from, Peter. That child needs to learn how to listen whenever I speak. No matter, she will one day soon. Get your things, Amalia. We're going home." The authority in Janet's tone stole any remaining oxygen in the room. She slowly sipped from the cup and crumpled it on the counter once finished with its contents.

Amalia stared at her father, pleading for his help, uncertain what to say.

Peter glanced toward Janet but at once darted away not daring to look his wife in the eyes. "I still need her help for a little longer. We planned to be home for dinner by—"

"I didn't ask you about dinner. I said I needed Amalia to come with me. She's got work to do before her brother gets home." Janet searched her purse for a piece of candy and pulled out an old butterscotch covered in lint. She removed the plastic wrapper and popped the candy in her mouth. The butterscotch banged against her rotting teeth swishing back and forth in a puddle of saliva.

Amalia grew hopeful that her mother had been confused by the dates. "Momma, Greg's not coming home until next week. I can fix up his room tomorrow." Her cheeks flushed.

Janet stood from the chair and slammed her hands on the desk. "I've had enough from the both of you. Greg is coming home tonight. His friend Carter will be driving him home instead of taking the bus this time. He's got all those boxes since school is over." Her head shook in disgust. "Come *now*, Amalia."

Peter's hand blocked Janet as her heavy steps trampled by the copper pipes hung on the side wall. "When did Greg change his mind? He told us last week he'd be home at the end of the month."

Janet brushed Peter away ignoring his hand as it fell to the side. "Greg told me yesterday. I'm certain I informed you both... not that either of you listen to me. It doesn't matter. Amalia needs to get the house ready for his friend." Janet stopped, turned, and searched for her daughter with her left eye fixed in a permanent empty glower.

Amalia grabbed her bag and keys, shuffling everything together to leave with her mother. In her rush, she dropped the bag to the floor. The red blouse spilled from its only protection unaware of the trouble its presence would generate. It was the only article of clothing Amalia owned that made her feel special, nor did it try to hide her body from the rest of the world.

"What is that doing here? I told you to get rid of it yesterday morning." The room grew a few degrees cooler as Janet's icy expression penetrated the surface of Amalia's waning facade.

"I... I just... forgot it was... in my bag when I brought it here today," stammered Amalia.

"Give it here."

"No, Momma. I'm bringing it home."

"Someday, you'll understand, girl." Janet refocused her triumphant gaze from Amalia to her husband. "Have you got a pair of scissors in this store, Peter?"

Amalia pictured what could have been if she'd met Bryan at the lake. She chastised herself for foolishly letting down her guard, imagining the possibility of something positive happening in Brant. It was merely another one of her nightmares masquerading as a silly little girl's daydream. Fighting back was a lost cause, and so was her blouse. Amalia grabbed the scissors from the rusty mason jar and walked with unparalleled defeat toward her mother.

"Stay right there, child. I'm not gonna be the one to destroy it. Give those scissors to your father."

Peter grew angry with disbelief, despite focusing on a pile of dirt in the corner. "Janet, let her keep the shirt, please. She's not going to wear it anywhere."

"Cut it up now, Peter. The girl needs to learn another lesson. Apparently, so do you." Janet banged her fist against the nearest wall rattling the pipes. "Make it quick. Greg will be ready for dinner in three hours."

As the harassment in Janet's voice punched holes in his body, Peter's courage went limp with burden. His shaky fingers, normally quite firm and adept from building his model trains and boats, slid into the scissors. Amalia turned away at the nagging graze of one blade against the other, grateful when the fabric muffled the awful scrape of her last hopes being dashed away for the summer. "I love you, Daddy," she mouthed and walked behind her mother to the car, praying for silence on the ride home.

* * *

Thirty minutes later, Janet leaned over to inspect the spare cot in Greg's room. She lifted the corner of the green comforter Amalia had just tucked under the mattress. "You call this making a bed? Fix this mess, child. Your brother hasn't been home since Christmas. The least you could do is show him and his friend some respect."

Amalia nodded, but her mind focused elsewhere. Bryan had been waiting ten minutes at the magnolia tree for her. She would never arrive in time to meet him and felt disheartened about his reaction to her standing him up. As Amalia placed the pillow on the bed, Bryan's dimples and a winsome smile danced inside her head, leaving an even more unsettled feeling deep within her. It wasn't often she'd found herself smitten with a boy, no less someone she'd known most of her life who might have been interested in her, too.

With the bedroom prepared and dinner cooking in the oven, Amalia completed the remaining chores on her mother's list. She needed to shower before Greg made it home, but once a car pulled up out front, it was too late. Amalia raced to the hallway window eager for a glimpse of her brother's arrival and shifted her grandmother's home-sewn draperies. Made of antique white lace and edged with blue trim as delicate as snowflakes in early winter, the curtains were one of the only decent items they'd inherited when her grandparents had passed on. Amalia's mother constantly reminded everyone the lace had been in the family for over four generations. She'd planned to give it to Greg when he got married.

A red Corvette idled at the end of the driveway. Greg lifted only a few bags from the trunk. He didn't have many pieces of luggage or boxes from his college dorm room. He also needed a haircut. His normally well-trimmed chestnut brown hair strayed a few inches down his neck, and he hadn't shaved in at least a week. Amalia opened the window the two inches the swelled wood and her strength would allow.

"Welcome home, *Shaggy*," she called to the street in his general direction.

Greg winked as he slammed the car trunk shut. "I'm just trying to keep up with you. Momma says you've let yourself go wild since I've been gone." He threw a canvas bag over his shoulder and pushed open the side gate.

A piercing creak floated through the window crack. A car door closed and from the other side appeared Greg's friend. Carter's dirty blond hair formed a tall spike in the middle of his oval-shaped head and shined from the gel product he'd spent twenty minutes applying that morning.

Amalia sped down the stairs reaching the door as Greg walked through it. He was more disheveled than she'd noticed from the upstairs viewpoint—his shirt untucked and his jeans stained with mustard and catsup. A faint smell of cigarette smoke and beer emanated off his skin.

"I'm so glad you're home. I might actually survive the summer now." Amalia rushed toward him in need of someone who empathized with what she'd been through. "You're a mess."

"Monster, I'm wiped. Final exams nearly killed me, but I'm done. I wish I could have been here when you graduated." Greg tightly hugged her dropping his bags on the floor near the staircase. "But I had to finish one summer class, or they wouldn't give me a degree."

*Monster* had been his nickname for her ever since she ran into his room at seven years old afraid of the creatures who lived under her bed. Greg let her stay up late to watch *Frankenstein* after their parents had gone to sleep. Amalia was frightened at the over-sized bolts and screws sticking out of the monster's head. She hadn't noticed his green skin color, but the very same objects their father sold at the hardware store were enough to give her nightmares. Greg let her sleep in his room that night, but she kept coming back during the rest of the week. He was afraid to tell their parents he'd let her watch the film, instead choosing to convince Amalia the best way to frighten a monster was to become an even bigger and scarier monster. Though it cured her nightmares, she spent that entire school year jumping out of his closet screaming '*Grrr*' and walking like Frankenstein.

"You do look tired." Amalia pulled away from Greg and peered out the front door in search of Carter, but he wasn't anywhere in sight. "Your room is ready, and I put out the cot for your friend."

"Thanks. I can't wait to sleep in my bed. Where is everyone?"

"Daddy's still at the hardware store. Momma's taking a nap. You know how she gets tired so quickly."

After several hours at the church selling her crafts that morning, Janet had given instructions on what to cook for dinner, criticized the quality of Amalia's cleaning skills, and retired to her bedroom. Amalia knew her mother had eaten too many lemon cakes at First Baptist inflating her blood sugar sky high. The only other reason for the sudden bedridden state, besides nursing the aches and pains of her ailments, was the thought of having to clean the house.

"Are things still tense between you two? She means well. You know that, right?" Greg snickered as he ruffled Amalia's hair. He walked into the kitchen and grabbed a glass of sun tea. "I left my gear on the porch. Will you get it for me?"

"Yep. Who's this Carter you brought home?" Upon reaching the front door, Amalia pushed open the screen and stepped onto the cement stoop.

"I'm his best friend. We played lacrosse together." A youthful boy extended his hand toward Amalia after leaning the sticks against the yellowed siding. "I'm the one you've been looking for." His sarcasm was the first thing Amalia noticed, then his mysterious eyes.

The top of Carter's head nearly hit the rusty chains that held the door from swinging all the way open. With his baby face and boyish smile, he appeared no older than Amalia—possibly even cute if she allowed herself to dream of anyone other than Bryan. "I just asked who you were. I didn't say I was looking for you." Amalia ignored his hand and stared at the Corvette they'd driven home in.

Carter pulled back his unaccepted friendly gesture. "No sweat, aren't you a charmer?" He pushed past Amalia and handed her the lacrosse sticks without even a glance. "Carry these like your brother said, will you, Monster? I'll take you for a ride later if you're a good girl."

Amalia stepped backward from the force of his handoff. She gathered the bulky equipment, navigated them through the doorframe, and backed into the living room. "I'm not your sister. Only Greg calls me that." She dropped them in the corner as Carter sauntered into the kitchen like he'd belonged there for years. "I'm not getting in that heap of junk."

Greg poured a glass of sun tea for Carter, then plopped down at the small kitchen table, where years ago he and his sister had built Lego castles and rocket ships to pass the time before their father came home from the store. "I see you two have met. What's for dinner?"

"Pork chops with homemade applesauce and baked potatoes. Momma splurged since you were coming home. You're her favorite, you know." Amalia monitored Carter while he took a seat across from her brother. He had on loose, black gym shorts and a form-fitting gray Nike tank top. His piercing glare penetrated her skin in a way that made her uncomfortable, but she didn't know why.

"Sounds delicious. And you made that for me?" Carter's lips simpered after he gulped down the contents of his glass. "Mind pouring me some more, Monster? I mean, Amalia." He waggled his brows, confident she understood he was playing with her.

She grabbed the pitcher off the counter and filled his glass, then Greg's. "I let a fresh batch soak in the sun for a few hours. And no, the dinner is Greg's favorite. I don't know anything about *you.*"

"If your dinner tastes half as good as this tea, I'm gonna owe you big-time. Haven't had a decent home-cooked meal since I was at my mother's last Christmas."

Greg tucked in his shirt after scratching off the dried condiment stains on his jeans. "Carter's mom sold their house right after the holidays and moved to Europe. She's traveling around with her sisters. That's why he needed a place to crash for a few weeks before he goes back to school later this month. They're doing repairs and painting his fraternity house while he's gone." Carter was a year younger than Greg and still had to complete his senior term before graduating.

Amalia shifted her weight against the counter, suddenly self-conscious over her appearance. She fidgeted with the dish towel in her hands and was about to speak, but her mother's voice frightened her back into submission.

"Don't slouch, child. You look like one of them hunchback girls who've been working in the fields picking cotton all day. Stand up straight."

Carter stood as Janet walked in the room. He had some manners, despite his rude introduction when first arriving. Sweat poured down the side of Amalia's face, and a faintly sour smell emanated under her arms. She wanted to crawl into the pantry closet over the way her mother had embarrassed her. A knot formed in her stomach when Greg embraced their mother.

"You look beautiful, Momma. I've missed you. Amalia told me all about the dinner you two planned. Thank you. We're both starving." Greg pointed to Carter after stepping back from the hug.

Janet assessed the stranger in her home. "Carter, it's good to meet you. Welcome to the Graeme household. Please make yourself comfortable." She took a seat at the table where Greg had been sitting, then gaped at her daughter. "Amalia, a good host always keeps her guest's glass full. Get him some more tea. The poor lad's thirsty."

Carter turned when Amalia filled his empty glass. "Thank you, Mrs. Graeme. She's already gotten me some and has been a perfectly charming hostess."

Janet grunted, then focused on Greg. "Your daddy should be home any minute. He's excited to have some help at the store this summer. We couldn't do too much on our own while you were gone."

Amalia frowned while bending down to the oven to check on dinner. She'd been helping her father update the shop's inventory to increase sales. Greg wasn't the only one with clever ideas in the family.

"Carter wants to help. He's getting his degree in economics and will run his own business someday." Greg placed his glass in the kitchen sink. "I need to shower and shave. I'll head down before dinner's ready." He walked toward the living room and ascended the stairs. "Are you coming up, Carter? I'll show you around."

Carter smiled at Janet. "I appreciate you letting me stay until I can move back into the fraternity house on campus." He dropped his glass in the kitchen sink and walked past the counter where Amalia stirred a pot of applesauce. His hand gently brushed her back as he whispered into her ear. "I'm looking forward to spending time with you, too, Monster."

Carter's proximity annoyed Amalia. The soft hairs on his legs tickled the back of her knees when he leaned close. Her shoulders crunched forward as he pinched her waist. She didn't respond, willing herself to focus on tasting a spoonful of dinner and not his hot breath on her neck.

"Don't eat it all now, girl. We have five mouths to feed tonight. Honestly, where are your manners?"

"Yes, Momma." Amalia closed the lid on the pot and finished setting the table. Showering would have to wait until after dinner. Being happy would have to wait much longer since attending college in the fall wouldn't come fast enough. She needed to find a way out of Brant before becoming permanently trapped in its menacing summer grip.

# Chapter 4

# Brianna, June 2004

Shortly before midnight, Brianna and Shanelle disembarked the train and walked through New York City's Penn Station toward the subway entrance. When Shanelle leaned in to hug her goodnight, Brianna unconsciously turned her cheek and rushed through the turnstile without realizing she hadn't said goodbye. Brianna buried her ability to interpret the near kiss on the train, instead focusing on cornering Lenny in the jazz club once arriving home. She was certain he might have information about her father or clues to her mother's past.

Brianna exited the subway car ten minutes later, jumping over a pile of vomit and two broken beer bottles—another reason she couldn't wait to attend college somewhere other than an urban hell. Though home was only a few blocks away, it could have been miles as she waded through the debauchery and corner drug deals. Upon reaching her building, she stepped down a few stairs and high-fived the bouncer standing guard at the door. Lenny didn't mind if Brianna popped in on quiet nights to listen to a few sets. She shouldn't be there on a Friday, but it was emptier than usual, and no one had stopped her.

The cool and lunar tone of Miles Davis crooning through the speakers comforted Brianna as she hunkered down on a rickety stool. She asked the bartender—an unfamiliar Russian guy—to fetch Lenny. She fussed with a cocktail napkin and drank a Shirley Temple while waiting for him to arrive. As a child, Brianna spent several afternoons a week sipping the non-alcoholic beverage while sitting at Lenny's bar. Her mother worked late many nights, but Brianna had to return home when the after-school programs ended by four-thirty each day. Lenny would watch over her, mixing a Shirley Temple for her to drink, so she felt cool, then send her upstairs to the apartment once his jazz club opened for business at six.

A random patron walked toward her, smiling with a glassy sheen. He took the seat next to Brianna despite several other open spaces that would have been more ideal. "Aren't you a sight for sore eyes. May I buy you a drink?" he slurred his words. A few drops spilled from his martini while trying to drag the stool closer to the bar.

Brianna shook her head. "No, I'm just stopping in for a minute."

He leaned forward, resting sweaty, hairy fingers on her forearm. "You look like a musician. Do you sing?"

Brianna controlled a growing desire to laugh. He tried to say *musician*, but it came out more like *muslin*. She'd learned to speak drunk talk by nine and translated what he'd meant to say. "Really, I'm just waiting for the owner. Have a good night." She pulled her arm away and shifted her body in the opposite direction.

He snorted as the stool shuffled closer inch by inch. "One drink. That's all, honey."

"Thank you, but no thank you." Brianna stood and tried to step away, but the patron grabbed hold of her waist. She went to push him off, but Lenny had already grabbed the guy's shoulder and shoved him away.

"Let's go, your friends are waiting for you." Lenny waved over the bouncer who escorted the drunk back to his table.

"I could have handled that." Brianna cocked her head toward him and downed her Shirley Temple.

Lenny tossed a few pieces of mail on the bar. "I'm sure you could have, but I was here, so I took care of it. What brings you downstairs tonight?"

Brianna brushed aside his assistance and initiated her inquiry. "I had a few things on my mind and wanted to talk to you about something important." She picked up a piece of his mail and fanned herself while debating the best approach.

"I don't mind when you stop in, but weekends aren't the best time, Brianna." He tried to grab the envelope from her hands yet missed when she ripped it further away. "Random age checks by the city, you know."

"It won't take long. I wanted to ask you about my..." Brianna stopped when the *addressed to* name on the envelope surprised her. Confusion stole her ability to concentrate on what to say or how to decipher the information.

"Give it back. That doesn't belong to you." Lenny's face flushed a deeper shade of red than normal. He collected the envelope during her distraction and guided her closer to the door.

Brianna stiffened with uncertainty by the name on the piece of mail. "I... I just... wanted to ask if you'd known my mother... you know... when I was born." She pretended not to recognize anything, hoping to get him to talk. As far as she knew, his name was Lenny Flint, not Lenny Porter. *How could she not know they shared a last name?*

"Why do you ask?" He motioned to the bartender. "Scotch, please."

"She won't tell me anything. I want to know who my father is. I thought maybe you might know." *Porter could be a common name.*

Lenny grabbed the drink and consumed it with one large gulp. "Your mother told me you might ask some questions."

"So, you do know?"

"You need to discuss this with her, not me." Lenny reached for her arm, but Brianna stepped away.

"No, that's not fair. You're hiding something." She tried to formulate the right question but ultimately decided to digest the recently acquired news of his alternative last name, then re-approach him once she was better prepared.

"Let's go. I've told you before... *no weekend visits to the club.*" He ushered her out the front door. "It's late. Your saint of a mother is probably curious where you are."

Brianna rolled her eyes. "Fine, but I'm coming back after I talk to her. I'm just asking for some information on my father. Not very difficult, is it?"

"Life is always more difficult than you expect it to be. Take my advice... push gently with your mother. She's not as strong as you think."

Brianna stepped to the sidewalk and climbed three flights of stairs to access her apartment. When she reached her floor, Tippy, an orange tabby cat belonging to her neighbor stretched out a paw to catch Brianna's attention. Mr. Pollardo, the crotchety man who owned Tippy, often forgot to let the cat back in at night, and she'd wander the stairwells in search of some comfortable place. Brianna perched against the wall petting Tippy and listening to a soft purring from her belly. "I know how you feel, kitty. Sometimes I'm just looking for someone to open the door, too."

As Brianna cradled the cat to her chest, it became apparent how much heavier Tippy felt than she had several weeks earlier. "Either you're gaining weight, or you must be pregnant again. Tell me, Tippy... are you expecting another litter?" Tippy had been hanging around the last few years, probably a stray before Mrs. Pollardo took her in one miserably chilly night. The cat had a good life until Mrs. Pollardo unexpectedly died from pancreatic cancer. Mr. Pollardo lost interest in Tippy, who found herself suddenly roaming the streets most nights for food and shelter.

Tippy jumped from Brianna's arms and rushed down the stairs when a door creaked open on the floor below. "Just gonna leave me as soon as I try to comfort you, huh? I would have taken you in tonight even though Mom's allergic."

Brianna grabbed the stair rail and lifted herself to a standing position before opening her apartment door. Her mother slept silently on the couch, another night where she'd waited up for Brianna to get home and failed to crash in her own bed. It was both a comfort Brianna wouldn't have to lie about her trip and a frustration that she couldn't ask more questions about Lenny's last name matching hers. Settling on being grateful the squeaky apartment door hadn't roused the whole place, she tiptoed into her bedroom, peeled off her clothes, and pulled the covers over her restless body. *Was his last name Flint or Porter? Were they related somehow? Could Lenny be her father?*

Brianna eventually fell into a deep sleep, dreaming she was a flag tied to the middle of a rope in a game of tug-of-war over her life. A life with no control except to fall to the ground dragged through the mud wherever someone wanted to take her. Helpless as though she couldn't even speak unless spoken to first.

\* \* \*

As soon as Brianna awoke the next morning, her mind replayed the moment she shared with Shanelle on the train returning from Woodland College. Being that close, even among a crowd of passengers, awakened more inside her body than the last time they almost shared a brief kiss on the soccer field. The uncomfortable sexual desires had intensified to the point where Brianna waffled chaotically between hiding from her urges and wanting to jump blindly into the unknown abyss.

Turning on her phone indicated there were eleven missed messages from Shanelle. The last asked if she'd died in her sleep to be sure she visited as a ghost with the answers to the final history exam. Brianna's mother had also left a note that indicated she was working at the office until midday.

Brianna had slept away half the morning. It was time to decide about Woodland. The tour had gone so well that it convinced her to upload her confirmation acceptance to the college website verifying her attendance in the fall as a freshman. With the first of her priorities completed, and one less indecisive item to address, she switched gears to deal with Shanelle. After apologizing for missing the text messages and confirming what time her best friend would arrive to help her dress for prom, Brianna showered and scarfed down a salad for lunch. She flipped through *MySpace* and other websites on her computer to check what happened in the world overnight, then pondered how to deal with the impending decision to lose her virginity to Doug.

They'd met her junior year in high school after sharing homeroom and biology class together. He'd moved into the Lower East Side a few blocks from her when his parents divorced, unfamiliar with city life or the public school system. Brianna and Doug bonded over living with a single parent, swapping stories to help each other deal with the disappointments in their lives. She'd grown reliant on him to provide a cover for everything that kept trying to gnaw its way out. Not even Doug had known she lusted after Shanelle. By senior year, he'd become one of the popular kids earning his spot on the basketball team and claiming her as his girlfriend. Doug had also grown more territorial and co-dependent once joining the squad, abruptly dictating who Brianna could hang out with or talk to on the phone.

After she lost interest and any remaining feelings for him, Brianna invented excuses to create space and find her independence. Soccer practice suddenly took more of her time, or her mother needed help at the office. Shanelle even started pushing Doug to go their separate ways, generating discordant tension whenever the three of them hung out. Brianna broke up with him a few times, but he kept convincing her to take him back. She found herself willing only as an escape from accepting the truth about the entirely different level of unmanageable attraction harbored for Shanelle. Having *someone* always felt better than having *no one*. At least, no one society would accept.

Brianna watched a movie on HBO and flipped through a few magazines to settle on options for doing her hair for the prom. Shanelle would find the best style—she always did. When she finally arrived thirty minutes late, Shanelle complained about one of the subways not running that weekend. "The city needs to fix this damn mess with the MTA. It's ridiculous that I had to take a taxi." She plowed through the living room, dropping her makeup kit and a bag of shoes on the floor.

"Did you bring your whole closet?" Brianna laughed, hoping to avoid discussing the incident from the prior day. "You never take the subway. What are you sniping about?"

"I like to bitch. You know that." Shanelle walked toward her, grabbed her chin, and turned her head from side to side. "It looks like you got enough sleep. I'll be able to convert you into a goddess for tonight." While Brianna wasn't a tomboy, she also had little interest in being ultra-feminine.

"I know you're still disappointed with me for not taking you to my prom." Brianna's school had frowned upon taking a same-sex date even if it was only as friends. She had to register any outside guests well in advance. Shanelle attended a different high school, a private all-girls academy on the Upper East Side, one that scheduled a class trip to the Hamptons instead of a formal prom.

"I'm over it. Let's move on. There's more pressing stuff to talk about."

A deep pit grew inside Brianna's stomach. "Such as?"

"What are we gonna do about Doug?" Shanelle grabbed Brianna's wrist, led her to the bathroom, and situated her on the toilet seat. She opened one of the boxes from the heaviest bag and considered what to do with a few curlers. "He's gonna push you to sleep with him. Maybe I should show up to protect you. I could taser him if he does anything wrong." Shanelle rifled through her cosmetics bag, pulling out three types of eyeliner. "Choose."

"Does it matter?"

"If I taser him? Probably not, though that asshole may get turned on. Hell, I might enjoy watching him piss himself from the electric shock." She freakishly shook her body and feigned surprise after pretending to become incontinent.

"Not Doug, the eyeliner." Brianna held up the makeup clueless about which color to select. She'd worn extraordinarily little of her own, following in her mother's footsteps. *Less is more* was a motto often chanted around their apartment.

"Oh, my lovely little Bree. We'll make a woman out of you someday." Shanelle chose the thickest one and applied a generous line around Brianna's eyes. "I'm jealous of these high cheekbones. They so perfectly shape your face."

"Umm, thanks." Brianna, often incapable of accepting praise, glanced at the mirror, then updated Shanelle about the information she discovered on Lenny's mail in the jazz club. "Maybe I've got a new lead, huh?"

"It's possible. That would be a tremendous help." Shanelle shrugged, then excitedly changed the subject. "Ooh, grab the bag on the floor."

Brianna tried to reach for it but couldn't without bending forward. Shanelle's hand slipped and traced a line of dark black liquid across her cheeks. "Bree, you're such an awkward mess."

"Just finish, will you?" Brianna grabbed the bag and shook a small blue box with a white bow. "You bought me something from Tiffany's?"

"Yeah, even though you don't deserve it." Shanelle capped the eyeliner and opened a tray of varying shades of blue eyeshadow. "You need a darker, smokier color to highlight your eyes."

"You shouldn't have bought me anything after the way I behaved last night." Brianna pulled the bow off the box and removed the lid. A pair of diamond teardrop earrings caused her to swoon. "They're beautiful."

"I bought them last week way before you went all psycho on the trip back from Woodland." She gently pushed Brianna's head back against the white-tiled wall and tested a deep blue powder on her skin. "Perfect. Now close your eyes."

Brianna patiently waited for her to finish, then stood in front of the mirror. As expected, Shanelle had picked the right colors. Brianna held up the new gift near her ears and smiled at the way they shined in the light. "You really are amazing."

"Yes, I am. Now put on your dress while I go check on something." Shanelle clapped her hands while leaving the room so Brianna could finish dressing. "Chop, chop."

When Brianna returned from the bathroom, Shanelle was chatting on the phone. "Who's that?"

"Your mother can't make it home." Shanelle threw her hands in the air and switched it to speakerphone. "It's a gorgeous dress!"

"I'm sure you look amazing, honey. I'm so sorry I can't be with you. I wish I could get a glimpse of the prettiest girl at prom tonight."

"Thanks, Mom. We'll take a bunch of photos." She raised her free hand and fist bumped the blank air while smiling at Shanelle. Though she was happy not to deal with her mother in person, Brianna was curious to witness the woman's reaction when her daughter put on a dress.

"Be careful tonight. Tell Doug I said he better stop by soon to say hello. He hasn't come around in weeks."

Brianna hadn't brought Doug back to the apartment since initiating the most recent off-again part of their relationship. Her mother didn't need to know every little thing in her life, especially not the breakup. It was also too soon for Brianna to divulge her attraction to Shanelle. She was certain her mother had already noticed a few of the clues. The guilt over keeping too many secrets ambushed Brianna while considering her response. "Speaking of Doug, I need to finish getting ready before he shows up."

"Okay. Are you still sleeping at Shanelle's tonight after prom?"

Brianna didn't want to reveal the hotel room rented for Doug that night, instead leading her mother to believe she would crash at Shanelle's for an early morning hike in the Cloisters. They'd spent a lot of time climbing the rocks and wandering the park after soccer during the last few months—an outlet to vent frustrations. "Yes, I'll be home late tomorrow morning."

"I'm so sorry. A mother should help her daughter get ready for prom. It's part of a parent's acceptance that their child is growing up."

Brianna knew her mother meant well, but it only emphasized how much more she wished her father had also been present. A throbbing lump materialized in her throat, compelling her to redirect the conversation. "Umm, so I saw a piece of mail last night with Lenny's last name on it, Mom. I thought it said *Porter*. Isn't that kinda weird since that's my last name, too?" She imagined her mother on a date with Lenny, immediately bewildered—possibly nauseated—by the thought of them sleeping together. "Is there something you need to tell me?"

Silence flooded the room for a few seconds. "Let's discuss it another time," said her mother with a curt voice.

"You always say that, but then you go dark and avoid me." Brianna's face flushed to match the tenacity of her temper. There would be no stopping until she got all the answers.

Shanelle must have noticed, prompting her to grab the phone. "Yeah, so sorry, but we need to run. I'm really glad we connected for a minute tonight before Brianna's prom. Let's talk soon. Bye, *Proud Mary*." Shanelle clicked the disconnect button and tossed the phone onto the bed. "Oops. Did I accidentally hang up on that lesbian?"

Brianna needed the intervention more than she was willing to admit. It brought a moment of levity to calm herself down and laugh. "She's not a lesbian. Do we have to go through this every time you talk about her?"

"Yes, we do. You're not helping the situation the way you approach her. Stop asking direct questions. Let her trip herself up by accidentally revealing something."

"Maybe now that I know what I might be looking for, I'll find something if I ask direct questions. If she doesn't say anything, I'll just point blank ask Lenny. I still don't understand why his last name on the apartment mailbox is Flint."

"It makes no sense, but maybe he doesn't know he's your father. Let it go just for today."

"I'd think he would know." Brianna reached in for a hug, resting her face on Shanelle's shoulder. "You're probably right about forgetting it for tonight."

"I'm always right." Shanelle pushed her best friend away and sighed when looking at Brianna's face. "Don't ruin your makeup. It took me over an hour to get you all fixed up."

"Thank you." Brianna's voice was low and distant.

"For what?"

"Everything. I'm sorry about last night. I'm having a tough time dealing with this shit."

"I didn't bring up last night. You did." Shanelle turned her back toward Brianna while fumbling in another bag filled with shoes.

Brianna had hurt her best friend, but now wasn't the time or place to discuss the train incident. "Can we talk about it tomorrow?"

"Sure, if you're ready. I told you I wouldn't harass you anymore." Shanelle handed her a pair of silver pumps with five-inch heels. "These might work."

"Umm, no. I'm not a hooker." Brianna squished her eyes together at Shanelle's choice. "You mean the world to me. There's no one in my life as good as you are."

"Don't forget that when you're with him tonight." Shanelle handed a different pair of shoes to Brianna. "Try these, they'll be perfect. Less *hoochie-mama* and more *hot babe*!"

Brianna slipped her feet into the pair of pumps, leaning on Shanelle for support. "Now these are some fierce shoes."

"Shows off your legs." Shanelle winked and licked her lips. "You don't even know how sexy you are, do you?"

"Ugh, no!" Brianna sashayed to the mirror to check her image. She glimmered in a sequined purple dress and three-inch Manolo Blahniks peppered with rhinestone flowers. She rarely wore dresses, choosing jeans and a t-shirt as school attire, then rushing into her uniform for soccer games. It clung beautifully to her body, but the discomfort of revealing too much skin rattled her nerves. "I've got more cleavage than I know what to do with."

"You're stunning." Shanelle softly moaned. "Yeah, so… are you ready to meet the douchebag downstairs?"

"Can't you be nice for just one night?"

"Umm, that was me being nice."

* * *

A few hours later, Brianna and Doug made small talk with their friends while nibbling hors d'oeuvres on the seventh floor of a midtown hotel overlooking Park Avenue. Her snug dress hadn't allowed her to eat much, but a few carrots and dollops of hummus wouldn't burst its seams. Deciding how far to go that night with Doug was the primary problem disquieting her not yet certain decision. They'd indulged in heavy make-out sessions and fooled around many times, but she always stopped them before the physical act of intercourse. It wasn't about the fear of losing her virginity, she wanted it over with months ago. Whether it should be with him, or Shanelle, whom she couldn't stop dreaming about, was the primary reason preventing her from taking the cherry-popping plunge in the past. She wanted to be certain the earth would dance under her feet when she was physically with someone for the first time—to feel an animalistic and magnetic attraction where no one existed but her and her partner during those few moments.

Though she wrestled with the options, Brianna rationalized that the only way to confirm her sexual orientation was to sleep with Doug after prom. If the earth moved enough to ignite her passions, then maybe she could stop thinking about Shanelle. If it barely limped or hiccupped, then maybe she had her answers about which team to play for. Testing the waters with Doug was the only approach that made sense to her at the time—starting with the easiest path.

At six feet, Doug was a few inches taller than her but still a bit shorter than the rest of the guys on his basketball team. He made up for it in his dexterity and ability to jump higher than most. He looked quite debonair in his well-fitting tux, especially around his slim waist. Brianna was jealous that his skin had already bronzed from multiple days at the beach, and his dark blond hair had lightened from the sun. No matter how hard Brianna tried, her skin burned whenever she tried to get a tan in previous summers until finally around Labor Day when she'd normally get a little natural color. She'd inherited her lighter skin tone from her mother and assumed the same of her father, not knowing anything about him or how DNA and family traits worked.

"You ready to bounce?" Doug asked as he placed his arm on the curve of her lower back. He'd behaved the entire evening, bringing her several glasses of punch and pulling out her chair each time they sat at one of the tables.

Despite lingering doubts, she whispered into his ear with minimal confidence. "Sure, seems about time."

Doug led her off the dance floor while Green Day blasted from the speakers in the over-decorated New York City hotel ballroom. Her dress sparkled in the strobe lights as they pushed through the crowded space searching for the exit to the elevator banks. As Doug shoved open the ballroom's door and they entered the lobby, Brianna convinced herself everything would be okay. Something had to be, the anxiety and lack of communication from Shanelle in the last three hours had depressed her more than usual. Brianna squeezed her fingertips together until it hurt, to distract her from checking her cell phone again for a response.

Doug pushed the button for the elevator, and the doors opened a few seconds later. Another couple pawed at one another in the gold-trimmed car. Doug grabbed Brianna's hand and stepped inside. He nibbled the back of her neck while he selected their floor, then realized it was already on its way there. "It's gonna be a fun night."

The elevator continued to the eighteenth floor, stopping with a jarring bounce before the doors opened. The other couple stepped out first, then the guy turned to Doug with the sarcastic tone of an intoxicated frat boy sending his recent conquest down the walk of shame. "Bump and grind that hottie, dude." His date slapped the back of his head before slinking away.

Brianna filled with gratitude over the interruption. "Drunk, huh?"

After leaving the elevator, Doug pulled the keycard from his pocket and handed it to Brianna while swaggering to their room. "Yeah, definitely blitzed. He's being an ass. Ignore him."

Green and brown woven carpets in a mid-century modern design decked the hallways. Checkered wallpaper with giant pineapples in the center of every panel adorned the walls. Gold sconces appeared every few feet to create ambiance. It was too stuffy for Brianna's taste, but the room was close enough not to back out. Arriving at the door, Doug pushed Brianna up against the wall and reached for the zipper on her dress. He paused when she stiffened in shock. "This is what we're here for, right? To have sex."

Brianna admired the desire he blanketed her with. It felt good to be wanted by someone who wouldn't push society's buttons even if it'd done little to physically excite her so far. "Let me open the door first." She flipped the keycard against the access panel. It blinked red twice. Nothing happened.

Doug pulled the zipper down her back, slipping his hand onto her ass. "You're so hot."

Brianna's pulse quickened, leaving her with the onset of clammy skin. "Shouldn't you wait?"

"Don't you want me to make you feel good?" Doug reached for the keycard in her hand.

"Yeah, but out here? We should go inside." Brianna let him take the card.

He waved it in front of the access panel with one hand while the other gripped Brianna's waist. Two more series of blinking red lights and a scratchy buzz told them it hadn't worked.

Brianna tried to step away, but his grip was too tight, and her dress had tangled. "Is the lock broken?" Queasiness percolated in her stomach despite not having drank any alcohol. *Was it another sign?*

"Hold on, gimme a minute. Shit. Why won't this door open?" Doug tried the card a third time, twisting the door handle in the hopes it would grant access. When the green lights flashed, the door swung open, and they fell to the floor, laughing. Doug rolled on top of Brianna and kissed her with a wet, sloppy mouth.

When their lips pulled apart, a heightened sense of apprehension materialized inside her body. "You got it opened."

"Guess I did." Doug stood, locked the door, and led Brianna to the bed. He threw his jacket and belt over the back of a chair, then undressed in front of her leaving on only his shorts.

He was attractive and had an athletic body. He'd been a cool guy to hang out with the last few months, when he wasn't a jackass. But it didn't feel right. Would it make more sense if Brianna slept with Shanelle first? No one said sex with Doug would prove she wasn't gay—that was just her own uneducated guesswork. Was she naïve and gullible? "Maybe we should take it slower."

Doug laughed. "You're funny. You rented the hotel room, you told me tonight was the night, and *now* you want to stop?" He reached for her hand and pulled her closer. "Or are you role-playing with me?" He lifted his brow and bobbed feverishly. "I dig that."

Brianna stared back when he dropped his boxers to the floor. He stood naked in front of her forcing her to close her eyes. She wasn't feeling the earth move below her, in fact it was so still she'd thought for a second the place had frozen over. Was it a sign? "Umm... well, I—"

"No sweat. I can play this game. Why don't you get on your knees and take care of business? I've been waiting a long time for this, Brianna." He pulled her forward and forcibly guided her shoulders down until she knelt in front of him. "Come on. You owe me."

Brianna leaned in close, convincing herself this was supposed to happen. At his last line, her stomach churned as viciously as a hurricane ripped trees from the pavement. Doug started another battle over who controlled her choices. "Owe you? What the hell does that mean?" She tried to move away, but his grip was too strong.

Doug's glare pierced through her core. He didn't care about her. Getting off was the only thing on his juvenile mind. "You've teased me for months about finally being ready to have sex after the prom. It's here. Let's do this. Take off that dress and hop the fuck on it, babe."

The nerve of him to say something so disgusting ignited a fire inside Brianna. "Listen, don't talk to me that way. I'll have sex when I'm ready to have sex. Hop on it? Is that how my first time should be? Hop the fuck on it? Screw you."

"Don't be that way. You know you want me." Doug grabbed her hand and jerked her arm toward him. "Come back, baby. I'm not waiting any longer. Is this about that lesbian you hang out with wanting to be your girlfriend? What, are you gay for her now?" A petulant child was less obvious in their immaturity and contempt.

Brianna tore back her arm, lifted her leg, and sent a driving kick straight to his gut. A force had built up over years of anger at the idiocy of men who thought they owned women, lashing its powerful blow against his body. Doug was at the receiving end of her well-placed fury and flew across the other side of the bed. "No, asshole. You can wait all night."

Doug sat, clutching his stomach. "What the hell... is wrong... with you? I can... barely breathe." His chest rose up and down, his breath wheezing as he searched for more words.

"Nothing is wrong with me." She grabbed her purse and rushed to the door. "We're over for good this time."

Doug drew in deep breaths of air. "Fine. You don't deserve me, anyway. Cock tease."

Brianna stopped in her tracks with the ferocity of a cornered animal who'd suddenly turned the tables on her captor. "You're right, I deserve better. Whether or not I'm gay doesn't change the fact I wouldn't want that tiny little prick anywhere near me, jackass. Grow a real one and grow up if you really want a woman to let you inside her."

# Chapter 5

# Amalia, August 1984

After church services the next morning, Janet demanded her daughter wait in the parking lot while she spoke with the minister about the congregation's upcoming annual banquet. Peter had a meeting with a supplier at the store and wouldn't be home for hours. Greg had been allowed to skip that morning given Carter, who was not a Baptist, stayed with the Graeme family. They'd gone for a swim at the lake and planned to return in the afternoon.

Amalia's nerves jittered when a group of her softball teammates approached from the side entrance to the church, reminding her she failed to attend their private celebration at Lake Newton. Amalia had never been invited to go with the rest of the girls before, but her triple in the last game enabled her teammates to score the winning runs. Sally with the double piercings and flawless sun-kissed skin took pity on Amalia and offered to bring an extra wine cooler if she found a way to show up at the lake. Amalia's desire for their friendship, and a need to escape her mother, outranked knowing that the girl's generosity had been forced purely because of a lucky hit.

As the leader of the group, Sally taunted anyone who didn't conform to her petty standards. Her ruthless gaze and boisterous voice zeroed in. "Hey, Amalia. We missed you on Friday. What happened? Were you too afraid to sneak around behind Mommy's back?"

Sally's best Sunday outfit, a hunter-green, empire-style frock cut just above her knees and three-inch white heels, mesmerized Amalia who didn't even own a pair of dress shoes. She wore beige flats with her ankle-length skirt and blue, long-sleeve blouse, also known as her *repeat church outfit* to anyone who bothered to notice. "Sorry, my father needed help at the store, and I couldn't make it."

Brant's small population meant there weren't a lot of girls her age living close by. Janet had refused to let Amalia join the public school system which meant she attended a First Baptist religious school where there were only six other boys and girls in the entire class. Amalia struggled to make friends partially out of fear if anyone had met her mother, but also because she rarely had time between her schoolwork, the softball team, and working at the hardware store. Amalia had been allowed to join the county's softball team only because of the scholarship opportunity it could offer as a way to attend college. Janet refused to pay for Amalia's tuition, explaining that any family savings had been spent for Greg's education. Amalia desperately wanted to find at least one friend, but fate threw too many family roadblocks her way, and it was futile for any spark of friendship to ignite.

Sally rolled her eyes. "You know our invites are special, right? It's not every day we lower our standards to let someone else in our group."

Amalia's head dropped with shame and discomfort when Sally said she was less important than the rest of the team. But Amalia needed them, or at least she thought she did, to understand how to behave on a date, especially if Bryan gave her a second chance. "I'm sorry. Maybe I could come next weekend. We could talk about boys and everyone's college plans." She grew hopeful about convincing them to extend another opportunity to attend their famous Lake Newton parties.

Lauren, the team's catcher, stopped talking to the rest of the bunch and leered at Amalia. "Do you even have a boyfriend to talk about?"

"You know she's never had one," said one of the other girls who liked reminding everyone that she fooled around with the captain of the football team behind the school bleachers after practice. The visible grass stains on her knees and a permanent crick in her neck had been dead giveaways to the entire team.

Lauren chimed in, "You've probably never even been kissed, have you, Amalia Graeme?"

Amalia had once been discussing *Great Expectations* with a boy from her class in the courtyard behind the hardware store. Unfortunately, it was one of those rare days when Janet came to the store to visit Peter. As the boy leaned over and kissed Amalia's lips once she said Pip and Estella were her favorite characters, Janet rushed through the back door and yanked her daughter away from the table. It was hard enough that the boy's lips snagged on Amalia's tooth and started bleeding. He cried when Janet screamed at him to leave her property. Amalia ran back inside, feeling mortified, and hid in the store. Janet warned her daughter to stay away from boys, threatening if she ever let one touch her body again, she'd end up a pregnant whore living in the streets. Although Amalia knew it was impossible to get pregnant from kissing, she'd little knowledge of physical intercourse since her education at First Baptist's religious school wouldn't allow any discussion or knowledge about sexuality. The church encouraged parents to provide the necessary basics for their children when it came to *the birds and the bees,* as they referred to it. All Janet would tell her daughter is never to let a boy put his demon seed inside her until she married him. Peter always assumed Janet had explained it all to Amalia. His list of inaccurate assumptions had grown far too long throughout the years.

"I have, too, been kissed." Amalia held a bit of confidence in her voice, but it wasn't enough to prolong the inevitable. She'd already been relegated back to the bottom of the pool of choices for someone new in their group.

Sally tossed her shoulder-length hair to the other side. "I bet you're still a virgin." Her laugh resembled a high-pitched boiling tea kettle ready to blow its lid. "Have you ever had sex? Because that's what we're talking about right now."

Lauren laughed as though she were a cackling bird. "And how to make sure he pulls out before he gets you pregnant."

Amalia's curiosity peeked, though her voice's timbre dropped a few decibels almost to the point no one else heard her. "What do you mean?"

Lauren grabbed the other girl and shook her head wildly. "Come on, let's leave this little baby alone with her daddy." The two linked arms before prancing across the parking lot. "That's as close as she'll ever get to having a man touch her."

Sally turned to Amalia before sauntering away. "Let me educate you, since no one else ever has. Pulling out is when you're having sex with a guy, and he's inside you without any protection. You make him pull out before he gets too close and shoots his gunk. Then you can't get pregnant from his sperm."

Amalia nodded. "Oh yes, I knew that. I thought you meant something else." Her stomach sank and grew twice as heavy. She shifted her weight to her left foot and hoped Sally couldn't see how much her legs had been twitching. "Maybe I'll see you at the lake next weekend?" *Exactly what were gunk and sperm?*

"Sure, you can tell us more about your first time. We'll let you know when we have another opening."

As Sally dashed away to catch up with the other girls, her pompous words stirred new heights of irritation within Amalia. She scowled, eager to learn more about having sex. She considered asking her brother again, but that made her stomach revolt with horror. When Amalia previously inquired about his first sexual experience with a girl, he cautioned his sister to ready herself for pain and tears when the boy ripped something in her body. Greg claimed he was trying to prevent his sister from letting any boys get inside her panties, referring to sex as '*getting your whistle wet.*' She planned to check the county's public library to find any available books that could explain everything, cursing her mother for being a prude who kept her daughter in the dark. But the library was at least ten miles away and difficult to get to, even on the bus.

Janet's acid voice jostled Amalia out of the distraction when she returned from the minister's office, limping and clutching something in her arms. "Don't stand there. Take this from me, girl. I can't carry it all by myself."

Amalia grabbed the picnic basket from her mother and tossed it in the back of the car. She was grateful for the temporary reprieve of silence on the ride home. Just as she stepped out of the car, Janet directed Amalia to bring sandwiches to the lake for her brother and Carter. "Mabel Newton brought them for the Pastor, but he was considerate enough to give them to us, knowing we're trying to save money for you to attend college. Not all parents are generous like I am. You know that, right?"

Amalia nodded. "That was kind of him. I'll bring them after I change clothes and eat something."

"Don't make your brother wait, Amalia. You are so selfish. Get down there right now. It won't take you but a few minutes."

Amalia opened her mouth to ask why they couldn't have stopped at the lake on the way home from church in the car, but she'd little energy even to reason with the woman. "Yes, Momma."

She grabbed a few sandwiches and bags of chips from the picnic basket, handing the lightened load to her mother, and lumbered down the driveway. While navigating the twists and turns of the half-mile distance, she nibbled on the sandwich, still hungry from skipping breakfast that morning. She'd taken a muffin with her, but her mother had eaten it in the car on the way to church.

Mississippi's infamous scorching one-hundred-degree temperatures had finally settled in the area. Large oak trees and wisteria bushes overtook most of the path and provided some shelter from the sun's penetrating rays, but the oppressive heat index wore anyone down. The air was thick and humid, and Amalia built up a small sweat from the repeat church outfit clinging to her body. Upon arriving at the entrance to the lake, she searched for her brother but was unable to find him. Amalia approached the grassy area and stepped down the old wooden planks over the shallow end of the lake. Distracted by the birds swooping down hoping to discover any fish to eat, Amalia failed to notice someone swimming toward the edge of the dock.

Carter jumped up from the lake, splashing her with drops of water when he leaned on the edge. "Looking for me again?"

As he grinned, Amalia noticed his blue eyes matched the color of her blouse. His bright white and perfectly straight teeth called attention to a handsome face she hadn't fully appreciated earlier. "You've gotten me all wet." Amalia brushed off the remnants of his unwelcome invasion, frustrated by his presence.

"Got you wet, did I? How clever you are." His shoulders and elbows rested on the wooden planks. The rippled muscles on his upper arms flexed while thin patches of hair glistened underneath. As he shook the water from his ear, thick blond hair that once formed a sharp spike above his head fell flat against his face, curling behind his narrow ears.

"Where's my brother?" Her voice blasted more intensely than she intended.

"Greg went to take a leak up in the woods somewhere. It's just you and me. What's in the bags?"

Amalia smiled. "Sandwiches. Do you want one?" She unwrapped the largest in the bag. "It's turkey and cheese."

"I'm also a bit wet." He nodded, then winked. "Maybe you could feed it to me?"

Amalia, befuddled by the boy her brother had brought home, again questioned his manners. Sometimes his rude and unabashedly direct behavior prevailed. Other times, his smile encouraged her to warm up to him. "As in hold the sandwich while you bite it?" She covered her lips, fearing bits of turkey stuck in between her teeth. "That's silly."

"I suppose. Or you could break off a piece for me?"

She listened and followed his suggestion. As she leaned in toward him, expecting him to reach for it with his hand, a devilish gleam appeared. "You're not gonna try to pull me in, are you?" She suppressed a wary giggle deep in her gut. Or maybe it was excitement. She wasn't sure.

"Did you *want* to come in the water with me?"

Amalia pulled her bottom lip inside her mouth, running her top teeth over it, contemplating how to respond. "I don't have a swimsuit." She lifted her hand in his direction, her fingers still nimbly holding a small piece of the sandwich. "Here, take it."

Carter raised himself a few inches higher and brought his mouth to her impatiently waiting fingers. His full lips gently sealed the temporarily open gap between them. Amalia's hand, uncertain what he was doing, twitched. Carter reached up with his right arm while his other held his body against the dock. He enveloped her hand with his, steadying her fingers near his lips as he slipped the morsel in his mouth. Swallowing the length of her index finger and thumb, he pulled back with delicate ease. When he reached the tip of her fingers, he paused and immersed himself in her gaze. "You taste delicious." Carter blinked in slow motion for what could have been thirty seconds but had barely been two or three.

"You mean the sandwich does." Amalia traced her finger against the soft patch of skin above his chin. His face was as smooth as her own flesh. A shiver meandered the curves of her dampening back.

"If you say so." Carter pulled himself fully out of the water landing near the other side of the dock. Barely two feet separated them, but he was careful not to drip any water on her a second time.

As he laid across the wooden planks dropping a handful of chips in his mouth, Amalia noticed not a single spot of hair on his chest or stomach. But Carter didn't have a stomach. He had a set of eight curved ridges that spanned the distance from his sternum to the top of his black trunks, a solid washboard of muscle. His dark swimsuit highlighted a sharp contrast to his golden skin, leaving her increasingly curious about what lurked beneath the trunks. She'd noticed other guys without their shirts, but none resembled Carter. Her hand quivered at the thought of his body nestled against hers. Amalia forced herself to look away, certain she shouldn't extend the reach of her fingers to his flesh.

"How's the water?" She stared in the opposite direction, fumbling with the button on her blouse. The heat had broken down her barriers.

Amalia considered taking off her shoes and dipping her feet into the lake. There wasn't any danger in showing her toes.

"A bit cool for me. I'm used to the Mediterranean in the summer. I usually spend them with my mother's family in Europe." Carter leaned back on his elbows and stretched his legs. His knee knocked the bag of sandwiches and chips on its side. "Are you gonna feed me any more treats?"

Amalia turned toward him with discomfort and anticipation growing inside her body all at once. She reached for the bag as he sat up and stopped just short of crashing into her. His eyelashes were long and thick. He was close enough to smell the sweet coconut scent of the suntan oil he'd applied earlier to his face. "Can't you feed yourself?" Temptation built inside her to wipe the smudge off the crease between his upper lip and nose. Amalia's heart pumped faster than normal, reminding her of times she'd considered stealing second base on the softball field—confident in wanting to take the risk but uncertain if she should.

Before Amalia had a chance to decide, Carter's lips pressed against hers with riveting pressure. His nose brushed against hers. She wanted to kiss him back, but something prevented her lips from moving. Letting him lead, her muscles relaxed. Carter's hand cupped the back of her neck. It cooled her off and built a fire inside her chest as each sensation undulated.

As his bottom lip pushed hers apart, Carter's tongue probed the roof of her mouth, pushing until it synchronized with hers in a sensual pattern. As if instinct kicked in when their tongues embraced, the fire in her chest sent a flood of warmth throughout her body. When the sensation traversed the path to her waist, she found herself squeezing her thighs tightly together and lifting toward him. Amalia trembled at the strength of his arms in the powerful grip he had on her neck. An urge to open her mouth wider, as if she wanted to bite him, beckoned.

A small gasp escaped Amalia's mouth as Carter separated. "Yeah, I was right. You do taste delicious," he whispered.

She shuffled back a few inches, overwhelmed by what had happened. Amalia had never experienced anything similar, excitedly questioning the rush of energy that surged between her legs and inside her chest. She'd less than a few seconds to bask in the pleasure before her brother's voice called to them in the distance.

"Amalia, what brings you here?" Greg briskly jogged down the dock toward them. "We were just gonna head back to grab some lunch."

Amalia nervously covered her chest, afraid her brother had caught them kissing, or that he'd noticed her nipples still poked through the fabric of her blouse. *What is going on with my body?* She lunged for the bag, smacking into Carter, who'd thrown his hands over the front of his trunks. Amalia looked down at the bulge he unsuccessfully hid. She shook her head back and forth as if to detach the images and thoughts, then grabbed a sandwich from the bag and tossed it to her brother.

"Nothing. Just going. I brought lunch. Bye." Amalia rushed off, unable to glance back at either her brother or Carter. For the second time that weekend, a boy had shown interest in her, and she recognized feelings inside her body she'd never experienced before—the things she feared her mother had been warning her all about when referring to the temptation of a demon's seed.

* * *

At dinner that night, Amalia avoided becoming trapped alone with or talking to Carter. She spoke to her father about his new train set and to Greg about his impending job search. Greg revealed he planned to work at the hardware store before starting his own job. After clearing the dishes, Amalia returned to the dining room and joined the conversation to determine what they spoke about while she'd been gone.

"Why did he go to New York City?" asked Peter.

Greg shrugged. "He took his uncle's job offer to work in a warehouse at the shipping yards. He thought he might earn good money."

Peter nodded. "He's a smart boy. I always admired him for having a good head on his shoulders."

While adjusting the collar of her repeat church outfit—she still hadn't found time to change out of it—Amalia listened to figure out who they discussed. As her bare feet stretched under the table, something gently rubbed against her ankles. Amalia wanted to check, but her mother had been glaring at her.

"Quit your fussing with that collar and sit still. You're more nervous than a man reciting his wedding vows." Janet scooped another spoonful of ice cream into her mouth. It dripped from her chapped lips as she dropped the utensil into the bowl.

"Yes, Momma." Amalia tried shifting her foot, but it was caught between the table and someone else. It could only be Carter or her brother, as both sat across from her. She was certain it wasn't Greg.

Carter pressed down harder as though it were a game of control between their separate desires. "I never had a chance to meet him, but I heard good things." Carter's toes trapped Amalia's feet against the floor.

Amalia tried to escape, but he wouldn't let her. "Who are you talking about?"

"Bryan took a train to New York City today," whined Greg, shrugging as if he were annoyed by her question.

Amalia pulled her foot back with such force her knee banged the underside of the table, knocking over her glass of milk and spilling her father's coffee. Her heart sank upon learning Bryan had left town.

"What is wrong with you, girl?" Janet shouted and waved her hands furiously. "Get a rag to clean this mess."

Peter jumped up when the hot coffee poured over the edge of the table onto his lap, stirring him from a distraction. "It's okay, honey."

"Yes, Momma." Amalia rushed from the dining room into the kitchen, incapable of processing the news.

Greg followed her into the kitchen. "I'll help."

Amalia's hands trembled at the kitchen sink, willing the forming tears not to betray her. "Why did he leave?"

"Who, Bryan?" Greg tore several paper towels from the holder.

Amalia splashed some cool water on her face. Bryan must have thought she didn't want to see him again. She was certain something had changed at the train depot when they were talking. "He said nothing to me."

Greg laughed. "Why would Bryan tell you he was gonna leave? When did you two become friends?"

Amalia ran to the dining room to wipe the coffee from her father's section of the table. She dropped off a replacement cup and returned to the kitchen with the dirty towels.

Carter followed her and whispered in her ear but out of Greg's range. "I enjoyed our moment at the lake earlier today." His hand cupped the small curve of her back above her hips.

Annoyed by Carter's words, Amalia groaned with angst. "Bryan and I *are* friends. We talked a few times while you were away, Greg. That's all." She didn't want him to know about the potential date with Bryan the day before. "Why did he leave?"

Greg turned from the sink. "He thought some girl was interested in him until she never showed up when they were supposed to meet. He'd been thinking about sticking around but figured if he couldn't even get a girl to keep a date with him, it was time to leave good old Brant." He went back into the dining room with more towels, mumbling about the pretty chicks he could find if he were going to New York City.

Amalia sneered at Carter, suddenly becoming angry with him. If he hadn't offered to drive Greg home, Greg wouldn't have shown up for a few more days, and she would have been able to meet Bryan at the magnolia tree.

"Seems like you didn't want this Bryan guy to leave, Monster?" Carter dropped his plate in the sink next to Amalia, resting his shoulder against hers. His mouth remained firmly set with a smirk that conveyed both curiosity and disappointment to Amalia.

Though he confused her, the same warm sensation from earlier in the day tingled inside her body. "Maybe, I didn't. Maybe I did. I told you to stop calling me *Monster*. I'm not a kid anymore."

"Right." Carter caressed her cheek, tracing his thumb across the outline of her lips. "Kids definitely don't act like you did at the lake. At least not the ones I know." His gaze was glued to her as he stepped backward toward the hallway.

Amalia struggled to breathe when her throat closed. "Shut up. You're such a jerk." She threw the wet towel at him, then shoved him into the counter as he caught it. "You've no idea what you're talking about."

"What is going on with you two?" Greg shouted as he walked back into the kitchen. "We've been here less than twenty-four hours, and you're already fighting. Come on, let's play some hoops. I need to work off that ice cream." He lifted his shirt and patted his flat and hollow stomach. "I'm not nearly as ripped as my boy, Carter."

"Sorry." Carter followed Greg through the mudroom, stopping behind Amalia on his way to the door. "I thought you liked it when I teased you."

Amalia busied herself with shelving pots in the cabinet and stopping images of his half-naked body from amplifying her reactions.

"You left some dishes on this table, Amalia. Come, take them away." Irritation accompanied Janet's voice worse than a cat violently letting the world know it was in heat.

Amalia refused to look up as Carter backed out the door with his glare firmly planted on her body. He winked, but she ignored him and entered the dining room to clear the plates.

"Are you still talking about Bryan?" Janet's determined gape and voice that sounded like nails on a chalkboard burrowed under her daughter's skin. She poured herself another cup of coffee, as black as her heart, then added three packets of fake sugar substitute.

As the crystals disappeared into the bitterness that was her mother, Amalia lifted her head and cringed at Bryan's name. "He came here for me?"

Janet belched loudly before speaking again. "He came by looking for you while you were down at the lake. What did he want?"

A brief blip of happiness surged followed by anger once realizing she'd lost her only opportunity to explain her absence at the lake. "Why didn't you tell me before?"

Janet scoffed. "Why does it matter? I didn't think about it earlier. I just did now when I heard his name. What's wrong with you?" She leered at Amalia, who sat in the chair and stopped collecting dishes. "Take this stuff into the kitchen. I told you we were done."

Peter grabbed the remaining plates, but as he reached over for Janet's, she pulled it away. He retreated with confusion. "I'm just helping to clear the rest of the table."

"It's not your responsibility. Let Amalia do her job." Janet shoved the plate across the table, but it slid too far and landed on the floor. "Stand up and get the plate, girl. Why are you sulking like a child tonight?"

"I needed to talk to Bryan before he left. You took that away from me, Momma. All you had to do was give me one message." Tears dripped down Amalia's cheeks as her head rested on the tabletop.

"I won't allow you to talk to me like that. Clean up that floor before I get back down here." Janet turned to Peter before hobbling out of the room. "You better knock some sense into your silly little daughter thinking I'm supposed to take messages for her."

"I'm sorry, Momma. I didn't mean to be rude." Amalia lifted her head and bent over to pick up the plate. "Please tell me what Bryan's message was. I promise I'll behave." She desperately needed to know what Bryan had meant and would say anything to get the update from her mother.

"You should think about that before you speak next time." Janet's large nostrils swelled as she breathed in. "He didn't say much. Never does that boy. He mentioned I should tell you he's sorry for any confusion."

Amalia pleaded with her mother for the full story. "What did you say to him?"

"I told him you mix things up all the time. What exactly did you do, Amalia? I warned you before about behaving yourself." The rapid thump of Janet's rubber sole hitting the wooden floor echoed throughout the room, jostling Amalia with the full force Janet had intended.

"Nothing, Momma. We talked about when Greg would arrive home so he could say goodbye to him. That's all." Amalia collected the rest of the plates and lumbered to the kitchen.

"You're gonna get yourself in a heap of trouble one day for all these little lies. It won't be my problem much longer. Once you're out on your own, you can clean up your own messes." Janet marched up the staircase, calling back halfway, "Bring me some tea in a half hour. It helps me sleep better."

Once he was confident Janet had closed the bedroom door, Peter approached his daughter. "Come here, my pet. Give me a hug."

Amalia dropped the dishes in the sink and ran to her father. "Oh, Daddy. I want to get out of here. I can't take it anymore."

"I know. Sometimes it's better not to argue with her. She just gets riled up. You'll be off to school in a couple of weeks." He suggested Amalia head outside for fresh air. "I'll clean up these dishes and get your mother the tea. I need to have a little talk with her about the things she said to you. I know she has her beliefs and values, but sometimes she takes it too far."

Amalia dropped her head and plodded to the front porch. She curled up in the wicker chair as the lights from the cars on their way toward the lake, or on their way out of Brant, flickered in the distance. Either way they traveled, it would be better than remaining stuck in the house with her mother and Carter for the rest of the summer. Soon she'd be leaving for college and find her happiness, even if it was the last thing she accomplished.

# Chapter 6

# Brianna, June 2004

Twenty minutes and one subway transfer later, Brianna arrived at Shanelle's townhouse. As Brianna reached for the bell, the door swung open. Shanelle, who had the place to herself for the weekend with both parents away at conferences, licked a spoonful of Nutella. She wore a long t-shirt that covered only what needed to be covered and left her bare legs glistening from the incoming light.

"You wouldn't answer my messages." Brianna should have apologized first, but Shanelle's beauty made opening with a grovel impossible.

"You had nothing good enough to respond to."

"That's not fair. I'm here now."

"Did you sleep with him?"

Brianna tilted her head toward her shoulder and pushed her lips out in a small pout. The flame of the gas lamp protruding from the entrance's gray brick lit her face as though she were on the red carpet. Her expression, an innocent yet playful grin, did not go unnoticed to Shanelle.

"You didn't, did you?"

Brianna shook her head. "Not unless you count my foot connecting with his stomach as foreplay."

Shanelle smiled. "Come on, I've been waiting for you. Let's watch *The L Word*. You need a reminder of what you're missing."

Brianna followed Shanelle inside, happy to land where she should have been all night. As they curled up on the bed together, Brianna shared a step-by-step blow of everything at the prom, including the choice words she'd said about a certain part of Doug's body.

They watched a few episodes of their favorite cable drama, screamed at the TV, and drank a shot of Shanelle's father's expensive liquor whenever someone kissed. Within two hours, both had collapsed under Shanelle's plush comforter and fallen fast asleep.

* * *

The next morning, Brianna's eyes blinked open with uncertainty where she laid. Clarity appeared upon noticing her much lighter-skinned leg entwined within Shanelle's smooth, dark caramel-colored thigh. The beautiful contrast in colors reminded her of their personalities—opposite in so many ways, yet always drawing out the best in one another.

She slipped from the embrace, careful not to wake Shanelle, and tiptoed to the bathroom. They'd moved a solid step forward in their friendship that night, but it was still too soon to take their relationship to any intimate levels, especially while Brianna worked through the choices in her mind. Cuddling had always been part of their camaraderie, but the line was kept firm when it came to full indulgence in her deepest fantasies. Brianna would only allow herself to cross that divide upon a certainty that she could accept who she was and what she wanted. It wasn't about labels. She couldn't care less if someone called her queer or a dyke. Brianna simply cared too much to lead her best friend on if there weren't any genuine hope of her ever accepting the sexual attraction as anything more than confusion or experimenting while still young.

Brianna showered and dried off with a towel from the nearby linen closet before pulling on panties and a bra. The whole bathroom was the size of either bedroom back in her mother's apartment. Purple towels, wallpaper, and tiles—like everything else in Shanelle's life—the only color she truly loved. Regal. Royal. Powerful. It also happened to be the same color of the dress Brianna had worn to the prom which she now quietly searched for upon returning to the bedroom. It was nowhere in sight.

"I hung it up while you were in the shower." Fully dressed in a low-cut green blouse and pair of dark, skinny jeans, Shanelle sat at her desk and typed on a laptop. "I'm making reservations for brunch. Are you hungry?"

Brianna walked toward the other side of the bed to locate her overnight bag. She'd packed another outfit, giving it to Shanelle to bring home the previous day. "A quick bite, but then I should head home. I need to talk to my mom."

Shanelle swung the chair around and focused across the room. She held a pair of tortoise-shell eyeglasses in one hand while her lips nibbled on one of the frame's arms. Her hair was pulled back and tied in a bun on the top of her head, except for a few rogue strands that fell against her cheek. She looked sexy in the morning, while Brianna needed at least an hour before daring to show her face in public. "Are you sure you're ready to tell her about us?"

Brianna adored Shanelle. They'd been best friends for two years, but the girl went from zero to sixty faster than any car on the market. "No, we're friends, maybe more. Just because I didn't do anything with Doug last night doesn't mean I'm ready to buy some flannel, listen to Indigo Girls all day long, and build a log cabin with you."

"We're not a lesbian couple in the eighties, Bree. We can choose our own version." Shanelle began making the bed. "Seriously, stop being so scared of giving this a chance."

"You're in a funky mood this morning." Brianna tossed her towel across the room and laughed when it landed on Shanelle's head. She pulled some clothes from her bag while Shanelle fixed her hair.

"Damn, that smells good," said Shanelle, holding the towel up to her nose. "It's like you're near me even when you aren't."

"Let's get out of here. You're delirious from not eating."

"Yeah, you don't want to miss the appointment I made before you head home to receive the daily dose of Proud Mary's smothering."

"Who are we meeting this early?" As Brianna pulled a tight-fitting t-shirt over her head, she found herself with one elbow stuck in the fabric and in need of rescue. After struggling for a few seconds, she gave in. "Help, please."

Shanelle moved forward to undo the constraints and pull the shirt to Brianna's waist, but her nimble hands never stopped upon reaching the tempting curves of her best friend's hips. Brianna had been blessed with a slim body, just curvy enough in the areas that counted. "You're the worst kind of mess."

"Thank you," said Brianna, huffing. "But I should put on some pants if we're meeting someone. Do I get any hints?" She enjoyed being close, but if Shanelle didn't stop, it could lead to more.

"Your wish is my command, Lady Bree." Shanelle grabbed a pair of jeans from the bag and knelt on the ground in front of her. "Let me finish dressing you."

Brianna rested her hand on Shanelle's shoulder, balancing on one leg as she lifted her other into the jeans. Once her first leg went fully through the hole at the bottom, she shifted her weight to allow Shanelle to pull through the other leg. Brianna jumped up a few times, stretching the tight denim across her butt and waist. She brought her hands around front to fasten them but was interrupted.

"That's for me to do." Shanelle pulled Brianna's back tightly against her own chest, tracing her fingertips across the outline of Brianna's jean pocket until reaching the zipper. She gently clasped it, rubbing her nimble fingers against Brianna's body, careful to stop every few centimeters and apply a slight bit of pressure against the flesh hiding behind the fabric. Brianna's eyelids fluttered, and she inhaled a deep breath. Slowly zipping the jeans and fastening the button closed, Shanelle brushed her lips against Brianna's neck, then slid her fingers just under the hem of her silk panties. "I suppose I'm all done for now."

Brianna enjoyed every moment of it, wishing her mind would concede to her body's demands, but she'd already decided to hold off until there was more certainty about the truth. "You know how to make me feel special."

"Trust me. I'm only demonstrating a small sample of what I plan to do after you let me in."

Brianna, pushing every desirous thought from her mind, packed her bag and followed Shanelle to the quiet street. It was mostly residential, and although there were a few doctor's offices, none were open on a Sunday. "Let's come back for the dress later. I need to take it to the cleaners to get Doug's stench off it." She broke out into laughter over the comment, then filled with nervous curiosity about what Shanelle had arranged that morning.

Upon arriving at the coffee shop, Shanelle opened the door and searched the large and bright space. Exposed industrial ceilings and lighting flooded the seating area, and the smell of freshly baked scones and a rich, nutty brew permeated the air. "I'll get a table. You get the coffee."

"You never said who we're meeting." A bit of concern weakened Brianna's confidence in her best friend's plans. Shanelle often sprung the craziest ideas on her at the last minute, but Brianna's fears of being trapped always edged out the potential fun it would bring.

"Can't you just trust me?"

Brianna relinquished, then approached the counter and ordered two tall coffees. She smiled at a man who got in line behind her. Late thirties. Dark suit, striped pink shirt, and blue tie. Light beard trimmed close to his cheeks. He resembled Matt Dillon in *There's Something About Mary*—it was her favorite movie. After paying for her coffee, she filled both cups with milk, avoided the sugar, and returned to the table.

"Friend of yours?" Shanelle lifted her head and frowned.

"No, being friendly. There's a difference." Brianna shook her head and removed the plastic lid from the cup. "Mmm… delicious."

"The guy from the line at the counter?" Her voice, flat and direct, left no room for argument. Shanelle always had the last word, even when she was just trying to be humorous.

"What are you talking about?" Brianna checked on the man paying for his beverage. "Well, he is cute, but I meant the coffee."

Shanelle folded her hands together, exhaling a large breath of noisy air. "Let's play a little game… *What kind of guy does Brianna find attractive?*" She scanned the length of the coffee shop, skipping the teenage girls dressed in too-tight halter tops and miniskirts who were standing in the corner giggling at their phones, then counted aloud and looked back toward Brianna. "There are four eligible guys in here. What about that one in line for the bathroom?"

"Does this have something to do with who we're meeting? This game makes no sense." Brianna sighed with deep exasperation and groaned excessively while waiting for a response.

"Do me a favor, just play along, babe. What do you think of Mr. Gets-Off-Watching-Himself-Flex-in-the-Mirror-Muscles?" She jutted her head toward a young guy wearing a black crewneck short-sleeve shirt, acid wash jeans, and heavy dark military boots. His biceps were the size of oranges, and the bulges in his neck reminded her of large chunks of spiral ham.

"Fine, I'll indulge you. He's too built and as big as a giant side of meat. Probably a dumb jock who plays football and calls his girlfriend *Princess* all the time like she's so special because he chose her."

"And that one, over in the corner table." Shanelle pointed out another twentyish guy, pale skin, lanky with reddish hair and large plastic-framed glasses. "What about Doogie-Blows-His-Load-Too-Soon?"

"Umm, no. He belongs with that chick over there in the Birkenstocks and jean shorts." Brianna pointed to a slightly heavy girl biting her hair and listening to music on her iPod. "You know, a convention of Star Trek freaks and Clay Aiken fans."

"You love Clay Aiken." Shanelle threw her hand up in the air and grinned widely. They'd been binge-watching *American Idol* that season.

"I only like one song, so it doesn't count. Why are we playing this game?" Brianna grew impatient, gritting her teeth and tapping her sneakers against the metal rod in between the chair legs. The nerves in her neck pulsed with annoyance.

"Two more. Let's just finish. The tattooed and pierced guy near the front window."

Brianna shook her head. "That's Darcy's boyfriend. He rides his motorcycle to our games and watches through the chain-link fence without ever coming inside. Rumor is… he joined a cult."

"Answer the question. Do you find him attractive?"

"No."

"But that guy behind you in line was hot?"

"I didn't say that."

"You didn't have to."

"Yeah, I guess he had a nice smile, seemed cool and collected." Brianna was out of patience and considered storming out of the coffee shop. "That's all."

"That's not why you were into him." Shanelle sipped from her cup. The steam rose from her lips and clouded by her forehead as she gazed intently at Brianna.

"Who the hell said I was into him? Why are you being so bitchy?" Brianna pushed off her chair, not realizing the Matt Dillon look-alike she'd been talking about had walked up behind her.

"Hey, how's your day going?" His voice was smooth and confident. He tilted his head toward Shanelle while backing up to avoid the collision. "Sorry, I got stuck chatting at the counter."

Shanelle laughed, clearly enjoying the game more than Brianna, who huffed while wiping coffee from her hand. "It's fine. I haven't yet told her about you."

He glanced at Brianna and tasted his cup. "I'm Malachi, a pleasure to be of service." He reached a firm hand toward her. He sounded like Matt Dillon, too.

"I'm Brianna. It's nice to meet you." After shaking his hand, she turned toward Shanelle. "Am I supposed to know who this is?"

Shanelle jumped up from the table. "I should probably leave you two alone."

As Shanelle paraded away, Brianna grabbed her arm. "Wait, I don't understand."

"He's here for you. Not me." Shanelle clenched her jaw and grunted. "I need to let off some steam."

Malachi interjected. "I'm a private detective. I work for Shanelle's mother's law firm. She asked me to meet you here to talk about a search for your father."

"Really?" Brianna's temper cooled down upon understanding what was going on.

Shanelle yielded. "Yes, I was trying to be helpful, but then you pulled that stunt."

"Am I interrupting something?" said Malachi, backing away from the table again.

Brianna ushered Shanelle to the front door while shouting behind her shoulder. "Malachi, give me five minutes, I'll be right back." They stepped outside. Brianna usually let Shanelle have her way, at least most of the time. Occasionally, things went too far, which meant Brianna had to stand up for herself. It only happened when a situation became too tense over the boundaries in their relationship or Brianna's inability to open up more. Despite the frustration, she liked the way Shanelle challenged her, even if it made her angry at first.

"I need to go," said Shanelle.

"Were you serious with that attitude back there? I wasn't interested in him. I was being friendly. You know... like how people are when they meet someone new. Not a nightmare like you." Brianna's hands fell to her hips, willing herself not to release her frustrations at Shanelle. It would only be misdirected as her problem with being too controlling was with her mother and not Shanelle. Even if Shanelle had mistaken the conversation Brianna had with Malachi as flirting, Brianna knew it came from a place of love. The delivery just needed to be better packaged next time.

"Fine, let it go. Let's get back to Bree's search for a daddy." Shanelle's feet stomped down the sidewalk past a nail salon and flower store, putting out its *We're Open* sign.

"That's not fair. You have a father. You're not an orphan."

"You have a mother. Orphans don't have any parents." Shanelle's voice grew more enraged as she reached the corner of the street. "I don't understand the big deal."

Brianna shouted to Shanelle and motioned for her to come back. "Please stop for a minute and let me explain." She switched her bag to her other shoulder while waiting for Shanelle to comply.

"I'm listening." Shanelle trudged a few feet closer but stopped short, forcing Brianna to meet her in the middle.

"You have an enormous family with a mother, a father, and tons of siblings. You celebrate with your grandparents every month at the big, happy Trudeau lunch. You guys all go to church together and have family vacations with deep connections and memories to hold on to in the future."

"Yeah, but they're also a pain in the ass. My brothers are always eating the last piece of cake or leaving the kitchen a mess. My grandmother tells me I need to stop playing soccer and put on more dresses. My father constantly tells me how I gotta follow in his footsteps as a doctor. It's not all happy moments." She huffed loudly between each example before settling against the wall with her hands shoved in her pockets in frustration.

"But you have the moments, whether they're good or bad. There's someone to share each day with. I've got no one. Do you hear me? No one!"

"You've got your mother."

"You know that's not what I mean. She works all the time, but someday she'll be gone, and I'll have no one by my side."

"You've got my family and me. They love you. Besides, you control who you let in your life. Stop holding me back."

"That's different. I'm grateful your family cares about me, but I never had a father supporting me in the audience at dance recitals. There was no one to pick me up and swing me around in his arms at the park. I won't have two parents to congratulate me when I graduate high school or go to college." Brianna threw her hands to her face and covered her eyes. She wouldn't let herself cry in public on the street. "Seriously. Do you know what it feels like to be the only kid who doesn't have anyone show up at their soccer games? Or to wonder if you're the reason your father's no longer around?"

Shanelle leaned forward and reached for Brianna's hand. "I'm sorry. I know it's been hard for you, but you don't know why your father isn't around. Maybe there's a valid reason. You can't blame yourself, babe."

"And let's not forget that there might never be a sentimental dad to walk me down the aisle when I get married. Or to tell me how proud he is of the woman I've become."

Shanelle purred while rubbing her fingers against the palm of Brianna's hand. "I didn't know you wanted to get married. That's good news."

"Stop changing the subject and be serious for a moment with me." Brianna idolized Shanelle, often put her high on a pedestal, but every time she tried to convey her actual emotions, Shanelle tried to make light of it. "I can't help how I feel."

"Okay, but what does that have to do with you flirting with guys in a coffee shop? I don't understand it especially after I hired him to help you out."

"You're being entirely too jealous. I thought you were stronger than that."

"I'm not jealous. I'm... worried... concerned you're not getting the right help. You've been canceling on me a lot lately. You can't make up your mind about Doug or whether you want to test the waters with me. I think you're depressed over how being fatherless makes you feel. I can't argue with why you're feeling it, but trust me, it's loud and clear lately. I just want to help you."

"Shanelle, I can't keep trying to explain something even I don't understand. I wasn't flirting. I'm attracted to you, and I find women beautiful. I liked Doug at one point, and yes, I said Malachi was cute but only after you forced me into that silly game. I didn't even think about him that way when I was standing in line. I don't know what's going on with me holding myself back from experimenting with you. I'm trying to deal with it as best I can."

"I know I'm being tough on you right now, but there's a reason for it. I'm not about babying people I love just to lift their spirits for a few minutes. I'm about the long-term solutions and telling you the truth." Shanelle pulled Brianna closer and rubbed her shoulders. "You have a pattern with this behavior. Where do you draw the line over being real with yourself?"

"If I knew, maybe I wouldn't be so scared." Brianna slumped against the wall next to an open stairwell leading underneath the florist shop. "I want to figure this out. I can't deny how I feel or avoid taking risks my whole life, but I can permit myself to explore both sides for a while. Right?"

"Are you're saying I have to let you do this? To flirt with strange men in a coffee shop, even though you aren't really interested. To go to the prom with a guy, even though you say you don't have any feelings for him. To watch you get hurt because you won't listen to me or trust me? Even *that* kind of patience would test the grand Zen Master, Gandhi."

"I'm not gonna learn a lesson because you tell how to do something. I need to live, breathe, and experience it myself. Just like I gotta push my mother to tell me who my father is, so I can figure out the truth. Once I have an answer about that, maybe I'll finally let myself freely explore a relationship with you." Brianna stepped away from the ivy-covered wall and breathed deeply to calm herself. "I work better by putting everything in buckets, tackling one problem at a time."

"I hope you realize it's not that I don't *want* to wait for you." Shanelle reached for Brianna's hand. "You're worth it, but I can't stand to see you so hurt and lost."

"I'm not lost when I'm with you. I'm just being cautious about jumping in too quickly."

"What do you want me to do while you're figuring this out?"

"We're gonna be together at Woodland. Away from your family. Away from my mother. All in less than two months. Can't you give me until then to find out more about my father?"

Shanelle pulled Brianna's hands to her lips and kissed them. "I suppose I can do that."

"Let me talk to Malachi and my mom to get some answers. Then maybe we can focus on what's going on between us."

"Okay, I understand, but I need a little breather right now. I'm gonna head to the field and kick some soccer balls around. Let's catch up later tonight. We'll both feel a little better, babe."

Brianna smiled as her best friend walked away knowing she was the most generous albeit pushy person she'd ever known. "Promise me you will stop being so sensitive every time I talk to some guy."

"Fine. I'll never doubt your intentions with another guy. That what you want to hear?"

"Don't make more out of this. It's nothing. Do you believe me?" asked Brianna.

Shanelle turned the corner without responding. Brianna pushed away her trepidations, returned to the coffee shop, and joined Malachi. "I'm sorry. She's having a bad morning." Brianna gulped the leftovers from her cup and paused while pulling herself together. "Okay, so you're a private investigator?"

Malachi explained his role at the law firm. "Yep, I often need to find missing people or long-lost relatives as part of estate planning. Shanelle thought I might help trace your father's identity or maybe determine where your mother lived before New York."

"I know nothing about my mother. Nor do I really have any money to pay you."

"Money's already covered. Shanelle took care of a few days' retainer to get us started. Let's discuss whatever you do know. Name, date of birth, *any* previous addresses?"

Brianna laughed, recalling the many times she'd asked her mother for information. She then provided Malachi with any known facts, which ultimately amounted to practically nothing. She hadn't even known her mother's place of birth or social security number but thought she could find something in their apartment. "What's your next step?"

"The Internet. Lots of opportunities to research people based on information they left behind without realizing their mistakes. I'll begin with a basic background check, then chat with my guy at the DMV who owes me a few favors. If you can get me her social security number, or any cities she once lived, it would be easier to narrow down my results."

"She doesn't even have an email account. It's like she's always lived off the grid." Brianna didn't want to get her hopes up, but this was her first potential lead. "Do you think you can still find anything?"

"If you only have a little piece to go on, I might locate her parents, then determine where she lived just before you were born. That could point us in a better direction to find your father." Malachi shook her hand and left a business card on the table before stepping away. He turned back just before exiting the door. "Listen, I don't want to lead you on. Usually, in cases like these, the person is running from something they've done in the past. She might have been incredibly careful about leaving behind any traces of her former life. Call me in a few days to see what I've found out."

Brianna left the coffee shop and leaned against the storefront, excited at the prospect of finally making progress in the search for her father. Any information might help her move forward, even if it was news she didn't want to receive. When her phone rang, she accepted the call without looking at the display screen. "I knew you couldn't walk away from me." She pushed off the brick wall and ran to the corner with hopes Shanelle hid on the other side, but she wasn't there.

"Hello. Is this Brianna Porter?" said an unfamiliar voice.

Brianna snapped the phone away from her ear and checked who called. It was a number she hadn't recognized. "Yes, this is her. She." *Do grammar freaks just make up these rules?*

"I'm calling from the admissions office at Woodland College. Do you have a moment to speak?"

"Sure. Did you receive my acceptance submission?"

"We received your confirmation email, but unfortunately, it was incomplete."

"I thought I didn't need my mother's approval since I turned eighteen already." Brianna's pulse accelerated. "I have to attend Woodland."

"Yes, I understand, and you are temporarily enrolled. There's no issue with you attending Woodland, except you've marked all the forms as requiring financial aid in order to proceed. We need more information regarding your parents' income, their approval for any student loans, and confirmation they can pay for the portion listed on the acceptance terms, Miss Porter."

Brianna had only submitted the acknowledgment form, indicating she chose Woodland, forgetting about the entire financial side of the process due to her preoccupation with everything going on around her. "When do you need this information?"

"We have some of it, but there's nothing mentioned about your father or his income. A parent also needs to co-sign the electronic form you returned to us. We have about a week to get this all sorted out."

Brianna's heart plummeted. "What if I've never met my father?"

"That's fine, but we'll need proof he isn't in the picture or has passed on. We only need one parent's signature if that's who will send payment. Perhaps we should schedule a call to discuss everything with both you and your mother?"

Brianna hadn't considered her father might be dead. Her stomach started churning again. "This won't stop me from attending in the fall, will it?" She leaned against the entrance to the subway, kicking her sneakers against the cement divider. "I can fix this."

"It won't as long as you provide the remaining information by the end of next week. Why don't we have a call on Tuesday at one o'clock to discuss everything?"

Brianna agreed and hung up the phone. She debated on the best approach with her mother, uncertain how to reveal she'd applied to an entirely different college without ever mentioning it before. They'd saved enough for her to afford to go to Woodland along with several student loans and other financial aid but living somewhere other than home and attending college out-of-state needed her mother's consent and additional funding to proceed.

trunks? Let go of me." She tried to push away, but his grip was too strong.

"It's hot out. Who needs to wear a swimsuit? Over-dressed much?" He clenched his muscles until her hands cupped his hard butt.

"You're so rude."

"Don't you find it sexy having me in your arms with your fingers inches away from certain parts of my naked body?" He sneered at her while delivering each word, leaning in to kiss her neck.

Amalia was too flustered to speak and struggled against his arms before freeing herself from his clutches. "Sexy? I barely know you." She wavered between wanting to scream and yearning to be even closer.

Carter disregarded her response and guided Amalia toward the edge of the lake. "I think you're just acting shy."

Amalia let him lead until reaching a spot where they could both walk. "You go first, but then turn around."

Carter capitulated. "Okay. We'll play it your way." He let go of her hand and waded through the water back to the grassy area. "Enjoy the show."

His broad shoulders emerged, followed by his back, rippled with muscles from playing lacrosse. Within seconds, Amalia stared at his butt, flustered as his perfectly round cheeks bounced from side to side. She'd never seen a man's naked backside before, but it was certainly an attractive part. She now understood what bubble butt meant. "Put on some clothes, Carter," she demanded.

Carter turned around once he was out of the water, his entire body displayed as though he'd modeled in a storefront window. "Sure, just about to. I thought you might want to look at the front side, too. I play fair, you know."

Amalia focused on his devilish grin plastered ear to ear. She allowed herself a quick glance downward, admiring his chest and the V-shape forming just above his stomach. His body had tempted her the last time they'd been swimming, but she had more to appreciate this time around. She let herself roam past his waist, curious what she'd see without his trunks. Amalia had a two-second view before he playfully covered himself up, unsure if she was amazed or scared by what he had to offer. "I... didn't mean to look... just..." Shyness stole the words from her lips, but her focus remained transfixed.

"That's all you get today. Only a quick peek. Got to leave you wanting more, right?" Carter laughed as he pulled on his shorts. "Now you."

Amalia shook her head. No way was she getting out of the water while he watched. "Cover your face or turn around."

"Okay, I don't want to make you uncomfortable." Carter placed his hand over his eyes, careful to leave enough of a crack between his fingers to allow an unobstructed view.

Amalia emerged from the water with her hands and arms crossed over her chest. "Thank you."

She reached for her shirt, but Carter also lunged for it. When they grabbed it at the same time, he pulled her close and kissed her. She didn't fight him off. As they separated, his gaze grew wide. "Don't be nervous. Your body looks beautiful."

Amalia's face flushed. "I've only been kissed once before." She wasn't sure if she could let herself trust him. "I'm not really sure..."

Carter nodded while reaching for her hand. "I can teach you. I mean, you're great, and I would love to spend time alone with you. Get to know you better." His finger rubbed circles in the palm of her right hand.

Amalia, anxious over being exposed, yet excited at Carter's attention, giggled. "I don't know how I feel about you."

"Let's go on a date. We'll take it from there. Don't you trust me?"

Amalia rested her head against his shoulder, conjuring memories of different happy moments from when she was younger. When her father brought home their dog, Buttons, who slept in her bed every night. When her brother made the dollhouse for her ninth birthday, carving two figures that resembled him and her. When she received the acceptance letters from several colleges, knowing she would finally escape from Brant. "Let me think about it."

She traced her fingers across the prominent collarbone outside the base of his neck, scared and curious at the same time. Carter was the her acclimate to college life, acquainting her with sororities and social clubs, but clarified that his priority was networking with local businesses hoping to attain an internship.

It'd been Amalia's first time away from her parents, and while she dreamed of finally getting out of Brant, her new home was strange and full of uncertainty. She felt younger than the rest of the people in her class. They'd traveled to other parts of the country, had friends on campus already, and knew how to socialize with the rest of the students. Carter also wouldn't ever visit Amalia's dorm room, claiming it was better for her to get out and meet new people. He explained that the rest of his friends would tease him if he went back to visiting the freshmen dorms. She agreed that he knew best.

Amalia tried to build a friendship with her roommate, Rachel Abernathy, but it started out poorly from the first day on campus, as they had truly little in common. Less than ten minutes into their introduction, Amalia had flashbacks of Sally and the rest of the softball team. Her new roommate had papered the walls with posters of *Miami Vice*, rock bands, and a couple of movies that were unfamiliar to Amalia. Rachel and her piercing, saccharine voice planned to rush Sigma Tau when she was eligible in the spring. She spent most of her nights hanging out at the sorority house with her older sister, who was in Carter's graduating class.

Amalia was stuck with the top mattress on the bunk bed, an arduous climb given her body type. Rachel had arrived earlier with three times as many boxes and claimed a larger part of the space in the room. Between her roommate's hair products, shoes, and clothes, there was little space left for Amalia. Asking sweetly if they could switch beds was Amalia's first approach, but Rachel's look of death soon caused her to back down. Later, realizing she'd brought nothing with her but one suitcase of clothes and a few books, Amalia hoped they could become friends down the line if she kept her mouth shut. For now, they ignored one another to keep the peace, especially when Rachel badmouthed her to others on the floor and throughout the dorm. Unfortunately, it meant Amalia still struggled to find a group of girlfriends to grow close to. She felt as though Woodland was only duplicating the trends and experiences she'd suffered through in high school.

In mid-September, Amalia received a package for her eighteenth birthday. She'd rushed home from the school mailroom to open it, excited her father had not only remembered her birthday but had sent a gift. The square box was small, no bigger than a deck of cards. She unlocked the door to her dorm room, dropped everything in her arms except the package, and shakily climbed the ladder attached to the metal-framed bed. Amalia settled on the mattress, her red and blue checkered comforter pushed to the side wall. Nimble hands ripped at the shiny silver paper she recognized from a roll they had at the hardware store.

After tearing the package's wrapping in two, Amalia lifted the lid off the white cardboard box and found a brief handwritten note and a small pendant necklace laying on a firm white bed of stuffing. She dropped the lid and removed the chain from the plastic piece that held it in place. A small gold heart with a sapphire gem in its center stared back at her. It had an inscription that read *For My Daughter*. Amalia clasped the necklace against her heart and let a few tears rain from her misty eyes. The note read:

> *To my sweet Amalia,*
>
> *Happy 18*th *Birthday. I'm sorry we couldn't be together on this special day, but I'm sending this gift instead of being with you. I saw it at the jewelry store the day after you left for college and knew it would look perfect on you. I'm sorry we fought, but it's hard for a father to accept his little girl has grown up. I wanted to inscribe it 'To Daddy's Little Girl,' but it is no longer appropriate. Please be careful out there all on your own, and don't let Carter push you into anything too soon. I can't wait until Christmas when you come home.*
>
> *Love,*
>
> *Your Father*

Amalia reached for the phone, confident her father's voice would comfort her. It was Sunday when he'd be at home building another model train. She dialed the number and listened to it ring a few times before someone finally answered.

"Who's there?" A hard candy swished around a muffled mouth.

The small lump in Amalia's throat grew three times the size upon recognizing the voice. "Hi, Momma. How are you?"

"I'm fine. Why are you calling? Long distance is expensive. We can't keep paying all these bills of yours, child."

"Momma, this is only the first time I've called since arriving a few weeks ago. Is Daddy home?" Amalia twisted the cord around her fingers, welcoming the distraction as it cut the circulation off from her hand.

"Nope."

"Where is he?" Amalia knew her father hadn't told her mother about sending the necklace. It was better not to bring it up.

"He's out with your brother. Now get back to your schoolwork. We're not paying for you to make phone calls."

"Yes, Momma. School is going well. Will you tell him I need to talk to him?" Amalia was saddened her father wasn't home to thank.

A loud and persistent dial tone blared on the phone. Her mother had hung up. Amalia jumped off the bed, then opened her wobbly closet door. She threw her arms around the back of her neck with childlike excitement to fasten the clasp on the necklace. It landed below the small indentation at her neck but high enough to still show when she wore a shirt, as all her clothes covered up every part of her chest.

She smiled at herself in the mirror and ignored her red and blotchy eyes and the quivering in her upper lip. Amalia missed her father, not having spoken with him for more than two minutes in the car on the way to the bus stop the morning she'd left for Woodland—even then, he couldn't look at his daughter when saying goodbye. She'd have given up anything to have a few minutes to thank him for the birthday gift, but the odds hadn't been in her favor for an awfully long time.

Amalia gathered her softball equipment and dashed toward the field a few blocks down the road. As she wandered by the library, the familiar smell of ripening fruit trees, mulled cider, and a distant campfire reminded Amalia of her favorite moments back home with her father. They'd watched the moon rise on Friday nights from her bedroom window and played a game to discover who found a hundred stars first. Whoever won earned the last slice of an apple pie she'd baked that afternoon. She'd always hid it in the back cupboard where her mother couldn't find it. Her father had always let her win.

As Amalia jogged across the quad, she contemplated letting her guard down to start trusting her life would change for the better now that she was away from her mother. Just as she reached the athletics building, the familiarity startled her, almost mocking her in Rachel and Carter's close embrace. She paused, wondering how the two had met before, then reasoned they'd probably seen one another at Rachel's sister's sorority house. Amalia ignored the voice in the back of her head that warned her to be careful and called out to them both. Neither heard as they trooped into the building. She wanted to run over to them but couldn't afford to get on the coach's nasty side by being late for practice. She quickly changed in the locker room and joined the team for several hours of practice, reminding herself to check with Carter that evening upon returning home to her dorm room. But when she called several times to talk with Carter that night, his fraternity brothers said he wasn't around and hadn't planned on returning soon.

# Chapter 8

# Brianna, June 2004

After leaving the coffee shop, Brianna approached her apartment building and waved to Lenny, who sat at a small table outside the entrance to his club. "I'm sorry." A small amount of guilt scratched at her conscience for the way she'd treated him. "I was immature the other night." Her focus dropped to the pavement with embarrassment over her behavior.

"Darling, you're still young. It's all you know how to do." He dropped a packing receipt on the table and smiled at her. "What's your end goal with all these questions?"

Brianna cocked her head to the side. "What do you mean?"

"Why do you need to know who your father is? What's eating you up inside about not knowing?" He leaned back in the chair and crossed his arms. "A lotta good people don't have relationships with their father."

Brianna considered his words, certain she knew the answer but unwilling at first to tell him the truth. "Maybe I just don't like secrets being kept from me."

"Nah, that's not the reason. No one likes it when other people know more than they do. Dig deeper, kiddo." He busied himself with paperwork while she pondered the question.

Brianna let it rip. If he wanted to experience her reality, she'd drown him with it. "I'm alone. I don't know where I come from. I'm scared to admit what I might be feeling for someone else. I feel like I'm not worth having a father. I worry that no one will ever love me. I keep asking if I did something wrong when I was a baby to make him leave. It's like I live in this fucked-up fake life where I don't belong, and no one's ever gonna rescue me." Brianna breathed in deeply, closed her eyes, and trudged up the steps. "Pick any of them while I disappear into the *Land of Lies* suffocating me upstairs."

"Sounds rough. Possibly an exaggeration, but I can see how much this is hurting you." Lenny shuffled toward the metal railing that prevented him from hugging her, even though Brianna desperately needed someone paternal to provide comfort. Or smack her. Either way, it wasn't his job. "I'll answer one question for you, but then you have to discuss the rest with your mother. And don't ask me who your father is because that's not something I can tell you."

Brianna glowered as her veins filled with fire. She couldn't understand why everyone kept secrets from her. The truth made simple sense to her. If you know who someone's father is, you tell them. Why be so cruel as to hold them back from something that might be the only thing they needed? As she cooled off, her brain rummaged through a list of possibilities. Of all the questions she could toss out, there was only one he'd be willing to answer that might give her a clue. "Why do we share the same last name?"

Lenny stepped toward the entrance of his jazz club, brooding over his response. "A long time ago, I got into some trouble with a loan shark when I worked down at the docks. I had to disappear for a while, but then I was forced to change my name to avoid being caught. Flint was my grandmother's maiden name, but I used to be a Porter. My family sometimes still sends letters to me with the old name. The loan shark's dead now, so I ain't got anything to worry about. But it's too much work to change names again."

"That doesn't answer my question." Brianna's eyes begged him in their quiver, to be honest. As her hand dragged across the bars, her chunky rings clanged in the space between them. "Why is your—"

He interrupted. "I don't know why she chose Porter as your last name, but she must have had a logical reason. She's a smart woman."

"Did you know my father? Help me, please."

"One question, darling. I answered it. I don't know the whole story. You need to talk to her." He disappeared into the club, leaving Brianna standing alone on the stoop.

"Thanks for nothing, Lenny." Brianna climbed the final steps, unlocked the front door of the building, and nodded at her neighbor who was shuffling through the hallway. "Hey, Mr. Pollardo. I picked up Tippy the other day. Is she gonna have another litter of kittens?"

Mr. Pollardo stopped in his tracks and sneered at Brianna. "That little bitch got herself knocked up again. I hear her whining outside all the time. I ain't got no time or money to deal with it." He gestured irately, mumbling how he'd put an Italian curse on Tippy, then he kicked a box of phone books littering the floor.

Brianna yelled after him, but either the door had muffled the sound of her voice or he'd ignored her. "Someone needs to take care of her, why don't you see if..." She gave up when the door slammed shut and wondered about the father of Tippy's kittens. *Has he just abandoned her, too?*

Brianna bound up the staircase to her apartment, placing all her hope in Malachi's search for her father. She now had more information to give the detective, but she wanted to elicit more facts from her mother before updating Malachi.

The comforting smell of vanilla buttermilk pancakes lingered outside the apartment door as Brianna searched for the keys in her bag. They were caught between her hair clips from the day before and the cell phone she'd thrown inside after getting a call from the Woodland College Admission Office. She inserted them into the lock, jiggled the knob a few times, and pushed the door open with her right foot. The irascible scratch of metal scraping against the wooden floor echoed in the hallway as her calf throbbed from the door's weight.

Brianna tossed her bag in the corner of the entrance foyer, kicked off her shoes, and entered the tiny kitchen on the right. "Mom, you need to get someone to fix this door again. The entire building cringes when I try to get into our apartment." Her voice contained its usual melodramatic whine as she dropped her keys in the dish on the old corner table they'd stolen from the curb on the way home from a late-night Chinese dinner a few years back.

"Good morning, sunshine. Isn't that the story of my life, every door in need of a repair?" A cheerful woman dressed in jeans and a long-sleeve Henley grinned at Brianna.

"What's that supposed to mean, Mom?" She crossed into the kitchen.

"Nothing." Brianna's mother, Molly, flipped pancakes on a griddle while leaning in to kiss her daughter. She had shoulder-length dirty blonde hair that bounced as her head bobbed and bare feet danced to the beat of pop music playing the background. "You're home earlier than I expected. Did you and Doug have a good time at prom?"

Brianna reached for the door of the corner cabinet, the white laminate particle board kind, picked up two plates and arranged the small breakfast table. "No Doug conversation allowed." Coffee cups banged heavily against the top metal surface. Another glimpse instead of actual words for Brianna's mother into how the night had gone.

"I'll be done cooking in a minute. How was the hike with Shanelle?" Molly accepted her daughter wanted the subject changed, something she'd grown accustomed to while raising a teenager on the cusp of becoming an adult.

"No Shanelle conversation allowed either." She pulled a container from the refrigerator, opening the sticky cardboard seal to smell its contents. Drinking sour milk was at the top of her list of things that caused immediate vomiting. "Is the coffee ready yet? I barely had a cup before leaving this morning."

"Yes, go ahead. Maybe it'll change your attitude, sweetheart." Molly ladled the last batch of pancakes onto the griddle, grabbed the syrup from the microwave, and approached the table. "Pour me one, too, please. I can't wake up this morning. I didn't get home from work until almost midnight."

"I don't believe you. You're lying to me again," shouted Brianna.

"You don't get to act this way, young lady. I'm the mother. You're the daughter. Don't change the subject. Where did you apply to school?"

"Woodland College in Pennsylvania." Brianna set down her fork and placed her hands on the back of her neck, fingers tapping against her tensed muscles in the same way she'd done it ever since early childhood. Sitting still was not one of her strong points. "You've probably never heard of it."

All the color disappeared from Molly's face. Her pupils dilated as she entered a temporary trance. The dish towel fell from her hands and glided to the floor as if it were carried by a chilled autumn wind. "Oh, I've heard of it." Molly turned the water off, moved to the table, and parked herself in front of her daughter. Her knees pressed close together, and her hands rested on the slightly worn denim covering her lap. "How could *you*?" The fine lines around her eyes grew deeper than before the conversation had started.

"Shanelle's going to Woodland. It might be good to try living somewhere other than New York City. You know, to experience what else is out there. That's all."

"It's not the right school for you. You will choose one of the state schools. They have the programs you wanted. We can afford that tuition." Molly reached for her daughter's hands and pulled them into her own. "It's for the best."

Brianna breathed in deeply. "I already sent in the acceptance letter to Woodland and the rejection letters to the rest. It's done. We can't change it."

"No, I don't want to hear that, Brianna. You should have waited. I'll fix it." Molly pulled her daughter in, hugging Brianna's torso so tightly her eyes popped wider and wider with each passing second. Any added pressure would expel them from their sockets.

"Mom, chill. You're hurting me. It'll be fine. I'll have Shanelle with me." She paused and waited for her mother to respond but received only her silence. "I'm excited about it. We took a tour again recently."

"You've been there before?" Molly stepped away, pushing the chair back several inches. The grinding of the metal feet against the wood floor blasted throughout the apartment, shivering the skins of every tooth inside Brianna's expressionless mouth.

"Relax, Mom."

"Why have you been hiding all of this from me?" Molly paced in and out of the kitchen aimlessly.

Brianna placed both hands on her hips as she stood. "Mom, listen to me for once. I need a change. I want to live on a campus where there are trees and places to hang out with other students. Where professors hold chats in the library, and there's a cafeteria to crawl out of bed and meet friends on Sunday mornings. To lie on the quad and watch everyone play frisbee. I want the whole college experience. I can't get that here."

"Woodland is a long drive from New York. You'll have no ability to come home on weekends. You should go out to Long Island or upstate for that kind of experience." Molly wiped the sweat from her forehead and scratched at nothing in particular on the back of her scalp.

"I want to go to Woodland. There is something familiar about the campus, almost like I belong there." Brianna needed to exercise caution with her words, biding time before bringing up the financial aid part of the situation.

"You're too young to make this decision. The world is a lot bigger and scarier than you think it is. You can't rush into growing up."

"I'm aware of that. You don't need to preach to me day after day." Brianna knew her mother would be difficult. Part of her wanted to reach out and hug Molly, but she had to wait it out. Just as she did as a child whenever she asked for something her mother was keen to veto. They always found their way back to one another while curling up on the sofa, eating popcorn, and watching something silly on the television. "I've heard enough about being careful around boys."

Molly said, "Do you really think all I do is preach to you? I'm just looking out for your best interests. You've no idea what goes through a guy's mind sometimes. Especially when he claims to be mature yet still puts pressure on you."

"I made my position clear to Doug." Brianna couldn't hold back the smirk when the image of Doug almost crying on the bed popped into her head.

"You didn't want to talk about him, at least that's what you said."

"You want the full truth? Fine, but don't be upset. I rented a hotel room last night. We didn't go to the Cloisters this morning. I shouldn't tell you, but it shows how mature I am. I made the right decision." Brianna hoped her point might land with a positive reception, especially when a girl revealing to her mother that she almost had sex usually led to awkward discussions.

Molly leaned against the refrigerator. Condensation from the fake stainless steel on its door saturated her forehead. "I don't even know who you are right now."

"Because I almost slept with Doug?"

"No, you've been lying to me for months about everything."

Telling her mother how she felt about Shanelle crossed Brianna's mind, almost throwing it in her face how much she'd been hiding to date. But it wasn't the right time. She could only take so much parenting at once. "I wasn't lying. I didn't tell you I did something. You don't need to know everything I do, Mom."

"I do if you expect me to pay for it." Molly shook her head back and forth. "Did you think about that?"

Brianna knew her mother was intelligent but had forgotten how intuitive and ironic she could often be. It was time to grovel a bit if she wanted to accomplish her goal of leaving New York. "Well, now that you mention it, there is something I need from you."

Molly's eyebrows shot high enough to resemble one of the plastic-surgery-gone-wrong cases on all the cheesy reality TV shows they'd watched. "And you just think to ask me now? Is Shanelle forcing you to do this? I worry about how she treats you sometimes. That girl is very pushy."

"No. It's not about her. It's about you."

"What about me?" Her eyebrows relaxed finally, but her lips puckered as if she'd tasted something bitter.

No time like the present to aim for the heart of the problems. "Why are you alone? Did something happen between you and Lenny?" Brianna tested the waters with something simple in the hopes of learning more about her mother's past.

"I'm not alone. I have you." Molly's face grew pale with exasperation. "If anything happened between Lenny and me, it's none of your business. He's not your father, I've already told you that."

"You know that's not what I meant." Brianna leaned on the counter and pushed several rogue curls away from her mother's forehead. Even their hair had the same tendency to have a mind of its own. "Why haven't you gone on a date? Like ever. I've never seen you with a guy who treats you right."

"In case you're forgetting, I'm pretty busy working and raising you." Molly poured a glass of water, drinking nearly all of it in one quick gulp. "College is expensive. Life's not about finding a soulmate. It's okay to focus on yourself first."

"I know other single parents who still have a life. Some even go on dates and meet friends at bars on the weekend. Shocker, huh?" Brianna's sassy side was coming out to temper the growing rage.

"I'm not other people. I also don't need to explain myself to you. You're crossing the line with this conversation, Brianna."

Brianna let her mother cool down for a minute, recognizing the vein throbbing in her upper temple. It threatened to burst through the thin layer of skin it hid behind. "I want you to find happiness. That's all."

"I am happy. I love my job. I have a beautiful daughter who, until an hour ago, was a near shining example of perfection." Molly finished the rest of the water and carelessly tossed the glass into the sink. Drops of water ricocheted everywhere when the glass cracked into pieces.

Brianna flinched but pushed through the tension. "I'm the same girl I was before this conversation started."

"No, you're not. What changed to cause this revolution?" Molly reached for a paper towel to clean up her mess.

"I happened to make my own decision for once. I'm eighteen. I can do that, you know." Brianna slammed her hand into the cabinet door out of frustration, not anger. She couldn't get through no matter what angle she tried to reach her mother. Why couldn't Molly be proud of her daughter for finally choosing something herself?

"Hiding things and hitting closets doesn't demonstrate your maturity." Molly dropped shards of glass into the garbage pail and ran the water to flush the small pieces in the drain.

Brianna threw her hands in the air as her mother washed away all hope for an easy future at Woodland. "Let it go, Mom. I made the decision. You can be supportive, or you can complain. I don't care. I've got to search for a summer job." She plodded into the foyer to grab her bag, mumbling to herself about how insignificant she felt, then slunk to her room. After slamming the door, Brianna sprawled on her bed and squirted moisturizer into her hands.

Her mother didn't handle it well, but she knew that would be the case. Molly was never one for surprises, and this was the first time Brianna had ever made a huge life decision without asking for her mother's advice. Rubbing the orange-scented cream on her tense legs, she thought about their life growing up together in the same New York apartment—never anywhere else. Her mother had the same job she's always had. There were no other friends as far as Brianna knew. Had something forced her mother into hiding behind a life of utter boredom and complete shelter?

She fidgeted with the newspaper's want-ads, repeatedly reading the same lines, shoving them to the floor in a moment of sheer frustration. Brianna glimpsed her reflection, suddenly reminding her of the difference between the beautiful woman Shanelle had created the night before and the angry, disappointed girl she'd returned to today.

Her life hadn't been difficult. She couldn't act the part of a poverty-stricken girl from New York City who had to ask for handouts. Molly had a decent job, bought nice things for their home, and often cooked delicious meals. She may have worked too much and occasionally pressed her thumb down too tightly, but she always understood if Brianna had failed an exam or skipped class a couple of times. Molly had been tolerant of her daughter's teenage attitude whenever it'd kicked into high gear, quick to find a solution to their disagreements. She truly was an amazing mother when it came to most positive things—yet being claustrophobic and secretive exploded on the negative side of parenting.

In return, Brianna had treated her mother poorly and pushed the limits in their conversations whenever she could. For Brianna, there had to exist something better than going to school or work, playing soccer, and crashing from exhaustion every night. Molly had wasted years of her life without any true enjoyment other than being a mother. There were no girls' nights out, Sunday single ladies' brunches, or sisterly bonding moments in her mother's life. How could Molly get through each day on her own without a best friend to talk to or family to help take away the stress when work got too hectic? Brianna needed to find a path that would force her mother to accept their separation was important for Brianna to grow up *and* for Molly to build her own life.

An hour later, after dozing in and out of sleep, Brianna's phone buzzed. She hoped it was Shanelle, but it was from the hotel where she'd rented the room during her prom. The reservation desk called to let her know there would be an invoice for additional damages beyond what her room deposit had covered. Though anger seethed at the surface, it wouldn't help the situation to take it out on the wrong person. She'd already accomplished that a few times during the weekend. Brianna called Doug to insist that he pay for the charges, assuming he trashed the room after she ran out. He suggested that if she wanted him to pay for the damages, he'd be happy to involve the cops. He hinted that he could charge her with assault and battery for kicking a minor given he still hadn't turned eighteen—the reason the room had been rented in her name.

Brianna didn't mind having to pay the additional costs once she sent out a few emails to all their friends and told them she'd dumped Doug. She cited her reasoning as when he dropped his pants, it became obvious that he'd fallen too short of being a real man and couldn't quite live up to her expectations. She'd deal with his petty wrath the following day. Brianna clicked the phone off and rested her head on the pillow. Just as she was about to nod off again, a knock on the door startled her. "What?" she grunted.

"May I come in?"

"Only if you're going to have a reasonable discussion." Brianna propped herself up against the headboard.

The door opened slightly, and Molly's head poked through a narrow crack. Brianna noticed the puffiness around her mother's eyes—swollen as though her skin had been allergic to some toxin, refusing to relent.

Molly stepped cautiously into the room. "Yes, let's talk. What's this all about, Brianna? It's not normal for you to make this type of decision in secret." Molly's gaze darted to the photo of them from a sweet sixteen party two years earlier when everything was so much more innocent. All the meals they'd cooked together. Every trip to the free museums to learn about art and history. Even the silly games they'd played trying to talk people down on the price of knickknacks and locally farmed vegetables. Molly was always able to find the best bargains by negotiating with the salespeople.

"Sometimes you still treat me like I'm a little kid," replied Brianna. Her shoulders sloped forward when she scratched at a cuticle on her left ring finger. She reached for her nightstand drawer and pulled out an emery board.

"I know you feel that way, but it's a mother's job to shield her daughter. To protect her from things she doesn't see for herself." Molly took the emery board and attended to her daughter's fingernails.

"Does that include high school boys who keep pressuring you to sleep with them?"

Molly brimmed with sympathy and filled with pain when the words escaped her daughter's lips. "Is that what happened with Doug?"

"I took care of it. I know how to handle myself."

"What did you do?" Molly's body withdrew, fearing the next words that would come from Brianna.

"Let's just say soccer came in handy. I didn't know I could land a kick that harsh to knock the wind out of someone." Brianna laughed, allowing her mother to pull her into a hug. "You taught me well."

"That's my girl. I knew those lessons would pay off."

"Exactly. You showed me how to defend myself. How to think for myself. How to make my own decisions." Brianna laid across the bed on her stomach.

"No one ever taught me. I wasn't as lucky when it came to helpful parents." As Molly breathed in, she grew weary and disconnected. She tapped the emery board against the comforter a few times until Brianna stopped her.

"But you had two parents, right?" Brianna used the opportunity to ask more questions about her mother's past. It'd come unexpectedly, but she needed to take advantage of the opening to get any information for Malachi to research.

"There's nothing worth discussing when it comes to my parents. It has no bearing on the present." Molly laid next to her daughter, her hand rubbing the small of Brianna's back. "Is this about me not telling you more about your father?"

Brianna scanned the room. It was tiny, and she didn't have many things, but it was all hers. She knew where every poster had come from and had picked out the carpet and the wall colors, even the side table lamp, which was more expensive than they could afford. Her mother had surprised her for Christmas with a few extra presents that year. "I don't know anything about him. It's a complete void, and whenever I bring it up, you go silent for days. Did something bad happen to him?"

Molly shook her head. "I accepted your decision not to tell me what happened with Doug. Or whatever squabble you're having with Shanelle. You owe me the same level of respect." She smoothed a wrinkle in the pillow, leaning against the fabric-covered headboard they'd built together the previous summer. "What does your father have to do with you going to college?" Her voice carried a heavy tone full of love but desperation to limit the conversation.

"Maybe he would have understood why I need to get out of here. I don't see why it's such a secret. Where was he from? Is he alive? Tell me something, Mom." Brianna buried her face in the comforters, unwilling to allow any tears to form or to control her in front of her mother. The pain had become too much of a burden to remain clueless any longer.

Molly sighed and ambled toward the mirror. She pushed curls away from her face, covered her mouth with both hands, and stared at a reflection that brought unwelcome memories. "He was in the Air Force and on a temporary leave one weekend. I fell for him quickly when I felt very alone." A hollow pitch carried Molly's voice across the room, as though she stood in a tunnel with no exit in sight.

Brianna hoisted herself up. "What is his name? I thought he was a hotel porter until I realized you borrowed Lenny's last name." The incident on the train with Shanelle floated through her mind, but she pushed it away. One question at a time.

"No, I only had that one weekend with him. That's why I'm so hard on you about waiting until you meet the right guy." Molly continued to stare in the mirror as she backed up a few steps to take in the whole picture. When her shoulders stooped forward, she focused on a pair of breasts that began to droop, highlighting a fortyish body fading into oblivion. "Lenny and I were good friends, and he wanted to help me focus on the future. He suggested I use his last name since he was gonna be around while I raised you on my own. He'd known I didn't want to carry on my family's name. It wasn't right after what happened while I grew up."

Brianna ignored her mother's last comment, even though it concerned her that something bad had occurred in the past. She concentrated on what she'd learned about her father. "Are you really saying it was a one-night stand with some random army guy? Just a hook-up?"

"Air Force. Not the Army." Molly nodded in the mirror, catching her daughter's gaze. She adjusted the sleeve on her shirt and turned back toward Brianna. "I've said enough for now. Can you let this go today? We have to deal with your decision to go to that awful place."

"What's wrong with Woodland?" Brianna always assumed her mother had been hiding things, especially now that Lenny's explanation not to know why Molly used his last name contradicted her mother's claim. Absolute certainty now filled Brianna's thoughts. Molly never got this angry or upset with her before. There was something big in her past. Did Woodland have anything to do with it?

"Nothing. I just meant living outside the city." She paused while collecting her thoughts. "Unfortunately, I need to head to work again today. Some things came up, so you're on your own for dinner. We'll talk about this again tomorrow." Molly cupped her hand on Brianna's cheeks and frowned. "I'm not pleased you kept a major decision from me. You might be old enough to make them, but it doesn't mean you should. We need to do better next time."

Molly had reached the door by the time Brianna responded. She was angry with her mother and had no intention of letting the conversation end. "That's all you're going to tell me about my father? Just walk away and leave me guessing. What the fuck?" She regretted the words the instant they left her mouth, but her rage was uncontrollable at that moment.

"Watch your language. I didn't raise you to say those words." Molly spoke without lifting her head, as if it required too much energy to finish the discussion.

"I'm sorry. This is so frustrating."

"I don't know a lot more. He had to leave for some training in the Middle East. He never contacted me again. I couldn't ever find him, but I did try, honey."

"That's not fair. What city were you living in? You won't even tell me about your past. I can't survive in complete darkness about both my parents' lives before I was born. Come on."

As wrinkles formed in her brow, aging her a few years during the brief span of their conversation, Molly brushed off Brianna's pleading.

"Sometimes a mother needs to have a few secrets from her daughter. The past is in the past."

"Didn't you just tell me I couldn't have any secrets from you?" Brianna's anger was soon replaced with disappointment that she might never find her father. She threw a pillow at Molly. It missed, hit the wall, and slid to the floor. "Come on!"

"I'm the mother. You're the daughter. I told you that before."

"Please, don't leave it like this, Mom." Brianna knew she couldn't get any additional information from her mother at that point, but gratitude soared over the little she'd learned and could give to Malachi as viable leads.

"I'm not leaving it *like* anything. I'm simply going to work to earn a few extra dollars this weekend, so I can afford to send my baby to Woodland College this fall."

Brianna's body twitched as hope clawed its way from a well of doubt. "I can go?" Her voice cracked with anticipation of good news.

"I heard everything you said today. I listened. I know this is important to you. I won't stop you, but we have to talk about it."

"Thank you for letting me go. You've no idea how much this means to me. I need to experience the rest of the world, and this is just my beginning." Brianna theorized about all the possibilities in the future if she could go somewhere other than New York. She'd finally gotten through to her mother on something.

Molly grabbed the pillow and placed it back on the bed, then perched on the edge next to her daughter. "I know you think you're an adult. In many ways you are, but there are things you need to know before you go off on your own. You dodged a bullet with Doug. At least it sounds like it. Some girls aren't that lucky."

"We need to talk to some admissions person at Woodland on Tuesday to cover the financial plans. They need your approval."

"Then they shall have it." Molly leaned in to hug Brianna. "But no more secrets. You need to talk things through with me before making decisions. That's how adults do things. We seek opinions and then weigh the pros and cons before acting on impulse."

"I understand." Brianna's mood improved knowing she secured an approval to attend Woodland. If she achieved that in only one day, she would convince her mother to share more information about her father in the coming weeks. If the man was in the Air Force, records had to exist somewhere. Maybe her mother didn't try hard enough in the past to find him. Or maybe now that more was digitized or electronic, Brianna could find a viable lead.

Molly left the apartment to complete the reports her boss had requested. Brianna called Malachi to tell him about the connection with the Air Force. He planned to start his search the following day. She then called Shanelle to update her on the news.

"How did it go?" Shanelle's voice was solemn and distant, almost distracted.

"She didn't fight me on it. At least not in the end. I'm going with you to Woodland in the fall." Brianna began jumping on her bed like a small child waiting for Santa Claus to arrive.

"That's awesome. Did you tell her anything else?"

"Such as?" Brianna wasn't sure what Shanelle had meant.

"What happened between us? Or that nasty *MySpace* post you sent out about Doug? That was the ultimate revenge."

"I told her that Doug and I are over. She started telling me a little about my father. Baby steps."

"I count that as progress."

"Definitely." Brianna updated Shanelle on her conversation with Malachi which reminded her of their earlier disagreement about flirting with him. "I'm sorry we fought at the coffee shop."

"It was silly, let it go. I've already forgotten it." Shanelle was unfazed by what'd happened and ready to move on. Brianna wasn't sure if it was a front Shanelle had put up or if it was the truth.

"Me, too, but listen, my mother is stuck working tonight. What time do you want to get dinner later?" Brianna craved the comfort only Shanelle could offer, missing her best friend despite only separating a few hours earlier. The good news she'd just received about going to

Woodland reminded her how much she relied upon Shanelle to cele-brate the wins in life.

"I'd love to, but I'm meeting someone else tonight. Maybe we can talk tomorrow?"

Brianna, worried over Shanelle's response, fell against her head-board in a huff. "Oh, maybe we could meet afterward? Take a walk or something."

"Sorry, Bree. I made other plans after you told me to give you some space this morning. I'll call you soon. Gotta run." Shanelle hung up the phone.

Shanelle had never said *no* to spending time together. Something was not right. Disappointment and alarming concern tugged at Bri-anna's heart as she buried her face between the pillows, uncertain how to handle her feelings for Shanelle. Every time she made progress in one area of her life, a setback forced its way into another. She theorized Shanelle might be going on a date, which made her jealous.

Brianna pondered her next steps. How was she supposed to decide whether she was straight or gay? Was she strong enough to choose a complicated life? How did anyone decide these things? Was it sexual? Physical? Why was there no one in her life to help her understand things she knew little of? Better yet, why wouldn't she let herself trust anyone else to help her through the analysis. Was her destiny to end up alone like her mother?

Chapter 9

# Molly, June 2004

Molly smiled as Tippy snuck through her legs and ran behind an antique table in the lobby's corner. She loved pets and always wanted to adopt one for Brianna, but ever since moving to New York, Molly had developed an allergy to cat dander. Her eyes would water, she'd sneeze uncontrollably, and her face would turn bright red if she ever came in contact with one. Molly once attempted to adopt a kitten when Brianna was small, but after the air pathways in her throat and nose closed up—the cat had to go. Brianna was disappointed for a long time, but eventually found an alternative solution by volunteering at a local shelter for a few hours each week.

Molly descended the stairs and hoofed it to the nearest subway station while focusing on how pushy Brianna had become with all the questions about the past. For years, Molly had avoided discussing Brianna's father or her grandparents, yet it worsened in the last few months. When they completed the college admissions paperwork, Brianna had endlessly drawn out the process of trying to navigate every path to discovering the man's identity. It wasn't something Brianna ever needed to know, but Molly feared an inability to continue keeping a lid tightly sealed on the past.

Molly stepped into the metro tunnel and rounded the corner until the turnstile blocked her ability to enter the subway platform. She searched her purse for the metro card and slid it into the opening while wishing the city hadn't discontinued the use of the subway tokens the prior year. She preferred using cash whenever possible given the concept of loading money on a blank card only added to her worry about one more thing to lose or that could be stolen from her.

While standing on the platform and waiting for the train to arrive, Molly recalled a promise concerning Brianna's father that she'd made many years ago. A few days after Brianna was born, Molly had asked Lenny to babysit for an hour, so she could run an errand. She'd been desperate to stand in that special spot in the middle of a bridge where you could look south across the East River and watch the ships arriving from the Atlantic Ocean in the very tip of the New York Harbor. The man who would have been Brianna's father once told her stories about how he'd disappear on the bridge to think about his future. Molly always wished she could have stood there with him, but it was never meant to be. Especially not after everything that'd happened between them years ago.

The subway car screeched as it came to a stop just a few feet away from Molly's anxious feet. She waited for the doors to open and passengers to exit before stepping inside and taking a seat against the wall of the car.

*What if you were still around to raise her?*

It was the question that'd plagued Molly for the last eighteen years, ever since Brianna came into the world. As the subway doors shut, Molly buried her head in the palms of her hands, closed her eyes, and summoned forgotten memories of the past. Her feet were tucked under the seat, tapping against the floor of the car, but the whirr of the subway hid the sound as it traveled through the tunnel.

She always believed he wanted to raise the baby, but fate intervened and left Brianna in Molly's hands with no help or support from anyone else. When Molly had finally made it to the middle of the bridge all those years ago, she leaned against the thick stone of the bridge's pedestrian pathway as a few tears rolled down her cheeks. She was alone and had to put everything that had happened behind her. A blustery wind sprinkled frosty snowflakes on her face as Molly spoke to him that day, as if he was right beside her.

> *"She was always meant to be yours. You should have been the one to raise her. To help her become an amazing and intelligent woman. I'm not sure I know how to raise a child. No one ever taught me. And I'm not sure I deserve her. But they tell me you've disappeared. Taken from me. Were you really ever mine to dream about? I keep reading the note you left before you walked out the door. You told me how much you wish you could take care of this baby and how excited you were to become a father. I can't think of any other way than to believe you should raise her. But there are consequences to everything that's happened, I suppose. She's in my hands now. And I promise you, I'll take care of her. She'll always be your daughter, at least in my heart and how I feel about you. She can never know the truth. I'm not even sure I know the whole truth. I promise you with all my heart that I'll keep the past buried in the past for her sake and for yours. If she ever needs to know who her father is, I'll tell her you disappeared—that I never had a chance to find you. But you were a good man. A good man I will love until the day I die."*

When the subway arrived at the first stop, a few passengers shuffled in and out just as people did throughout Molly's life. She never believed anyone ever stayed very long, at least not to help support her. She'd always been second best or pushed around with little care given to her desires and needs. Molly had put the past in the past, but Brianna wanted to bring it forward again. It wasn't imaginable to revisit what'd happened. There was too much pain, and there were too many unknown factors that could make things far worse for everyone involved. Molly couldn't handle revealing the truth or hurting anyone else in her life. It was impossible to explain without destroying both of their futures. It needed to remain buried, if not for her sake, but for the consequences it would mean for Brianna.

When the subway arrived at Molly's stop, she exited and wandered through the underground tunnels, reaching her company's building. She unlocked the door, staggered through the hallway until finding the third right turn, and flung herself into the familiar office where she spent all her time. It was a small six-by-six space, barely big enough for her desk and a guest chair, but it was her private oasis where all she had to worry about was focusing on a client or a project. No complicated past that brought up acerbic memories. No swinging pendulum of doubt forcing her to debate what to reveal to her daughter. No one pressuring her to toss more gasoline on an insidious fire, still refusing to die out inside her. No matter how hard she'd tried, forgetting what'd happened twenty years ago had become impossible.

# Chapter 10

# Amalia, October to December 1984

As the weeks passed by, the full breadth of autumn arrived, bringing brilliant oranges, reds, and yellows to all the giant oak trees around campus. Fall was Amalia's favorite season, full of cinnamon and pumpkin spice smells, crisp cool breezes, and fun Halloween parties. She and Carter dressed up as Bonnie and Clyde, an ode to Carter's love of old-fashioned criminals and interest in all the great bank robberies.

Amalia had grown close with him throughout the first semester on campus, but after the incident in Brant, she wouldn't let him touch her very often. She worried about her father walking in on them or her mother threatening that she'd turn into a pregnant whore on the streets. Amalia eventually let Carter get further each time they were alone, which wasn't often between him living in his fraternity house where people were always coming in and out of each other's rooms without knocking and his refusal to hang out in her dorm room.

Though Carter had said he understood, he was frustrated whenever Amalia stopped his roaming fingers from peeling away her clothing layer by layer. He'd been a good boyfriend, buying her flowers a few times and paying for all their dates. He even bought her a new dress, encouraging her to wear it their last night on campus together before the holiday break. Shock pervaded the room when she opened the box and held it up to her body. The dress had a plunging neckline and would show off way more than she'd ever revealed before, not to mention cut just above the knees, so she could barely sit without having to cover up her legs.

Amalia wasn't falling in love with Carter. He was intelligent, kind, good-looking and friendly, but they were in separate places in their lives. She wanted time to grow up, figure out who she was away from her parents, and understand what the world had to offer. He hinted at settling down after graduation and beginning a life together, possibly back in Brant. Amalia wasn't ready for that type of commitment, but she also didn't want to lose him. She worried about trusting him around other girls, even though he'd never truly given her any reason to doubt his genuine affection. It just always seemed like something unusual was going on behind her back.

When Amalia questioned why Rachel hugged Carter in front of the academic building weeks earlier, he claimed he was just being friendly since she was the younger sister of one of his sorority friends. When Rachel belittled Amalia's apprehension, it left a shade of doubt inside her mind, especially when her roommate's personality changed as the semester unfolded. Rachel had numerous fights with someone on the phone, nervously jumped every time Amalia came into the room, screamed during the night while sleeping, and started dressing differently. Amalia tried to ask questions but ultimately grew tired of being told to shut her face or mind her own business.

Amalia instead focused on her classes and getting to know a few of her softball teammates. While they were friendlier than her former teammates back in Brant, Amalia still felt disconnected in a way that made her reluctant to befriend them beyond the field. She'd chat with them in the locker rooms, say hi around campus, and eat lunch together before practice if they happened to be in the cafeteria at the same time. It never extended to hanging out at night or on the weekend, especially because her teammates were solidly against the Greek social life and Amalia dated one of the more well-known fraternity guys. Most of her free time away from Carter was spent studying in the library or volunteering at the local homeless shelter. She was content with her college life but knew something was still missing. Others around her seemed happier and more confident, whereas Amalia worried what everyone thought or said about her each moment of the day.

When Thanksgiving approached, Carter told Amalia that he, Greg, and some other frat brothers would take a ski vacation on the West Coast. Amalia was at first concerned, but once learning it was an all-boys trip, she filled with excitement over having a few days on her own. She hadn't planned to go home for Thanksgiving, given her parents would dine with several families from the church and not cooking at their house. When Amalia also checked the bus schedule, the times didn't line up to make a quick trip to Brant. It would be a perfect opportunity to explore Woodland without worrying about upcoming final exams or having to keep Carter occupied instead of flirting with all the sorority girls who hung out at his place all the time.

The school cafeteria closed for the extended weekend, which meant a long hike to the downtown grocery store to buy supplies and food to cook for herself in the dorm kitchen. No one else was around except for her roommate—unexpected given they were still barely on speaking terms ever since a disagreement over the hug with Carter.

Rachel wandered into the kitchen and put on a pot of Ramen noodles as Amalia was cooking a meal. Amalia hypothesized what'd changed with Rachel in the last few weeks, unsure if she'd been popping pills or drinking excessively. Her roommate had gone from sorority princess to dark Goth overnight and still acted as though they didn't share a room together. Amalia found the courage to start the conversation, even though she expected another nasty reply.

"So, you're stuck here, too, huh?" Amalia hesitated while mashing potatoes.

"Yup." Rachel adjusted one of three metal rods in her ear, visibly enjoying the sensation as it moved in and out of the cartilage.

Amalia pulled a chair to the table and offered it to Rachel. "How come we haven't ever talked? I mean, we've been rooming together for almost three months, but you're always a bit short with me."

Rachel threw her hands in the air. "Whatever."

Amalia tried every way to connect but watching paint dry went faster than a conversation with her roommate. "How's your sister doing? Carter said she got a great internship."

"Yeah, she's working at a medical clinic. You know... we don't *need* to talk to each other just because we're roommates or I know your boyfriend."

Amalia grimaced and grew perplexed at the frigid attitude cast in her direction. She turned back toward the stove when the pot of noodles bubbled from the rapid flame underneath them. The rising heat matched the temperature of her frustration. She was tired of everyone's constant arrogance and decided not to accept it. "Well, I think that's stupid because you're here and I'm here. We're by ourselves. It's Thanksgiving. What's the point in being miserable? We're lucky to attend a great college. I don't know about you, but I'm glad to be away from my mother. Being nice to people matters to me. I care about other people." She grabbed the spoon and stirred Rachel's dinner in determined circles. "Your soup is ready."

The room was silent for a few minutes while Rachel poured the contents of the pot into a bowl and slurped each spoonful from a chair in the corner. She finally responded in a meek tone, "I'm sorry."

Amalia sliced open the chicken she pulled out of the oven to check the inside color. "Would you like to sit at the table and eat dinner together? I've got extra chicken and potatoes."

"That'd be cool, thanks. I'm going through some crap right now, and I guess I've been taking it out on you since we didn't hit it off so well in the beginning."

"Come on over. Let's start fresh. Like we just met." She removed the bowl of gravy from the microwave and rested in on the counter. "I'm Amalia Graeme from Brant, Mississippi. I still don't know what I want to major in, but I love the campus so far. How about you?"

"I'm Rachel Abernathy from Bethlehem. It's a few hours away from here. I think I want to be a teacher." She rolled her eyes, then giggled. "Or maybe a nurse. I don't know."

"Ugh, they make us choose so quickly. Totally not fair, right?" Amalia turned the stove off and carved the rest of the chicken.

"My dad is awful about it right now. That's part of the problem. Ugh. Do you hate your family, too?"

Amalia began plating the food using an extra dish stored in the cabinet. "No, I don't hate them. Maybe my mother a little. I mean, she's not very nice to me, but I could never hate anyone. She's a spiteful person, and I don't want to be like her."

As they popped open two cans of soda, Amalia recalled the last time her mother had hugged her when she was eleven years old. During PE class when she'd changed into her gym shorts, Amalia noticed her underwear had been bloodied on the inside. She'd been so scared of anyone finding out, she threw on her clothes, ran from the school, and rushed up the front stoop of her house. She was afraid she'd somehow cut herself and would die from all the blood loss. She flew through the front door and passed her mother who was still wearing a dirty old nightgown and laying on the couch watching one of her TV shows. Janet yelled at Amalia to stop, but she refused. Janet followed her daughter and banged on the bathroom door until Amalia finally had to open it. Amalia needed someone's comfort, even though it might end up worse. She was frightened and didn't have anyone else to turn to. Amalia shared what'd happened, a few tears rolling down her cheek and a sniffle forming in her nose. For the first time in a long time, the wicked Janet Graeme patted her daughter's back, told her it was normal and explained a bit about what was happening inside a woman's maturing body. Not a lot of details, but enough that Amalia calmed down, certain she was no longer dying. Janet hugged Amalia and drove her to the store to pick up what they needed at the pharmacy. Yet, by dinnertime, Janet had returned to her normal self and hammered away at her daughter over the burned rice pilaf.

Rachel's knife scraped against the plate while she sliced the chicken into pieces. "My mom went to jail after getting caught selling drugs on the street. My dad dropped me off in August and told me not to screw up, or he wouldn't pay for another semester. He hasn't contacted either my sister or me in three months, even though I called him a few times." She shrugged and pushed potatoes around with her fork. "Maybe it's better that way. Who needs them anyway?"

As Rachel ate her food, it occurred to Amalia that the girl barely had enough money to take care of herself and devoured Ramen noodles for every meal. Amalia suddenly accepted things might not be so bad in her own life. "My dad is good to me, but I haven't talked to him in a few weeks. We fought before I left. Our relationship has been different ever since then."

As Rachel spooned food quickly into her mouth, the utensils banged against her new tongue piercing. When Amalia winced, Rachel flicked her tongue back and forth several times. "Just got it on Monday. It doesn't hurt, but it took some time to get used to it. I've had a bad few weeks and needed to chase away the depression."

Amalia laughed. "You seem pretty cool. I'm glad we're finally talking." After finishing their dinner, she and Rachel cleaned the dishes and watched an episode of *The Facts of Life*, the first time for Amalia. Rachel had to repeatedly explain each of the relationships between the different characters, but Amalia was glad to make a new friend—one who didn't care whether she was still a virgin like the girls on her old softball team. And especially not like Carter, who kept trying to get her to finally give up her virginity.

When a commercial aired, Rachel disappeared to the bathroom. After twenty minutes, Amalia grew concerned that she'd been gone for a long time. Amalia checked every stall before finally finding her roommate trembling on the floor with a plastic device in her hand. "What's wrong, Rachel?"

"I think I'm pregnant." A dark trail of tears and mascara trailed both of Rachel's quaking cheeks. "I was worried earlier in the week but didn't want to believe it until I took a test. It has a plus sign."

\* \* \*

The next day, after finishing a paper in the library, Amalia took the long way back to her apartment while circling through the western end of campus. Woodland College's property divided into three major sections with student housing in the southern area, academics in the northern area, and everything else in the central part. Amalia lived at the last dormitory on the southeastern end, not too far from Carter's frat house. It was only a quarter mile to cover the entire length of the campus, but if she went around the outer perimeter, she could stroll through the tree-lined pathways near the residential neighborhoods to where the beauty of the town blossomed.

Amalia thought about Rachel and wished she could help her roommate get through a challenging time. Rachel admitted that her boyfriend told her to get an abortion—he wanted nothing to do with her after she started dressing Goth, partying, and found herself pregnant. She planned to finish out the semester and then deal with the baby situation when she went home for the Christmas break. Amalia was grateful she'd not been in Rachel's condition and relieved that Carter had been supportive of their decision to delay having sex together. She was uncertain why he agreed to wait, but hoped it meant he'd understood her fears about moving too quickly while she was still very young.

Amalia wandered the cobblestone walkway from the library to the admissions building and noticed someone standing between the two pillars that held up the Woodland College sign. His sinewy legs stretched several feet in front as he angled against the column, his elbows and shoulder propping him up. Strands of wavy dark hair blew in the wind underneath his loose-fitting baseball cap. As she drew closer to him, he seemed only a few years older than her, but his eyes looked dark and heavy, almost black.

"Hi. Do you mind if I pass through?" Amalia smiled at him.

He nodded but didn't move. "Where are you going in such a hurry, pretty thing?" He crossed his arms a little higher on his chest and wildly chewed tobacco.

"I'm heading across campus." Amalia tried to step over his legs, but he reached for her arm and his fingers locked on her right elbow. She jerked her arm when he grabbed her, a sudden sense of anxiety percolating on the skin beneath her sweater.

"Mighty nice shape to you, darling." When he winked, the repellant leer lurking on his face made her even more nervous. "Don't see many girls as pretty as you around these parts."

Amalia withdrew from his grip and stepped backward. "I need to go. Would you mind letting me through?" Despite the cool breeze, a bit of perspiration formed under her arms and dampness soaked the small of her back. She didn't trust the steely vacancy in his heartless eyes, uncertain whether he'd even been aware of the sleazy appearance he projected.

"You're not getting away that easily. What's your name?" He blocked the only open entrance and reached for her hand. "I'm Riley. Just like you ladies like 'em."

Amalia looked around in the hopes someone could intervene, but she was alone. There was no chance of circumventing him, nor defending herself if he tried anything. He had at least eight inches on her and solid muscle on his wide frame. "I'm late for a meeting with a professor. Please let me go."

Riley moved to the side. "A professor, huh? I know a few of those types who think they're smarter than me." There was a hint of self-deprecation in his voice. "Well, don't let me hold you up. I'm sure we'll meet again sometime, maybe take a class together."

Amalia's shoulders relaxed as she stepped beyond Riley. "Are you... a student here?" Her voice was quiet and distant as she continued shuffling backward to get away from him.

"Something like that, honey." He lifted his hand to his forehead and saluted in her direction. "Nice meeting you, Amalia Graeme."

She wanted to turn back but getting further away was her first priority. Her second was to figure out how he'd known her name. While stumbling across the admissions building courtyard, she crashed into someone coming from the opposite direction.

Amalia dropped her folder full of papers and bent down to grab them from the dewy grass before the ink bled. "I'm so sorry." Her face was pale and ghostly.

"Are you okay? You look a bit frightened if you don't mind me saying so." An authoritative voice beckoned as she tried to calm her furiously beating heart.

Amalia smiled as a tentative wave of peace drifted across her like fog settling above a still sea. A man in his early forties knelt beside her and collected her strewn papers. The sun glistened off his eyeglasses as they teetered on the bridge of a strong and patrician nose. Amalia suddenly smelled the familiar cologne she'd given her father every year for Christmas. "Yes, I'm fine now." She brushed some dirt off her knees with one hand and pushed her hair behind her chilled neck with the other.

The man wearing a brown corduroy jacket and khaki pants smiled back at her. His full lips and cleft chin stood out on his clean-shaven face—one with distinct features and a strong jawline that sculptors would love to mold in their wet clay. "I'm certainly glad you're okay. It's not every day I knock over an upset young lady."

Amalia, finally catching her breath and relaxing her nerves, bobbed her head. "Is that Old Spice?" Her eyes switched their focus from the man she'd crashed into in search of the one under the Woodland College sign. "It reminds me of someone else. I'm Amalia. Thank you for saving me."

"It's good to meet you, Amalia. Let's see... that's a lot to respond to... Yes, it is. Of whom? I'm Dr. West. How exactly did I do that?" His laugh was innocent, full of charm and honesty.

Amalia squinted her eyes in confusion. "I don't think I understand you."

"Oh, I apologize. I do that sometimes when I have a lot on my mind. Yes, it's Old Spice. Of whom does the cologne remind you? That covers your first two questions. Let's see... I'm Dr. West, Department Chair of Accounting and Finance. And well, the last one was a bit obvious. How exactly did I save you?"

"I think that guy over there harassed me." Amalia shuffled her papers together and pulled them closer to her chest. Curiosity whether Riley was in the fraternity with Carter or knew Rachel crossed her mind. "He creeped me out a little, that's all. It's nice to meet you, Professor, I mean, Dr. West."

Dr. West raised his head and peered into the distance. "I don't see anyone."

Amalia checked again, but Riley had disappeared. "He must have left. He knew my name, yet I'd never met him before." Her breathing labored, and her heart raced faster.

Dr. West turned back toward her. "Well, those papers you're carrying might have given you away. Your name is on the top of them. Amalia Graeme. English Literature 101. You must have Dr. Shope. She teaches all the freshmen."

Embarrassment at something she should have known caused Amalia to blush. "Yes, of course. It makes sense now. He didn't let me pass by at first. It scared me a little, but he's gone now." Her fingers began twirling a lock of curls that'd fallen back toward her cheek.

"I'm sure it felt that way with it being so empty around here this weekend. Most students left since it's a holiday. I wouldn't worry about it. Woodland is a very safe campus, but you should always use caution."

"Right." Amalia suddenly remembered she never answered his earlier question. "My father."

"I beg your pardon." Confusion flooded his face as he cocked his head to the side.

"The cologne you're wearing, it reminded me of my father. I'm missing him a lot right now." Amalia shifted her weight from one foot to the other when her nerves fluttered. "What brings you to campus today, Dr. West?"

"I'm grading papers, and I wanted to get a few things out of the way before all the students returned. What about you? Why aren't you home with your parents for Thanksgiving?" Dr. West placed his briefcase on the pathway, then reached out to flick a blade of grass from Amalia's flushed cheek. "Pardon, you've got something near your eye."

Amalia let him remove it. His fingers were cool against her warm skin. Her heart, which had just slowed down, sped back up from the intense sensuality of his touch. "Yes, thank you. What was your question?"

"You didn't visit your parents this holiday weekend?" He smiled while waiting for her reply. He paid attention to her words and responses way more than Carter. She quickly picked up on it.

"Oh, no, it's a long story. It's fine, and I love being on campus, especially when the weather cools down. It reminds me of happier times."

"Me, too. I've been a professor here for almost fifteen years now and wouldn't want to live anywhere else." He lifted the sleeve of his jacket off his wrist and glanced at his watch. "It's getting a bit late, and I need to drop off this advertisement with the printer."

Amalia studied his lips as he spoke. He was confident and mature. She could tell he was a generous man, even though she barely knew him. He was the type of professor who cared about his students. "What are you selling?"

He laughed again. "No, not selling. I'm searching for a student assistant for next semester. My former one quit this morning, and I have to admit, I can't survive without the extra help."

Amalia was quite fond of him at this point. "I considered taking on a few student employment hours besides my schoolwork next semester. Maybe I could apply?" A brief hesitation surfaced in her voice, but it receded when his expression brightened at the suggestion.

"That might be a splendid idea. Why don't you stop by my office before you leave for winter break, and we'll verify it's a good fit? You've certainly brought a smile to my face, and that's something I'd enjoy having around each day." He reached his left hand toward hers.

"I'm left-handed, too. How funny! It's always weird when someone shakes my hand, and I have to use my right one." She shook his hand while nimbly trying to hold the papers in her arms. "I look forward to chatting again, Dr. West."

"My students call me Dr. West, but my colleagues and staff call me Jonah. I prefer to keep it a little less formal when we're working together." He pulled his hand back and collected his briefcase. "It's very nice to meet you, Amalia. I hope you enjoy the rest of your weekend."

"You too, Dr. West. I mean, Jonah." Continuing down the path, she turned her head back and inhaled his comforting scent as he sauntered away. A wide grin and sense of tranquility escorted the walk home to her dorm room. Birds cheerfully chirped to their mates, chipmunks rambunctiously crossed her path in search of nuts and berries, and the crisp, cool air playfully danced on the surface of her skin.

* * *

The next morning, Amalia awoke and cooked waffles and pork sausages that she'd found on sale at the local market. Rachel helped proofread Amalia's English paper, and in turn, Amalia paid for the food. She didn't have much money herself, but knowing she'd have a job upon returning to campus after the Christmas holiday, her generosity was larger than normal.

When Amalia pressed Rachel to learn more about the boyfriend who threatened to dump her, Rachel suddenly remembered a meeting she'd forgotten to attend and rushed from the dorm room. Amalia let Rachel leave, knowing it was unfair to pester her but wanting to do whatever she could to help. By the time she'd finished all her homework assignments, a sense of restlessness had unnerved her body, and Amalia debated going for a run around campus.

After throwing on long pants and a sweatshirt, she braved the cold front settling in overnight and jogged through the neighboring residential areas. All the homes were small cape cods housing most of the professors and school administration staff. Though Woodland wasn't a small town, many people who lived there also worked for the college or the bottling factory on the outskirts of the northern district. After a few miles, her legs weakened, and she power-walked the last quarter mile, stopping to stretch out her muscles at each corner.

Dr. Jonah West had been a welcome surprise the prior day, proffering an opportunity for an on-campus job to earn some extra money. She was excited to spend time with someone who might encourage more intellectual conversations and who could help her understand how to prepare for the future. Amalia missed being around an older and mature crowd as it reminded her of the times she'd cherished with her father. Carter, though not a bad boyfriend, always behaved childishly wavering between a partying frat boy and an insufferable juvenile who couldn't keep himself occupied for more than a minute—always needing her attention, hanging out with friends, drinking, and talking her ear off about nonsensical things. He knew nothing about literature and books, nor did he ask questions about her classes or softball team anymore.

As she rounded the last corner, Carter crossed in front of his dormitory's front entrance, a surprise since he was supposed to be away on the ski trip. She tried to capture his attention, but he had Walkman headphones on his ears. When she finally reached him, he startled. "Who's there?"

"Carter, it's me. What are you doing back?"

Carter turned and scooped her into his arms. "Amalia, I missed you so much. We came back a day early. Umm, one of the guys broke his leg and needed to have surgery."

"Oh, that's a shame. Did you have a fun time? I never heard from you." Amalia kissed his lips, leaving her hands clasped behind his neck. She sometimes liked to hang off him, although it made her look too clingy.

"Yeah, totally. I'm glad to see you, but I'm all sweaty. I need to take a shower." Carter backed up quickly and pushed her away.

Amalia pulled her shirt down from riding up too high and revealing part of her body. "Do you want to come over tonight after dinner in the cafeteria?"

"You know I don't eat in there unless I have to. Slop, more slop, and a bunch of tasteless shit." Carter hesitated and bit his lower lip. "Isn't Rachel going to be around?"

"I don't know. I'm sure she'd be fine with you coming over." Amalia rested her hand on his forearm. "We got closer this weekend. Things are a lot better."

"Really?" Carter swallowed hard and hesitated before further responding. His eyes looked anywhere but at Amalia. "How about I go clean up, and we can go out for dinner tonight? It'll be my treat."

Amalia agreed, and they set plans to meet up later that evening. She went home excited to tell Rachel that Carter had come home early. When Rachel wasn't around, Amalia kept busy studying for her upcoming exams and daydreaming about working with Jonah in the spring semester.

Carter took her to a fancy restaurant in the neighboring town, claiming he didn't want to run into anyone they knew. He was romantic and interactive, which relieved Amalia since he'd been acting so weird the last few weeks. He asked about her weekend with Rachel and if she'd learned anything new about her. Amalia wanted to tell him that Rachel was pregnant, but decided it wasn't her secret to reveal. He ordered a chocolate souffle to share and even took her on a moonlit stroll around the village when dinner was over. By the time they arrived back on campus, she tired and tried to convince him to stay over at her place to cuddle.

"No, I can't tonight, babe. I've got an early interview tomorrow for this amazing internship next semester. Maybe tomorrow night if Rachel's not around." He dropped Amalia off in front of the building, kissed her goodbye, and nipped back toward his fraternity house.

When Amalia stepped into her room, Rachel was in bed already but initiated a conversation. "Hey, what kept you out so late?"

Amalia giggled. "Carter came back early. We went for a romantic dinner. It was fun." She pulled off her clothes, threw on pajamas, and grabbed her toiletries.

"Oh, cool. Yeah, I was with him earlier at my sister's sorority house. Everyone was blitzed. I so wanted a drink." Rachel rolled to her other side and adjusted the covers. "He's such a cool guy."

Amalia cocked her head to the side, wondering why Carter had come back early and gone to a party without first stopping to see her. She'd ask him the following day but was more concerned about her roommate attending parties. "Have you made any decisions about the baby?" Amalia opened the door to leave the room while wondering whether Rachel had truly stopped drinking now that she was pregnant.

"No, not yet. I thought about trying to talk to the father again. Maybe he'll be more open-minded this time." Rachel checked the clock and rested her head on the pillow. "I've got an early meeting tomorrow. Sleep tight."

"Okay, keep me posted. I'm here for you." Amalia nodded and left for the bathroom to get ready for bed. She whispered, "Good night, friend," as the door shut.

\* \* \*

A few more weeks passed before Christmas break arrived. Amalia and Carter finished their final exams and planned to head off campus the following day. Carter would fly to Europe to meet his mother and aunt at one of the family estates in Italy. Amalia had been invited, but she missed her father and wanted to reconnect with him ever since the fight they'd had before she left Brant. When she declined, Carter invited a few of his fraternity brothers who were psyched to travel with him.

It was the last day before she and Carter would separate for an entire month, and Amalia was second-guessing her decision to finally sleep with him that evening. She was worried, but Rachel had previously told her the first time having sex wasn't always awkward or painful. Carter planned for her to sleep at the frat house, as everyone else had left for winter break. When Amalia arrived, he offered her a bottle of beer, but she was too nervous to take that many risks at once. They sank into his futon, kissing and necking while a cassette played Peter Gabriel songs in the background. Amalia's insides fluttered as though a rollercoaster had jostled her back and forth. It wasn't a comfortable feeling, but she rationalized it was only fear of the unknown.

"So, is tonight still the night?" Carter whispered in her ear as he stripped to his boxers.

Amalia pulled away from him. "You've only slept with one other girl, right?"

Carter's face flushed. "Don't worry, just a few girls. I only did it twice with the last girl, and then I dumped her. She was a total bitch all the time and turned into some weird freak. I wasn't putting up with it afterward."

The temperature in the room was too warm for Amalia. She had trouble breathing properly in dry heat. "I know, but I'm a virgin, and I don't want it to hurt." She fanned herself with a nearby record case.

"I'll be gentle." On his way back from opening the window, Carter lifted her from the futon and pulled her sweater over her head. "You do have a magnificent body." He buried his head in her shoulders, kissing her neck.

"Yes, you've said that before." Amalia's shoulders tensed as he slid her skirt to the floor. She stood before him in a bra and panties. Her throat would barely let the words leave her lips. "Please go slow."

"I know, baby." Carter unfastened her bra and pulled it off her chest. "Damn, you're hot."

A song ended on the cassette, leaving them suddenly trapped between tracks. Silence devoured the room, increasing her need to escape. The quiet was incapable of hiding the thump in her heart and the heavy panting rising from Carter's lips. His fingers inched their way toward her waist, thumbing the only remaining fabric covering the one part of her he'd still not touched or seen. "Slower, please."

Suddenly her father's shock and disappointment—when he'd caught Carter nuzzling her on the couch in the family living room—weighed heavily on Amalia's mind. As the song started up again, Carter kneeled in front of her. "Relax, I know what I'm doing. Just listen to the music. Put your hands around my neck and rub my shoulders." He slipped the panties to her ankles and slid a few inches away from her. "Naked looks hot on you, especially this spot right here."

He leaned in close, but her hands instinctively fell from his neck and covered herself. The image reflected in a mirror across the room confirmed she wasn't ready for the next step. Her legs trembled. She considered lifting her hands to wipe away the tears but was afraid to stop them from preventing his access to her waist. "I'm not sure anymore." Her legs swayed with uneasy trepidation.

He led her to the bed and began gently pushing her onto the mattress. "Yes, you are. Trust me."

At that moment, Amalia pictured the wet, greasy Vicks VapoRub on her mother's neck as her mouth flapped back and forth. '*You're a dirty little whore.*' She closed her eyes, trying to forget the image. As Amalia focused on pushing the memories out of her head, a shiver crawled up her spine an inch at a time, and she sank into the lumpy mattress. The chill settled at the base of her neck, leaving her suspicious something horrible was happening at that very moment.

Amalia flinched and pushed Carter's hands away from her chest. "No, I can't do this. I don't want to tonight. Please," she cried out.

"Are you serious?" Carter stomped across the room to shut off the stereo system. "Look, if you still aren't ready, maybe we need to take a break. It's been four months. I just turned twenty-one, and my girl-friend still won't sleep with me. Every other girl around here would lift their skirts for me. What gives, Amalia?"

"I'm only eighteen. Please stop pressuring me so much." She stood from the bed, re-fastened her bra, pulled on her panties, and searched for the rest of her clothes.

"If you leave, don't bother coming back. This isn't fair. I've been a patient boyfriend." Carter punched the wall. "Ugh, fucking A."

Amalia shuddered from his outburst. "Please don't be upset."

Carter noticed her reaction and walked toward her. "I'm sorry, baby. I don't mean to act like a jerk but come on... ever since that day at the lake, I've desperately wanted to be with you. We're so close right now."

"I'm sorry, but I'm not ready," she begged. "Something feels wrong. I know how important this is to you, but I don't feel comfortable." Tears streamed as Amalia pleaded with him to be more patient. "Maybe I should go home."

"Listen to me." Carter held her hands. "I hear what you're saying, but I can't deal with this tonight. How long am I supposed to wait for you?" He stomped away in his boxers, pulled a shirt over his head, and leaned against the wall, throwing back a huge chug of beer. "I leave tomorrow for Europe and won't get back until the end of January. Take all the time you need to figure this out. I guess I'll find another way to get off tonight."

The air held a strange and ominous quality to Amalia, a foreboding over losing someone she deeply cared for, while she finished dressing. "We could try again on Valentine's Day, that's our six-month anniversary. I don't want to break up over this."

"We're not breaking up, but I need to be alone right now. We can talk again when I get back from Europe. I'll try to call you while I'm away." He swallowed the rest of the beer and cracked open a new one as he paced back and forth in the room.

Amalia wanted to stay and fix it, but she knew he wouldn't openly talk once he started drinking. She walked toward him and tried to kiss his cheek, but he turned away. She whispered, "You mean a lot to me. I'll call you in the morning before I catch the bus home."

"No, don't bother. I'm gonna drive to the airport tonight and try to catch an earlier flight. I need to get out of here." Carter began packing the rest of his bags with deliberate force.

"I'm so sorry." Amalia put on her jacket as Carter threw all his toiletries in a backpack. "Are you gonna sleep with some other girl?"

"Just go. We'll deal with this when I get back."

Amalia gripped the door handle and exited the room. As she turned the corner to head down the stairs, a beer bottle slammed into the wall, cracking into small shards no one would clean up. She reminded herself to stop back the next morning and tidy his room before leaving for Brant, wishing he'd know how sorry she was for making him wait even longer.

Amalia plodded through the fraternity house's front doorway, ignoring the sharp slap of the frigid wind against her cheeks. She crossed the road and jogged back toward her dorm, hoping Rachel hadn't left already. Amalia needed a friend to talk to but also wanted to check with Rachel before her roommate went home to the clinic to discuss the options for dealing with the unexpected pregnancy. Amalia prayed that the father had changed his mind and would be there for Rachel.

It was eerily quiet when she tiptoed onto her floor and stuck the key in the knob. Amalia pushed the door open, disappointed the lights were off, and Rachel wasn't around to talk.

She tripped over a pair of shoes rushing to her desk and flicked on the light, flooding the room with brightness. On the top of her textbooks was a handwritten note.

> *I had to leave early. My sister knows I'm pregnant. I'll be in touch. Check the machine's messages. You need to call home as soon as possible. There is something about an emergency. I'm so sorry about everything. - Rachel*

Amalia's stomach squeezed into a knot as her body grew agitated with a burning rumble. Small bits of dinner dangled at the base of her throat, threatening to explode. She reached for the phone, untwisting the cord from the wall while dialing the numbers. Knowing something felt wrong, Amalia was unwilling to listen to any messages that would delay her call home. Her skin was clammy with wet tension all night, believing her next steps with Carter as the cause. Now she knew differently.

Amalia's fingers punched in each digit, but when she hit the wrong last number, a screeching signal boomed back at her. She dialed again, pausing slowly above each button and praying that she pressed properly. The phone rang once, then a second time. It rang a third time before someone finally picked up. The voice was unrecognizable.

She gulped deeply, holding down the fury of her personal hell from reaching out to swallow her whole. "This is Amalia Graeme. What's going on?" She listened to someone else on the other side of the phone speaking. It was a voice she'd never forget. Cold. Distant. Hollow. "What kind of an accident was it?" Ten seconds later, the phone dropped from Amalia's hands. As the world closed in all around her, she cried out, "Oh my God, what about..."

## Chapter 11

# Brianna, July to August 2004

In the first few weeks after Molly agreed to support Brianna's decision to attend Woodland, they kept their distance from one another out of anger and apprehension. Both were furious that the other had been keeping secrets. Brianna worried that her mother avoided her or was reliving some former nightmare. Molly worked twelve-hour days claiming there were larger college payments to consider now. She'd called Woodland College to deal with the financial expenses and confirm there was no father in the picture. The first tuition payment's impending due date obligated Brianna to approach her mother for the money earlier than she'd planned. Though a soccer scholarship had covered most of the cost, Brianna still needed to pre-pay for room and board, meals, and other expenses before the semester began.

Brianna picked up a part-time job working in a second-hand bookshop shelving all the donations and helping customers find copies of their favorite author's novels. She'd grown tired of hunting down inexpensive versions of the latest bestsellers. Patrons rarely understood people dropped off old books, not brand-new ones they'd finished reading the previous week.

Shanelle prepared to leave on a two-week vacation to Greece, a graduation present from her parents. Brianna declined the invitation as the guilt over leaning on them for money consumed and prevented

"Hey. Mr. P. What's going on?" Brianna asked.

"None of your damned business, princess. Leave me alone." He moved to the right to block her view of whatever he'd been intently focused on before she arrived.

Brianna never liked the man. She occasionally visited his apartment to have cookies and milk after school with Mrs. Pollardo while the elderly woman was still alive. From his easy chair, Mr. Pollardo barked orders at his wife to bring him tea, fix his pillow, and iron his work shirt for his night shift. When Brianna once told Mrs. Pollardo that she didn't like gingerbread cookies, Mr. Pollardo jumped off his chair and declared that she was an awful little ingrate who should never complain about something that'd been given to her for free. He later raised his hand to her, saying she needed to be taught a lesson, but Mrs. Pollardo calmed her husband and ushered Brianna out of the apartment before anything more serious had happened.

"It *is* my business if you're doing something wrong. Is that Tippy under the table? I haven't seen her in days. She should be ready to have those kittens soon, right?" Brianna stalked to the back of the hallway to get a better look at Mr. Pollardo's clandestine activities.

"Stay out of it! Get yourself upstairs now," he yelled and waved a newspaper at her like she was a small child again. "You're always causing trouble."

"No, I won't stay out of it. Are you hurting Tippy?" Brianna shoved Mr. Pollardo out of the way while she bent down to check under the table for the cat. Mr. Pollardo slammed into the wall and fell to the floor, moaning in exaggeration.

"You pushed me, stupid little witch." He tried to stand up but couldn't grab hold of anything to help stabilize his weight. His feet slid out from under him a few times before he gave up and sank to the floor in disgrace.

Lenny came running up the steps and into the foyer as Brianna began screaming about what Mr. Pollardo had been doing before she arrived home. Tippy cowered under the table, barely breathing, and was covered in blood after Mr. Pollardo had beaten her into submission. "What is going on? I could hear the poor cat downstairs," Lenny asked while rubbing a handkerchief across his face to dry the sweat.

"She's an alley cat. Just a little bitch about to give birth to more feral beasts. Damned thing is always in heat, tempting all the male cats. Deserved much worse."

Brianna stroked Tippy's fur, hoping to comfort the cat in her final moments. She could tell the innocent animal was dying by the trembling fear in her badly tortured and weakened body. "You're a monster. She's just a harmless cat."

"She ain't got anyone to take care of her. We don't need more living things who can't take care of themselves around here." He'd finally stood up and scuffed toward Brianna, pointing his finger and raising his nose. "I'm doing us all a favor."

Lenny held Mr. Pollardo's arm back to stop him. "You've done enough, old man. Go upstairs and don't let me see you down here again tonight."

Mr. Pollardo turned to Brianna. "That cat's just like your mother and probably like you someday soon, too. Pregnant and alone. No morals or consideration for the rest of us. This whole world's going to hell soon enough."

As Mr. Pollardo ambled up the stairs, Brianna cradled Tippy in her arms, knowing she was already gone. "How could he, Lenny? She's just a poor, helpless animal."

"I know, sugar. Some people are vindictive. He's never gotten over losing his wife. It doesn't give him an excuse for what he did, but we can't change it now." Lenny bent down and threw an arm around Brianna to comfort her. "It'll be okay. Let me take care of it."

"Just give me a minute with her, please. I'm not ready to say goodbye," cried Brianna. "I was hoping to take one of the kittens with me to college in a couple of weeks. I guess now I'll never get that chance." Brianna planned to surprise Shanelle with a kitten as a gift when they moved to Woodland. At first it was just to have something to take care of together, but after Shanelle had rented the apartment for the two of them, it became Brianna's only way to show how she truly adored her best friend.

Lenny shook his head in empathy while Brianna rocked back and forth with Tippy in her arms. "Life's gonna toss you around more than you know, honey. It punches you in the gut sometimes just to see if you're still alive."

"I've already been punched enough, Lenny. I know what it's like to feel dead inside."

\* \* \*

A week passed with little progress in Malachi's investigation to find Brianna's father. He tried cornering Lenny, but the guy was on high alert anytime someone asked about his past. Malachi abandoned that angle and pressured Brianna to search for any additional hints around the apartment when his DMV leads also never came through.

On a night in late August, Brianna was able to get home from work early enough to ransack her mother's bedroom for clues. She'd been inside it tons of times before but had never searched for any keepsakes or memories her mother might have hidden. She first checked under the bed, but it only had a few boxes of shoes and a couple of winter clothes stuffed in those bags people vacuumed all the air out of, to conserve space. Brianna often felt like all the air had been sucked out of her, too. She also found one half of a pair of gold earrings her mother had been looking for earlier that summer. They were a Christmas present from Brianna, and Molly had been heartbroken when she lost it one evening at a movie theatre—the place either had last seen both. At least now Brianna could make her mom happy again.

Brianna lifted the mattress but found nothing within the bed's pristine display—her mother was fanatic about proper tucking at the corners and lines between each layer of blanket or duvet cover. She pulled open the nightstand drawer with trepidation over finding something any daughter would never want to come across. If her mother truly wasn't dating, she had to be addressing her physical desires somehow, unless the woman really was *Proud Mary*. Two magazines, an empty water bottle, a bookmark, and a bunch of bangle bracelets from the 1980s occupied the space. No clues there other than her mother had bad taste. Brianna noticed a picture of her mother with a few other unknown people caught between the drawer and the side panel of the nightstand. As she perused the image, trying to decide when it was taken or if she recognized anyone in it, the front door squeaked. "Hello?"

"Are you home, hon?"

Brianna tossed the photo back in the drawer, verified all the lights were off, and strolled down the hallway to the kitchen. "Yeah, I'm coming."

Molly stood on the tips of her toes, unpacking a bag of groceries and tossing a few boxes of pasta onto the top shelf. "I'm cooking us a special dinner this weekend. I picked up some salmon, dill, and a couple of ears of corn."

Brianna had forgotten the bookstore closed for repairs, and her mother had off from work for a few days while her boss was away at a conference. It would be just the two of them stuck in the apartment together. "Great. You cook. I'll clean up."

"Just as we always do. I'm gonna miss times like this when it's just you and me. Remember when we…"

Brianna cut her mother off before memory lane hijacked the entire conversation. "No, don't. I can't listen to you tell one more story about our cozy little New York holidays." She made a noise resembling an animal puking up a hairball.

"Maybe I won't really miss everything about you when you leave for school next week." Molly smirked as Brianna flicked a few drops of water at her from the sink. She'd just started washing the dishes leftover from earlier in the day, having previously forgotten to finish her chores.

Brianna was in no mood for a lecture. "You're funny, but you know I can still call and harass you every day, Mom." She rinsed a glass, dropped it in the drain, and turned the water off. "Oh, guess what

I found?" After drying her hands on a towel, she pulled the earring from her pocket and cupped it inside her fist.

"If that's a roach, I swear you're cooking dinner for the rest of the week." Molly backed up and made a squishy face.

Brianna cornered her mother against the counter. "Come on… you know you wanna check."

"Ah, fine," Molly screeched, then held her hands out. "Eww… I hate bugs."

Brianna dropped the earring in her mother's palm. "Surprise. I found it under the bed when I was looking for… dryer sheets. It's my turn to do the laundry tomorrow, and I couldn't find them in the closet." It seemed like the best explanation rather than tell her mother she was still prying into the past. It really was her turn to do the laundry, too, a realization that made her hiss with frustration.

"Oh, that's so wonderful. I knew it had to be here somewhere. Thank you, thank you, thank you." Molly's face shined with astonishment while hugging her daughter tightly until forced to stop when Brianna squirmed away.

"Ugh, you're such a needy mother. It's just an earring." Brianna stepped to the side and poured herself a glass of seltzer. "Want some?"

"No, I'm fine. Let's figure out something fun to do this weekend." When Molly finished storing all the groceries, she shut the cabinet door, crumpled the brown paper bag, and tossed it under the sink.

"How about we watch a movie? There's no need to fill the air with useless conversation."

"Useless? Is there something on your mind, honey?" Molly grabbed an apple from the bowl and bit into it. For ten seconds, the only sound in the kitchen had been Molly's teeth crunching into the core while waiting for her daughter to respond. Everything around them had seemed to stop in that moment.

Brianna noticed the clock read 10:20 p.m. and grew irritated that she couldn't finish searching her mother's room. "Is that your dinner?"

"No, I had some soup from the deli before I left the office. Someone else didn't want it and was gonna throw it away."

Brianna shook her head. "I don't know how you're gonna survive after I leave. Do you ever cook a meal for yourself or has it always been about cooking for me?"

"I've learned not to waste things. I cooked the entire time I grew up. Sometimes it's okay to skip a meal or two or eat something light." She finished the apple and tossed the remains in the garbage pail. "Since you're in a funk tonight, I'm gonna head to sleep. We can talk tomorrow morning about planning our fun weekend." She squeezed her daughter's shoulder while leaving the room. "Love you."

Given searching the hallway closet was now the priority, Brianna let her mother leave without pushing the issue any further. "I love you more." When the bedroom door closed, she began rifling through the closet's contents. Brianna had been through it hundreds of times before, but never with any intention of discovering something from her mother's past. Vacuum cleaner bags, spare batteries, and extension cords were plentiful. Molly had to have hidden a high school yearbook, old photo albums, or letters from family inside some forgotten box—something that could help.

Just as giving up seemed to be the only solution, Brianna stumbled on an old address book that'd gone through a few ringers in its lifetime. As she flipped the pages, finding very few entries, a scrap of paper with the name Rachel Abernathy and a phone number and address in Bethlehem, Pennsylvania fell to the floor. It was the only thing in the whole book that stood out as particularly odd or hopeful. Brianna called Malachi and gave him the information. He promised to conduct some research the next day and get back to her if it was anything useful.

Brianna fell asleep while watching an episode of *Sex and the City* and researching various self-help topics on her laptop. When she woke up the next morning, the laptop was charging on her desk, and a light cotton blanket had been thrown on top of her. She stomped to the kitchen where Molly relaxed at the small table, drinking a cup of hazelnut coffee. "Did you move my laptop?"

"I'm sorry, did you just say '*Good morning, Mom. Thank you so much for taking care of me last night. Can I refill your coffee?*'" Molly waited for her daughter to respond, but only a pair of eyes filled with teenage annoyance glared in return.

"Whatever. Thank you." Brianna worried her mother had found the scrap of paper with Rachel's name on it. The last she remembered it was on her nightstand next to the laptop. "Did you find anything else when you were in my room?"

"Such as what, honey?"

"I lost an address last night. Umm… a house where a teammate is staying this summer."

Molly studied her daughter for a few seconds, then turned her attention out the window. "Nope. Is there anything you wanna talk about? You've never been this rude before." Molly quickly stuffed her hand deeper into her left pocket and sighed. "Pour me another cup of coffee, please?"

"I'm sorry. Thanks for cleaning things up last night." Brianna recognized she'd been too hard on her mother and theorized that the address must have fallen to the floor or gotten caught up somewhere under the covers. "I miss Shanelle. I'm bored. I don't know what's wrong with me." She dropped off the steaming mug and searched through the fruit bowl for something to eat.

"Nothing's wrong with you. You're in a transition and leaving the nest for the first time very soon." Molly crossed the room and leaned against the counter near her daughter. "Stop dwelling on the past and start focusing on the future."

"Yeah, I know. It's like I'm at a standstill waiting for something to happen. I'm not comfortable with uncertainty." Brianna peeled a banana, offered her mother half, then bit off a small chunk on the remaining piece.

"Did you resolve things with Doug, or do I need to get involved?"

Brianna nodded while swallowing a mouthful of coffee. "Yes, he got the message. I'm done with dating for a while."

Molly laughed. "I've been there before."

"You've been there every day of your life." Brianna gagged.

"Let's not go down that path again. You'll meet someone else. A nice boy who cares about you. When you're done with college. After you've decided what you want to do with your life. Don't rush it." Molly ran the sponge across the countertop to clean drops of coffee Brianna had spilled, then trashed the discarded banana peel.

"I'm not you, Mom. I haven't decided to remain celibate the rest of my life. I'm not rushing off to find matching habits to grow old together in this apartment." Brianna stifled rising laughter upon recalling the conversation with Shanelle on the train.

"No one said you needed to wear a chastity belt, just take your time." Molly tossed the sponge in the sink. "Leave my love life out of it. That's none of your business."

"Fine, I'm going for a run." Brianna conceded to her mother's requests while reading an incoming text message from Malachi, revealing he'd found something to discuss in person. She replied with a time and location to meet. After swallowing the remains of her coffee, Brianna shuffled through the hall toward her bedroom to check under the bed and beneath all the sheets and pillows. It seemed the scrap of paper with Rachel's address had disappeared, like her hopes for ever getting answers from her mother.

Brianna changed into shorts and a t-shirt, left the apartment, and escaped toward the East River pathway to run for a few hours before meeting Malachi. Upon clearing midtown, she detached from the insufferable conversation with her mother and focused on her other dilemmas. *Perhaps they needed identification numbers to properly keep track.*

Brianna's mind pulsed with questions about the purpose of life, how to figure out who she was, and what she wanted to be when she grew up. Everyone said you're still a kid, you're barely at the beginning of your future, or you're still not ready to decide on your own. Yet, there was such an incredible amount of pressure to figure everything out before you graduated from high school—they wanted you to know exactly what college to select, how to be an adult who could make proper decisions, and which direction to lie out your entire life plan. Could making decisions too early in life lead normally sane and productive people to experience a mid-life crisis? If life were truly that easy, why had so many people fallen into depression, killed themselves, or turned to drugs and alcohol?

Even though she'd matured quickly throughout her teenage years and stayed away from those invasive temptations, Brianna hadn't yet settled on a future career and couldn't choose a major at Woodland. She loved reading and writing, thoroughly intoxicated by thrillers, mysteries, and suspense novels because there was always something to solve about the past. But did she have the right skill set to make a career in publishing? There was a lack of savvy and worldly people who knew more about her, who could give her advice, or who would keep her from the pitfalls she was bound to stumble into on her own. Where would she go to get answers?

There were too many others struggling with the same identity crises, calling excessive attention to themselves, and begging for any-one to tell them they were pretty or smart or adorable. She'd always wrestled with apprehension at sharing her wavering opinions and ex-pressing the growing desires inside her heart with the people nearest to her. Brianna worried the world would accuse of her being immature for not knowing what she wanted or judge her for the choices she'd already made that they couldn't understand. Her dreams demanded authenticity and depth in life, a truth that would close the gaping hole in her heart over being abandoned by her father and stuck merging too many conflicting desires that left her flummoxed about the future.

Brianna's legs gave out before her breath expired, forcing her to stop on the return trip at a small park across from Roosevelt Island. She'd taken the tram across once before with Shanelle walking all around the small island in less than thirty minutes. Thirty minutes in which they'd strategized new offensive plays and potential ways to invigorate the rest of the team's spirit before the final state con-ference. Brianna just spent several hours running and couldn't even solve one of her own problems, suddenly afraid of having become too co-dependent on Shanelle to help drive things forward.

There were days when Brianna wanted to bolt in the opposite direction of every standard part of civilization. Live without any boundaries writing books while gallivanting around the world, stumbling upon ancient wonders, and saving the rainforests. Desperation to feel something real, or simply to connect to people with inspiring stories, propelled her to choose a life where she *could* make a difference in the world. Yet, she also craved that normal future, even though it would make her just another regular, common member of society. Whenever she witnessed a couple kissing, the anticipation of one day finding the perfect life partner filled her with hope. Discovering a tangible connection to another person or soulmate was what would make her happy and fulfilled. Part of Brianna longed for the traditional family life where two parents built a home with several children, pets, and familiar love. She longed to create task lists for delineating who had which household responsibilities, to plan elaborate vacations where they could bond and laugh together, and to buy property in the suburbs with gardens, workshops, and a basketball hoop on the garage wall.

When Brianna had the privilege of seeing two women passionately kiss—only a few times on television and once on a street corner—the possibilities she'd yet to fully explore thrilled her. But when she socialized with straight couples, a paralyzing fear they'd pick up any scent of homosexuality consumed Brianna to the point she overcompensated in the opposite direction. She never questioned that her physical needs or desires for other women were wrong, but she also had no one to talk to about it, except Shanelle, who was obviously biased. Keeping them hidden from everyone else was the only remaining option.

Brianna wanted to believe life was a journey that allowed each person to explore however he or she deemed fit, selecting friends and sexual partners based on one's internal desires, derived from those who treated them well and who made them feel special. One of the priorities at Woodland would be to surround herself with other people, both men and women, who in some influential way opened doors to the rest of society. Brianna needed to find the freedom to explore who she truly was without rampant concerns someone would try to dictate her path toward things she didn't even want to explore. Her indecision between all the different options seemed to grow larger and more untenable each day. Doing nothing had always offered the most navigable route to maintaining her sanity. Leaving New York would finally change those circumstances.

She stretched her muscles to kick-start the journey back home, then finished a slow jog across the pathway. It was time to get out of her head and focus on getting answers. As Brianna rounded the corner, Malachi hiked toward her. "Right on time. Thanks."

He lifted his head and replied, "A runner, huh? I imagine you've stuff to work out."

"Yeah, tell me about it. What did you find?" She was confident he had good news.

Malachi motioned for her to sit on a nearby bench. "I was able to track down Rachel Abernathy at that address and number."

"What did you say to her?" Brianna wondered if she'd taken too big of a step in giving him the lead. It could have been no one, not even someone her mother had known.

"I claimed I was a reporter and that a mutual friend had given me her number as a potential interview. I was just making things up to see if Rachel would take the bait. When she asked who, I told her your mother's name."

Brianna's heart began racing. There was truly little patience left inside her body. She leaned forward, wishing Malachi would just tell her everything as quickly as possible. "Did Rachel recognize it?"

"Seems so." Malachi hesitated before responding and tapped his feet on the ground. "Although she clammed up, Rachel was surprised your mother would ever be willing to connect me with her."

"Meaning she did know my mother before New York?"

"Rachel said something a bit alarming. I'm not exactly sure what… " Malachi stared at a group of birds cackling and settling in a nearby tree, a welcome distraction to the news he was about to deliver.

"Just tell me." Brianna's mind grasped at every possible outcome. Any information had to be better than no information.

He clasped his hands together and rubbed them nervously in circles. His eyes were cast on the sidewalk, and he cleared his throat. "She asked if this was about the adoption from almost twenty years ago."

Brianna's heart stopped beating at the word *adoption*. Her shocked body flinched, resembling the chill one felt when the shower quickly turned freezing cold after only pouring a minute of hot water on your skin. "Whose adoption?"

"I'm not sure. I tried to be vague and get her to talk, but Rachel must have figured something was up." Malachi paused as a group of schoolchildren shuffled between them. He awkwardly smiled at the guardian huddling the kids closer and patiently waited to finish explaining to Brianna what he'd learned on the call. "This bit of news caught me completely by surprise. All I could get Rachel to confirm was that they'd known each other for a few months."

"What does this have to do with the search for my father?" Brianna tried to piece the information together, but it made little sense. Rachel's story could have been a lie, and it might have nothing to do with Molly or her father.

Malachi jumped right to the key question, wasting no time to let Brianna get sidetracked or further annoyed. "This is difficult to ask, but is there any chance Molly isn't your birth mother?"

A sharp pulse of electricity surged through her body and zapped all remaining energy until Brianna became lightheaded over learning she might be adopted. The last image in her line of sight before passing out was Malachi's puzzled expression as he stopped her from hitting the cement.

Chapter 12

# Amalia, December 1984 to January 1985

A blustery cold front littered the entire southeastern part of the country with unexpected thick and icy snow that winter. Amalia bundled up in her father's old black and gray parka, three sizes too large. It comforted her and kept the wind from spreading the chill to her bones. She'd been home from college for just over two weeks, grateful at passing all her classes with high marks, but disillusioned Carter still hadn't called since their disastrous last day on campus. She was certain his lack of communication meant he'd planned a sweeping end to their relationship when he finally returned from Europe. No other explanations were plausible in her weakened state.

Despite the freezing temperatures, Amalia settled into the swinging chair hanging from the front porch ceiling. She'd scraped off the frost earlier that morning, but an inch of powdery white dust already covered the cement stoop again. For as far as her eyes could see, nothing but a pure white cloud of snow and glistening crystal shine existed around her. The winter wonderland persisted since the funerals had ended a week before, though, in her mind, she was certain any minute both her father and brother would drive up the road in the beat-up family Dodge.

A fire had claimed both their lives while working late one night at the hardware store. The sheriff blamed faulty wiring recently installed in the cigarette shop next door and cited a blaze that'd ignited within the interior wall between the two stores. It'd spread quickly, tearing through the first floor and burning the staircase, trapping Peter and Greg in the basement. With no other escape from the cellar, both had died from smoke inhalation before the volunteer firefighters could attempt a rescue.

When she arrived home by bus two agonizing days after learning the news, Amalia's mother barely spoke to her. They'd planned the funeral together, avoiding any major disagreements, but neither would share their severe heartache with the other. Amalia knew her mother had been devastated at losing Greg, probably wishing it'd been Amalia ravaged by the fire. Thoughts of losing her mother as opposed to her father crossed Amalia's mind a few times, too, but she wouldn't let them linger as it only made accepting the truth harder. Her father was gone. The only person in her family who'd shown her genuine love or tender emotion had been ripped from her life. Amalia would miss Greg, but they'd grown apart while he'd been away at college, never finding time to rebuild a bond, especially once Carter had moved in with them the previous summer.

The front door opened, and Janet shouted, "Did you make dinner yet? I'm hungry. My diabetes is acting up, and I can barely move, child."

Amalia stared into the open field across from their house, refusing to turn back. "No, Momma. I'm not hungry tonight. I'll fix you something in a minute." As if she'd nothing to do but cook meals for her mother. Wasn't it supposed to be the other way around?

"Hurry. You never bought any cakes this week. I've got nothing to snack on, and the neighbors haven't brought food over in three days. What a shame they've brought to their houses! I lost my family, and no one comes by anymore." She backed into the living room, oblivious to the harsh intrusion of her selfish words.

Amalia drew in a deep breath, the back of her throat burning at the bitter sting from the ingestion of fresh oxygen. "No, Momma.

They won't come around no more now that it's just you and me." She stepped off the swing, clicked her boot against the doorjamb to shake off a few clumps of icy snow, and slipped into the living room. The house was warm, too warm. Her mother had jacked the heat again, and if she didn't stop, the furnace would eventually give out. Amalia had little idea how much money her mother had left, or if anyone would even come around to fix it.

Amalia thought back to her conversation with Rachel the prior week when she called her roommate to explain what'd happened to her father and brother. Rachel hadn't been surprised that Amalia wouldn't return to Woodland in the spring, but she'd also recommended it might be better to stay away, too. Amalia wondered what Rachel had meant by the comment, "*Things aren't always what they seem to be back at Woodland*," but never had an opportunity to find out. Rachel hadn't returned her last two phone calls.

While the soup warmed on the stove, Amalia poured a cup of hot tea and stood beneath the arch separating the living room and kitchen. Her mother rested on the couch while the Christmas lights from the tree cast a bright silver glow on the room. Her father had brought out all the decorations and set them on the floor the night before he died, knowing Amalia would soon return home to decorate the tree together. He'd even wrapped her present and stored it under the tree, certain she'd find it before anything else. It still sat in its lonely six-by-ten-inch space next to the decorations, everything untouched as though no time had passed since he last stood in the room.

"Why did you put on the lights, Momma?" she croaked with little care about the response.

"I can't see in here when it's so dark out. What's it to you?"

"Nothing. Your soup is ready. I'll bring it to you." Amalia poured a bowl full of homemade chicken noodle soup she'd found in the freezer. It was from the winter before, still edible given nothing else lasted for very long behind the cupboard doors. She placed two cups of tea and the bowl on a serving tray and stepped to the coffee table. "Here you go."

"What's this?" Janet mumbled. "I said I was hungry. Where's dinner?"

"That's all we have right now, Momma." Silence perforated the room for the next few minutes, allowing Amalia time to think about her father, though he never left her mind since she'd learned of his death. Without him, Amalia's entire world crumbled into tiny pieces of sand filtering their way through the narrow center slit of an hourglass. It would all soon empty from the top half of the timepiece, standing still, alone, and hollow, just as she did on the inside.

"When are you going back to school?" Bits of chicken stuck to Janet's chin in a way they could become permanent additions.

"I'm not going back. There's nothing left for me anymore at Woodland. Who's gonna run the store once they rebuild it?" Amalia's voice was curt, emotionless. She'd already disconnected herself from Graeme Hardware Store's burned charcoal facade—a mere shadow where positive memories of her father had once bloomed.

"It'll take them a few months to finish. The insurance man said he'd help expedite some money from your father's life insurance policy. It will help me survive until the store opens again." Janet slurped the last spoonful of soup. "Got any more?"

"No, just the one bowl." Amalia sipped her tea, shaking her head at everything her mother had dumped at her feet. "I'll get a job at the café. They'll find a few shifts for me. It should be enough money to pay the bills around here."

Janet was about to respond when a knock at the door interrupted the conversation. "Who could that be? Answer it, girl."

Amalia placed the teacup on the coffee table and moseyed toward the door. Maybe one of the ladies from the church had finally come by to give Amalia a break from sitting with her mother. Ever since the funeral ended on Christmas Eve, they'd spent the entire week stuck in the house, no way to get out with the old Dodge on the fritz. She pulled the wooden door open and rubbed a frosted-over spot on the storm door's glass window with her bare hand.

"Open up, Amalia. It's me," said a muffled voice.

Amalia thought only something she dreamed about had come true. It couldn't be. She unlocked the switch on the door handle and struggled to hold firm when the wind pulled it away with substantial force.

A man with a thick cotton hat and a woolen scarf wrapped around his face stumbled inside. "It's freezing out there. Has Brant ever dealt with a massive snowstorm?" Carter tore off his scarf, revealing a red-cheeked, frozen baby face Amalia had missed more than she knew how to convey. "I'm so sorry for what happened to your father and brother."

"Oh, Carter," she cried, falling into his arms. "You're really here." Amalia dragged him inside and dusted a layer of snow off his coat. She turned back toward her mother, suddenly realizing not only were they *not* alone, but the last time Carter had been there, he'd been thrown out of the house.

"Momma, it's Carter. He came to visit me." The joy in Amalia's voice was clear—its presence had been long gone for many weeks. Any small moment of happiness was welcome in their prison.

"I see that." Janet stood and walked toward Carter. "You weren't very well behaved the last time you showed up here, young man. I should throw you out on your bum right now."

Carter lifted his hands in her direction, thwarting Amalia's attempt to intervene. "Let me handle this." He motioned to Janet to take a seat on the couch.

"What do you want to say that I haven't heard already from other foolish young men before you?" Janet sneered deeper with each word delivered from her spiteful lips. As she settled back into the couch, her leg knocked the coffee table a few inches, spilling Amalia's tea. "Clean that up, girl."

Amalia grabbed a napkin and wiped the tea. She cared extraordinarily little for her mother barking orders at her, curious only to learn Carter's intentions.

"Mrs. Graeme, you are right," Carter replied. "Last time I was here, I took things too far with your daughter. You were correct to throw me out." He nodded in her direction to show he was genuine.

"There is no need to tell me what I already know. Get on with it."

"The way I see things, it's time we focus on the future." Carter reached out his hand and guided Amalia to the remaining seat on the couch. "Sit for a minute, baby, will you?"

Amalia deferred to him. "Okay, we can talk." The emptiness inside her chest filled with a small morsel of hope, uncertain whether Carter wanted to fix things between them or showed up only to announce he planned to walk away forever.

"You've both lost two very honorable and loving men. I've lost my best friend." He lifted both hands to his face and rubbed his temples. "One of the guys traveling with me got a call from a friend at school explaining what happened to your father." Carter's empathetic glance focused on Amalia as he told his story.

"It's been awful. I missed you so much." Amalia's eyes welled to the brim, taunting her body with a fear of spilling over in a cascade of rain that would never end. No one else had known about the deaths except for Rachel. Had Carter or his friend spoken to her?

Janet continued to glare at Carter, impatiently waiting for him to finish. "Let him get on with it, girl."

"I rushed back here as soon as I could. Took the train out early this morning and caught a ride with a trucker who was passing through." Carter rubbed Amalia's hand, relaxing her as he continued speaking. "I had a lot of time to think about it all."

Amalia grew confident he'd come back to fix things. "What do you mean?"

Carter explained that he wanted to return to Brant to finish rebuilding Graeme Hardware Store after he graduated from Woodland in a few months. He disagreed with his mother over her spending the rest of his father's inheritance and planned to start his own life separate from her. Carter offered to stay in the house with Janet, helping contribute to all the expenses, relaunching with a new store opening in the summer. Amalia would assist, but once the summer ended, she'd have to go back to Woodland to finish the last three years needed to obtain her degree.

Janet spoke first, but only after staring down Carter for enough time to chip away at any confidence in a positive reaction. "You've been mulling this over a lot. It's not a bad idea if I do say so myself." She refocused on Amalia. "This boy does have a good head on his shoulders, even if he's got a few problems behaving himself around you. I can fix that mistake. Your daddy should've taught you those lessons a long time ago, Amalia, but he never did stand up when he should have until it was far too late."

Amalia's horror at her mother's comments about her father thrashed her core. It was as if he'd been gone for years, and the loss wasn't still so fresh. She turned to Carter. "I'm so happy you showed up, and it's wonderful you want to help. Could you give me a few minutes with my mother to discuss this?" She kissed his cheek, hoping he'd understood her intentions. "Alone."

"Definitely. I would love to take a hot shower and warm up if you don't mind, Mrs. Graeme. Could I stay here for the night? It is New Year's Eve after all." Carter smiled and tilted his head, resembling a puppy who knew it'd done wrong yet wanted to cuddle with its owner for forgiveness.

"Yes, that's a possibility for tonight on account of it being a holiday and all. Go on up. While you're shaking off the chill, I'll listen to what my daughter has to say. Not that it is anything important, I'm certain." Janet waved him off. "Now run along, young man."

Once Carter left, Amalia tore into her mother. "How dare you say something about Daddy? He was a good man. It wasn't that he couldn't stand up, you wouldn't let him. You're awful!" She stomped to the window, turning her back toward her mother. Sometimes the devil spewed the words coming from Janet's lips.

Janet glared. "Don't you sass me, Amalia Graeme. This is just what we need. I don't care much for that boy putting his grubby hands all over you. But it ain't even his fault. I always said you were a little harlot. You don't know when to say no, do you?"

"No, Momma. You have no idea what you're talking about. I told him *no* back at school. He wanted to do things I wasn't ready for. That's why I haven't talked to him. He pressured me more than I know how to tell you." Amalia's heart raced, and her pulse quickened to the point where she couldn't stand still. She cared deeply for Carter, but he was too immature to trust completely.

"Listen to me, child. You have a choice. You go back to school and finish getting your degree, or you find somewhere else to live. You won't receive a dime of that insurance policy if you don't do what I tell you. That's the only way you'll have money to pay that hefty college bill. We need that boy to help us rebuild the store. Get yourself some intelligence before you speak. Life ain't as easy for other folks. You've got it pretty good and don't even have the sense to know it."

Amalia stopped listening halfway through her mother's speech. Staying in Brant wasn't a possibility. There was no other choice but to return to Woodland if she ever wanted to get away from the misery.

Janet grabbed Amalia's shoulder and spun her around. "You hear me?"

"Carter is being very generous. I understand what you want, but I don't know if this plan will work." Anger seethed through Amalia as she pulled away from her mother and rushed out of the room.

"You better figure out how to fix things with that boy. He's our only hope right now. I can't do this by myself. You ain't no help even when you have your head screwed on properly." Janet followed her daughter into the kitchen, pointing her finger with increasing rage upon each step as Amalia poured water from the teakettle on the stove. "That boy is husband material. Figure out what to say to keep him interested. Using your wiles comes naturally to you, anyway."

"Carter is not a pawn for you to move around as you choose." Amalia dropped the kettle on the stove and tossed the cup into the sink. "I'm done talking to you tonight, Momma. You're a nasty old woman who will get hers someday." She bounded up the stairs, slammed her bedroom door shut, and climbed into bed.

* * *

Amalia awoke to Carter knocking at her door the following morning. He mentioned he'd brought her breakfast in bed. "It's not much, but I found a few pieces of bread and milk to whip up French Toast."

Amalia rubbed the sand from her itchy eyes and glanced at the clock on her wall. She'd slept through the New Year's Eve ball dropping in Times Square. "It's open, come in."

Carter twisted the knob and appeared in the doorway dressed in Flintstone flannel pajamas. "Your mother let me borrow some of Greg's clothes. I had nothing warm enough." He placed the tray on her dresser and knelt beside the bed. "I didn't want to disturb you last night. You could use the extra sleep." He caressed her cheek and pushed misplaced strands of greasy hair behind her ears.

"Where did you sleep?" Amalia yawned, then noticed she still wore her heavy clothes from the day before.

"In Greg's bed. I watched the New Year's celebration with your mother. We talked a bunch about how you missed me and that she might have misjudged me." He kissed her cheek with a soft peck. "Maybe she's repenting!"

"I've never missed watching the ball drop without my father by my side." Amalia shook her head. Every day delivered a new blow to her sense of trust and confidence. "My mother is not turning over a new leaf, but I can't get into it right now. Tell me how you found out about the fire."

Carter pulled away, and his eyes dropped to the floor. "Oh... Rachel must have told her sister. I heard it from one of the guys in the frat house who probably heard it from her."

Amalia considered his response, uncertain how the news had traveled so fast to Europe. "Have you spoken with Rachel in the last few weeks?"

Carter shook his head. "No, but let's not talk about her. I was a jerk before you left campus. I should never have pressured you into sleeping with me if you weren't ready. I promise I'll be good from now on. Let's put everything in the past." He walked to the dresser, grabbed the tray, and handed her the dish of French toast with its sad, single strawberry tossed in the center.

Amalia recollected his anger and attitude from the night they'd almost slept together in Woodland. "Okay, but how do I know you're not just saying it? You were upset. Did you do anything with another girl while you were in Europe?"

Amalia wasn't sure if she wanted him to say yes or no. She didn't want him to leave her, but she was still processing her father's death and Carter's selfish actions. Things were moving too fast again, leaving her little to no control of her own life anymore. Not that she had any to begin with, but she'd amassed some fragment of strength since attending at Woodland.

"Let's just leave it all in the past. A few girls flirted with me, and one tried to kiss me on Christmas, but I behaved while I was away the last two weeks. I kept thinking about your beautiful face and amazing body. And how sweet you've been. I wanted to come back to you." He pursed his lips and nuzzled her nose. "I love this little button. It's a good thing you got your father's nose. Your mother sure has a honker. She kept twitching it last night while we chatted."

They both laughed. Amalia was relieved and nervous over his words. "We can give this plan a chance. I've missed you, but you need to let me decide when I'm ready to be with you again. Promise me? Scout's honor?"

"I was never a scout, but I'll do whatever you ask of me. I love you. Someday, I want to marry you."

Everything in the room swirled around Amalia. The formidable force of her father's death pulled her into depression. The albatross around her neck, the woman she called Momma, squeezed the life out of her day by day. Everyone wanted Amalia to make a choice, to decide what to do with her life at that very moment. Now Carter hinted about getting married someday. Amalia wanted to let everything settle, to process, to understand what it all meant in a time when the ground shifted beneath her no matter how hard she tried to stand firm. Knowing little remained in Brant for happiness to crawl its way from the depths of her pain, Amalia accepted that going back to Woodland with Carter was the only practical choice, despite the discomfort niggling deep inside.

"Okay. I believe you, but let's take things slow, Carter." She hugged him and ate several bites of French toast, unable to remember the last time anyone had done something for her without asking for a favor twofold in return.

# Chapter 13

# Brianna, August 2004

After Brianna took a nosedive off the bench upon learning Rachel had given up a baby for adoption, Malachi whistled for a taxi and dropped her off at home. Lack of eating anything other than a half of banana that day, as well as the general anxiety infiltrating her body, left her susceptible to passing out. She didn't want to tell Shanelle via text messages what Malachi had learned. They hadn't been able to talk much while her best friend was in Greece. Brianna's entire world crumbled into pieces, and no one could protect her. With nothing left to fight for, she contemplated what it would be like to become a recluse or join a convent—ostracizing herself couldn't be all that bad compared to accepting the potential truth she'd just learned.

Malachi tried to obtain more from Rachel, but she refused to speak about it claiming she and Molly had a falling out years ago. Rachel knew nothing about what'd happened to Molly over the last twenty years, nor did she want to speak any further about the adoption. It was part of her past and needed to stay buried. Malachi continued to research different angles to disprove Molly had adopted Brianna, but once he learned Rachel's adoption files were sealed, it was fruitless. Something had happened years ago between the two women, and it would take a miracle to figure it out.

Brianna considered asking her mother if she was adopted, but never felt confident enough to say the words aloud. Brianna rationalized that they also looked too similar for Molly not to be her biological mother. Then she feared maybe Rachel was Molly's cousin or sister, which would partially explain the resemblance if Rachel was actually Brianna's birth mother. Accepting the possibility was true meant that she knew even less about herself than before. She couldn't stomach that level of disappointment, instead choosing to pretend the whole connection to Rachel was just a misunderstanding or red herring.

After a trip to the public library to borrow a few books, Brianna ran into Doug on the walk back home. He'd tried to cut through a crowd of people, but a group of noisy tourists asking for directions trapped him from escaping her path.

"Doug, don't be an ass. You know I'm standing here." She wasn't even sure what made her call out to him as opposed to pretending not to notice the jerk.

"You've made it clear we're over. There's no need to talk anymore." He refused to focus on her.

"We were friends once. Before you became a giant dickhead," replied Brianna.

"Move, people," Doug grunted, but the light had turned red. They would be stuck until traffic cleared. "How's your new girlfriend, *Bree*?"

"Shanelle and I are just friends. You're making way more out of this than there is." Brianna wondered what she ever liked about Doug. Did he always have a pompous and nasty attitude?

"I've moved on. I don't have to deal with your desperate fear of being alone. Or your inability to make a decision. God, you were awful."

He knew exactly how to press all her buttons, but she wouldn't let it impact her this time. "I'm sorry we didn't work out, but you can try to let it go."

"I guess it's better to know sooner rather than later. Besides, I've already met someone new." He beamed with excitement. "And guess what… it just goes to show you what happens when you are patient. My parents are also getting back together. It's been nothing but great news since I dumped your paranoid ass."

Brianna wanted to fight back, but his words stung too deeply. *She* dumped *him*. It served no purpose to correct him. It then dawned on her what he'd just revealed about his parents. "Are you kidding? I thought they hated each other."

"Yeah, things changed. My mom has grown up a lot since being on her own. That's something you need to do, too."

"You're one to talk after everything you've pulled. Our friends even think you're a douche."

"*Our* friends? Are you serious? They talk about you behind your back all the time."

Brianna cocked her head in disbelief and huffed. "Don't be a loser. Our friends all know what you—"

"I'm serious. Used to be just whispers. Now they know you're queer. Haven't you noticed no one's been calling to hang out with you ever since we broke up?" Doug flung his hands in the air to make his point.

Brianna ran through the list of friends, suddenly unable to recall the last time she'd chatted with anyone since prom. No one other than Shanelle. Was he right? "You're just jealous because I—"

"Ha! You're delusional." As the crowd dispersed, he stepped off the curb to cross the street. "Good things happen to *normal* people, Brianna. Maybe you should rethink the woody you've got for that dumb bitch. You'll be punished one day."

Brianna screamed, scaring several people standing nearby. "Fuck you! You're just a loser with nothing to…" Doug didn't stick around, knowing it would devastate her even more to lose the argument. He'd always been homophobic but had never slurred anything directly at her before. She wanted to believe he was wrong, that his ego had been bruised after the hotel room incident. He had no outlet other than taking his retribution out on her with full force. But then she worried maybe she'd been the one whose head was screwed on the wrong way.

Brianna couldn't control the floodgates. Everything was going wrong in her life. She rushed home and drew a bath to relax. Slipping into the warm water, she pondered whether there were alternative options to deal with her problems. Brianna had little remaining strength to keep fighting for herself—no one else was going to protect her. She rolled the razor's handle between her fingers, keeping her focus on the future, though it was barely enough to combat the dark thoughts growing more intense inside her head. Brianna couldn't afford to lose her final grip on hope, especially when she wasn't certain how far she'd go to stop all the pain.

\* \* \*

When Shanelle returned two days later, Brianna recounted all the new information, uncertain how to proceed with the investigation. Shanelle pushed Brianna to *ask* her mother if she was adopted, purely to get a sense if the woman could be hiding the information, or to validate that a continued search for the records and pressuring Rachel would even be fruitful.

Brianna wanted to find her father, but all her leads had been exhausted. Nothing of substance came from Lenny, the DMV, Rachel, or any memorabilia around the house. Molly held all the clues, and she refused to talk about it. Brianna suggested that Malachi put the search temporarily on hold until she left for college, theorizing Molly would be more vulnerable if she weren't around. She spent the last few days of the summer shopping and preparing for her upcoming move to Woodland, then asked Malachi to propose the best way to meet Molly on his own, where he could trick her into revealing the secrets of her past. He said he'd give it some thought and get back to her once she settled in at Woodland.

When moving day arrived, Brianna was close to a nervous breakdown over getting ready to leave home for the first time with everything still unsolved in her life. She hadn't selected a major, couldn't bring herself to ask her mother questions about the potential adoption, was no closer to finding her father, and still hadn't determined if she was ready to consider the next step with Shanelle.

Brianna had just finished choosing a couple of winter outfits in case the temperature dropped too low before she came home for the first break at Thanksgiving. She'd little room for anything else in the luggage and sulked on the bed. Molly came into her daughter's bedroom to ask if she'd needed any help. Clothes were strewn everywhere, from the top of the floor lamp to under the wheels of the desk chair. "It looks like you haven't even begun to pack. What blew up in here?" She removed a green hoodie from under the chair and folded it.

"I'm never gonna fit everything in this suitcase. I haven't even found all my soccer crap." Brianna thrust her solid frame against the bed's headboard and pouted like a child.

"What do you want me to do about it?" asked Molly.

"I started, but I can't fit everything. Do you have a bag I can borrow?" She slid off the bed and dragged both her suitcases to the doorway. "We're leaving in thirty minutes." On her return, Brianna grabbed the hoodie and threw it in a pile on the bed.

"Yes, I'll find something." Molly left the room to search the closet in her bedroom.

"You're the best, Mom." A lump grew in Brianna's throat every time she said the word *mom*. She had to find a way to hint about an adoption if nothing but to prove it wasn't true. When Molly returned to the room, Brianna forced herself to blurt out the question as though she ripped off a Band-Aid that'd been there too long. "Are you sure you didn't adopt me from someone else?"

Molly lifted her head, then refocused on the floor. A few seconds later, she responded. "Adopt you? Where did you get a crazy idea like that?"

"Oh, I was just checking. Sometimes parents have deep, dark secrets. Things they fail to tell their children until it's too late." Brianna laughed while sorting the remaining piles on the bed.

"I don't think I'll forget the twenty-four hours of labor it took for you to show up." Molly tossed a heavy blue duffel bag with several side pockets at her daughter. "Try this one. I'd completely forgotten about it at the bottom of my closet. It has enough room for all your stuff." Her eyes, heavy and glassy, refused to blink.

"Thanks. Where did you get it from?" For a moment, a sense of relief over Molly's response about the adoption comforted Brianna. But she still had no answers about her father and had never gotten to check the rest of her mother's bedroom for more clues. Now that she was leaving, there wouldn't be another opportunity until a break near the end of the semester.

"I don't remember. I've had it forever, but it's time to pass it on to you now." Molly sighed heavily with a distracted concern over the topics in their conversation.

Brianna hugged her mother, holding tight as though she'd almost changed her mind about leaving the nest that'd both protected and smothered her entire life. "I'm glad you're cool with me going to Woodland."

Molly jerked her head to the side. "I never said that."

"I meant you didn't try to stop me. I know you're not happy I chose to leave home." Brianna unzipped one of the pouches on the duffel and tossed in some soccer gear.

"You're my daughter. I can't hold on to the past forever. I just wish you told me sooner about considering schools other than New York." Molly strolled to the far wall and straightened the picture of the two of them taken at a Broadway show. Molly's boss had given her tickets to *Phantom of the Opera* as a holiday gift that Christmas, a thank you for all her work at the accounting firm that employed her for ten years. "Do you remember the day we took this photo? You'd just turned twelve."

Brianna was concerned her mother had gotten too nostalgic and would begin crying at any moment. "Yeah, it was a fantastic day. Can you toss me the cleats on the floor by you?" As Molly slowly turned away from the wall, Brianna noticed the detached emptiness in her mother. "Don't get all weepy on me."

"I can't believe how much time has gone by. It's okay to say you're gonna miss me, you know."

Brianna smiled back at her mother. "Of course, I'll miss you. It's been you and me for so long. I won't hear you singing in the shower, then arguing with me that you're not tone deaf. Or kick your butt playing a game of checkers before bed. I won't know if you've remembered to cook yourself dinner, or if you stay at the office until the cleaning people show up. It's gonna feel different."

"I don't need my daughter to tell me to eat." She smacked her hips and snorted. "I've got a little extra around here that says otherwise, don't you think?"

"You're so dense. I wish I had your hips and chest. That would have been a good thing to inherit." She made a sizzling sound upon placing a single finger on her mother's butt. "My mother, the hottie. Seriously, didn't you need to get away from your parents when you were my age? You haven't even told me where you grew up." Brianna knew she trod on volatile ground with that line of questions, but in less than an hour, many miles would separate them. Desperate times called for desperate measures, wasn't that the saying?

Molly's fingers mindlessly smoothed out wrinkles from the comforter that weren't present. "Nothing good ever comes out of discussing the past. Yes, it was hard to leave home, but I needed to. I know what you're feeling right now, that's why I had to let you go away."

"Why don't I know anything about my grandparents?" Brianna laid on the bed across from her mother, resting her head on her hands with both elbows propping her up. "Where do they live?"

Molly pushed her weight into her daughter, letting their feet gently bounce against one another. "Do you need to know about them? How does this change your life?"

"I'm lonely sometimes. Like even though I have you, what if you suddenly got sick or disappeared. I don't know anyone else in my family. It doesn't feel right." Brianna hoped her mother would recognize a hint of sincerity in her voice and relinquish control to finally share something, anything, about her past.

"I left home many years ago. We didn't have a good relationship. I couldn't talk to them about what I wanted or who I was." A withdrawn solace surfaced in Molly's demeanor as the disconnected breaks in her somber voice haunted the discussion.

The room grew smaller as Brianna and her mother talked, stifling the remaining options to learn anything new about the past. "I'm sorry you didn't have their support."

"Why is this so important? Have I failed you as a mother?"

"No, you didn't, but one person can't provide everything. You can't be the mother who teaches me how to grow into a woman, the grandparents who watch over me when I'm sick, and the favorite aunt who buys me sexy clothing my mother would disapprove of." Brianna's voice rose higher as she rattled off her list. "Or the father who always lets me be his little girl, even when I'm all grown up." She stood with her hands on her hips, waiting for a response.

"Are we back to that again? I told you everything about your father I know." Molly turned away, her body language revealing a heightened proximity to shut-down mode. "It's sad and unfortunate, but I have no way of getting in contact with him."

Brianna desperately wanted to shake Molly. Shake her until some tidbit of information accidentally fell from the impenetrable safe that was the woman who raised her. "It makes little sense, that's all. You won't talk about anything, and the details are very fuzzy. What girl wouldn't have curiosity about her father, especially when her mother goes out of her way to hide who he is?"

"I've said enough for today. I don't enjoy talking about my past. There are too many painful memories. I'd rather focus on us and the future." Molly reached to the front of the bed and picked up the stuffed rabbit, witnessing their struggling conversation. "Are you not taking Bunny?"

During the winter when Brianna had turned seven years old, she suffered several bouts of strep throat and tonsillitis. The doctor opted to remove her tonsils, which didn't sit well with Brianna. She refused until finally Molly bargained with her daughter to undergo the surgery. Molly promised to buy a rabbit if she'd let the doctor do his job. Brianna, excited at having her own pet again, had finally relented. Upon waking up, the first words she whispered in her gravelly voice were *"promised me a rabbit."* Molly had always meant a stuffed animal, but Brianna had been under the assumption it was a live one to pet and feed. On the day Brianna was set to come home from the hospital, Molly brought the stuffed rabbit with her and handed it to her daughter as they signed the final release forms. Brianna, upon realizing she'd been tricked, threw a tantrum the whole hospital wing witnessed.

"No, Bunny should stay with you. That way, when you miss me, you have something that I love close by." With increasing pressure, Brianna smoothed the fur around his nose. "He can watch out for you while I'm away."

"I love you, Brianna. Someday we can talk more about where I grew up and how I ended up in New York. For now, remember that you need to use common sense wherever you go. Not everyone was raised in a cheerful home with loving parents who want nothing but the best for their child."

"This conversation isn't over, Mom. I'm not giving up on finding out my father's identity, especially now that you've told me you had a terrible relationship with your parents."

"You need to stop pushing me on this." She caressed Brianna's cheek. "Focus on college."

"You're hiding something, I can feel it. I just want the chance to meet my father, so I can decide for myself what I want to do. Is that so wrong?"

"It's not... I guess maybe you do deserve—"

A voice shouting in the hallway interrupted any opportunity to truly unleash the history that needed to be shared. "Hellooo... hey look at that, the door no longer squeaks... Let's go, Bree, I'm double-parked. We need to get out of here soon. We got a new life to start, babe."

Molly pulled away from Brianna and walked into the hallway. "Hi, Shanelle. Lenny fixed the door. But you know, you could still knock and wait for us to open it, hon. Tell me, how are your parents dealing with you being gone for a few months?"

Shanelle ignored what she didn't want to answer. It wasn't from being rude, she just felt she had full access to Brianna and the apartment.

"Oh, I didn't realize you were home. They'll miss me, but my parents still have the rest of the crew around."

"I still can't believe I've never met them." Despite Shanelle and Brianna being best friends and playing in the city's soccer league for two years, Molly rarely made it to any games. And on the few occasions she did, Shanelle's parents had been busy traveling. They'd spoken on the phone once or twice but never found time to get together in person. Molly always assumed Shanelle had them wrapped around her finger, given what she'd seen of her thus far.

Brianna zipped the last bag and tossed it over her shoulder. She needed to interrupt the conversation to get things moving more quickly. "I'm almost done, then we can leave."

"I know you're worried about Brianna leaving home, Molly. I promise to protect her. She's my girl. No one touches my girl without going through me first." Shanelle grabbed Brianna's wrist, rubbing her thumbs against the sensitive spot that always caused her best friend to shiver and giggle.

"You girls need to stay away from the boys at Woodland. I know you think it's tough here in the city, but even scarier dangers worse than drug pushers and drunks lurk on a college campus." Molly cradled Bunny against her chest, her weepy gaze cast toward both girls. "You never know a person until you see them at their worst."

"Don't worry. Bree's got me to protect her." Shanelle grabbed her friend by the waist and pulled her close, unwilling to let her step away. "No boys will bother her with me around."

Brianna's toes fidgeted against the leather on her sandals as her mother judged her best friend. "Why don't you bring those two bags to the car? I'll say goodbye to my mom."

Shanelle let go of Brianna's waist and embraced Molly. "Bye, Molly. See you soon." She carried both bags down the hallway with effortless ease. "I'll meet you downstairs. Don't take too long."

Molly turned to her daughter once Shanelle shut the front door. "May I ask you a question?"

The back of Brianna's throat shrunk and cut off her ability to breathe. She knew what her mother would ask. It was an inevitable discussion at some point. But not at that moment. She wasn't ready. "Make it quick."

Molly hesitated, but then blurted out her question. "Is Shanelle... gay?"

That wasn't the expected question. It was an easier one to answer than what lingered in the back of Brianna's mind, but one that would still lead down a dangerous path. Brianna recalled watching the movie *Ghost* with her mother a few months earlier, fascinated by Demi Moore's scene at the pottery wheel. The curves of her shoulder as her fingers delicately manipulated the clay and spun art in her nervous hands. The sense of inner femininity not only being born but transcending from her very existence as if she'd been a glowing goddess. Brianna always feared her mother had guessed the truth in those few seconds—how her daughter had longed for Shanelle the way she once stared at the television screen and adored Demi.

"Yes, I thought you knew." Her voice barely allowed her to squeak out the words.

"I suspected, but it was different just now." Molly pushed both hands into her pockets. "Is Shanelle in love with you?"

Brianna choked on her spit as it nervously slid down her throat, mixing with a few tiny pockets of rising bile. "Umm, she's my best friend."

"I know, but I also spotted how she looked at you."

Brianna's panic overtook a proper goodbye to her mother. "I need to go. We have a long drive." Her priority was getting away from the conversation, and she rushed out of the bedroom.

Molly called after her daughter. "Surely, you recognize it. Is it true?"

Brianna continued down the hall, unnerved by the fifteen feet between her and the front door. After twisting the knob, she mumbled into the air, "Sometimes a daughter needs to have some secrets from her mother, too."

"Brianna, wait. Be careful, please."

"I have a full course load with soccer practice every day. I need to get a job. I need to choose my major. I have to join a few clubs to put on my resume. There won't be much time for anything else." Brianna dropped the duffel bag and nervously glanced at her mother.

"I can't believe this day arrived so quickly. That you're leaving, and I won't see you again for months." Molly's heartache swelled with each word that betrayed her weakening composure.

"This happens to every teenager who goes off to college. I promise I'll email you every day if you need me to. I'll call every week, so you hear my voice." Brianna threw her hands around her mother's neck. "Please don't make this a bigger scene. I'm struggling, too, but I need to hold it together, so I'm not in a ten-hour car ride of nonstop waterworks."

Molly squeezed tighter, then let go. "Okay. But check all around you. Find a group of friends you trust. Focus on your studies. Don't let Shanelle boss you around."

"And stay away from boys. I've heard the speech all summer. I get it, Mom. Can I go now?"

"Don't be a brat. Someday you'll walk in my shoes."

"That's decades away. I'll worry about it later." Brianna hadn't even decided if children were in her future. How could she extend the family line when she knew nothing about the family?

"It creeps up on you more quickly than you realize. Some days, it's like you smiled at me for the first time… when the nurse handed you to me, and I…" Molly wiped her cheeks and sniffled.

"What are you gonna do with yourself when I'm gone? Will you focus on your own life for a change? Tell me something to make me worry less about you." Sorrow overtook Brianna, more than expected. She'd assumed once the door closed on her life in New York City, there wouldn't be a need to look backward. Now, as it was about to happen, it suddenly occurred to Brianna that her mother would truly be alone.

"Don't worry about me. I've told you that before. I'll keep busy. I don't need someone to occupy my time for me." Molly clasped together her hands and sighed. "Really, I know how to take care of myself."

"You need someone to treat you well, too. I wish you'd consider joining one of those online dating sites. Every guy would want to chat with you."

"I'm not looking for anything. If it finds me, maybe I'll think twice. I don't see myself putting up a picture and profile to entice some man based on my appearance."

"Make a few friends. Visit a bar. Go downstairs to the jazz club and find a handsome stranger worth talking to."

"Not that you need to know, but someone came in to ask questions about his tax payments today. He asked me out for coffee."

"Really? What's his name? Is he hot?" Brianna was excited her mother might have finally met a guy.

"He's an ex-cop, very disciplined. Trim beard. Tall, too."

Brianna swallowed deeply to hold back from choking. Could it be Malachi? "He sounds cool."

"He has very kind eyes."

Brianna checked the time on her phone, realizing they were already late. "I need to go. Promise me you'll give it a chance."

"I promise you, I'll think about it. I'm not committing to anything else."

"That's good enough. I love you, Mom."

"I love you, Brianna. Call me when you get there. I don't care what time it is."

"Ugh. Go wash your face. You kinda look a mess." Brianna left the apartment and jogged down several flights of stairs to the front entrance of the building.

Shanelle leaned against the car door, tapping her foot on the curb. "Are you ready, Bree?"

"I believe so. Guess what… I think Malachi might have asked my mother on a date."

"If he did, it's pure genius. A bit cruel. It might backfire, but worth the chance." Shanelle shook her head.

"Yeah, I didn't expect him to ask her already. He was supposed to schedule an appointment for his taxes, then meet her in person once

I was gone." Brianna glanced up at the window, worried at the blank expression occupying Molly's face.

"He knows what he's doing. Let the man do his job."

"I asked her for the truth about being adopted. She sidestepped the conversation by bringing up how long labor was, but never said it was her who gave birth to me." Brianna opened the passenger car door. "Almost like she was playing word games."

"Does that mean you'll contact Rachel Abernathy yourself?" Shanelle walked around the front of the car and jumped in the driver's seat. "I'm not sure that's a good plan, but I'll help however you need."

"I know you will. It means so much to me." Brianna waved good-bye to her mother before closing the car door. "I'll wait a few days while Malachi tries to get any information on their fake coffee date. I'm worried about my mom being on her own or getting hurt."

"She'll be okay. I had the same reaction from my mom when I left a little while ago. Come on, we'll do this together." Shanelle placed her hand on Brianna's knee. "You're in charge of music. How does that sound?"

"Are you serious?" Brianna laughed. "You never let me pick the tunes."

"You agreed to come with me to Woodland. Now it's time I let you take the lead. I trust you. I believe in you. I'll support you however you need me to."

Brianna's emotions got the better of her as they began the long drive to Woodland. "I couldn't ask for a better best friend."

Chapter 14

# Amalia, February 1985

After several weeks back on campus, the days grew busy enough to distract Amalia from a paralyzing grief over the death of her father and brother. She stood before the photocopy machine, printing materials for a finance theories class later that afternoon, anticipating what the professor needed as handouts and reading assignments for the uninterested freshmen required to take his intro course.

On the second floor of the liberal arts academic building was Dr. Jonah West's office, a ten-by-ten box he'd crammed full of books and journals, the occasional scraps of ledger paper discretely shoved between issues of *Business World* magazine, and the hopes of someday publishing his own college curriculums. As Amalia stared across the hall from the floor's admin area, he scribbled notes on a student's first draft paper. Jonah's profile reminded her of a strong and commandeering captain, one who exuded confidence, but no ego. She'd not been around men like him before yet found herself smitten with Jonah perhaps more than she should be.

Amalia's father, whom she loved more than all others, might have once been as robust, at least before Janet had come into the picture. She'd once asked him why he stayed married to her mother, despite the way she treated him. He explained that Janet had been a good woman once before, and he wasn't the kind of man to kick someone when they were down. Although Amalia understood her father, she knew that wasn't the type of marriage she ever wanted to have. She and her husband would treat each other respectfully and lovingly every minute of their time together.

Jonah interrupted her thoughts. "Amalia, do you have a minute?"

She dropped the papers on the machine and pushed a few loose curls behind her ear. "I'm on my way, Jonah." Before entering his office, she pressed her skirt down, smoothing the fabric as it surreptitiously draped her shapely hips and thighs. Though it was still only February, spring had made an early appearance, offering Amalia a small hope for things yet to come. Jonah's kindness also had that effect on her.

He glanced upward from his desk, the outline of his lips rising in the corners as Amalia came into view. "You look nice today. How was your weekend?"

"Pleasant." The fingers on Amalia's right hand tapped the top of his wooden desk. "I went for a long walk around campus and attended a few of the student concerts in the music building." Her focus fixated on the ceiling moldings as she pulled her bottom lip inside her mouth.

"Have a seat, please." Jonah extended a hand diagonally across from his desk to a low-seated, comfortable brown leather chair. "I'm sure you spent time thinking about your father and brother. I'm so very sorry you're going through this horrific ordeal."

Amalia bounced nervously at the edge of the chair. Though he was informal in his ways, she still sat upright and poised for an adult conversation. She hadn't wanted him to think of her as a child, despite being so much younger than him. "I miss them every day."

"I lost both my parents when I was younger. Cancer. Although it happened a few years apart, it unfortunately never gets any easier. In time, you'll focus on the positive memories." He leaned forward, placed his elbows on the desk, and crossed his arms. "It's still too soon right now. Don't rush through the range of emotions you've yet to explore. Each person's grief is unique and requires its own very special acceptance process."

Amalia searched her mind for something to concentrate on. She appreciated his truthfulness. Anyone else who'd known about the accident treated her like a sullen and weak young girl, uncertain what to say, or pushed her to get through it quickly. "Thank you. How was your weekend?"

Jonah shifted in his seat, then slid off the cap on his red ballpoint pen. "Quiet. I don't work on Sundays. It's my day to relax and forget about all the papers and outlines. I watched a few movies. Have you seen *Gone with the Wind?*"

Amalia shook her head. With only one television in their house, there had rarely been opportunities to watch anything she was interested in, not even to mention the rules her mother had dictated when it came to the types of permitted shows or movies. "No, tell me about it."

"You must be kidding. Ah, you've missed out. It would take hours to explain the complexities of such a brilliant film. It was a book first. You should read it." The whites of his eyes grew brighter as his shoulders relaxed into the tufted padding of his chair when he leaned back. "We could discuss it each week. I'm certain you'd love Scarlet."

"I'd like that." A hint of comfort, one not prominent for many months, brewed in the back of Amalia's head. She filled with curiosity to learn more about him. "Did you watch it on your own? I mean, I know little about your life outside campus."

"We must change that." Jonah rambled toward his office door. He glanced back at a perplexed Amalia, whose feet anxiously tapped on the carpeted floor. He reached a hand toward her. "Come, let's get a cup of tea and talk about life. It'll do us both some good."

After grabbing two peppermint blends at the student café, they settled into the giant sofas in the library's reception lounge where Jonah revealed to Amalia all the pertinent facts of his life outside of Woodland.

"I was married once, but it didn't last. She was young and foolish, never really wanted to settle down," responded Jonah when Amalia asked him if he was in a relationship. "It was different for women in the sixties. Traditions and societal expectations still trapped them from ever being treated equally."

Amalia considered her response, careful to choose her words. Did he think she was young and foolish, too? "I think that's still happening today. At least where I come from. My mother has always told me I didn't need to go to college. She expected me to stay home and take care of a family."

"That's sad to hear. You've so much more to offer the world with your intelligence and wit." He sipped from his cup and broke off a piece of a chocolate chip cookie to nibble on.

Amalia blushed thinking about his compliment, then reached for the other half of the cookie. "Do you have any children?"

"A son, but we never spent much time together. After I caught my former wife cheating on me, we tried to make it work. I don't think my heart was in it after what she'd done." Jonah loved his ex-wife despite her cruel actions and constant need to cuckold him. When she requested a divorce and moved to the West Coast, Jonah had little opportunity to fight for custody at that time. "The courts always sided with the mother." Jonah considered himself a neglectful father, given he'd only visited his son for one week each summer and every other Christmas. When he finished talking, hope overtook the nostalgia that'd cloaked his face.

Amalia reached to his cheek and brushed away a smudge of chocolate, bringing him back to their conversation. His smile shined brightly at the smoothness of the skin on her fingers as he rested his hand against hers on his face.

Jonah explained that once his family left town, he spent most of his time and energy obtaining a doctorate, studying the market, and analyzing financial regulations. When he received his Ph.D., there was no one supporting him in the audience to watch as the President of the University handed off a diploma to the top student in the class. Though Jonah dated a few women over the years, nothing ever clicked well enough to move to the next phase in a relationship. He lived off campus, a few blocks away in the middle-class part of town, owning a small colonial home where he spent most of his time outside of Woodland.

Amalia grew fond of her conversations with Jonah each week, considering him a friend as well as a boss. As they bonded, she became convinced getting a degree in accounting and finance was the best path for her. She envied his excitement when he'd come bounding into the office, newspaper in hand, challenging her to explain recent decisions made by Fortune 500 companies over tax laws and finance policies. She soon found herself reading the newspaper each morning before arriving at work to impress him with her questions or be ready with the right responses to his. Though her father's memory never trailed too far from the surface, her time with Jonah made it easier to accept what'd happened. Despite the twenty-five-year age difference—he was old enough to be her father—they developed a strong connection, one in which they trusted each other in sharing their thoughts and emotions. Amalia enjoyed having someone who would listen to her without judgment or any expectations, someone who comforted and protected her the way she'd almost never been attended to before.

Carter, who followed through on his promise to let Amalia control the evolution of their relationship, had taken an internship for his final semester in the sales department of a local bottle distributor. He'd wanted to gain experience in various marketing practices and business operations as part of his plan to help rebuild Graeme Hardware Store. He'd assumed a larger course load than normal and worked at least thirty hours each week. Friday nights were date night, where Carter would take Amalia to a movie at a local drive-in still in operation despite the decline in attendance, or out to a romantic restaurant to try new cuisines.

When Valentine's Day arrived, Amalia preferred not to celebrate with a fancy, starry-eyed rendezvous. She couldn't keep her mind from recalling all the greeting cards she'd handmade from construction paper and glue as a child for her father, preferring to forget the holiday. Carter convinced her to give him a chance by suggesting he could cook dinner for her in the fraternity house. Amalia had found a few rays of sunshine in her life and agreed to his plans, recognizing how hard he'd been trying to impress her with his newfound patience and open-minded attitude.

An hour before their Valentine's date, Carter called from his internship, his voice hesitant and distracted. "I'm so sorry to cancel our dinner, Amalia."

"It's fine. I didn't want to do anything special tonight, anyway. My mind isn't focused, and that wouldn't be fair to you." A sense of relief flooded Amalia's body when he told her his boss demanded he stay late to fix a shipping issue. It hadn't been Carter's fault, but he'd look like the hero if he were able to get the order released in time.

"I won't finish until at least eleven, and then I have class early tomorrow morning. Let's meet for lunch before you go to softball practice?"

"I can't tomorrow. The bus leaves at twelve o'clock for our afternoon game at the Coyotes' field. I'll call you when I get home," she explained, resting against the refrigerator on the floor in her dorm room. Her mind wandered to the game for a moment, hoping they'd finally beat Millner College's cunning Coyotes. The school rivalry had been going on for at least a decade. It was their turn to win.

"Okay. I love you, baby."

Amalia flinched at his goodbye. He'd been saying he loved her at the end of every conversation lately. She still hadn't said it back. Love wasn't something she understood anymore. Amalia wasn't ready to accept replacing love for her dead father with someone else who'd still left her concerned about his sincerity. Even though she'd grown comfortable with Carter, nothing told her it was love. If she loved him, that meant it was time to sleep with him. "I know you do."

"Do you love me?" Carter's voice echoed like nails on a chalkboard. "It would mean the world for you to say it."

Amalia pulled the phone from her ear and covered the mouthpiece. An unappreciated silence occupied the room and a better part of her mind. She mumbled to herself, willing the right message to formulate, but it wouldn't come. He acted childish and immature, needing her to say the words. He was still a boy who knew little of reality other than his own needs and desires. "Yes, I do, but..." By luck, the door swung open, and her roommate wandered into the room. "I gotta go, Carter. Rachel's back."

Grateful for the interruption, Amalia hung up the phone and turned to her roommate. "Hey, what's going on?" Rachel had become distant again ever since returning to campus after winter break, choosing not to reveal anything about her trip to the doctor or the decision about the baby. She'd put on more weight, but it wasn't completely obvious. It'd only been about four months since she'd gotten pregnant.

Rachel laughed and shot back a quick glance in Amalia's direction. "I'm just changing before I head out to a party at my sister's sorority house. Wanna come with me?"

Amalia wrestled with the decision to attend the bash with her roommate, curious what other girls would do that night and hopeful to discover a way to make new friends on campus. In the end, she was more concerned about Rachel's well-being. "Are you sure that's a good idea... with the baby and all?"

"I haven't decided what to do about the baby. I have a few more weeks before I need to make that decision. I'm not planning to drink tonight."

Amalia uncrossed her arms and leaned closer. "Is the baby's father still in the picture, or..." She wanted to ask for more details, but an awkward uncertainty stole the moment.

"He still comes by from time to time. I don't really know anymore. He's a little older than us. I'm not sure he wants to be around me anymore. Maybe I shouldn't say anything..." Rachel hesitated with her response, clicking her tongue ring and shifting her eyes to the floor at several points in the discussion.

Amalia worried that her roommate wasn't very trusting of their friendship. She decided to share something about herself in the hopes it would be enough of a trigger to bring them closer together. "I understand. I have a bit of a complicated situation going on, too."

"Really?" Rachel's interest crested.

"I have a crush on one of my professors." Amalia covered her face and giggled. "I shouldn't say anything."

Rachel dropped the shirt she'd pulled from the closet. "Tell me, tell me... that's scandalous."

Amalia confessed to thinking about Jonah as more than a friend. She explained how they'd met the previous semester, why he'd offered her a student job, and even the couple of times she'd thought he stared at her from his office. "But don't say anything. It's just a silly crush, and I don't want Carter to know. He's already very jealous," Amalia replied.

"Who would I tell? Don't worry!" Rachel made light of the discussion and changed into a new outfit.

Amalia considered asking Rachel if she knew her pseudo-stalker, Riley. She also wanted to ask more about the baby's father, but ultimately decided her roommate would reveal the truth when she was ready. Amalia was concerned by pushing too much, she might lose her only friend. "Thanks!"

Rachel tossed a silk blouse on the bed toward Amalia. "This would look hot on you."

Amalia checked her closet and searched for a pair of pants or jeans to wear with it. Her eyes fell on a box in the bottom corner, realizing she still hadn't opened the gift her father had left under the Christmas tree. "No, I'll pass for tonight, but thanks. I've got something else to do."

After Rachel left, Amalia tore open the box hidden beneath her luggage. She was desperate to unwrap it but afraid to open the last gift she'd ever receive from her father. Tossing the ribbons and the bow into the wire trash basket, Amalia lifted off the top and peered inside. Pink tissue paper covered what resembled a leather-bound book. She quickly shredded the paper, sending delicate scraps floating through the air, then sat on her roommate's mattress to admire the gift—a journal with the Woodland College logo embossed on the front, full of blank pages and opportunities for hope.

Amalia flipped the cover and scanned the inside page where an inscription summoned her to read its words with a pull stronger than gravity. As she did, watery tears fell, knowing her father had forgiven her for that night he'd caught her on the couch with Carter.

> *A girl should always have a place to keep her innermost secret thoughts. The blank pages of your life need to be filled with treasures and hopes for a future you deserve. Don't ever be afraid to tell your story or to fight for who you want to be. It's been my privilege to watch you grow into a beautiful and intelligent woman who's made her father the proudest man that ever lived. - Dad*

Amalia hugged the book to her chest tighter than a dog's grip on its favorite bone. She scanned the room for the nearest pen. After locating one in the desk's top drawer, the room offered freedom she hadn't ever known before. Amalia uncapped the pen and wrote about how much she loved her father in the first entry. She then talked about her roommate, Rachel, being pregnant and not wanting to have an abortion even though the baby's father demanded it. Amalia questioned why she continued to date Carter, even though he kept pushing her to sleep with him. The journal became her place for confessions, truths, and random thoughts. The scent of the paper comforted her. Its texture brought out a smile. The present from her father lifted her from the haze that'd enveloped her soul ever since his death. Content with the first entry of her future life, she stood from the bed to change clothes. Her phone rang, and she picked up after the second ring. "Hello."

"Hi, Amalia. I'm so sorry to ask this of you on Valentine's Day, but I need some help. Is there any chance you have some time available?"

Amalia's cheeks grinned widely and released a laugh free from a numbing pain and constant hurt. "Yes, definitely. I've got nothing at all tonight. What can I do? I'd love to help you."

\* \* \*

One hour later, Amalia sat across from Jonah in his office. She'd changed into jeans and the dark, low-cut flowery blouse she'd borrowed from her roommate, accenting every curve of her voluptuous body. Though Rachel had a smaller frame, it'd been loose enough to still fit Amalia, yet snug in all the right places. For the first time, confidence rose over her image in the mirror, even though she'd been uncertain why she chose to get all dolled up. She'd added rouge, eyeshadow, and a few dashes of mascara with a darker shade of fire-red lipstick coating her full lips. Rachel had taught her how to appear more feminine and sultrier, not like an innocent young girl who was afraid to wear makeup.

"You're a savior." Jonah leafed through the pile of notes on his desk. "I got back from class earlier, rushing across campus to meet a student who, it turns out, had stood me up. I was so careless; I spilled my entire cup of coffee all over everything."

Amalia lifted the closest sheet to her and tried to read from it. "You have quite a mess here. Did you need me to help rewrite them?"

"Yes." He breathed out deeply while relaxing in his chair. "I have a meeting with the editor tomorrow where she expects a final draft. These were all the changes I'd planned to type tonight, but I barely understand half the words."

Amalia read aloud from the page. "Hmm... this one either says the fundamental principles of accounting are... to offset the debits and credits, so your books are always balanced, or," she giggled, "to upset Didi and Claire, so your bottom is always bouncing." Amalia dropped the paper on the desk. "I personally prefer to think it's about your bouncing bottom."

Jonah's jaw dropped a few inches. He was about to say something but cracked up laughing so hard he snorted. "You did not just say that."

The color of Amalia's skin brightened a deeper shade than her lipstick. "Oh, I'm so sorry. I can't believe I actually did. It sounded so funny."

Jonah walked within inches of Amalia as an imaginary force enveloped them in a bubble. "You are busted! And yet you've always come across as such a quiet young woman." Laughter filled the room as he knelt next to her and placed his hand on her forearm. "I know better now, Amalia." He leaned too far backward and landed on the carpet against the side of his desk.

Amalia turned her head downward in his direction and covered her face in humiliation. "No, seriously. I'm so embarrassed. I... I have no idea where that came from."

She hadn't laughed that loud in months. He'd brought out a different side of her, one she'd never known existed. Even as a child, she'd been reserved and always fearful of saying the incorrect thing. One wrong phrase or glance, her mother would act quickly. Discussion of boys and dancing, or even someone's rear end, were never topics she'd thought about out loud with other people, least of all her father or a professor.

"Don't worry about it. You made this whole situation fixable. I see what needs to happen next. I must turn my accounting textbook into a romance novel to keep the readers' attention." Jonah raised a hand toward Amalia, almost begging for her to touch him. "Help me stand up. I've lost all energy from laughing this hard."

Amalia grabbed his hand and pulled with all her strength, but it wasn't enough. Quite the opposite. The weight of his body on the floor, along with the playful nature of gravity, sent her toppling onto him. She landed with her torso against his chest and her head less than six inches from his lips. Amalia's eyes caught Jonah's as they laid twisted together on his office floor—Jonah in his Oxford shirt with the top button open and a few patches of light hair sneaking out from the top, and Amalia in a low-cut blouse, her chest pounding heavier than she'd expected.

Images of Carter plagued her as she studied Jonah, remembering her sweet but immature boyfriend who'd canceled their Valentine's dinner. Memories of Bryan, who once offered her a chance to experience another side of Brant, a potentially good one, flooded her vision. A wish to again see her father, torn from the world in a way that left Amalia with no remaining love to find or give, flashed before her.

Jonah was strong and masculine. He had an intelligence she'd always admired and the allure of a confident and stable man. As her fingers grasped his, Jonah's soft yet rugged skin revealed he wasn't afraid to work hard in achieving his goals. Time was still for those moments they laid on the floor together, offering Amalia an escape from the distractions in her life. She ran her finger across the back of his hand and onto his forearm. The sharp bristle of his hair sent a shiver down her back. Jonah was beyond attractive. Kind. Handsome. Powerful.

The warm air turned to a fine mist between their lips, and the strength of his hand cradled Amalia's neck. Jonah pulled her into a kiss—his lips were soft yet commanding. When they pressed together, energy soared from her toes straight through her entire quivering body. She'd been waiting for this kiss throughout her whole life, not just at that moment. It was passionate yet gentle, full of desire but innocent. When she pulled away, reality hijacked the room.

Jonah spoke first. "I apologize. I don't know where that came from." He quickly adjusted the button on his shirt and backed away toward the other side of his desk. Both fear and a renewed interest in a life he'd once abandoned dominated his countenance.

"No, it was me. I got lost in a moment thinking about too many other things." Amalia paced the floor and focused her mind on the situation. He was her supervisor. She was dating Carter. It was just misplaced emotions while remembering her father and Bryan and everything from the past. "We should work on your notes."

"Yes." Jonah shuffled a few papers. "Why don't you read aloud, and I'll type? You have a knack for reading my chicken scratch better than I can."

Amalia agreed, and they spent the next two hours transcribing his coffee-stained notes from inscrutable messages to finished copy.

Something had awakened inside Amalia despite years of Janet's vicious attempts to leave her daughter afraid of physical connections and interactions with men. Sensuality and femininity developed within Amalia, and she wanted to experience her seductive side—unsure why it'd taken only a kiss with Jonah to elicit such an animalistic urge when months with Carter led to her protecting her virginity.

Jonah thanked Amalia for reassembling his portfolio and led her to the outside of the building. As they said their goodbyes, he left for home and Amalia called Carter. Some fraternity brother said he'd gotten home hours earlier and went to the pub with a friend. Amalia decided to talk with her mother as soon as possible, knowing it was necessary to sort out a few expectations for the future that'd suddenly changed inside her.

# Chapter 15

# Brianna, September 2004

Brianna finished her last class of the day, excited but exhausted by her arrival on campus a week earlier. The students seemed friendly, the administrators were open-minded, and the faculty treated her as an equal. Woodland was everything she'd hoped it could be, but it was Friday and time to take a break from academic life. She was anxious for news from Malachi's fake coffee date with her mother that afternoon. Once she finally got hold of him, all he'd learned was that Molly had talked about relocating from somewhere else many years earlier. When Brianna called her mother, she never even mentioned the coffee date—the woman would hide things until the day she died.

Brianna left the classroom, crossed the entrance to the library, and began the trek home. She scrolled through her playlist, stuffed a pair of small white buds in her ears, and jammed her way across the courtyard. As the Nine Inch Nails' track she desperately needed to hear surfaced on the iPod, Brianna glimpsed someone leaving through the library's front doors. She stood at the end of the half-circle, waiting for him to walk past the rose garden and onto the pavement path, hoping to get closer as something seemed familiar about his face. When he lifted his head, revealing light-colored eyes, blond hair, and a kind smile, no immediate memories came to the surface as to where she could have previously met him.

The stranger caught her glancing at him, then motioned to check if she had the music on or off.

Brianna pressed pause on the device and smiled. "Hi. Wanna sample a bit?"

He reached out a hand while staring her down from head to toe. "I'm Professor Villing, and that all depends on what you're listening to."

She extended one earbud and pressed play while he held it near his ear. "I'm Brianna Porter. It's a few nineties bands. I'm a bit old school."

His head rocked back and forth as he sang out the cathartic lyrics. "I grew up listening to this stuff when it first aired." He winked at her as he settled into the groove of the music and their conversation.

"Oh, that's cool." She searched the fine lines on his face to guess his age as a way to stop her mind from going places she wasn't prepared to go.

"Are you a student here?" When he handed the cord back to her, their fingers briefly connected. He wore a pair of light-colored khakis, a green polo shirt, and a checkered jacket that molded perfectly around his well-defined torso.

"Yes, it's my first week. I love it already. What do you teach, Professor?" She assumed he dabbled in philosophy or something in the humanities field based on his casual yet stylish appearance.

"I'm an adjunct faculty member in the Woodland's business school, mostly in their MBA program. I just started two years ago."

"Damn, I had it all wrong. One of those corporate types, huh? You fooled me with those Italian loafers." She moistened her lips, given they'd grown parched in the last few moments.

"No, definitely not me. So, where are you from?"

"New York City. Just got here a week ago."

"And what are you majoring in?" He held a direct gaze while leaning against the stone wall behind them. "Wait, don't tell me. Three ear piercings. Sandals. Bohemian style about you. Lit. You're a literature major. Women's studies. No, hmm… writing, you're focusing on creative writing. Am I right?" His lips grew a half-smirk, and he cracked his knuckles before placing them behind his neck.

"Undecided... but leaning toward something creative. Don't let the appearance fool you." Brianna was intrigued by his confident attitude. "I'm also a striker on the women's soccer team and know how to play just as hard as I work." The words spilled from her lips, yet she'd no clue where they came from.

The professor laughed loud enough to scatter a few robins who'd landed in the nearby trees. "Aren't you a breath of fresh air?" He dropped his hands to his waist, inserting a few fingers in the hoop of his pants where a belt should have been. As he hooked the fabric, a small patch of skin near his hips captured Brianna's attention.

"Yeah, well, I prefer to be upfront about what I'm capable of." Brianna kicked off her sandal and rubbed her toes against the back of her other leg. Studying him more closely, she decided he was incredibly attractive. His facial features were clean and simple and revealed a man somewhere in his thirties.

His left hand disappeared into his pocket. When he pulled it out, he handed her a business card. "You should stop by my office sometime. I could verify how much you actually know about nineties grunge rock." He paused for a few seconds, waiting for any response from her, but she stared back with no expression and a plentitude of silence. "Or we could test out how well you play... on the field, of course."

Brianna re-engaged as his wit charmed her. "Definitely. *Playing* sounds like a lot of fun." Her mind floated back to the night with Doug in the hotel, suddenly feeling a wave of nausea overcome her ability to keep composed in front of the man.

"Indeed, it would." His vocal tone and facial expressions dripped with a coy allure she was unprepared to handle.

Brianna cautioned herself to reign in the flirtatious thoughts before her mouth shot off any further. "I should probably go. Things to see. People to do." She scrunched her brow when realizing her mistake. "Vice versa, I mean."

He bellowed somewhere between a sinister mock and a hearty guffaw. "I believe that's called a Freudian slip, Miss Porter."

She half-smiled at him and continued down the path, refusing to look back in near shame over her words. "Goodbye, Professor."

After jogging far enough away to avoid his gaze, she finally let herself draw a full breath. Caught between severe embarrassment and excitement, Brianna pounded a tree to calm herself back to normalcy. She'd totally flirted with the guy and was unclear how or why it even happened. She'd only meant to get a better look at him, to figure out where she'd seen him before. Maybe it was on the tour earlier that year or in an orientation seminar. Brianna was never flirtatious or outspoken around her friends, usually even less so around men, instead choosing to ignore them as much as possible. Professor Villing had a unique quality about him, one that intrigued her.

As she stepped back on the path, Shanelle hollered to her. "Bree, I've been searching for you everywhere. We need to get this weekend started."

Brianna flicked her head in the opposite direction while worrying about what she'd just done. "Hey. I've finished my last class for the week. And I met another new professor. Villing, have you ever heard of him?" She showed Shanelle the business card.

"No." Shanelle shook her head back and forth. "I'll ask my cousin. Is that the dude who you just walked away from?"

"Yes." Brianna murmured while holding in her emotions. "He was a funny guy, but he seemed like—"

"Yeah, well forget about him. We've got plans. Let's go." Shanelle grabbed Brianna's arm and yanked her down the pathway. Brianna was glad for the distraction.

Twenty minutes later, they parked themselves in the Resident Advisor's (RA) apartment listening to the recommendations from Woodland College about safety and security on the first weekend. Tina, their building's RA, had called all her freshmen together to discuss staying away from underage drinking, partying, and drugs. Tina, in her pink polo, baggy jeans, and ponytail, had been conversing with a few other girls, allowing Brianna and Shanelle a chance to talk privately during the reprieve.

"So, as soon as Tina's done with the *don't be a badass* lecture, we're gonna head back to the apartment and have a few drinks." Shanelle lifted her Woodland hoodie, revealing a half-filled bottle of vodka she'd swiped from under the RA's desk when no one paid attention. "We've got a bunch of mixers back home and can have ourselves a little fun."

"Crap. You're gonna get us in trouble on the first weekend. Keep it hidden," replied Brianna.

Shanelle had already taken it out and couldn't cover it with her shirt quick enough. Brianna turned toward Tina, giving Shanelle full access to her backpack to hide the bottle. Tina went on for a few more minutes to the rest of the group before telling the girls they were free to go. When Shanelle and Brianna approached the door, Tina called to them. "Girls, wait up. I need to talk to you." Her high-pitched voice grated on their nerves and served as a reminder of the prima donnas on the soccer team.

Brianna created excuses, thinking they'd been caught red-handed. "We're so sorry, we didn't mean to..."

Shanelle smacked her in the stomach. "Will you relax, girl? Ugh, sorry, Tina, this one's a mess. She's bloating or some shit. Go ahead, Bree, go to the bathroom. I got this."

Brianna rushed out of the room, trying not to call attention to the bottle poking through the top of her bag. They'd been waiting for Shanelle's cousin to get them fake IDs and couldn't yet buy their own alcohol. At least they'd lucked out for tonight. While waiting for Shanelle, she pondered the call with Malachi and why he was taking so long to find anything. It unnerved her to be stuck waiting on someone else's timetable.

A few minutes later, Shanelle returned laughing hysterically. "That was close!"

"What was that all about?" Brianna wandered the staircase to their apartment on the second floor.

Shanelle began mimicking Tina's hollow tone, waving her hands and tiptoeing like she had a pole shoved halfway up her ass. "Well, girls, it's so nice to have such good freshman ladies who want to set examples for the rest of the building. I expect you'll join my squad as assistant RAs in the building. Don't you feel special?" She accentuated the word special, rolled her eyes, then broke out in complete hysterics.

"Did she really say that?" As soon as they'd unlocked their door and shut themselves inside, Brianna fell to the floor, clutching her stomach. "That girl's priceless. Oh, we are so awful."

Shanelle grabbed two glasses from the cabinet, poured them each a shot, and began a toast. "To Woodland College and our freedom. Babe, this is what I was talking about. Aren't you glad you followed me here?"

Brianna thought about her mom back in New York, probably still at work on Friday evening, having no one to go home to. The guilt persisted over leaving her mother behind, but the woman had chosen to remain single, not talk about her family, and keep everything private. Brianna loved her mother and wanted nothing but happiness for her, but that was not the life she intended to live. Sure, she had a few things to work out before feeling truly comfortable. *What was that weird connection with Professor Villing in front of the library? How did she really feel about Shanelle? Was she gay or was it a phase? Could she be bisexual?* That's why she chose Woodland, to get away and have a few years to date whomever she wanted to date without everyone knowing her business until she made her own decisions.

"Hello, where did you go?" Shanelle snapped her fingers to interrupt Brianna's bizarre distraction. "You disappeared on me while I was talking to you. Aren't you psyched?"

"Yes, this is exactly what I needed. Pour me a real drink now, please!" Brianna turned on the sound system and flipped to their party playlist. Nickelback blasted across the room as they danced for over an hour in the exhilaration of their first weekend on their own.

"Did you bring that Avril Lavigne t-shirt we got at the concert earlier this summer? Let's both wear them tonight. We'll look awesome," Shanelle screamed across the living room, its walls painted a crisp blue and nothing yet hung on them. The plan for the next day was to fix the place and to finish unpacking so they could throw a party at night.

"Yeah, it's in the bag in my closet. Let me get it." Brianna strutted to her bedroom and flipped on the lights. Without the distraction of the music, she felt the vodka cranberry and shots filtering through her system while the brightness of the room stimulated all her senses. She sat on the bed enjoying the sensation, thinking about how different her life was a week ago. Since then, she'd turned in a formal creative writing assignment, flirted with some random professor, played her first college soccer game, and stolen a bottle of vodka from another student.

Brianna was actually having fun for a change, at least until she began thinking about her father. The need to meet him popped into her head all the time when she least expected it. Confusion tortured her when trying to surmise whether he was a pilot or mechanic in the Air Force. A curious desire to know where he'd flown would flood her imagination when commercials for joining the military aired on the television or a cadet in uniform passed by on the street. Had he ever fought in battle or been forced to drop a bomb? Brianna envisioned a decorated captain who'd risked his life every day to protect the innocent, feeling confident he was an admirable and honorable man.

Brianna craved answers to her questions, incapable of trusting in herself and growing frantic with anxiety over all the decisions she needed to make about her future. Though she significantly resembled her mother, someone else helped contribute to her appearance and personality. She'd been compelled on occasion to create lists of untraceable physical features. Did she inherit her weird longer toe from him? Or her slightly darker hair and complexion? Why was she so adept in soccer, yet her mother held no interest in sports or even exercising?

Wearing no shirt and a purple lacy bra, Shanelle bustled through the door with another drink in her hands. "Let's go. Did you find it?" She stood close, the tempting curves of her chest within an arm's reach from Brianna.

"No, I'm still looking." She tore open the closet door while taking a swig from the new glass. "What's in this drink, it's a different color? And where's your shirt?"

"I'm not putting it on until you find yours. I added orange soda to the vodka. I found it in the refrigerator when we ran out of cranberry juice." She spilled part of her drink on the floor. "Whoopsie!"

Brianna tossed a few shoes out of her way, then found the duffel bag her mother had lent her. She lugged it to the floor near the edge of the bed, falling quickly when its bulk became too much for her slightly intoxicated body to maneuver. "Damn, this is heavy. I thought I emptied most of it out."

Shanelle began unzipping the side pouches nearest her, finding them all empty. "Are you sure it's in here?"

Brianna hesitated. "I thought so, but maybe it's in this one." She ripped open the bottom zipper. "I don't remember ever opening this pouch, but something's packed in there."

Shanelle leaned forward and surprised Brianna with a soft kiss on her lips. "You're so hot when you relax and savor the moment."

Brianna wanted to let herself fall into the kiss. When Shanelle let go of her always-on-alert attitude, just going with the moment, she was so much more attractive. "You taste good, but I believe I just found something." She pulled an object from the duffel and tossed it on top of the bed.

Shanelle reached for it first. "This ain't no Avril Lavigne shirt. It's just a thin baby blanket... oh wait, something is wrapped inside it. Open it up." She grabbed the remote to lower the volume on the speakers. "What is it?"

Brianna unfolded the blanket, not recognizing it from anything she'd seen before. "I have no clue, but I know it's not mine." She lifted the last piece of fabric, which revealed a leather-bound journal with a Woodland College embossed logo on its cover. Confusion peppered her face, her eyes bulging as she flipped open the first page.

"Maybe your mom bought you a gift from Woodland as an apology for her initial reaction." Shanelle swallowed another gulp of her sticky drink. "That'd be cool."

"No, I don't think so." Brianna's muffled voice became distant. "It says *'Property of Amalia Graeme'* on the inside cover." Many thoughts materialized inside her head, but none settled with any comfort or ease.

"Who's Amalia Graeme?"

"My mother. Molly is her nickname, it's short for Amalia. This is her journal." Brianna fell back against the side of the bed, dropping the journal on the comforter.

Shanelle picked it up and scanned the page Brianna had opened to. "It's dated February 1985. Does that mean your mother went to Woodland College?"

"If so, she never told me." Brianna's stomach sank, and her head throbbed when she thought about the supposed adoption Malachi had learned from Rachel Abernathy. "My mother is worse than Agatha Christie with these damned twists and secrets."

"You know what this means." Shanelle smiled wide like a Cheshire cat while twirling her imaginary Hercule Poirot mustache. "I love a delightful read."

"No, that would be so wrong." Brianna threw her hands to the top of her head as her eyes bugged out twice as large as normal. "Can I?"

Shanelle clinked the rims of their glasses together with force. "If you want to know who your father is, you certainly can. Maybe we don't need the brilliant detective's help anymore!"

## Chapter 16

# Amalia, February 1985

Amalia tried to reach her mother several times since sharing the kiss with Jonah the previous night. The latest phone call rang for thirty seconds before a machine switched on and brought her father's voice to life. It was the first time she'd heard the answering machine message after her father had died. They'd forgotten to create a new greeting while she was home during winter break.

Amalia remembered five years earlier when her father had finally agreed to buy an answering machine after a concern surfaced that they'd miss phone calls from admissions counselors while Greg applied for college. Greg and Amalia had both wanted to leave the greeting, but their mother wouldn't yield. Janet insisted on recording her voice on the tape but kept speaking too low and painfully slow. As a last-minute compromise, their father agreed to record the greeting. *Graeme residence. Leave a message.* That's all it said. Monotone. No accent. Plain. Just like Peter had lived his life.

Amalia hung up, knowing her mother wouldn't ever listen to a message even if she'd left one. The need to speak with her mother suddenly evaporated from her mind, only to now be filled with the emotional baggage one lugged around in a desperate attempt to connect to the only person she couldn't reach. Her father would know what advice to give Amalia regarding the growing attraction to a professor she'd not realized began materializing inside her.

Being around Jonah had truly brought her peace and comfort for the first time since seeing her father. A replacement for the innocent care and affection she'd missed most of all when he died. Jonah lifted her spirits every day since she'd returned to campus, but now it'd turned into something stronger. Amalia needed a distraction, something to keep her from reflecting on what'd happened in Jonah's office the previous week. Referring to him as Jonah was part of the problem. She should call him Dr. West. Why did he insist on a more personable and intimate relationship?

Amalia called Carter, but he wasn't home and wouldn't finish with his science labs until later that afternoon. She finished changing clothes, left her dorm to meet the bus, and rode to the Coyotes' field for her softball game. Though it was a close game, they lost by one run that she'd unfortunately given up in the last inning. The entire afternoon had been wasted as her mind wouldn't relinquish her body to focus on the game.

When Amalia returned home that evening, she straightened up her bed, organized her notes for an upcoming paper, and checked out the hallway bulletin boards in search of any club meetings to attend. There was nothing. Rachel wasn't home either. She'd been acting weird, claiming it had something to do with her father not being able to pay the tuition much longer and growing anxiety over what to do about the baby. Rachel had very few days left to decide about ending the pregnancy before it would no longer be a viable option.

After an hour studying for a psychology exam, Amalia caved and escaped the confines of her room. Deciding a workout at the gym might help, she changed into a pair of sweatpants and short-sleeve shirt, then threw on her father's parka to keep warm. Amalia had hidden it in her luggage, assuming Janet would either toss it in the garbage or try to sell it at the church. The smell of his cologne permeated the hallway as she jogged through the lounge and into the fresh outside air. Jonah also still lingered on her mind. She couldn't release his foothold on her concentration. It petrified and excited her all at once.

Amalia crossed the quad and noticed the beginnings of spring budding among the scattered leaves on the ground. Daffodil stems broke through the loosening dirt in many of the flower beds. The grass grew a few shades greener. Seeing life pushing its way through the frosty winter with a bourgeoning persistence finally cleared Amalia's confusion. What happened with Jonah wasn't about Jonah. Perhaps it was her way of pulling herself from an uninvited depression when her father had passed away. All she needed to do was to focus on her relationship with Carter, push herself harder in classes, and conserve her energy for what would undoubtedly be a painful summer at home alone with her mother. Carter had said he wanted to come back to Brant to help rebuild the business. Maybe that would eventually come to fruition and offer Amalia the opportunity to escape her mother's clutches at home.

Nearing the athletics building, Amalia stumbled upon potential trouble. Riley, the guy who'd blocked her path the day she met Jonah, stood outside the glass-walled entrance. Too late to find an alternative door, Amalia's skin crawled, encouraging a sense of alarm and caution throughout her body.

"If it isn't the lovely teacher's pet. You're Rachel's roommate, Amalia, right?" His voice lingered on the last '*a*' in her name as he rolled his tongue between his teeth, resembling a serpent showing off its venom.

"Yes, and you're Riley." She crossed her arms and kept at least four feet between them while her eyes darted quickly to the left, then the right, checking if anyone else was around. But no one was.

"You're pretty, but you'd look better if I opened this jacket to see what's underneath…" He reached for her waist and tried to unzip the parka.

Amalia had no experience with lecherous guys. Carter was more handsy than she preferred, but he never left her feeling slimy or smarmy like the oily grease covering her mother's neck. Jerking her body to the left, she side-stepped Riley's grip to gain closer proximity to the door. "Keep your hands to yourself, please. I barely know you."

"Aw, I guess you think I'm not good enough for you. Not as good as Jonah." When he said the professor's name, his jaw dropped at least two inches and hung open in a fixed state.

"How do you know about Jonah?" Amalia abruptly grew nervous someone had caught her kissing him that day in the office.

"I've seen the way you bat your lashes at him, sticking your tits in his face as if you can't wait for him to touch you." He reached a long, creepy hand toward her again, but she slapped it away. "Playful girl, aren't you? Trust me, Jonah can't make you happy, sweetheart. I'd suggest you drop him and give me a chance to show you an enjoyable time."

"Listen, I told you to stop that. Now leave me alone, or I'll call campus security." She looked for the nearest call box, but it was too far in the distance. She debated whether to scream, but that might be too drastic. Amalia's best escape was to hide in the gymnasium, yet she wasn't certain if anyone else was around. Being alone with Riley was not a possibility.

"Don't be nervous, honey." Riley's purr penetrated through her clothing and burned her skin. "I only bite if you ask me nicely. Do you wanna ask me? Nicely? Rachel always liked when I played roughly." He boxed her against the glass doorway, the handlebar pressed into her lower back as a reminder she'd gotten too close to him once before.

Riley's resolute tone pummeled her body with fear when she thought about him saying Rachel's name. Amalia prepared to knee him in the crotch, but as she grew the courage to tense the muscles in her leg, a pager strapped to his waistline beeped persistently. In the distraction when he checked the device, she pushed herself away from him and broke out into a sprint.

"You will one day, you know, ask me nicely, Amalia. You can count on that." He always ended his words with a drawn-out slur, as if the old movies he'd watched taught him a false way of sounding seductive. On him, it was sleazy.

She took off running as an icy chill ran down the curves of her back. Amalia raced to the library and ducked in one of the private study rooms. Catching her breath felt impossible despite the many times she'd run the length of the softball field without once needing a break. Grateful for men like Bryan and Carter, she quickly tried to ignore the ugliness, believing there weren't many men out there like Riley. She scanned the shelves in the history section, thumbing the books with no actual interest in reading at that moment. The distraction of their rich textures and intense smells brought her back to a calmer state.

Amalia called her room from the library phone to ask Rachel why Riley said her name or even knew about her, but her roommate still wasn't home. Amalia dialed her mother again, uncertain if the long-distance call would go through, but when the line transferred, she had success.

Janet answered on the second ring. "Who's there?"

"Momma, it's Amalia. You're home."

"Where else would I be, child? I live here. I worry about you sometimes." Her voice sounded distant as a tinny echo bounced on the line.

"I need to talk to you about something. It's important."

"I don't got all day. I'm about to go to sleep. Make it quick."

Amalia tapped her foot on the wooden chair while leaning against the windowsill. She wanted to ask if her mother ever had feelings for someone other than her father. Or how a girl knew when she was in love. But the words wouldn't come to her lips with any ease. "I'm feeling kind of funny about things with Carter. I... I'm not sure if he's good for me." Amalia fiddled with the phone cord.

"What are you talking about? That boy is our future. How else do you expect to fix things here at home? You've got responsibilities." Janet's abrasive voice blasted through the receiver. There was no mistaking her lack of interest in Amalia's concerns. Only an angry determination to ensure there wasn't any risk that Carter would alter his mind about running the hardware store.

"He's very immature, partying all night with his friends. It's different from when we first met." Amalia no longer enjoyed being labeled as his girlfriend once she accepted they had nothing in common. She wanted someone who read *Great Expectations*, watched *Gone with the Wind*, or knew more about what went on in the world.

"You need to learn something, girl. Life is not all cookies and milk like your father let you believe. That man never did have any sense to teach you about real life. It's hard out there."

Janet's deep wheeze followed by a series of hacking coughs paralyzed the conversation. Amalia pulled the phone from her ear, protecting what was left of her personal space and ability to hear.

Janet persisted. "Did you ever see your father and me have the energy for silly romantic dinners? Time alone together? Sitting on our bum? Reading books or worrying about the meaning of life? No, you didn't. We knew better. We had to raise our kids."

"There is more to life than listening to God, going to church, and staying at home all the time." Amalia knew the conversation would not end up any better, but she had to try. She had to elicit some sense of real emotion from her mother. The woman couldn't contain such a vapid emptiness inside her.

"Amalia, I warned you after your daddy's funeral. If you don't make it work with Carter, don't bother coming back. I'm counting on you to do the right thing. Marry that boy and take care of your home here in Brant. Both the store and your mother should be the priorities." Janet coughed a few more times and clicked a butterscotch candy along the roof of her mouth.

"I understand, Momma. I was just trying to think a little differently." She listened in for a response but had none—just a persistent loud beep. Her mother had hung up the phone, no longer interested in carrying on the discussion. It'd been her typical response whenever the conversation didn't meet her expectations.

The library, a place where she hid out to avoid the realities of life beyond its perimeter, brought her peace for a few minutes. Though Woodland had offered so much hope and potential in the beginning, it had all been crashing around her the last few months. People like Riley frightened Amalia from wanting to be alone. The dangers of letting herself get too close with Jonah pecked at the surface of her skin.

Maybe her mother was right. Carter was a good guy. He offered her a way to counter the gnawing irritation of life back in Brant on her own.

An announcement noting the library's closing in ten minutes blasted throughout its corridors, prompting Amalia to compose herself. She summoned the energy to climb back onto the dark paths on the campus. The disappointments of the day had given her reason to dread all the problems that lurked around her, but she needed to escape them.

Amalia stopped at Carter's fraternity house on her way home to check if he'd returned from classes. When she stepped inside, his housemate's erratic voice and panic surprised her. The guy first indicated Carter wasn't home, then said *he* would tell Carter she'd arrived. Amalia pushed by him, preferring to check for herself. As she ascended the stairs, voices carried from Carter's room, the first one at the top of the landing. Light and airy. Feminine. Pretty. Carter was with another girl. As she cleared the last step, Amalia turned the corner and tiptoed toward his room. His door was closed almost the entire way. She leaned near the crack and listened in.

"You're really sexy. If only I could," said Carter.

"Are you sure? It feels like you wanna do more with me. What's that in this pocket, stud?"

The fears in Amalia's stomach churned tighter than normal. He was with a bubbly sorority girl who fawned all over him. She tilted her ear an inch closer.

"Yeah, well, I can't help it. You're hot, but you should go. I'm with Amalia. She may be holding out on me, but I'm gonna be a little more patient. And if not, well, then you'll be the first one in my bed."

Amalia was angry with Carter for letting some trampy girl flirt with him in his bedroom, but he'd told the girl to stop. Maybe she was being too hard on her boyfriend.

Her mother's voice blasted against the insides of her exhausted head. *Keep Carter. Stay away from everyone else. Come back to Brant. Don't be selfish. Relationships aren't always about love.*

A loud noise rustled inside the room, as though they might be leaving. Amalia quickly hid in the bathroom down the hall, shutting the door behind her. It had a small crack on the bottom where she listened to their voices but learned nothing new. Carter walked the girl to the staircase, and she left on her own. He jogged back to his bedroom while humming a strange tune to himself.

Amalia flushed the toilet, then opened the door with the hopes she could get a glimpse of the girl leaving the fraternity house. By the time Amalia reached the bottom of the stairs, the girl had already exited. While Amalia wanted to run after her, she knew Carter had turned the girl down, which meant nothing had changed. She called out Carter's name while walking up the stairs on her way back to his room, assuming he'd think she'd just arrived.

"Amalia? Come on up. I'm in my room."

She entered his room smelling the girl's sweet perfume but acted oblivious. "What have you been up to?"

"How long have you been here? I mean, did you see anyone downstairs?" His voice held an uneasiness she'd not been privy to in the past.

It comforted Amalia to know things he didn't know about for a change. "Just for a minute. Umm... your housemate was downstairs, that's all. Why?" She twisted curls falling to the side of her face while debating whether to let him know she'd heard the girl in his room.

"No reason." Carter leaned forward to kiss her, then pulled back. "You're as cold and white as a ghost. Everything okay?"

Amalia had still been thinking about the run-in with Riley and how it'd nearly knocked the wind out of her. "Well, this guy seems to be following me around. I don't think it's serious, but it just freaked me out earlier."

"Do I need to do anything? No one else should be bothering my girl," replied Carter with genuine concern in his voice. "I'll make it stop."

Amalia didn't want to cause trouble, especially since she still worried about how Rachel fit into the whole puzzle. "No, no... I think he just enjoys being creepy. If it happens again, or he starts really stalking me, maybe you can do something then."

"Don't let it go on too long. You need to put jerks like that in their place to get them to stop. Sometimes guys don't understand—" Carter's phone rang, interrupting his thoughts. He glanced over as if he wanted to pick it up. "Umm, I should get that. I don't want to deal with a message on the machine later." He picked up and responded with a few "Mmms..." and several "Okays..."

Amalia considered her mother's advice while listening to Carter's vague conversation across the room. When he hung up, he shrugged. "Just something about my internship. Nothing to worry about."

A nervous chill tickled the back of Amalia's neck. "So, I've been thinking about us."

Carter stopped Amalia's train of thought by picking her up, dropping her on the bed and rolling his body next to hers. "Why would you do such an awful thing?" He kissed her lips gently, nibbling the top of her mouth as he pulled away. His cheeks flushed bright red.

"Oh, Carter, you're such a stud." Amalia ran her hand down his left leg, searching for the loop of the belt in his jeans. She smiled when her fingers found what they'd been looking for. "What's this in your pocket?" She couldn't help herself. He deserved to feel as uncomfortable as she had in the past when he teased her. Amalia hadn't meant to embarrass Carter, but wanted to hold firm in her approach.

Carter jerked away. "What did you say?" His eyes grew wide with curiosity and fear, like an animal caught in the headlights of an oncoming car.

"Oh, nothing. Maybe it's time we took things to the next step." She smiled at him, confident in her words, though uncertain of how to still be coy enough to win him over.

"Don't tempt me. We've been there before." Carter leaned back against his bed frame with one arm crossed behind his neck and head. "I told you I'd wait for a little while longer. You know how much I want to be with you." With the other, he grabbed and placed her hand on his heart.

"I know, maybe next week when everyone leaves for Spring Break. Rachel won't be around." She pulled her hand away and wrapped her arms around his shoulders and neck. She was curious how he'd react at Rachel's name, but he gave nothing away. "You could come to my place this time, and we could take it slow. I want my first time to be with you."

Amalia had mostly believed the words coming from her lips. It wasn't exactly an untrue statement. She'd been thinking about the next step, ignoring her concerns about him not being the right guy for her in the long run but also understanding the need to give it a chance. They'd been together for over six months at that point, and the next step was suddenly a more natural option.

"You know that's what I want." Carter climbed on top of her nervous body while lying on the lumpy mattress. "I love you and want to show you how much, Amalia Graeme." He pressed lips into the crook of her neck and kissed her with intense desire.

Amalia let herself forget the budding nerves dancing inside her stomach. It would all be okay. Carter would take care of her. Even though he was a boy, and she'd begun hungering for a man. This was the only way to stop the craving for Jonah. For Jonah, whom she couldn't think about anymore without yearning to be with him in a way her mother wouldn't approve.

## Chapter 17

# Brianna, September 2004

*The door was a shabby white. Black streaks from the rubber soles of all the sneakers that'd once kicked the solid pine barrier stood out as a painful reminder of the past. Silence perforated the room. An ominous one, enough to make her heart leap from her chest in fear.*

*"Are you there?"*

*No response. With tense knuckles, Brianna rapped on the door, startled when it creaked open a few inches.*

*"I'm looking for someone. Is there anybody here?"*

*As she stepped beyond the door into a small parlor, a faint murmur echoed in the room. A violin or a cello. She couldn't decide. The thumps of her steps were louder and more penetrating. Rounding the corner, the source of the music along with a few dozen people came into view. People that resembled her mother but older and strangely more familiar.*

*"Mom," she called out. They all turned to stare at her. Her body stiffened with alarm and fear at a coffin lurking in the corner.*

*Brianna stood in the living room of an unfamiliar apartment, though as she concentrated, it was not vastly different from her own. Emptier. Bigger. Frozen. Smelling of death.*

*"Can I help you?" The woman closest to her in the room leaned in as the words fell from her lips.*

*"I'm looking for my father. Do you know if he's here?"*

*"Can you describe him?" The woman's eyes opened wider and brighter as she finished speaking.*

*"I don't know." The strain in Brianna's voice grew more despondent, mirroring a child who'd forgotten where she lived and needed comfort. The desperation of being lost in an unfamiliar world swallowed her whole. "I don't know. I don't know."*

Brianna awoke drenched in sweat and screamed. She bolted upright, her hands thrown to her face and rubbing her temples. "I don't know."

Shanelle burst through the door fully dressed and holding a cup of coffee in hand. "Bree, are you okay? You don't know what?"

Brianna's gaze darted around her bedroom. A window still in need of curtains. An Avril Lavigne t-shirt on the floor. An unpacked duffel bag haphazardly thrown between the corner dresser and the closet door. An empty bottle of vodka on the table beside her. Next to it, the journal she'd found the night before. She breathed in deeply. A sharp pain in her head throbbed and a persistent concern pulsed over the nausea rising from her stomach. "It was just a bad dream."

"Was it about the journal? Should we read a few more pages to learn what your mom wrote about?" Shanelle handed a coffee cup to Brianna. "Drink this, babe."

"No." Brianna placed one hand across her lips, and the other waved the mug away. "I need to sit for a minute until this plague passes over me."

Shanelle put the coffee on the dresser, gathered the journal, and rested on the edge of the bed. "We ate little last night. You might need some food in your stomach to cure the hangover. It will soak up all the alcohol."

"I don't remember going to bed." Brianna recalled as much as possible from the previous night. Tossing the journal back in the duffel. Cursing her mother. Checking the Woodland College website's list of alumni. No mention of her mother, just pictures of a campus with the potential to hold all the clues to her past.

"I helped you get in bed after you tried climbing out the window to take the train back to New York in your drunken stupor. You wanted to talk to your mother, but she never picked up the phone." Shanelle brushed Brianna's hair behind her ears and massaged her neck.

"It must be a mistake. She never mentioned attending Woodland." Brianna blinked, and her head swirled. Everything trailed for a few seconds longer than normal after passing by her eyes. "Tell the room to stop spinning, please."

"Okay, that does it. I've had enough of the *woe is me* routine from you. Get up, now." Shanelle grabbed Brianna's shoulder and arm to pull her to a standing position. "Molly's obviously keeping secrets from you. She won't tell you about your father and never mentioned studying at Woodland. Let's get some clear perspective and put together a plan with Malachi."

Brianna groaned. "Slower, please. I don't want to get sick."

"You're in the driver's seat now, Bree. Call your mother again. Tell her you have the journal. Ask her nicely for the information you want. And if she doesn't, read it for yourself." Shanelle pushed her toward the bathroom. "First, go take a shower so you can wash off this self-doubt. I have an errand to run before I meet you at practice."

Thirty minutes later, Brianna prepared breakfast in the kitchen. The journal lingered on the counter, tempting her to read its secrets. The last thing Shanelle had told her before leaving was to flip through the diary to check for the approximate dates it covered. As much as she wanted to, it was an invasion of her mother's privacy. She tried to convince herself it might reveal nothing but decided it couldn't hurt to read a few entries to discover any mention of adoption.

Brianna nibbled a slice of whole wheat toast as her fingers casually turned a few pages, all dated 1985. March 4th. April 29th. July 8th. October 3rd. December 6th. She closed the journal, doing the math in her head. Brianna had been born shortly afterward, which meant Molly was likely writing in the journal when she'd gotten pregnant, assuming Molly was her birth mother. It wasn't a certain fact if there were any truth to Rachel's adoption comment.

Brianna shuffled to the living room and vacillated between telling her mother about finding the journal or just pressuring her for more information. She dialed the number and waited until Molly answered. "Mom?"

"Hi, sweetheart. I was just thinking about my baby girl. I'm picking up a few things at the market, wishing you were home to have dinner with me."

"I need to talk to you." Brianna threw herself back onto the sofa, her head hitting the arm and sending another wave of nausea throughout her entire body. "You never told me you were a student at Woodland." Nothing but silence filled the void between the two women. Brianna instantly recalled the dream she'd awoken to. "Are you there, Mom?"

"How did you know about Woodland? Where are you getting this information from?" Molly's voice carried irritation and heat as she spoke, almost lashing back at her daughter over something so simple to answer.

When she was nine years old, Brianna had been livid with Molly for not buying her the doll she'd wanted for her birthday. She'd torn open all the gifts and packages, excitedly hoping to find the newest *American Girl* that resembled her in every way, but it wasn't in any of the boxes. She'd run off that afternoon and hid under a table in the jazz club while Lenny was receiving inventory. After about an hour, Molly finally found her. When Brianna asked her mother how she'd known where to look, Molly told her daughter she'd left a trail of stuffing from inside Bunny who'd fallen apart.

"Breadcrumbs, Mom. Breadcrumbs. What difference does it make how I know? Why didn't you tell me?"

"It was years ago. It's part of the past."

"No, it's not just the past," Brianna shouted into the phone. As her emotions intensified, the unsettled nausea in her stomach from the prior night's drinking binge turned into a fierce burn. "I'm going to school *at Woodland*. We could have talked about the whole connection."

"Brianna, the two things have nothing to do with each other. I went to Woodland College for a semester. I hardly spent any time on campus after the holidays, and then I returned home. It wasn't the place for me. There's nothing else to tell."

Brianna flipped through the journal, firmly pressing her fingers against the dates on several pages. The ink, dried out for years, wouldn't smudge despite the salty perspiration forming on the tip of her thumb. "I don't believe you."

"What is this about? Your attitude can't be from not telling you I was a student at the same place you chose to go to school."

Brianna shook her head, biting her lower lip as she tried to achieve her real purpose. "You're right, it's not about Woodland. It's about you, and how you don't trust me enough to tell me about your past. Obviously, you didn't grow up in New York. I don't even know where my mother lived before I was born."

"Can we talk about this another time? Maybe when you come home over the holiday break. It'll give me some time to—"

"To make up another lie? Seriously, Mom, this is shitty. I can't even talk to you right now." Brianna hung up the phone, ignoring the repeated calls coming in afterward. She would not get the information out of her mother and had no desire to continue the game.

As frustrated as she was, Brianna couldn't bring herself to read any more of the journal entries. She was a good person, and reading from them would make her a bad person. The only thing she truly had left was being fair and honorable, like her father in the Air Force. She had to keep trying to convince her mother to confess the past secrets. It would come out in time, it had to.

Brianna left for soccer practice and jogged across campus until reaching the rest of the team playing on the quad. The hangover had mostly receded, but the disillusion sat firmly inside her chest, weighing heavily on her heart. She missed two opportunities to block another player from scoring a goal and ran foul several feet off the playing field at one point. She slid across the wet grass on the last shot before half-time and almost hit the goal post.

"Where are you right now? That girl with the braids is the slowest player on the team, and you couldn't even keep up with her." Shanelle hunched over and rested her elbows on her knees while trying to get Brianna's attention. "Did you talk to your mother?"

"Yeah, she admitted being a student but lied about how long she'd been here." Brianna moved to the sidelines and vomited bits of toast from earlier that morning. "I can't play. I'm still not feeling well."

Shanelle patted Brianna's back and reached for a towel from her gym bag. "Walk it off. I'll tell the coach you're done for today."

"Thanks." She wiped her mouth and grabbed a bottle of water, ingesting a few small sips to cut the pasty dryness on the insides of her cheeks. Getting sick again wasn't an option. "I don't know what I'm going to do. She doesn't understand that I deserve to know my father. I should have a connection with my entire family, not just her."

"I don't know what Molly's hiding, but if she's this determined to keep it secret, it must be pretty bad. Maybe she's humiliated by something she did or hurt because he left her?" Shanelle guided Brianna to the benches in the far corner and ripped off her shin guards as they sat. "What did Malachi say about the journal?"

"I haven't told him. He's got a second meeting, or fake date, whatever the hell it is, with my mom soon. He'll try again, but she doesn't enjoy talking about the past."

"I'm not on her side, but if she's got a legit reason, you might need to let this go for a while."

"I can't. I'm having nightmares. I'm afraid my mother's gonna die one day, and I'll never know the truth. And then there's..." Brianna had been too upset even to prevent the genuine fear from escaping her thoughts. She'd not told anyone yet as there was still an uncertainty what it all meant. "Never mind."

"Don't do that. Stop holding things in. If you've got something to say, say it."

"I don't know what I'm saying. Let it go." Brianna took another sip of water and rested her head against the bench. "I'm not making any sense."

"Spill it. You can't bitch about your mother hiding something and then do the same thing to me. What is it?"

"Fine, but don't get all in my face and angry about how I feel." Brianna wanted to be honest, but she also needed to protect their friendship.

Shanelle consented by holding up two fingers in a scout position. "I promise."

"What if this attraction I've developed for you... toward other girls... is really just about not having a male influence in my life?"

"I see." Shanelle wrinkled her nose. "Are you saying... lesbian by way of circumstance?"

"Don't get me wrong. I'm not saying I might be gay because I didn't have a father or brothers. I just mean... I only had my mom. Maybe I don't know any better."

"Do you want to know what I think?" Shanelle's voice was calmer than ever before.

"Yes. I'm not trying to hurt you."

Shanelle kissed Brianna's forehead. "You might be on to something, but you're not exploring it properly. You're going about it half-assed if I'm being candid."

Brianna cocked her head and leaned in closer. "I don't know what that means."

"Remember when you thought Malachi was attractive before you knew he worked for my mom?" Shanelle waited for Brianna to rebuff the idea and shake her head in disagreement.

"Not this again."

"And then the crush you had on the fifty-year-old substitute teacher last year? But how you weren't into Doug or any other boys at school, right?"

"What are you trying to say? I feel like crap. Stop speaking in riddles."

"Bree, think about it. All the guys you claim to like or have some sort of attraction to... are *older*... like father figures. It's a classic transference of your feelings from not having a father while growing up. I learned all about it in a psych class, and it's what's causing you to doubt you're a lesbian."

Brianna's shoulders tensed. She'd never interpreted it that way before. She'd always assumed older men were more attractive because of their maturity, something about their poise, intelligence, and charm. Could she have been hiding behind the truth the whole time? "I guess that could be part of it."

Shanelle nodded. "I'm no psychologist, but you've got some pretty hefty baggage over this lacking a father thing. You won't commit to me or even anyone else. I'm not gonna lie and say I'd be cool if you chose to keep dating guys. I know who you are inside, but I want you to be happy. You need to gain some confidence in yourself and accept the truth about who you are."

"How do I figure this out? I'm tired of an emptiness... a pit of fear... having my heart ripped out. It's stopping me from feeling like a whole person. Or from letting myself trust anyone."

"Piece by piece. First you read the journal. I know it's a dick move to your mom, but she's not exactly being helpful. Just check out one or two pages to get a sense for what your mother went through. You'll convince her to finally open up about your father." The coach blew the whistle and shouted at Shanelle to return to the game. "Then maybe you'll start feeling better about trusting people."

"Do you think that will clear my head enough to figure out my feelings for you?"

"It might, but so could going with me to this new bar my cousin told me about. How about we read the journal together to get some answers after the game? Then we can go out tonight to test the waters around other girls. Just as a comparison."

"You'd be okay with me flirting with another girl?"

"I didn't say that. I said let's see what happens. Maybe you'll start putting all the pieces of your life together and in time get more comfortable. I still want you to choose me, but I'm not gonna pressure you every minute of the day until you finally cave. When you climb into my bed, it's gonna be because you have it bad for me."

"I've already been in your bed, Shanelle."

"Sleeping doesn't even come close to what I'm gonna do to you when you tell me you're ready to climb into bed with me. Believe me. Ain't no man gonna make you scream like I will."

"Stop. I can't think about that right now." Brianna flushed red and gasped. "But it does sound kind of hot the way you put it."

Shanelle pulled Brianna inches away from her lips. Brianna stared back, relaxing her entire body as Shanelle kissed her with full lips and the intensity of her imagined passions coming to life. "That was a preview of things to come." When the coach screamed, Shanelle cupped Brianna's cheek and said, "You'll figure it out. I have faith in you." She stepped back a few feet, then rushed back to the field to finish soccer practice.

Brianna was stunned and uncertain how to interpret the kiss. She returned to the apartment still in a daze. Sitting on the sofa, she flipped through the journal and read the March 4th entry. She couldn't wait for Shanelle to get home and needed a distraction to avoid thinking more about what'd just happened on the field.

*Dear Diary,*

*My father gave me this journal for Christmas, telling me to share everything on my mind with someone who would always listen. I used to share things with him, but he's gone now, and all I have left is you... my Dear Diary friend... Carter is an okay boyfriend, but it's always felt like something's been missing. I still don't know if I love him. Or if I ever will. I want to, but I'm scared to let go of all the things Momma told me about boys back home in Brant. Maybe that's why I started thinking about someone else today. I'm afraid to get too close to one guy. He told me to call him Jonah, but he's my boss and one of the professors at Woodland. It felt wrong at first, but now whenever I see him, I feel different inside. There's electricity running through my veins. I don't know what it means, but I dreamed about him the other night. We were walking through the park, and he kissed me. I liked it more than I should have. I liked it more than when Carter kisses me. Jonah's lips had been waiting a lifetime to kiss mine, a depth I haven't ever known from Carter. Is it possible to feel something for two people at once? For someone you shouldn't have feelings for? Help me... I wish I had someone to turn to for answers.*

*Love,*

*Amalia*

The journal's words ran rampant and uncontrolled in Brianna's mind as she thought about the parallels between her growing interest in Shanelle with her mother's feelings for Jonah. "An affair with a professor, Mom... is that why you won't tell me about my father?" She buried her face in the sofa and screamed at the lack of anything to believe or trust coming from her mother anymore.

Brianna gasped when the pivotal clue she'd just learned in the journal filled her body with shock and hope. She called Malachi and left him a message.

"Jackpot! My mother comes from a town called Brant. I don't know where the hell it is, but please call me back as soon as possible."

# Chapter 18

# Amalia, March 1985

"Are you sure I didn't hurt you?" Carter's arms wrapped tightly around Amalia's body as they laid in the top bunk of her dorm room. "I tried to be gentle."

"You were. It was nice." Amalia laid naked under the covers after they'd taken the *big* step in their physical relationship. He'd done all the right things. Candles. A bottle of champagne even though she only took a few sips once the bubbles made her lightheaded. Soft music. He'd proceeded slowly and cautiously, letting her choose when to move forward. She knew he was trying hard to be a thoughtful boyfriend.

"Nice? That's all?" Carter's voice climbed a few decibels higher, as if he'd been going through puberty again. He turned to the side and looked directly at Amalia. "I hoped maybe I rocked your world, or you felt silly for waiting so long given how amazing I was." He laughed for a few seconds, then grew nervous at her silence. Amalia had closed her eyes, partially annoyed by his words and mortified by the awkwardness.

Nice was the best way to describe what'd happened. It had only hurt for a few seconds, but Carter listened when she pushed him away at first. His gentle approach encouraged her to relax, so they eventually found the right rhythm. As he lay on top of her, she stared at the ceiling, questioning how much longer it would take. His eyes suddenly shut, and he began grunting. When he told her he was getting close, excitement—maybe a little fear of everything her brother had told her about being ripped inside—took hold of her body. She leaned forward to kiss him when he looked ready to burst, but Carter suddenly pulled away. Something had happened under the sheets, but all she could do was turn to the side wall in embarrassment. Carter curled up next to her under the covers and threw his arm around her waist. She wasn't sure what to expect or do next, except to wait for him to say something.

The experience didn't impress her, but rather left her curious why people even raved about sex. She'd once felt the same way after eating a piece of pie that had been nothing more than your average slice of pie. A bit overfull knowing she shouldn't but wanting to try more, hoping the next time would be that amazing, delicious slice of sweetness. "Did I... I mean... was it..." She'd no idea what even to ask, choosing to let her voice falter rather than finish her thoughts.

"Yeah, it was hot. Was it amazing for you, too?" Carter brushed her cheek with his fingertips and flaunted his puppy dog eyes while waiting for a response.

Amalia wrinkled her nose and shrugged. "Sure, you were great, Carter. I'm just... still figuring it out." She lifted the covers and adjusted the balled-up sheet under her waist. "Are you sure we didn't need to use protection?"

"Yes, I promise you, I pulled out before anything happened. Trust me, I'm safe. I'm sorry I left the rubbers at my place, but it was your first time. Nothing's gonna happen." He sounded convincing, his voice was strong and persistent. "I love you. Let's get some sleep."

She kissed his cheek while reflecting on her decision to finally go all the way with him. Or how to avoid saying those three words in return. She hadn't been sure which caused more anxiety. Her mother had said to do anything to keep Carter. While this wasn't what Janet had in mind, it happened, and Amalia couldn't go backward. "I care for you, too." She fell asleep soon afterward, wondering what was really going through Carter's mind.

The next morning, Carter jumped off the bed and began dressing. His muscles twitched and flexed as he pulled up his jeans. There wasn't a single hair in sight on his chest, barely any under his arms or near his waist. He looked younger each time she saw him. "I need to jet. Gotta study for the rest of my exams this afternoon." His voice carried a feverish pitch as he stared up at her in the top bunk and prepared to leave.

"Good luck. Will I see you tonight?" A sudden need to hide her body from full exposure in the morning light compelled Amalia to pull the covers over her shoulders.

"I'm sorry, but I probably can't get together until we leave for Brant tomorrow. I have to put in a few hours at my internship sometime today, and if I don't get an 'A' on this midterm, the professor will probably fail me this semester. I can't risk not graduating in May."

Spring Break would officially start the upcoming weekend, but they hadn't planned to go on vacation like the rest of their classmates. Carter had insisted on driving her back home to check on the renovations at the hardware store, curious to monitor the progress himself. The insurance claims had been filed, and they had approval to begin the repairs during the month. The contractor would pour the new foundation after the ground had thawed. Amalia didn't want to go home, but they needed to get Graeme Hardware Store functional again.

"What about after you're all done tonight? I finished my classes yesterday, and everyone else is heading home already." Amalia was irritated that Carter was so distant after she'd finally gone all the way with him. Didn't he understand what a big step it had been for her?

"No can do. I'm out with the guys before they all head off for Spring Break. It's only one day. I'm sure you'll find something to do." He tied his sneakers and slipped into his treasured suede jacket. "Oh, would you be able to do my laundry? I have nothing clean that I can pack for the trip." He pulled himself up by holding onto the top bunk's bedframe, kissed Amalia, and paraded toward the door. "Love you, babe. I'm so glad you finally said yes."

When he left, Amalia threw on a robe, grabbed her shower caddy, and stepped down the hall to the girl's bathroom. As she undressed before getting in the shower, she checked her image in the mirror, debating what Carter loved about her body. Amalia knew he fawned over her breasts, he couldn't keep his hands off them. Beyond that, he rarely said anything. After what'd happened, she didn't know if she'd done everything the right way. He was inside her for less than ten minutes and then laid back on the bed as if it were time to fall asleep. Carter hadn't really cared what she felt or if she, too, had experienced any pleasure. Amalia hadn't been sure herself. Warm. A bit heavier breathing than usual. It was mostly nerves over letting him convince her not to use any protection, not that she'd known much about it, anyway.

After her shower, Amalia spent most of the day reading and watching movies, anything to keep herself from being bored or second-guessing what'd happened. By late afternoon, she went to the student union building to buy a cup of hot cocoa and a snack. Upon arriving, she found Jonah hiding at a table in the far corner.

"Hi, stranger," said Amalia while wiping sweaty palms on the back of the chair.

Jonah looked up at her. "How'd the philosophy midterm go? Did you remember the trick I taught you about how to sort out all the names?" When he smiled, his nose wiggled, and his cheeks flushed.

"It worked. I'm pretty sure I got an 'A.' I won't know until next week." She pulled out the chair and sat across from him. "Are you too busy to keep me company?"

"That would never be the case with you. You're one of the greatest rays of sunshine in my life these days." Jonah leaned forward and placed his hand on hers.

Amalia swooned as his thumb caressed and tickled her. They discussed the stock market's biggest winners and losers that week, then he quizzed on her some tax laws she'd been studying in the office the previous days. Each conversation became more exciting than the last as the time passed. When she checked his watch, a gasp escaped her mouth. "Is it really seven o'clock?"

"Yes. I should head home. I've got dinner plans with my neighbors. I looked after their house while they were on vacation last month. Just a little thank you from them, I suppose." He sorted through a few folders and packed his briefcase. "I'd invite you, so you weren't stuck home alone tonight, but I don't want to pressure you. What do you think?"

Amalia considered her options. While she wanted to go with him, it might make things between them more awkward in the future. She'd started falling for Jonah, and as much as she loved spending time with him, it'd gotten too dangerous. "I shouldn't. I need to do some laundry and pack. Plus, I'm leaving tomorrow. Maybe another time?"

"I understand. Walk back with me to the office? I have something for you." He rested his hand on her shoulder and motioned for her to follow him.

Amalia filled with curiosity and excitement. What could it be? As she strolled across campus with Jonah, an eerie sensation that someone had been following them prompted her to worry Carter had been spying on her. He'd said he was busy, but sometimes her boyfriend exaggerated the truth. She stopped and scanned the area before they entered the academic building but hadn't noticed anyone the second time. They went upstairs, and Jonah unlocked his office.

"It's right here on the desk. I thought I'd give it to you when you returned from Spring Break, but since you're here… it might come in handy when you go home." He struggled to contain his elation.

Amalia opened the bag and found several books, including a copy of *Gone with the Wind*, the novel he'd recommended to her a few weeks earlier. "Jonah, this is so wonderful."

"It's an early edition. I found it in an old bookshop right here in downtown Woodland. I want you to have it," said Jonah.

When she reached in to hug him, their lips met. As Amalia peered into his eyes, she was unable to break the connection this time. It was as if they were magnets destined to press together forever. She fell into the kiss with him, immediately swept up in passion and desire for his touch. His hand pulled her closer to his body. Her fingers reached for his waist and climbed up his back inch by inch. Though their bodies pulled apart a minute later, her head still rested against his chest. "I'm falling for you, Jonah. I'm scared."

He hugged her closer. "I know. I feel the same way."

Amalia knew it was time to leave and stepped backward. She had to put some space between them before things heated up beyond repair. "I should go. I think maybe this isn't a good idea right now. I'm all confused."

"Okay. Why don't we take a few days while you're away to think about what happened? We can talk when you get back." His stare begged her to stay, but his hands let her slip away.

In the rush, Amalia forgot to take the books and left them sitting on the corner of the desk. Jonah hadn't noticed either when he fell into his chair and threw his head on the desk with a sigh that even Amalia could hear while rushing down the staircase.

\* \* \*

Amalia kept herself busy that evening doing laundry on the first floor of her dorm building. She and Rachel talked about her first time with Carter and the kiss with Jonah. Rachel pushed Amalia to explore the crush rather than try to forget it, but Amalia wasn't convinced that was the right decision. Rachel had bad luck with guys and had stopped talking to the baby's father. A few minutes finishing the laundry, Rachel left to meet her sister.

Amalia called Carter but only got his answering machine. He was busy, but she was certain he'd check on her after their first time sleeping together. After brushing her teeth and writing in her journal, she went to sleep worried about why he'd grown distant again. Amalia suffered nightmares where men laughed at her while she stood naked at the edge of their bed. Carter's cold shoulder and flippancy were slicing away at her confidence.

\* \* \*

The next morning, Amalia returned from eating breakfast in the school cafeteria, ready to finish packing before she and Carter left campus and headed home. As she turned the doorknob to her dorm room, the phone rang. Knowing Rachel had been sleeping elsewhere the last few nights, Amalia rushed in, pulled her hair into a ponytail with a scrunchie, and picked up the call. "Hello. This is Amalia." A few drops of water fell to the floor as she began packing her suitcase.

"Hey, babe. My mid-terms are finished. I think I aced that stupid theory class. Just got a little more packing to do, and then I'll be ready to drive us back to Brant today. Are you excited?" Carter asked.

"I've been trying to reach you for an entire day. I know you were busy, but you could have called me back, Carter." Her voice filled with exasperation.

"Sorry. Exams were rough. My boss kept me longer than expected. And I was too drunk when I got home last night. Crashed in my clothes on the futon. Did you get to do my laundry?" he asked.

Amalia grimaced. "Yeah. It's all packed. I need to pick up some books at Jonah's office, but I should be ready to leave in a few hours. How about I grab some sandwiches on the way back and meet you at the fraternity house at noon?" Amalia wanted to read *Gone with the Wind* while she was home for a few days, convincing herself the reason wasn't because it would help her feel closer to Jonah.

"You spend too much time with him. I don't understand why you can't call him Dr. West like every other student. Seriously, I've noticed the way he looks at you." Carter had been a jealous boyfriend, occasionally raising concerns over her relationship with Jonah, often telling her to quit her job and find something else. Amalia kept coddling Carter until he stopped arguing about it, but she'd known he was right. It was a risky idea for her to spend more time with Jonah, especially since picturing him as more than a boss and mentor.

"It's fine. He's just a good friend, and he's very open-minded with his students. He won't even be there today, at least I doubt it. Jonah's on break, too." Amalia desperately hoped the vacation would help her forget the attraction to Jonah. She wasn't ready to tell Carter about her feelings changing for either of them. "Go pack. I'll be there soon."

"Being with you the other night was really special. Maybe we can do that again when your mother's not around." He chuckled, muttered an awkward goodbye, and disconnected.

Amalia finished packing, applied some light makeup, and began the stroll to retrieve her books. Ten minutes later she arrived at Jonah's office and focused on the spot on the rug where they'd fallen into an embrace. She contemplated whether her mind and body had split into two separate parts. It'd been as if she stood above watching herself nuzzle Jonah's face, his hands pulling her into the kiss. Her body instantly heated up, and a wet spot formed between her legs. As her fingers gently brushed the desk, Amalia soon breathed heavier, picturing Jonah's body, wanting his hands to stroke her cheek at that moment. Pulling her lower lip inside with her teeth, her tongue pressed against the top of her mouth, sending a shiver down her back. She was about to fall helplessly into her daydream when an interruption frightened her back to reality.

"Amalia?"

His voice pulled her from the distant trance. Jonah appeared in the doorway, stunned to find her inside his office. He wore a pair of tight jeans and a loose-fitting shirt untucked with a few buttons open at the top. The cleft between his chest muscles poked through patches of shiny hair. He hadn't shaved in two days, and his body offered a rugged intensity clearer than ever before.

Jonah rushed toward her. "I didn't expect to find you here, beautiful."

A case of bashfulness or longing stole her words. "I... I needed to..."

Jonah's leg brushed up against hers and caused her to shiver. Though she smelled his cologne, it couldn't mask the heavenly scent of his natural skin. There was a fire burning between them, and Amalia was uncertain if she could dampen the flame.

"You're standing in my office looking back at me with your lips pursed as they are... I don't know if I should turn around or take you in my arms." When he pushed closer to her, the hair on his arms tingled against her wrist.

Amalia grabbed his hand. "Don't leave," she whispered, placing his fingers on her hips.

"Are you sure we should, Amalia? I know you have a boyfriend." He moaned as his hand grazed down the side of her leg and touched her inner thigh.

"All I know is I haven't ever felt this way before."

"I know what you mean. You are so beautiful." He bent further down and dropped his lips into the crook of her neck, licking under the curve of her jawline right up to her ear. His tongue gently tickled the shell as his gentle breath cooled her off.

"Jonah, can we go somewhere? I want to be alone with you. Please." A small sense of guilt crept inside her body, but the sensation of Jonah's rough skin, the shape of his chest and shoulders, and the placement of his hands on her body outweighed any inclination to stop. She'd been hypnotized. "Maybe your place?"

"I've wanted you for weeks." Jonah squeezed her hand and kissed her lips with a passionate craving for more. "Yes, my car is right outside. We can be there in less than ten minutes."

By the time she reached his front door, Amalia had forgotten the car ride, the walk up the front path, and her boyfriend, Carter. All she thought about was the consuming energy soaring throughout her body—a shooting star with no end in sight. She'd felt none of it with Carter and all of it with Jonah. Upon reaching his bedroom, Jonah kicked the door closed with one foot and angled her toward the bed. When the door banged against the solid wood frame, the reverberation in the room intensified the pulsing within her body. Nothing Carter had ever done excited her with such fervor.

Jonah stripped off his shirt and pulled her black cotton dress over her head. He laughed at the wild curls that adorned her heart-shaped face and fell against her shoulders. Amalia settled on the bed as he leaned over to open the nightstand drawer.

She relaxed in his grip as he unfastened her bra with one hand and searched the drawer with the other. "What are you doing?" Amalia asked.

"I'm looking for a condom." Jonah shut the drawer with a quick force.

"Oh, yes." Amalia recognized how different Jonah was than Carter. Smart. Thoughtful. Safe. "Good idea."

"I may have one in the closet." Jonah heaved his body off the bed, pounded across the wood floor, and opened the cedar-planked door. "It's been a long time." He laughed with a hearty energy that electrified the room.

Amalia removed the rest of her clothes and shimmied to the end of the bed as Jonah leaned into the closet. The light outlined the shape of his body in shadows on the floor, the skin on his back and shoulders glowing before her. She wanted him desperately knowing it was wrong, but her flesh needed his arms wrapped all around her.

Jonah tossed around a few bags in the closet before turning around with excitement dripping from his words. "Success, it's a free sample I got months ago when the college had a *Safe Sex* campaign to stop the spread of diseases."

When he returned, Amalia unhooked his leather belt. With forceful eagerness, she popped open the button, pulled down the zipper, and ripped off his jeans. In seconds, his boxers fell to the floor. Her eyes brightened, and her lips grew wide in approval of his naked body.

They made love for the next hour, switching between passionate and sensual at different moments, fully encouraged by each other's sounds and reactions to their deepest desires. Amalia, for the first time, had climaxed, unable to contain the noises emanating from her throat. She knew Jonah was pleased, not only by his facial expressions and moans, but through the way his body moved with hers as if they were one synchronized machine. When finished, she laid in his arms, unable to hide the smile plastered across her face.

"I don't know what to say, Jonah. It was not anything I expected." Amalia buried her face in his neck, running her hands through the hair on his chest. "You're wonderful."

Jonah snuggled against her. "This wasn't your first time, was it? I should have asked before, but I got too excited in my office at the way you sparkled. It was one of the most erotic things I'd ever witnessed." He caressed the small of her back, and she pushed her body further onto his.

"No, it wasn't my first, but definitely my best," she cooed in response. "Thank you."

Jonah smiled and lifted his body slightly. "Let me take care of something." Jonah reached under the sheet and pulled the condom away from his exhausted body. After a brief silence, his smile faded. "Oh, no!"

Amalia's body stiffened with a concern that he'd been hurt in their lovemaking. "What's wrong?"

As Jonah shifted in the bed, a grim expression formed on his face. "The condom broke. It must have been too old."

# Chapter 19

# Brianna, September 2004

Brianna balanced on the edge of the bathtub in her apartment and slumped against the shower wall, her toes lifting and dropping the mat on the floor in front of her. Professor Villing and the conversation she'd shared with him in front of the library weighed on her mind. He intrigued her, perhaps as a friend if nothing else materialized, or she determined their encounter meant nothing. Brianna flicked the card between her fingers, tossed it in her purse, and checked her reflection in the mirror.

Shanelle banged on the other side of the closed door. "Let's go, we need to jet. I wanna get there before midnight."

Brianna applied some strawberry-flavored gloss and smacked her lips together. "Coming."

Shanelle wanted to give Brianna an opportunity to explore a different side of life at the new lesbian bar her cousin had suggested. Brianna had never gone to the ones in New York City, afraid she'd be recognized or labeled too quickly. She adjusted her cleavage, fixed the shoulder strings on her camisole, and dried her hands on a towel. "Too much skin."

When Brianna opened the door, Shanelle glimmered in a red miniskirt and see-through nylon crop top. "Should we take one more peek in the journal before we head out?"

Brianna's lips hesitated. "No, I've had enough for today. I feel awful for invading her privacy." She brushed imaginary lint off her skirt and walked toward the living room.

"Your mother had two boyfriends. What's wrong with that? You don't know she actually slept with both." Shanelle followed her outside to the parking lot and opened the car door. "Which one do you think was the Air Force guy she claims is your father?"

"I don't know. It's probably not the professor. At least maybe now I can start asking her some detailed questions." Brianna fiddled with her iPod in the passenger seat as she pulled up some tunes. "Let's forget about it for tonight. I'm excited about this new bar."

"The Willow? Yeah, my cousin said it's the only place around here worth anything." Shanelle switched gears and casually rested her hand on Brianna's knee. "You sure you're ready for this? You might get hit on, which won't make me happy."

"I'm not sure, but I told you I want to give it a chance. There's no way to be certain unless I push myself, right?" Earlier in the day, they'd discussed Brianna's concerns over going out to the club. Shanelle suggested Brianna find some male student on campus to have coffee with one day the following week, just as a way to explore both options for her future. Pick a guy, see if the date is awkward or comfortable, then decide which of the two paths would make her happy.

A few minutes later, they parked the car and walked twenty steps to a warehouse-like structure on the side of the road. The nearest building had been a quarter mile down the road when they made the last turn at the intersection. Music thumped through the windows and door as the bouncer opened it to let a few girls inside.

"Are you sure these IDs will get us access?" Concern about being caught breaking the law skulked throughout Brianna's body. She'd already crossed too many lines with her mother's journal. Was she heading down a path to hell by breaking every law or code of conduct in life?

Shanelle nodded. "Yup, my cousin printed them for us before practice today. Remember, we're twenty-two years old tonight. Eh, I guess they aren't too particular around here about that stuff."

Shanelle handed both picture cards to a tall brunette with arms the size of a football player. "Decent night?"

The bouncer tilted her head and leaned forward with a flashlight to check the IDs. "It's just filling up inside. Have an enjoyable time, ladies."

Brianna shuffled in behind Shanelle, gripping her elbow with determined force. "It worked. You were right."

"How many times must I tell you I'm always right?" Shanelle winked.

The room was large and dark. A few strobe lights flickered in each corner. The bar ran the length of the opposite wall. Two guys chatted in the corner drinking half-empty bottles of beer, hustled close with a bunch of older women. Otherwise, the crowd was mostly women in their twenties.

"Let's order drinks first." Shanelle dragged Brianna toward the bar. She swerved in and out of a few groups of girls idling on the dance floor as they navigated the path. No one had been dancing. It wasn't that kind of place. Women came to connect. Socialize. Collect numbers. Not to get sweaty and grind against one another.

"It's not what I expected." Brianna looked for an opening at the far end of the bar. "What about over there, those two might be leaving?"

"Perfect. You go order us something. I'm gonna hang back over here to observe how you interact." Shanelle pushed Brianna a few steps away as if she were a baby bird leaving the nest for the first time.

Brianna turned back. "You're not coming with me?"

"You need to act like you're alone. No one will come up to you if I'm hanging on your arm. Flirt a little. See whose attention you attract." Shanelle backed away, nearly bumping into a woman wearing too much eyeliner and three more layers of clothing than she should have been. "You got this. I'll be close."

Brianna complied and stumbled to the open space in the bar, standing between a platinum blonde in a halter top and a squat girl with a pasty complexion who resembled a wannabe hippie without the beads and hemp. She checked behind the counter, catching the eye of the bartender—a tall brunette with choppy hair and a vest pushing her breasts out the top. One had a beauty mark in the shape of a heart. Brianna was intrigued by the tattoos running up and down both arms and around the base of her neck. Uncertain if she should signal to get the girl's attention, Brianna absorbed the ambiance of the room to find a sense of comfort. As she laid eyes on a girl about her height throwing darts at a board in the corner, a voice with an Australian accent spoke behind Brianna.

"What'll it be, newbie?" said the bartender.

"What a cool voice! How's your night been?" Brianna encouraged herself to act more outgoing. Shanelle would be proud.

"A talker, huh?" The bartender popped open a beer and slid it a few feet down the slippery veneer. It landed in front of the platinum blonde who held a ten-dollar bill in her hand. The bartender leaned over the edge, her chest planted firmly on the wet surface. "The cash drawer is open, love."

The platinum blonde slowly pressed the bill into the bartender's cleavage, her fingers lingering a little too long. "Keep the change, Rita." She blew her a kiss and strutted toward a friend near the seated area in the back corner.

*You can do this.* "I'm Brianna. Nice to meet you, Rita." Discomfort was tossed to the sidelines, letting a breath of elusive confidence wander in for a moment. "What are the options tonight?"

"A bar full of women I need to serve." Rita tramped away with a few bottles in her hands and one under her chin delicately balanced in the curves of her cleavage. As she poured a steady stream of gold into a shot glass, her eyes sparkled.

Brianna scanned the length of the room, noticing Shanelle talking to a group of girls they'd met a few times on campus. She caught Shanelle's eyes and grew more poised when her friend winked back at her. Shanelle always appeared relaxed and self-assured no matter where they went—on the soccer field, in a classroom, or now even in a bar among dozens of strangers. Shanelle knew who she was. No provocative questions gnawed their way out from the inside.

"Drink this."

Brianna focused her attention back to the bar, noticing the shot glass sitting a few inches from her elbow. "Is that for me? But I didn't order yet."

"Time is money, newbie. I can't stand here all night and wait for you to decide. First one is on the house. When you decide what you want, give me a shout. Otherwise, let someone else have the spot." Rita wandered to the register to deposit a handful of cash.

Although the girls were tough in New York, Rita projected a different kind of hardness. In the big city, they'd beat the crap out of you in a back alley, steal your wallet, and spit in your face. It would hurt, but you'd recover. Bartenders in Woodland didn't even give you the time of day—the blisters were all from their words. Brianna opened her purse and retrieved a twenty-dollar bill as her eyes scanned the line of bottles across the back row on the counter.

On Rita's round-trip return, Brianna waved the twenty-dollar bill in the air. "I'll take two Vodka Tonics. Absolut, please."

Rita stopped in her tracks, grabbed the money, and turned toward the counter.

"Wait, don't I get to put it in the cash register, too?" Brianna teased.

"No."

"That's not fair, the blonde chick did." Brianna tried to act coy, but her nerves wouldn't let her find the right tone and expression. She instead came across as a whiny airhead, too bubbly for anyone to take her seriously. "What if I wanna flirt with you tonight, too?"

"Brianna, that's your name, right?" Rita adjusted her cleavage and dried a few drops of liquor from the top of her vest. "The blonde chick doesn't want to just flirt with me. She knows I want to nip her tits and make her feel special."

Brianna retreated on the stool as her lips formed into a frown. "Is she hotter than me?"

Rita strode back with both drinks in hand, slapped them on the bar, and leaned forward within inches of Brianna's face. "Not hotter, just ready to handle me, newbie."

"You don't know anything about me."

Rita's gaze bored through Brianna's weakened barriers. Her hands furiously made drinks as she spoke. "Tell me if I got this right. You broke up with a guy. You think you're bisexual. Your friend over there, the one with the crop top and short skirt, who keeps staring at you like she's ready to yank the leash back any minute, wants to be your girl-friend. But you don't know yet if you're a little lezzie, so she brought you here to figure it out."

Brianna recoiled, unable to speak. *How was it so obvious?*

"I'm not being cruel, newbie. It's cool. I get it. Just don't go expecting us to fawn all over the new girl in town. You've got to put in your time like everyone else." Rita drank the shot she'd poured earlier. "Enjoy your vodka."

"Wait, don't go." Brianna reached for Rita's forearm. "I'm sorry. I didn't mean to come across as a bitch. You're direct, Rita. I'll say that for sure."

"Only way to be."

"I don't know what I'm doing. Yes, I think I still have a thing for guys, but I'm into my friend, too." Brianna pointed toward Shanelle, who was engrossed in some conversation with the group of girls she'd befriended. "I'm trying to figure it all out. I thought you were kind of hot."

"I am hot, that's why they hired me. I can tease all night long and keep the drink orders pouring in. It doesn't mean I'm gonna say yes or go home with every doll walking through the joint."

"What about me?"

"Another day, another time? Yeah, maybe. You need to settle in still." Rita took another order and began mixing the drinks.

"My friend's great. I'm just not so sure if I'm done with guys, or it was the one guy in particular." Brianna remembered Doug, then Malachi. When the professor popped into her head, Brianna accepted Shanelle might have a point. Maybe it was just older men. "Ever been confused?"

Rita shook her head. "Nope, I've dated women all my life, newbie." She wiped her hands on her hips and capped a bottle before shoving a shot glass in front of Brianna.

"For me?"

"Yeah, you need one. If you're not sure which gender your body vibrates for, pick one and take it further. Find a guy you wanna mess around with or let your friend over there have a field day popping your girl cherry."

Brianna's eyes grew wider as she contemplated Rita's advice and searched for a response.

Rita's forehead wrinkled, and her lips puckered when she leaned closer. "Don't play the role of a poor little ingénue who can't even figure out how to cross the street without someone holding her hand. Grow a pair. No one can make your future happen but you."

"Thanks. Something to think about." Brianna recalled saying '*Grow a pair*' to Doug earlier that summer. *Was she as childish as him?*

"That's my advice, special to you, newbie."

Brianna liked Rita despite the rough exterior packaging and how she wouldn't coddle her with kid gloves when it was most desired. Rita was sultry and deep, vibrant and insightful. "Maybe I should push myself into something riskier. Just to test the waters." As Brianna turned her head, Shanelle came into view.

"How's it going?" Shanelle wrapped her arm around Brianna's waist. "I guess you got our drinks."

"Your friend here was telling me she wants you to yank her chain more. It makes her real hot-n-bothered." Rita glowered at Shanelle, then stepped away to take a few more drink orders from a gaggle of lipstick-laden thirty-somethings.

Brianna shook her head, amused by Rita's attitude, and searched for the motivation to choose a path that night. "Ignore her. She was giving me a tough time over the drinks I ordered. I need to run to the ladies' room."

Brianna stood in line, pondering everything Rita had suggested. What resonated the most was how Brianna would never know what she wanted until she permitted herself to try something new. The line had almost been crossed with Doug, but Brianna became too scared in the end. She had to find the courage to take a risk and to close the door to one part of her life if those ideas or sentiments never truly belonged to her. She wanted to figure out the truth, divert the anxiety, and force the unsettled urges to disappear.

Brianna recalled the entry she'd read earlier that evening in her mother's journal. Molly had a few similarly confusing situations when she was the same age, uncertain about being intimate with her college boyfriend or surrendering to the temptation of an older professor. Perhaps Brianna was more like her mother than she'd realized. Shanelle would be at a study group for a few hours the following night. According to what Rita's message implied, if Brianna didn't take the opportunities presented to her, she'd never get her answers.

When it was her turn for the next stall, she rushed in, shut the door, and grabbed her phone.

> **Brianna**: *Are you free to meet up tomorrow?*
>
> **Professor Villing**: *What did you have in mind?*
>
> **Brianna**: *We could get to know each other. Listen to good nineties music.*
>
> **Professor Villing**: *Want to come over to my place?*

Brianna hesitated before responding. She needed to push herself but being alone with him the first time they went on a date wasn't the ideal solution. At the same time, if she didn't start challenging herself, the answers about her sexuality would remain hidden. Brianna wracked her brain for a compromise, settling on a funky bar a few people previously mentioned in one of the meet-n-greet orientations.

**Brianna**: *Do you know Kirklands?*

**Professor Villing**: *I do. Been a few times before.*

**Brianna**: *Meet me there at eight tomorrow.*

**Professor Villing**: *Very much looking forward to it.*

As she washed her hands, a pang of guilt for not telling Shanelle about the date distressed Brianna. The last time Shanelle thought she'd been flirting with a guy, Malachi, her best friend had flipped out. Convincing herself to keep it a secret for a little while longer as the risk would end up being meaningless, Brianna exited the bathroom. Her phone buzzed when crossing into the lounge area.

**Malachi**: *Brant is in Mississippi. She moved to NYC to escape a difficult home life.*

**Brianna**: *She's from the South? Yikes. What's your next step?*

**Malachi**: *Not sure. Your mother's a pretty cool woman.*

**Brianna**: *Umm… what are you saying?*

**Malachi**: *We're going out again soon. You still sure you want me to keep digging?*

**Brianna**: *Yes. I need answers. Please find out who she knew there.*

**Malachi**: *I'll investigate more in Brant. Then I'll check back in.*

Brianna grunted. First, Shanelle tells her to abandon the search. Now, the private investigator wants her to drop it because he fancies her mother. When would it finally be her turn to get some answers? What did she have to do for someone to choose her side?

Chapter 20

# Amalia, March 1985

"That's not good." Uncertain how to respond, Amalia found herself suddenly more frightened about the things she knew little of. "Should I be concerned?"

Jonah pushed the covers away and turned toward Amalia. "I haven't been with many women before. You don't need to worry about catching anything from me." After leaning over to kiss her lips, he slid out of bed and traipsed to the bathroom. "I assume I have nothing to worry about either?"

She ran her fingers through her hair, collecting as much as her hands could hold, and tossed it behind her shoulders. "I'm not taking birth control pills. I mean, I know about them. But I... I wasn't allowed to when my mother took me to the doctor back home."

"I'm not talking about you getting pregnant. At least I'm not worried about that happening." Jonah walked back in the bedroom with only a towel hung around his waist. The movement of his body as he sauntered toward Amalia caused her heart to flutter. The calf muscles in his legs tempted her to ask for another opportunity to be with him, but concerns about the topics he'd brought up alarmed her.

"Oh, okay. Then what were you worried about?" she asked, focusing on the floor.

Jonah lifted her chin and smiled. "I meant any sexually transmitted diseases. There are a few new concerns popping up lately that they don't know a lot about. Are you familiar with AIDS?"

"Diseases? I never thought about that." Amalia shook her head and pinched the comforter, feeling distracted by the smooth texture as it slipped between her fingers. "I've never heard of AIDS."

Jonah knelt at the side of the bed. His hand reached up to caress her cheek. "Have you been with many other guys? Were you always safe?"

Foolishness set in as Amalia questioned whether she'd moved forward too quickly in exploring her sexual desires without knowing the facts one should know beforehand. "Carter and I only made love the one time. It was recent. I don't know a lot about this stuff. My mother wouldn't talk to me about it. And, I..." Amalia's eyes grew misty. "I'm sorry."

Jonah pulled her head toward his shoulder and explained the basics about the diseases she should consider familiarizing herself with. "Don't be scared. I'm sure everything is fine. I've been tested before. Are you sure you're okay with what happened just now?"

Amalia hugged him tightly and basked in his warmth and safety. It reminded her of the days before she'd met Carter, when she was still the sweet little girl her father had adored. "I am. It was amazing. I want to do it again, but we should take things a little slower for a while." While thinking about Carter, the room spun a little. She couldn't love him if she were willing to jump into bed with Jonah so quickly.

"That's a smart idea. I mean, you and I are also working together. We need to consider Carter and your schoolwork. I don't want to pressure you." He wiped a few drops from under her eyes, kissing both spots before pulling back. "I adore you immensely. We might have something here."

"I'm leaving this afternoon with Carter to go back to Brant for a week." Amalia drew in a gulp of heavy air. "I should tell him."

"I'm going away to a conference for a few days starting tomorrow, too. Why don't you give me your home number? I can call you when I get to the hotel."

Amalia nodded and wrote it on a scrap of paper sitting near the nightstand. "I'd like that." Shocked by the time on the clock, she quickly jumped from the bed. "Oh my, I was supposed to meet Carter an hour ago. I need to go." Amalia gathered her dress, shoes, and remaining clothes and rushed to the bathroom. Though shyness over being fully naked in front of him percolated on the surface of her excited body, she turned back and smiled at Jonah. His grin was twice as wide, and that's when she knew he could be something special, too.

Fifteen minutes later, Amalia ran across the quad to her dorm room knowing it would make her even tardier, but she'd been desperate to shower before finding Carter. The guilt had bubbled inside her and pushed her to remember all the cruel names Janet had called her. Amalia had morphed into the harlot her mother had once said she would become, upset at herself for crossing the line with Jonah before telling Carter she didn't want to date him anymore.

Carter was a wonderful boyfriend, but not good enough for her. Carter needed a girl who loved the things he loved, who was content to remain the arm candy he paraded around to all his friends, but this wasn't who she was nor who she wanted to be. Carter's passions only relegated her back home to Brant, the one place she never wanted to be again. Amalia would have to tell him the truth, even if it destroyed him.

As she crossed the other side of the quad and wandered the path around the boy's dormitory, her building came into view. Just outside on the front steps, a perplexed Carter anticipated her return. Amalia sensed the concern and frustration as his feet feverishly tapped the cement. His head hung low, bouncing up and down, nerve-wracked over what'd happened to her.

She called out to him upon reaching the front of the dorm. "I'm so sorry. I got distracted. I… I'm here now." Amalia instantly knew he hadn't been worried. He'd been angry. His teeth gritted down hard enough, and the twitching nerves in his jaw were now excruciatingly obvious a few feet away.

"Where have you been? You're over an hour late." He stood with his arms thrown in the air. "Where are the sandwiches? I'm starving."

Carter pulled at his hair and dropped his hands as angst assumed more control.

"I forgot. I'm so sorry, Carter. Can we go inside? To talk?" Amalia's heart pounded. No matter how much he wasn't the right boy for her, she'd never wanted to hurt him, to wound someone who'd loved her. She pictured the day they'd met, his flirtatious behavior and unabashed persistence in courting her. Had it really been less than a year? So much had changed for her since that fateful day he'd arrived in Brant.

"We can talk in the car. Just get your stuff," he yelled, motioning like a flight attendant for her to go inside for the luggage. "We'll stop at a gas station on the way out to pick up something to eat. Geez, Amalia. What's wrong with you? After what we did this week, I thought you'd be more committed than ever to making this work."

She looked up at him, unable to cry any tears at that moment. Though sad, Amalia wasn't the victim and had no right to ask him to hug her. "Carter, I don't think you should come home with me to Brant anymore." She waited for him to respond, but his silence was deafening. "Carter, did you hear me?"

Carter nodded once. "Yup. What's this about? I don't have time for your silly games today." His hands flew to the top of his head again.

Amalia struggled to find the words, choosing to announce the news as though it were part of a normal conversation. "I love Jonah. I want to be with him."

Carter's eyes were the first part of his body to betray his emotions. They first closed to contemplate his response, but when he opened them, they appeared dark and determined. The last time Amalia had seen someone as disheartened, perhaps sickened, was when her father had caught her on the couch with Carter. She recognized the irony when life switched roles so quickly among the men who'd once told her how much they loved her.

"I'm sorry. I didn't mean to hurt you." Amalia reached for his hand, knowing it would lead to rejection and expecting him to get angry. To scream. Even to smack her. Past experience allowed her to think she deserved it. No matter how much Carter had pressured her in the past, he'd never done anything to cause her outright harm. Amalia had been the bully in this situation. No different from her mother. If he'd chosen to slap her, she'd accept it with no anger or fear. Years of protecting herself against her mother's physical abuses had taught Amalia to bury her feelings deep. To ignore the pain in her body. Her head. Her heart.

Carter did nothing she'd expected. He stuffed his hands deep into his jean pockets and angled his head directly at her. When he looked toward her, he raised his brow, and a bitter smile appeared. "I thought I loved you, Amalia Graeme. But that can't be true. I couldn't love someone with no heart. You're nothing but a tease. An empty, foolish, stupid little tease I no longer have time for."

"Carter, please. Let me explain." She reached for his arm, but he stepped backward and spat on the cement beside her.

"I knew you'd pull this crap again. It's a good thing I've got girls lined up to be with me. You've always worried there was someone else. Remember Rachel's sister? She's been after me for months. Maybe it's time I chose her instead of a fickle little fish who can't stop thinking about her daddy." He trudged past Amalia, down the walkway, and took off in a heated dash across the quad.

Amalia wanted to call after him, but as part of the consequences of her actions, she had to let him go. If not for his sake, for her own. As much as it churned inside her, she needed to make peace with her decision and tell her mother she wouldn't return home. Amalia jogged to her dorm, hoping to first talk to Rachel about the breakup with Carter and then find out if she knew anything about her sister's relationship with him, but it seemed like she'd already left for home without saying goodbye. Rachel's half of the room, while still a mess, was emptier than usual and felt abandoned. When Amalia thought about Carter saying he was smitten with Rachel's sister, she was glad he had someone else to turn to. It made her worry less about breaking his heart.

She dialed the phone, preferring to hear the machine's outgoing message rather than her own mother's voice. But Amalia had never been that lucky of a girl.

"Who's there?" Janet's husky tone blasted through the receiver.

"Hi, Momma. How are you?" Amalia searched for the proper words, confidence growing inside her as she listened to the irate voice coming through the phone.

"Aren't you on the road yet? I thought Carter said you'd be here soon. What did you do now, girl?"

Amalia pulled the phone away from her ear to avoid any damage from the volume of her mother's hysterics. "Relax. There's been a change of plans. I'm not coming home today. I'm not coming home at all anymore, Momma. It's time you knew that."

"What on God's good green earth are you spouting off about? Carter needs to be here to help me with this store. Now get a move on it before I—"

"Before you what, Momma?" Amalia needed to crank the pressure on her mother if she had any chance of getting her point across. "Hit me again? We're done with that. Now you hear me, I'm not gonna take this abuse from you anymore."

"Amalia Graeme, you have twenty-four hours to get home with that boy. If you don't, rest assured, there will be consequences. I've had enough of your attitude and you…"

Amalia slammed the phone back into the cradle. The echo of the handset's harsh bang against the desk resounded inside her dorm room. "We'll see what kind of consequences there are, Momma. I'm the one deciding now."

She leaned over on her bed and grabbed the journal hidden beneath her pillow. Though she trusted her roommate, it'd always been dangerous to leave the diary in an accessible location in case Carter came around. Amalia's deepest intimacies had been recorded in its contents, things she feared he would find and read at some point. Now her secret was out in the open, so she could be with Jonah. Shaky hands began writing…

*Dear Diary,*

*It's been an eventful couple of days since we last chatted, my friend. And you'll never believe what's happened. I took the big step with Carter this week. It was sweet and innocent. He held me and listened when I asked him to take it slow. When we were finished, I kept thinking something was missing. I thought it was me, that I was inexperienced and didn't know how to make love to a man. I was wrong. It wasn't me. It was him. And he isn't a man. Carter is just a boy.*

*He just left to study for exams and go to his internship before our trip back to Brant. I don't want to go home. Too many memories of my father and realities with my mother. She's an awful woman. I'm never going back to Brant again. I have a new life to look forward to.*

*When I stopped by Jonah's office to pick something up, he found me there. After he touched me, it was as though everything lined up in a perfect row for the first time. He was so amazing. His hands were strong but passionate. Rough but sensitive. He took me back to his place where we made love for so long. When he was inside me, I thought I'd been rescued from all the horrors back home... like I'd have a new home here in Woodland. I know I've only known Dr. Jonah West for a few months, but I love him. I love him like no one else before. I love the little gray hairs growing in at his temples. The scar on his arm from when he fell off the swing as a child. The nervous laugh when he flirts. I can't wait to kiss him again. I've got some thinking to do about what happens next. Can't wait to talk again.*

*Love,*

*Amalia*

Amalia closed her diary and placed it at the end of the bed. She climbed down the stairs, excited about the prospect of seeing Jonah again. He'd mentioned leaving the next day for a conference, but now that she wouldn't return to Brant, maybe Jonah would want to meet her again that night. She called his house, but he didn't pick up there or at his campus office. He often left the phone off the hook to work without interruption. Checking his office in person seemed like the ideal solution.

Amalia exited the dorm, distracted by everything that'd happened in the last twenty-four hours. She raced toward the academic building, paying little attention to her surroundings. While rounding the corner, Amalia misjudged the height of the small metal fencing around one of the flower gardens and tripped over it, flying toward the ground. She skidded a few feet and banged her shoulder into the trunk of the tree. When she tried to stand, a shooting pain blared across Amalia's shoulder and down her right arm. Amalia lingered for a few moments, rubbing her muscles until the ache became more tolerable. Wooziness from the injury filled her body before she returned on a path toward Jonah's office.

The sun began its slow descent as the evening's dark mantle arrived in Woodland. The brilliant blue and purple hues in the distance and the image of Jonah's arms circling around her body teased and comforted Amalia. Excitement to reveal she'd broken it off with Carter—and had chosen Jonah—fueled her motivation for the new future she'd been waiting for all her life.

Chapter 21

# Brianna, September 2004

The morning after her trip to The Willow, Brianna kept busy writing a paper and studying for her first English quiz. By late afternoon, she convinced herself that it would be okay to read a few more pages from the diary, but soon realized she'd invaded too much of her mother's privacy when intimate details of the past came to light. Not only had Molly fallen for two men, Carter and Jonah, but she'd slept with them both in the same week. Though Brianna was desperate for answers, some unknown force compelled her to walk a fine line that nudged the boundaries with her mother yet wouldn't erase them entirely. She didn't want to read the answers from a book. Brianna wanted her mother to finally confess the truth. It was time to expose what she'd learned about the past in the hopes Molly would recognize things had gotten too far out of control.

Brianna was certain Rachel's adopted baby had nothing to do with her own search for her father, but she also couldn't figure out how the Air Force guy and any connection to Lenny Porter fit into the puzzle. There'd been no mention of either in the few entries Brianna had read, leading her to believe her mother must have lied about the Air Force one-night stand, or there was more to the story than what she'd discovered in the journal at that point. The facts weren't adding up to anything logical. Brianna dialed the phone and greeted her mother. "Hey, Mom."

"Hi, honey. How'd that history paper turn out? I'm sure you aced it."

"I won't know until next week." A nervous pause filled a few seconds of silence as Brianna debated how best to initiate the conversation. "I kinda need to talk to you about something."

"Sure, what's on your mind?" Several pots and pans banged in the background.

"Wait, what are you doing?"

"I'm making a roast chicken. A friend is coming over for dinner."

"A friend?" Brianna wondered if Malachi's approach was working. "Is this that hot guy from the tax office?"

"Maybe. I'd rather not discuss it with my daughter right now."

"Hmm, I'm glad you're taking chances." Brianna worried about Malachi revealing he'd been hired to investigate Molly instead of just searching for clues. She needed to get ahead of the situation without revealing how underhanded she'd been between hiring a detective and reading the journal. "So, I need some advice… not sure what I mean quite yet, but… have you ever had feelings for two different people at the same time?" Brianna focused on her budding relationship with Shanelle, but also on the upcoming date with Professor Villing. The parallels were a little too close for comfort.

"That's an unexpected question. Why do you ask?" Molly's voice was low and distant.

"I've been meeting a bunch of people on campus, and now I'm wondering how to handle dating. It's been a while since Doug and I broke up." Brianna wanted to ask more specific questions but preferred her mother volunteer her own experiences. "There's this guy I met on campus the other day, and we're going out this afternoon. I also might have feelings for someone else I'm not sure what to do about."

Molly was silent for a few seconds. "Anyone I know?"

Brianna cringed, trying to ignore the concerns that her mother had noticed the chemistry with Shanelle. "No, Mom, I just started going to school here. How would you have met anybody from Woodland?"

"Right. So… take it slow. Don't rush into anything. School should come first. There will be time for boys in the future."

"You didn't answer the question about dating two people at once." Brianna wasn't getting the information she'd wanted. "Have you dealt with that before?"

"I have dated no one since you came along. You already know the answer to the question. I'm not sure why you keep asking it every which way from Sunday." Molly always emphasized her consonants when angry—it'd quickly become clear once their conversation took a downturn.

"Fine. Thanks for nothing."

"Oh, calm down. Dating is meant to be difficult, Brianna. It's how you weed out the bad seeds and germinate the good ones. You're too young to know who or what you want."

*God, her mother was cheesy.* "Isn't that the purpose of going to college? To explore?"

"Well, yes, but it doesn't mean you have to rush—"

Brianna interrupted. "But how do you know when you really like someone?"

"That's not a straightforward answer. Sometimes you just know it when you peer into his eyes. Other times, it takes some big event to knock you upside the head and tell—"

"Can your feelings change for someone over time?" Brianna tossed the questions in rapid fire. She was hopeful to keep it open-ended and not about anyone specific. Somewhere in the conversation her inquiries might have bled into her own jumbled and conflicted love life. "Maybe you fall for them as you spend time working together?"

"Are you sure this isn't about someone you've known for a while? Has someone told you... their... feelings have changed?"

"No, well, but..." Brianna encountered her invisible limit and needed to retreat. She wasn't savvy enough to tiptoe around the subject and still elicit the necessary answers. "Oh, I just remembered, I have to meet a study group. I'll call you soon. Bye." Brianna flung the phone on the bed and changed into a pair of skinny jeans and a black short-sleeve blouse for her date. She couldn't continue the charade with her mother without revealing the information learned by reading the journal or confessing how she felt about Shanelle. Letting another twenty-four hours pass would have to suffice before Brianna confronted Molly in search of answers about Carter and Jonah. Subtlety was not a skill she possessed.

Brianna rode the bus to Kirklands, an Irish pub a mile downtown where she could avoid the normal hangouts and prevent them from running into people from campus. The professor leaned against a wooden column, waiting to claim the next game on the billiard table in the back corner.

Brianna noticed his ruffled hair and rolled-up sleeves. He appeared more relaxed than she did. "Hey, stranger." She tilted her head in his direction playfully, uncertain how to address him. "I mean, nice to see you again, Professor Villing. I appreciate you agreeing to meet me for this class assignment." Brianna winked at him, then ran her fingers through her hair.

"You look gorgeous. I'm a lucky guy to be out with you tonight." His voice was thick and mellifluous—intense, yet comforting at the same time. "But maybe you should—"

Brianna interrupted, then sidled up next to him and rubbed chalk on the tip of the pool cue without moving her eyes from his face. "Rack them for me, please. Let's dive right into the game."

"You know your way around that stick, Miss Porter." He reached over and grabbed it from her. "Let me do the breaking. I'm good at banging things."

"Touché." In the dark lighting around them, a devilish aura overtook his face when he smiled. Brianna had to force herself to be stronger and more flirtatious tonight. She had to reach her goal to get her answers and discover the truth about her sexuality.

"You mentioned an interest in creative writing last time we talked. Tell me more."

Brianna's voice twinkled. Very few people had asked her that question, usually casting it aside as a hobby and not a profession. Not even her mother had understood the passion Brianna experienced when creating stories and characters. "Yes, I enjoy uncovering secrets and learning about dark histories of mysterious people. I'm keenly interested in understanding what happens to someone's psyche when they yearn to know more about themselves but can't get hold of anyone who can help them."

He stopped preparing for his first shot and glanced at her with an inquisitive gleam that made her nervous. "Is that a reflection of your own life?"

"It might be." Brianna took comfort exploring the answers in her head before responding. The man had a way of making her jumpier than speaking in front of a large group. "We all have questions about the past. I'm incomplete and unaware of all the important things. Typical family stuff, like where we emigrated from or what my grandparents were like." Brianna had been about to say more, but suddenly became alarmed at dropping too much baggage on a first date. "What about you?"

He motioned to a waitress to bring two drinks. "Nothing special about me. How are you finding Woodland? Do you have a boyfriend?"

She leaned over the table, purposely pushing her shoulders closer together, so the scoop of her blouse would drop low enough for him to notice. *Isn't that what Doug once liked?* "No boyfriend. Possible girlfriend. Still figuring that out." Shock permeated her body upon realizing she'd just outed herself in the attempt to be flirtatious. *How the fuck did that happen?*

"Sounds complicated." The streamlined wooden stick slid through his fingers, driving the white cue ball deep into the triangular pack. As he moved toward the far corner of the table, the three-ball smacked into the pocket nearest Brianna. "I guess I'll be shooting solids. Always did love things red hot." He sank another solid into the same pocket, then missed his next one. "Your turn."

The game continued, alternating barbs of sexual innuendo and strategic pool shots. He'd won the first round. She came back for him in the second leading by a narrow margin when he scratched the black eight ball in the wrong pocket. Agreeing to call the competition a tie, they grabbed seats at a table and ordered another round of beers.

"I didn't think you were old enough to drink, but you've said a few surprising things just now." His voice held a small amount of concern wrapped in an abundance of wanton desire. "You have a bit of a dark side. Tell me more about this girlfriend you may or may not have."

"I said I was still figuring it out." She stepped back from the table and away from the light, curious if he might help her understand things better. "Sometimes I find myself attracted to women. Sometimes maybe I could see myself getting to know you better." Brianna found a seductive tone she'd unearthed from deep within, something she'd not been fully aware of beforehand. She tussled with his hair, leaning in close until he smelled her perfume.

"I like this side of you, but you shouldn't have to choose between the two things. Maybe both you and this girlfriend of yours should come over to my place. I could help you figure out what you want." He pulled her toward him, his hand looped around her waist.

Brianna fell into his lap, uncomfortable at how quickly things moved. "I'll think about it. A girl needs to have options sometimes, right?"

He nodded. "Yeah, she does." His hand reached around her waist, landing just below her breasts.

Brianna's stomach plummeted as fast as her uneasiness rose. She'd been trying to step outside her comfort zone, but this might have caused too much anxiety. "And you?"

"Nothing as complex as that. Married a college girlfriend. It didn't work out. Been divorced for ten years. No kids."

When he said the word *girlfriend*, Shanelle's voice scratched at the back of Brianna's mind, pushing her to explore the attraction Brianna had felt to women, not to men. She staggered toward the other side of the table, eager to get away for a moment. "It's been a fun night, but I'm sure you have other things to do."

"Such as?" He appeared unwilling to give her up.

"Oh, I just meant it was getting late."

"It's not that late, and there are no classes tomorrow."

Brianna smiled at him until an idea popped into her head, compelling her to chase after it. "True, but I need to finish a paper. Hey... question for you... would you know if the dean keeps a master list of all professors at Woodland?"

He cocked his head to the side, uncertain at the change in topics and curious over what she'd wanted to know. "As in what courses they're teaching? Sure, it's online. You can find it with your student account."

"No, I meant a list of all professors that ever taught here in the past." Brianna sipped the last of her beer, grateful she'd only had two bottles as they'd made her lightheaded. "I'm just doing a minor research project."

"Maybe the library has that info? I've only taught here a few years, so I don't know the ins and outs of the different systems." He leaned forward and reached for her hand.

Brianna pulled it away when his tickling of her palm reminded her of Shanelle again. "Thanks. We should meet again soon." She pushed in her chair, desperate to leave.

His eyes danced with concern. "Did I say anything wrong?"

"No, I'm just taking things at a slower pace." Brianna had walked too close to the edge that night, and she wanted to escape to determine if Dr. Jonah West still taught on campus.

"Okay, if you're certain." He sighed.

"I'll call you during the week. Sweet dreams."

"Goodnight, Miss Porter. Dreams of you will not be of the sweet kind tonight. Dark. Yes. Intense. Yes. But not sweet."

She ignored his last remark and left through the front door. Upon reaching the street out of view from the front of the bar, Brianna leaned against the cold bricks of the building's facade. The first questions on her mind—who did she suddenly become tonight and was she coming out of her shell? The next question—how quickly could she get to the library?

Twenty minutes later, she dashed by the reception desk, ignoring the pimple-faced clerk shouting after her they closed in five minutes. Brianna found the library's computer terminals and logged in with the guest credentials listed on an index card taped to the side of the monitor.

"What the hell, security sucks around here." She deftly punched in a few words into the search field and scrolled through the results.

The first two responses returned course schedules and department rosters. Not what she wanted. She clicked the third, and the screen flashed. "Bingo."

Brianna scrolled down a few lines coming across a subject line. '*Dr. Jonah West, Woodland Professor.*' She pressed the link to expand the details and opened an article from just over three months earlier. Maybe it would reveal whether he still taught at Woodland or had transferred to a different college.

*Dr. Jonah West, Woodland College – June 23rd, 2004*

*We will hold a memorial for the late Dr. Jonah West, Associate Dean of Woodland College, who died suddenly last week after a perilous tragedy occurred on Main Street. Another school employee witnessed the accident after an out-of-control speeding car veered off the side of the road and crashed into the alumni building. Dr. West died of internal injuries a few hours after being rushed to the hospital. Faculty, friends, and students will meet on the campus quad for a candlelight vigil at 9:00 p.m. to honor this beloved professor, influential pioneer, and respected colleague with a thirty-five-year tenure at Woodland College. For more information, please contact Dean Clayrent in the Administration Office.*

# Chapter 22

# Amalia, March 1985

The liberal arts academic building, though lit by several lampposts guiding the pathway to the front door, appeared dark and empty. Shadows of great oaks loomed large over the structure, leaving Amalia's insides unsettled and waiting for something unfamiliar to spook her. She needed to apply ice on her throbbing shoulder before too much swelling had occurred, but first wanted to find Jonah to share her news.

Amalia looked around the front of the building, anticipating that the door would be locked, but the knob turned when she placed her hand on its cold metallic surface. If it were open, she assumed it meant Jonah might be in his office. She trod down the hall past the closed doors to the Education Department and then up the stairs to the second floor to search his office. As Amalia checked each one, the various noises in the building made her nervous—nothing but empty rooms and shadowed hallways. The distant buzzing hum of the refrigerator in the shared open administrative area filled the building as she stepped further into the darkness.

Stretching her neck against Jonah's door, Amalia listened through the barrier to determine if he was working inside. Nothing. She confirmed the door handle was locked, walked across the floor, and flipped on a small lamp on the secretary's desk. It wouldn't be too bright, ensuring her presence remained unknown. Students were supposed to be off campus by now.

Amalia opened the refrigerator door, grabbed a bottle of water, and applied it to her shoulder. Knowing there was no ice in the freezer, it offered a small opportunity to relieve the intensity of the sharp throbbing. She relaxed into the chair while her mind grew accustomed to the surrounding sounds. The refrigerator's constant hum. The wind rattling a few windows when it swept by. The pop and hiss of the heaters on the first floor as the pipes banged against the floorboards. The heat should have been turned off since the campus closed for Spring Break, but perhaps the maintenance guys had forgotten.

An eerie creaking near the stairs told her someone else had entered the building. It didn't resemble any of the other noises and quickly alarmed her. Amalia jerked forward, grasping her shoulder as the pain shot through the nerves beneath her skin. The water bottle fell to the floor and rolled across the room. Slanted floors had been a problem in many of the older buildings that had been converted from former mansions into offices for several of the college academic departments. Amalia switched off the light and hid under the desk, attuning her ears to the creak in the hallway on the other side of the wall separating them. She didn't want to be caught alone in the offices and hoped it was Jonah coming upstairs.

"Hello?" came a distant voice, followed by a few steps ending at the entrance to the admin area. "Is anyone here?"

Amalia didn't recognize the voice. She shifted her weight, balancing her good shoulder and back against the inside of the desk. Several keys clanged together in the hallway. It dawned on Amalia that it could be campus security doing a final sweep before locking up the building. Optimistically, the guard's patrol would end quickly, and she could sneak out once he finished.

A few seconds later, the steps of a heavyset man lumbered closer to the desk. From a small hole in the corner, Amalia watched his arm reach down and pick up her water bottle. Then the gasp of pressure when he twisted off the cap. Everything was silent in the room. Only the beating of her heart and the security guard's wheezing filled the vacuous air. Even the refrigerator's compressor had shut down.

Ten seconds later, he returned to the hallway and descended the stairs. When the front door slammed shut again, she breathed loudly, then coughed from the pressure the expansion of her lungs had placed on her sore shoulder. "That was close."

Amalia slid her body across the floor to a place where she could stand, then stepped toward the window and pulled back the shade a few inches to peer into the front walkway. The guard stood outside, gulping the bottle of water and tossing it into the garbage can at the far end of the path.

Amalia returned to the desk and picked up the phone, expecting to ask if Jonah could take her to the clinic for someone to check her shoulder. She tapped her feet on the floor, listening to the echo in the room while waiting for him to answer the phone.

"Hi, this is Jonah." His voice at once comforted her.

"It's Amalia. I'm so glad I found you."

"I thought you were leaving tonight. Is everything okay, beautiful?"

Amalia's eyes closed while picturing his warm and inviting smile. The way his hands had caressed her cheek. "Carter knows about you. I had to tell him it was over." She slid open the top drawer and retrieved a bottle of aspirin she'd found the prior week when searching for paper clips.

"How did that go?"

"Not well. Can you meet me right now?" She popped off the lid and swallowed two pills, using whatever saliva her mouth generated. Every pasty and sticky bump of the pill scraped at Amalia's composure as it bounced down her throat. "I need your help."

"I stopped home to pick up the last pages of edits we worked on this week. I'm about to have dinner with my editor." Jonah shuffled through papers in the background. "I'll be home in two hours. Why don't you meet me here? I believe you know the address."

She grinned as a flood of warmth overtook her body. "I'd like that. I'll see you soon."

"I can't wait. You're acting very quiet. Are you okay?"

Amalia wanted to tell him about the fall, but her priority was to check if the campus health clinic happened to be open, despite doubting her luck. "I'll fill you in later."

"Why don't you head to my house now? You can take a relaxing bath, and I'll return as soon as I can. The key is under the small frog statue by the back door."

Amalia smiled, comforted he trusted her enough not to only to let her stay in his house while he was away, but to reveal the key's secret hiding place. "Perfect. I have one stop to make, and then I'll be there."

They hung up. Amalia planned to take a bus to the eastern section of Woodland to the health clinic. She was certain nothing had been broken, but the fall had knocked the wind out of her, and she'd twisted a few muscles that would be swollen for days.

As Amalia tiptoed toward the doorway, footsteps again creaked up the stairs, allowing her no time to run behind the desk. Instead, she hid against the wall, praying the security patrolman didn't wander back into the admin area. His footsteps stopped outside one of the office doors on the other side of the wall.

The doorknob jiggled, and then the entire space became silent. Amalia pressed tightly against the paneled facade, wishing she could quietly peek around the corner. A shadow across the hallway floor moved closer toward her. Though the pain in her shoulder was powerful, the sense of fear in her stomach had grown much worse. The shadow was tall and thin. It couldn't be the security guy, or if it were, it must have been a different one this time. Then he spoke.

"Amaliaaa…"

A creepy drawn-out version of her name, a familiar voice she'd heard only twice before, yet each time an awful chill breached the surface of her skin. Her heart raced three times quicker than normal, and her chest heaved up and down with frantic exasperation.

Amalia stood in stillness, certain he hadn't known she was inside the admin area. His feet reached the entranceway, each step sending a small wave of movement under the floorboards until it vibrated at her toes. Her ankles shook from the sweat forming behind her knees and racing down her legs.

"I know you're in here. I watched you come inside a little while ago. But you never came out, did you?" It was the kind of voice one could never forget. One that instinctively rang warning alarms—a punch of danger packaged in a way that it was obvious the person had a vendetta against you.

Amalia tiptoed slowly away from the entrance, eager to find anything on the desk she could use to protect herself. Even her cautious steps were too loud in a room filled with nothing but silence. The normal hum of the refrigerator had disappeared long ago. The pipes had stopped rattling on the floor below, no longer keeping her every movement disguised. It was as if the room had wanted her to hear nothing except her own palpable fear buried within the floorboards shifting under her feet, and that of Riley as he rounded the corner with his flashlight beam dimly lit against his face.

His ruthless eyes appeared first. Glassy. Narrow. Raising their lids. The small fold of skin on the bridge of his nose lifted higher as he leered. Despite the sweat pouring from her body, he stood there perfectly calm. Collected. Cool.

"There's my pretty little girl." He angled the beam of light toward Amalia's unprepared face.

Amalia threw her hands up to block the brightness, but the pain in her shoulder shot back an angry retort. She let out a heavy gasp and pressed one hand into the muscles between her chest and the bones of her weakened shoulder.

"We're all alone, in case you're thinking about screaming. No one's gonna hear you even with that beautiful voice." Riley dropped the beam of light to the spot she'd been rubbing, then a few inches lower. "Look at those breasts, Amalia. I'm a lucky guy."

"Leave me alone, Riley. Just stay away." She turned her head once the light became too intense, but the inability to see what he was doing only increased her apprehension. "Jonah's on his way to meet me."

"Is he now? And I thought you agreed to go to his place. We can play it that way if you want. I'm not sure why you're acting so nervous." He stepped a couple of inches closer to her, his hot breath landing on her ear as he finished speaking. "Rachel always had fun until she no longer did."

Amalia stepped around him, attempting to squeeze between him and the front of the desk. "I don't know… what… you're talking… about." The hesitation in her voice was too apparent and revealed her doubts about escaping his clutches.

"Yes, you do. And you've been thinking about getting a taste of me, too, haven't you?"

Amalia now understood why Rachel had been nervous and scared the last few weeks. Maybe Riley was harassing her, too. "No, I have not."

"I know you were just practicing with Carter. And then with your Jonah." He drawled out Jonah's name again. "Third time's the charm, right, beautiful? Isn't that what he calls you?" When she backed away, he leaned forward and winked several times in a row. "I know everything about you."

Amalia's entire body tensed as she realized he'd truly been stalking her if he knew all those facts. She moved closer to the desk, her good arm stretching backward to grab the only weapon she'd been able to find. The three-hole punch was a few feet away, and it would be useful if she could access it. The pain in her sore shoulder kept her from reaching back that far. She begged her body's adrenaline to kick in and help her fight. "You need to go, Riley. Leave both Rachel and me alone."

"Don't worry. I already took care of her." Riley sneered, reaching his hand out to Amalia. He grabbed her shoulder. When she tensed and cried in pain, his lips formed a sinister smile. "Oh, did that hurt? I'm sorry. I'll be gentler next time." He yanked her forward until she was further from the desk and right against his chest.

Amalia tried pushing him away, but he'd twisted her around, so her back was against him. One arm held her firm at the waist, the other thrown around her front cupping her left breast. "It will be easier if you relax, beautiful. I promise you're gonna love being with me. Come on, let's take a little walk."

Amalia shoved back with force. "No, I'm not staying with you. Heeelllp." Her voice pierced loudly in the silence as she strained to escape the room.

Riley's arms were too strong, and her body was too weak. She was no match for his forceful grip and subsequent shove toward the floor. "We're going downstairs to the basement for a little while."

His syrupy voice and fiery breath filled the room with a musky scent. Amalia smelled the Old Spice he'd sprayed all over his shirt—another sign Riley had been planning this entire attack. "Please, let me go. You don't need to do this."

Riley bent down and lifted her off the floor, grasping her upper arm with a vengeance. "I'm not doing anything you don't want me to do. I've seen the way you drool over your Jonah. He's not good enough for you." He pushed her forward into the hallway, his hands tightly gripping her wrists as they trooped in unison toward the stairs. He matched her stride to gain maximum constraint, pushing her body forward with each step of the way. "If you walk slowly, I won't squeeze you any tighter. Though it might be harder on me, I don't want to hurt you."

Amalia filled with painful tears. When they reached the first floor, she tried to shout again. Riley's hands were too quick shooting up to cover her lips. His palm was sweaty, and she tasted a combination of salt and dirt in the cracks between his fingers. Her mouth opened and tried to bite him.

Riley ripped his hand backward upon the sensation of teeth grinding into his fingers, viciously thrashing Amalia until she went flying into the corner and banged against the windowsill. The shock and pain scattered throughout her body like fire ants rising from the depths of the earth, rendering her unable to move.

"Please don't, Riley. No." Amalia's sense of consciousness slipped away from the fear materializing inside her head.

Riley knelt in front of her, lifting her head to within an inch of his face. "You've got the most sensual lips, Amalia. I'm gonna kiss them right now, but let me warn you, if you try to bite me again, I won't be easy on you anymore. You got that?" His fingers dug into the skin on the back of her neck. Sweat dripped from his nose to his mouth. He hadn't shaved in days and looked haggard and drugged.

She knew she had to listen, but secretly hoped the security guard would find his way back to the office. Amalia nodded while anticipating Riley's kiss. Her stomach curdled, an instant gag reflex squashed down in fear of what he'd do to her if she hadn't controlled the urge to vomit. Riley pressed his lips against hers. Hard. Angry. As though he'd kissed no one before. It resembled a jackhammer driving her into the wall. "You're gonna love what happens next."

Tears rolled across Amalia's cheeks, mixing with both their sweat, the stench of his dirty body, and a familiar cologne. She couldn't help but think of her father at that moment. The fresh smell of him after he'd showered in the morning and kissed her forehead before he left for work. The way he'd comfort her whenever Janet spewed her venom against them both. Now, the scent of Old Spice would become her new nightmare.

Amalia focused on the throbbing in her head and shoulder, reserving any remaining strength to fight back when the right moment appeared. She'd been hit before. The pain of a monster's angry punch had swallowed her whole in the past. She'd even been butchered by someone who grabbed the full length of Amalia's golden curls and tore into them with a pair of vengeful scissors. But none with such a brutal force as Riley when he ripped a few strands from her scalp.

Amalia fell to the floor on her back and went limp while Riley dragged her across the smooth wooden surface. The bottom of her dress rode up to her waist. Her hands bitterly clung to his forearms to relieve the pressure on her shoulder. When they arrived at the stairwell to the basement, her head and neck dropped to the floor. It was quickly becoming a blurry, unknown world that was about to consume her.

"I'm gonna pick you up now. It'll feel nice to cuddle up in my arms. A real man's arms. A man who knows how to treat you right." He stepped forward, lifting Amalia against his chest and throwing her over his shoulders.

Amalia's head knocked into the doorframe as Riley bounded the first few steps. She cried out. Every step he took bounced her body against his. Her arms dangled down the side, almost lifeless. When they reached the bottom step, she raised her head and looked around the unfamiliar basement. Visions of the cellar she'd once been locked in as a child began terrorizing her.

"I've found the perfect spot." His breathing wavered from the effort to carry her down the flight of stairs. Riley leaned forward and dropped her on a slew of old comforters casually piled on the floor.

Amalia breathed in an unrecognizable, heavy chemical odor. It burned her nose as its pungency stifled the remaining air around her. "Please stop." She summoned the last of her strength from what felt like the bottom of an empty container someone had recently discarded, the remnants of any hope that she could still survive. Thrusting herself forward, her hands reached for his neck. The pain in her shoulder disappeared during those first few seconds, only to be replaced by something more formidable. The strongest of a long-forgotten desire to survive persisted. Amalia pressed her fingertips on his throat, hoping the length of her nails would slice his skin and cut off his circulation to render him temporarily weakened. Then she could run for safety.

Riley was too quick. As soon as the first nail reached his throat, he heaved her away with a vicious force, slapping her with the back of his hand. Amalia fell to the floor, her head hitting the cement hard and fast, leaving her body trembling.

Her eyes blinked a few times. In her mind, she was falling asleep. Tired from a long day of working at the store with her father. Counting the inventory. Organizing the tools. Tearing old clothes into rags to dust the shelves.

Except it wasn't rags being torn for the shelves. It was the fabric of her dress being torn, split from the bottom hem up to her waistline.

A noise she would not ever forget. The last thing floating in front of her was the jagged tooth that protruded over Riley's bottom lip. As he formed a smile—no, not a smile, but a huge grin running from one end of his sinister face to the other—Riley savored in his fated and desired moment.

A faint whisper wafted from Amalia's dry mouth. "Jonah."

She listened to Riley's last words before the world left her in his hands with no consideration for all she'd been through in her short eighteen-year life. Riley grabbed her jaw and cheeks, leaning in close while she emptied of any last hope for protection. "Jonah's not gonna want you after I'm done with you."

Jonah with his name drawled longer than she could stand, the last sound pummeling Amalia's consciousness before she cloaked herself with an invisible protective coating and prepared for the consequences of ever allowing herself to have faith again.

Chapter 23

# Molly, September 2004

Molly hung up the phone after Brianna ended their call in a rush to meet up with some forgotten study group. She was certain it was a lie but could do nothing when her daughter wouldn't answer any repeated follow-up calls. Brianna was growing up and changing, suddenly keeping secrets from Molly. It had started with choosing Woodland and now seemed to be centered on much more complex emotions. Brianna was no longer the baby girl who needed her mother for everything. Molly could feel her heart breaking in two over the pain she'd inadvertently caused Brianna by not revealing the entire story about the past.

*Was it time to tell the truth?*

It was a question crossing Molly's mind ever since Brianna revealed her decision to attend Woodland. Its campus was a place Molly struggled to forget for two decades. While there were a few positive memories in the beginning, it'd eventually become the impetus for everything spiraling downhill rather quickly in her difficult life. After things cascaded into oblivion, Molly found herself home in Brant dealing with situations no eighteen-year-old girl should ever have to deal with. As soon as she recognized the words inside her head, Molly remembered that Brianna was also eighteen years old. They were the same age when Molly's life changed forever in the building's basement where she worked with Jonah... with Jonah, whom she still thought about from time to time despite everything that eventually happened between them.

For years, Molly had tried to protect Brianna from all the horror and pain in the world. Living in New York City was difficult in the eighties, especially with all the drug busts, shootings, and theft, but Molly had been insistent on never allowing Brianna to be close to danger. Once Brianna came into the world, Molly had to overcome the past. She watched over the new baby like a mother hen, quick to defend her young no matter who or what tried to hurt them. It wasn't easy raising a child all on her own, too. In the early years, Molly worked part time from home, managing the books for many small businesses to be available to teach Brianna all the things she'd never been taught as a child. Things like how to love, support, and trust the parent who was supposed to cherish and protect you.

Lenny would look out for Brianna from time to time when Molly was working, but he wasn't the fatherly type in any real way that'd counted to Molly. He did what he could without putting in a lot of effort, but Molly only relied on him whenever she was in a jam. She'd luckily found a cheap babysitter, the daughter of a colleague who could watch Brianna while Molly attended night classes and passed her exams to become an accountant. Molly also moonlighted as a cocktail waitress at a sleazy dance club on Friday nights, earning enough in tips to afford everything Brianna needed for soccer. At twelve years old, Brianna had gone to her mother crying about how awful gym class was but would never explain who or what caused the problems. Molly's lack of faith in adolescent girls and her bitter memories of life in Brant quickly convinced her paying for soccer was the right thing to do if Brianna was that desperate to join the team and opt out of gym class.

Between the soccer tournament costs, the uniforms, and transportation, Molly often considered taking on more nights at the dance club. She wrestled with the decision to demonstrate a positive role model for her daughter versus earning enough money to keep Brianna off the streets and away from trouble. The manager at the club often groped

Molly behind the counter or cornered her in the back room when no one was looking. After the third time, she cried herself to sleep not because she was afraid of him or the pressure to keep her job but because it flooded her mind with images of Riley. Crying was the only way to ensure that her mind and emotions would block out the pain. Molly cried to have something to focus on rather than to remember the hem of her skirt ripping or the vile smell of Riley's sweaty body. His vicious attack rarely abandoned her memory despite every attempt she'd made to excise it.

*Was it time to tell the truth?*

After Molly quit her nighttime job, she struggled to pay bills on time. Although her daughter was the priority, being around sleazy men was a problematic trajectory and not something she could maintain. Lenny would let the maintenance payments slide for one or two months, but he reminded her he had to look out for the entire building and couldn't play favorites all the time. She always understood and cut back on lunches or new clothes that would have impressed the boss and possibly earned her a promotion. She'd asked for a raise twice but was told the company's salaries were on hold due to an economic depression impacting the whole city. There was no energy left to argue and ever since she'd run away from Woodland, there was no one to quiz her every afternoon on what was happening in the financial world other than bosses ensuring she was aware of changes to tax laws for her clients. It was a job. A necessity. No longer a passion. Just a way to support Brianna and keep her mind off the past. Life had little meaning other than protecting her daughter.

Her daughter would back down. College would take over her life. Shanelle was becoming a stronger force. It concerned Molly. She respected Shanelle but also worried about the pressure it put on Brianna to do or try things that her daughter was not ready to acknowledge. They say a mother always knows the truth. Molly always believed a mother also knows when to keep secrets hidden until the moment is right.

*It wasn't time to tell Brianna the whole truth.*

# Chapter 24

# Brianna, September 2004

"I can't believe Dr. Jonah West died. When I read that press release on the library computer last night, I freaked out." Brianna slurped coffee and swallowed a spoonful of cereal across from Shanelle at the dining room table.

"I'm so sorry I didn't pick up when you called last night," replied Shanelle. "Study group was intense. Everyone's worried about a pop quiz this week."

"It's okay. I'm still trying to decide what to do. What if he's my father? I have a right to know." The whole situation, all the situations, were becoming too much to handle.

"Wait, Bree. You reminded me of our trip here last June when that car accident happened. Could he have been the driver looking at you?"

Brianna replayed in her mind as much as she remembered from that afternoon. Her heart began beating more quickly, soon matching the pace of the memories that flooded her head. "Maybe he knew I was his daughter, and that's what caused the accident. Wait, there were two people in the car. The police officer pulled both the driver and a passenger from the wreckage. I'm so confused. Should I call the Dean to ask for more information about Dr. West's death?"

"You can't tell the Dean we were there. We could get in trouble for leaving the scene of an accident." Shanelle's voice was forceful and direct. "Plus, you don't even know if Jonah is your father. What if it's Carter?"

"Or what if it was Carter in the car with him? We need to find him, too." Brianna dropped her head against the table with a thud that bounced off the walls and perforated the entire room.

"We can schedule a meeting with the Dean to ask questions about the accident after we come up with a believable story, so he suspects nothing."

"I don't know if I can wait that long."

"Call Malachi and ask him what to do. I'm so sorry, I need to get to my biology lab. We're learning more about DNA today." Shanelle gathered her books and hugged her best friend.

Once Shanelle left, Brianna called Malachi to discover what he'd learned from talking to her mother, but his desire to cease working on the case surprised her. "You're the first guy she's taken a chance on. It'll devastate her to know I hired you to investigate her past."

"She's an understanding woman. I'm sure if I come clean this early, I'll still have a fighting chance."

"This isn't about you, Malachi. You're supposed to be helping me find my father." Everyone was against Brianna at this point. Things were getting hopeless. Soon, all she would have left was to read the journal, but it felt entirely too invasive and menacing. "Not falling for my mother and abandoning my search. I can't do this on my own."

"Maybe as we get to know each other, she'll tell me more."

"If she won't tell her own daughter, what makes you think she'll give you any clues, especially after my mother learns about the false pretenses of how you met?" Brianna had meant it sarcastically, but the anger in her voice was too strong and persistent.

"Are you threatening me?"

Brianna considered his question. She'd never been accused of being malicious before. Did it mean she'd grown a backbone? "No, I just want all the roadblocks to disappear."

"Maybe you should listen to my recommendation."

"Don't forget that you work for me. Start finding me answers." Brianna regretted the flippant words as soon as she'd said them. Her desperation showed, yet she'd no idea how to control it.

"You really need to grow up before you can tell other people what to do. That was uncalled for."

Brianna sighed heavily. "I'm sorry. I just feel all alone. Please, hold off on telling her that I hired you for a few more days. It'll be fine."

Malachi cleared his throat. "I'm in Mississippi. I'm trying to find out more about your mother's parents. I won't reveal anything to Molly for a few more days."

"You're in Brant? What's it like?"

"Desolate. This town barely has a few hundred people in it. I found some newspaper articles about a Graeme family owning a hardware store in the early eighties. Maybe they're related to your mother, but I've got some more research to do before I get on a plane home."

"Thank you. You're amazing. I can't wait to thank Shanelle for connecting us."

"You know how much Shanelle cares about you, don't you? What does she think about your news?"

"Shanelle wants me to read the whole journal. I'm not ready to do that until I have no other choices left." It might give Brianna the answers, but it would also destroy the relationship with her mother. "This is so frustrating."

"Can I give you some advice?"

"I guess."

"You're a smart girl, Brianna. You've obviously got a mother who loves you and a best friend who wants to help you in the search for your father. I know this is important, but you can't let it consume you. Sometimes you have to focus on the things you *do* have in life and not what you *don't* have."

"Aren't you a chipper dude? I appreciate the thought, but that's kinda the problem. Besides them, what *do* I have?" Brianna picked at a scab on her knee she'd gotten in the last soccer match. It was just healing, but she couldn't stop herself from opening the wound again.

"Well, for one thing… you have a chance for a great future if you put your mind to it. Stop worrying about what other people think, say, or do. You have the power here. It's your life. If you keep letting the unknown mysteries of the past color every aspect of your present, you'll wake up one day in the future with nothing but regret over lost time."

Brianna shook her puzzled head in an attempt to sort through his Yoda-like response. Did he have a point or was she just letting herself be talked out of another choice she'd already made? "Live for the moment, carpe diem. That's your advice?"

"Yeah, pretty much. Take advantage of everything you have while you can. Make sure you tell Shanelle how you really feel about her. Don't be afraid. Things will work out for you one day soon."

"You talk a good game. I just wish it were that easy, my friend," replied Brianna. She wanted to believe him more than her brain had the capacity of at that moment. "Let's see if you can help me find my father before you push your way into every other aspect of my life, Malachi. I'm not saying you're wrong, but your messaging is a little too *Pollyanna* for me."

"Fine. I'll save my *solid* advice for someone who can handle it." Malachi snorted. "Maybe I should come out to Woodland to check for clues since Molly spent some time on campus before living in New York?"

"That actually may work."

"Let me visit after this trip is done. I'll call you with the plan later in the week."

"And listen, I didn't mean to be rude or put you off. I just know how I feel."

"We're cool. I get it," replied Malachi.

Brianna disconnected the phone, then spent the rest of the day finishing homework and attending a required freshman seminar on conflict resolution. The key message she'd learned was to spend enough time planning and understanding your opponent's position before you did anything else. She made a list of her steps and prepared to address each one before moving forward—determination to obtain her answers before the weekend was at an all-time high.

Knowing Shanelle planned to spend part of the upcoming weekend with her father, who was in town for a small medical conference, Brianna called Professor Villing to schedule a second date, thus checking off another box on her plan. Things were lining up, letting her fall asleep for the first time in weeks without the fear of everything exploding in her face.

\* \* \*

The rest of the week went smoothly in classes and practice. Brianna earned a 'B+' on the English exam and an 'A-' on one of her papers. The soccer team started to bond and developed a strong defensive line. She joined a creative writing group, hoping it would encourage her to open up to other people.

Malachi called with plans to arrive that Saturday, so he could begin researching Molly's time at Woodland. He also hinted that he had some information to share about Molly's parents back in Brant, but he needed to have a final conversation with someone before he could tell Brianna anything. When Brianna told him about Jonah's death, Malachi asked her to find out when the dean would be around. Brianna checked with his secretary and learned the dean would work the first few weekends during the school year to help new students acclimate to campus life. Rather than schedule a meeting, Malachi convinced her to make it an informal drive-by once they'd found an opportunity to produce a list of questions.

Brianna motivated herself to put more pressure on her mother by revealing that she'd found the journal, in the hopes it would convince Molly to spill anything that could help Malachi's research. The only thing her mother—the opponent in this debate or battle—wanted to protect was the truth. The journal likely held that information, and after exchanging a series of vague questions and answers on a phone call one evening during the week, Brianna dropped her bombshell.

"Did you ever think about being something other than an accountant, Mom?"

"No, I'm a math girl. There's something about things balancing out that makes me feel comfortable. Having specific rules and formulas without any blurry lines," replied Molly.

"You never thought about writing or doing something more creative and personal?" Brianna slowly navigated the conversation toward her end goal.

"Me? No, I'm not one to share my thoughts or let people get too close. I prefer my privacy."

"Not even when you were younger?" Brianna hesitated but pushed herself to cross the line. Now or never. "Like maybe keeping a diary as a teenager?"

There were a few seconds of silence on the phone. "Umm... I don't really remember much from back then. I don't think I would... why are you even asking?"

Brianna's skin crawled with irritation, forcing her to stop the charade. "That's not true. I found the journal in that duffel bag you loaned me. You can't keep things from me anymore, Mom."

Molly gasped. "That's unfair. You were baiting me. Wait, how did you get my journal?"

"That's what you care about? Not that I know you've been lying to me."

"How much did you read?" Anger replaced the hesitation between each of Molly's words.

"I know all about Carter and Jonah. I read several entries, enough to know you slept with them both." Brianna kicked the leg of the ottoman, spilling a few magazines to the floor. "Which one is my father?"

Molly's distressed breathing blasted through the phone. "Brianna, I need you to listen to me. This is important. I know you want to know more about your father, but this isn't the way to do it. Those are my words and memories." Her voice waned as if the energy driving the trajectory of her life had suddenly given up, choosing to flee when it was most needed. "I'll call out of work for a few days and come visit you. We can have some mother and daughter time to talk about this in person."

"I don't believe you." Brianna grew tired of her mother's delays and avoidance. "You've kept these secrets a long time. It's almost like you can't be honest about your past anymore."

"Brianna, listen to me. I'll leave New York tomorrow after work to drive to Woodland. We can discuss everything when I get there. Promise me you won't read anything else until we talk."

Brianna considered her options. She'd finally gotten through to her mother, igniting the issue enough that Molly would drop everything to prevent her from reading the journal. Guilt consumed Brianna for reading her mother's confidential thoughts, knowing she'd have been far more antagonistic if someone had invaded her privacy. Waiting another day or two wouldn't mean the end of the world.

"Fine, but if you're not here soon, I'm going to keep reading until I discover whatever you're hiding from me. If I need to beat down every door on this campus to locate Carter or any information on Jonah, I will find my father. If you won't help me, maybe someone else will." Brianna wondered if her mother was even aware Jonah had died but couldn't bring herself to ask. It already hurt to consider if he were her father, she'd never have the opportunity to meet him. *Did she watch her father die in that car accident months ago?*

"Don't do that, Brianna. If you ever loved me, you would let this stay between us. I would never do anything to hurt you. You need to trust me."

When the call ended, Brianna reflected on the conversation. Molly had provided everything Brianna needed except the one thing she'd actually wanted—to know her father. If he'd been in her life, she would have had someone else to talk to about the unsettled feelings and attractions she'd been dealing with. Or maybe Brianna would have known for sure, early on, if she was meant to fall in love with men or women. Her father might have been open-minded and helped her through the discovery process. The guilt ate at her over not revealing the dates with the professor to her Shanelle, her best friend. Or girlfriend. She and Shanelle never kept secrets from one another. *What exactly were they at this point?*

Her problem was not having all the pieces to the puzzle and feeling unequipped to decide what was right for her own future. When Doug wanted to have sex, she'd known he wasn't the right guy. He was a player, an immature guy who wanted to get laid. He'd no charisma or maturity. Professor Villing, though potentially too old for her, offered a unique experience. Sensuality. Flirtation. Knowledge. Power. Charm. After thinking about how her mother had slept with a professor, Brianna convinced herself sleeping with a man was a necessary step to solving her own problems. It was time to lose her virginity and prove once and for all if she was attracted to guys. Perhaps if it felt like the earth moved below her while they were together, she'd find her answers. If not, she'd know for certain if her inconsistent attraction to men was just a way to protect herself from taking the plunge into the reality of accepting she was a lesbian—to keep checking the boxes. One at a time. That was the best approach to solving the dilemma.

* * *

After classes the next afternoon, Shanelle left to meet her father for dinner. Feeling desperate for a night of pampering, she opted to sleep in the guest bed in his five-star hotel room before returning to campus the following morning. Once Shanelle confirmed she wouldn't be home until the next day, Brianna invited the professor to the apartment and ordered food from a takeout place for their second date. She slid into a short black dress and checked her image in the mirror—sexy, not as hot as Shanelle made her the day of prom, but good enough for the date. And men liked dresses, right?

When the doorbell rang, Brianna reminded herself it was all to prove a point, to figure out the truth. "Welcome. Thanks for coming to my place."

"Miss Porter, an orchid for the table. None of that red rose tradition for someone as devilish as you." He leaned in as if to kiss her cheek, but at the last minute pulled her lips to his with a gentle nudge from his hand.

After recovering from the strangeness of the kiss, she invited him inside. "They're beautiful. Make yourself at home."

"I take it that means you want me to strip down to my briefs, pop on the TV, and drape myself across your sofa?" He smiled wide, then winked. "And stop calling me *professor*. It makes me feel so old."

"Then stop calling me *Miss Porter*. It's like we're living in the nineteenth century. I'll go get my corset, kind sir." She curtsied.

He bellowed with a solicitous tone. "Agreed. So, about that sofa?"

"Don't get me too excited. You just arrived." Brianna couldn't help herself. Something about him encouraged her entirely too direct and flirtatious responses. At first, she blamed it on his eyes. They were such a beautiful and intense color summoning her attention no matter what words crossed his lips. As she spent time with him, it was more his ability to straddle the line of charming yet seductive that excited her—his perfect balance between devil and angel. Brianna had often found herself equally trapped between two decisions but ill-equipped to handle the subtlety or the repercussions of a middle ground. His demeanor represented a confidence and comfort she longed to find within herself.

"No one said we don't have enough time for both flirtation and getting to know one another. They're not mutually exclusive, right?" He followed her into the kitchen, his hand folded in hers.

Brianna turned and pushed him against the wall, eager to get her first time over with. "Nothing with me is mutually exclusive right now." Despite what her gut said, it was time to push herself over the finish line. To decide for herself if she would enjoy being physically intimate with a man. Her hand detangled from his, then her fingers slid across his hips, locating his belt. "Maybe the sofa is the right idea."

"Are you saying what I think you're saying?" While their bodies pressed close together, he flipped her around, so she was against the wall. "Because I would love something pretty hot to happen before we eat dinner. If you know what I mean."

Brianna looked beyond him, down the hallway and into Shanelle's room. As her fingers wandered the professor's body, unbuttoning his jeans, and slipping her hands in between the fabric and his skin, his lack of underwear became obvious. "I thought you said on the sofa *in your briefs*. There are no briefs."

"It's just an expression. I thought you might try a little wishful exploration today." He undid the zipper on her dress, sliding his hands across the curve of her back. "I'm glad I was right."

Brianna struggled to keep her focus on him. On his body. On what they were potentially about to do. She kept looking back down the hall. As her gaze narrowed in on the small pillow on Shanelle's bed, the one Brianna had bought for her earlier that year on her birthday, she rationalized her actions. If she never slept with a man, she might not truly know. If she was meant to date Shanelle, then it's better to get this out of her system and know for sure. But if Brianna found herself truly excited and lusting for the professor, then it would be time to end things with Shanelle sooner rather than later. This alternative approach was for Shanelle as much as it was for Brianna.

She led him to her bedroom and slipped the dress off her waist. "I know I said the sofa, but my mattress is much more comfortable." She shut the door and shoved him toward the bed. Brianna undressed him, admiring the taut flesh and muscles on his body, uncertain if it was the athlete in her that found toned male bodies attractive or an actual interest in him sexually.

When they were both naked, he rustled several through his hair. "So, any chance you have a condom? In my haste to come over, I didn't think to bring one."

"You know, I do… seems like something important to keep around, right?" Brianna laughed and pulled him into a kiss. They soon fell to the bed and made love. While it was happening, Brianna's thoughts drifted from him to Shanelle, to Jonah West's accident, and to Molly's diary. All the things bouncing around in her mind stole prominence over their activities even when he was inside her and climaxed. Though he was skilled when he touched her, it had little emotional connection for her. The physical side of their encounter brought more pleasure for him, purely intended for him, but not fulfilling for her in a way that aroused or interested her in doing things to him in return. It was just an opportunity to expel directionless energy, a way to work off a few calories. The earth never moved once. If anything, it stood so still she thought life had ended.

When they finished, he caressed the side of her shoulder and upper arm, basking in the afterglow. "That was fun."

Brianna smiled. "I may have been a bit distracted. I'm sorry. I suppose first times are always a bit awkward, huh?"

He sat up with widened eyes and responded in a hollow voice. "That was your first time?"

"Sort of." Brianna's lips formed an awkward smile. "I told you I was still deciding how I felt about guys and that I kind of had a girlfriend."

"I wish you'd told me beforehand." He jumped up from the bed, haphazardly searching for his pants. "I would have been easier. More attentive. Maybe not done this all the first time." He reached for his shirt and covered the lower part of his body. "Are you okay?"

Brianna grabbed her bra from the corner of the headboard. In the rush to have sex, their clothes had flown in every direction. "It's totally fine. I wanted to do it. I've experimented before. Just never gone all the way with a guy."

He suddenly showed a more innocent side of his nature, mirroring a crushed lover. "Well, maybe we should eat some food and talk about it. I like you a lot, but I don't want to pressure you. I've learned that lesson before."

"Your ex-wife?"

"Not exactly. Someone who slipped away. You remind me..." he said, shaking his head. "Never mind."

They dressed in silence, then Brianna left for the kitchen to set the table with takeout Italian food. Though glad she pushed herself to sleep with him, there was a clear recognition it was not what she'd expected. He knew what he'd been doing, but it didn't excite her in the way she'd hoped it might. It was too soon to be certain what it all meant. When he returned from the bathroom, Brianna motioned for him to join her at the table.

They began eating and covering trivial items about Woodland, favorite colors, and the weather. It was one of the most uncomfortable conversations she'd ever had with someone in her life. He scarfed down his food, then stood. "I should probably get going." He grabbed his keys and wallet from a small table in the hallway on his way toward the door. "This got weird. Not you. Just the communication between us."

Brianna followed him, grateful he was choosing to leave. "Listen, I wanted it to happen. I don't know what it means for me yet, but I do like you. I'm just not sure what to think. It could have been my nerves or something." She leaned in and kissed his mouth with curiosity about what might change now that she'd finally taken a bigger step forward.

He pulled away and brushed a few wisps of hair away from her face. "You're very sexy. We should go out another time, but let's take a few days to figure this out before we meet again." He turned the knob and backed up to fully open the door. "I had a good time, Brianna. Call me soon."

As he edged through the doorway, he flinched when someone blocked his path from exiting into the hallway. Molly abruptly stopped, her face pale and skin a bit flushed. "Brianna, I didn't know you had company. I got here as soon as I could."

Brianna realized her mother left New York much faster than she'd previously indicated. "Umm, this is Professor Villing. He just dropped off a few notes for me on his way back to campus."

"Carter?" said Molly. Her eyes grew large and disappeared into a blank void where flashes of her past stole all sense of life.

"Amalia Graeme?" he replied. "I was just thinking about you."

Molly nodded. "Yes, it's been years." Her skin blanched a ghastly shade of white. "What are you—"

Brianna's gaze darted from her mother to the man she'd just slept with. "You know him? Wait, did you just call him *Carter*—"

"Not now, Brianna," Molly interrupted, shoving Brianna back into the apartment. She then pulled Carter a few steps into the outside hall. "I need to talk to my daugh… Brianna… about something important. It was nice seeing you again, Carter." Molly entered the apartment and slammed the door shut.

"Mom, was that *the Carter* from your diary?" The confusion plastered across Brianna's face set the tone for the conversation. She rushed past her mother and waited near the door. "It can't be. His name isn't Carter, it's…" Brianna struggled to remember his name, suddenly realizing she never once asked. Nor did he volunteer it. It hadn't been listed on his card either. Had she really been calling him Professor Villing the entire time she'd known him?

"Brianna, let him go. We need to talk." Molly's voice grew agitated. The veins on the side of her temple pulsed furiously. Blood rushed through them to bring oxygen to a brain quickly trying to adjust to the room spinning around her. "Malachi told me you hired him to investigate my past."

Brianna opened the door to check if he was still around. A stunned expression across Professor Villing's—Carter's as she now knew—face stared back. "I'm so sorry. I'll call you tomorrow."

Brianna shut the door and turned back to her mother. "I don't care about Malachi right now. Please don't tell me Professor Villing is the guy from your journal."

Molly interrupted. "Yes, that's Carter, and he's the same guy. I told you not to contact anyone. You promised me you'd stop reading that journal." Molly pulled her hands to her head, cupping her entire face and pressed her fingers to her eyes.

Brianna fell against the wall, her body sliding down its vast length in slow motion. When she reached the ground, her head slunk into her lap and her neck tensed. Nausea and despair convulsed deep inside the pit of her stomach over what she'd done. "I didn't meet him from your journal. I met him at Woodland. We went out on a few dates." Brianna's body twisted into a fetal position as disturbing thoughts raced through her mind about who she'd slept with.

"Please tell me you're joking." Molly dropped to the floor, shaking her daughter with an unparalleled urgency.

Brianna looked up. "Don't tell me he's my father. Please don't tell me I slept with the man who might be my father."

As the words flew from her mouth, Brianna agonized over the options. If Carter wasn't her father, that meant her father was Dr. Jonah West, who was dead. Either path leading to her father meant utter destruction, chaos, and a far worse emptiness than ever before. She wept against her mother's chest, heaving her body as though something dark was about to break free. "Please tell me which one my father is. Jonah or Carter. I can't handle this, Mom. Please." Tears dripped from her eyes. Brianna's hands jostled Molly feverishly while trying to shake free all the answers she'd been searching for her whole life.

Molly shivered on the floor, numbly letting her daughter toss her back and forth like a seesaw. "I don't know, Brianna. I don't know who your father is."

Brianna fell forward and clutched the sofa in a desperate attempt to control every nasty thought running through her head. "How can you not know which one it is? Weren't you safe? Didn't you use condoms with both?"

Molly shook her head back and forth. "You don't know what it was like for me growing up. What I lived through at home with my mother." She sobbed, mascara raced down her cheeks. "I don't know because it wasn't just Carter or Jonah. There was someone else... something else happened."

Brianna heard the words leaving her mother's mouth, yet she couldn't believe them. Not only was there a chance she'd just lost her virginity to the man who could potentially be her father, but she'd learned her mother had slept around years ago with multiple men. At least three, and the woman had no clue which one had fathered her daughter.

"Are you fucking serious?" Brianna pushed her mother away, violent enough that Molly flew against the table and smacked her head against the wall. "You're disgusting. Now I know why you never told me the truth about my father. I can't believe I've got a whore for a mother."

"I'm not a whore," Molly whispered. "I did nothing wrong."

Brianna reached for her keys, then stumbled to the door and tried to turn the handle. After gagging, she recovered, pulled it open, and looked back at her mother preparing to say something when Molly interrupted her.

"You don't understand, Brianna. It's not what you think." Molly held a hand against her cheek where a few drops of blood mixed with tears. Her fingers slowly crept to the back of her scalp as memories of her past came flying toward her from all directions.

Brianna ran out the door, incapable of listening to anything her mother said. "I don't care right now, Mom. I can't be anywhere near you. You better be gone when I get home."

# Chapter 25

# Amalia, March 1985

Waking up in the dark frightens many people, especially when unfamiliar with their surroundings. Often it starts out like a dream, a state of confusion with peculiar imagery flashing quickly before adjusting to the surrounding space. When Amalia's eyes fluttered open for the first time that morning, she assumed she'd awoken from a nightmare and forced herself to return to what should have been a peaceful slumber.

Then the throbbing pain in her shoulder sent sharp signals all throughout her upper body. Signals that carried memories of the last few hours her brain had permanently recorded before falling asleep or losing consciousness—she wasn't certain. Crashing onto her shoulder. Intense pain walking into the academic building. Searching unsuccessfully for Jonah. Listening to the security guard. Fearing the strange noises in the hallway. And then Riley. When Riley's image popped into her head, she shot straight up off the cold cement floor, stunned as a flood of the more dark and prominent memories surfaced. A chill shivering the course of her entire lower half replaced the pain in her upper body.

With her hands plastered against her clammy skin, Amalia breathed in deeply, hoping to teleport home to the safety of her bed. Not sure which home as everything she'd loved distanced itself from her at that moment. When her hands searched for the source of the chill, she noticed the long tear in her dress, red scratch marks on her raw skin and the absence of her undergarments. Her naked body ached with intense pressure. Almost burning where she knew it shouldn't burn.

Amalia reached with shaky fingers for a blanket from a pile of linens next to her on the cement. Her head nodded, and her upper body swayed with the hope of calming herself down, but she couldn't. One by one, flickers passed of everything that'd happened in the basement. Remembering where she was, Amalia tried to stand, but her legs wouldn't support her weight, a weight that was much heavier than she'd ever known before.

When her mother had beaten her as a child, it'd always left her hurt and confused. Her skin would blister. A strange numbness persisted for hours. But she could tend to her wounds so they would go away more quickly. While her mother had always been wrong to physically abuse her, Amalia had never fought back. Under the foolish notion children should always listen to their parents, she'd assumed responsibility for what'd happened years ago.

Kneeling on the ground with her hands grabbing hold of a rickety metal shelving unit to help pull her to her feet, Amalia knew she bore no responsibility for what'd just happened. She'd certainly not invited this wretched brand of evil into her life. She'd tried to fight back but wasn't strong enough. As she leaned against the cement wall, Amalia searched the room for anything to wrap around her waist and disguise her naked body. A sheet with dark stains lay on the floor near her. It had a few holes, but she tossed it around her waist. As her fingers tied a knot near her left hip, a wet substance saturated her skin.

Her blood. From where her head had fallen against the floor when he first pushed her down. She raised her hands to the back of her scalp and cringed at the beginnings of a scab that formed beneath clumps of dirt-soaked hair. Amalia needed to get home to inventory the insidious damage. And shower. To remove any physical reminders from the night as the emotional ones were certainly permanent. She stumbled up the steps, using the handrail to pull her forward. When she reached the top, the sunlight drenched through the windows into the hallway.

Amalia yearned for the sun to warm her skin. A way to cleanse herself. Her body. Her thoughts. With each step forward, the memories pounded through her unprepared mind. He'd hurt her. Physically. Emotionally. None of it mattered until her escape from the building was completed. She wasn't able to think about finding someone to help her, instead wanting to bury the event deep inside, somewhere it could eventually remain dormant and entombed. It could only ache worse if someone had known and pitied her over what'd happened.

Amalia found her way home briskly walking the outside perimeter of the campus so that no one would catch her on the main grounds. Her hands feverishly searched all around her throat for the necklace her father had given her. It was gone, probably lost in the pile of rags in the basement. She needed to retrieve it but wouldn't allow herself to go back. It was too soon.

When she arrived at her dorm, Amalia couldn't locate her key and assumed it had been lost somewhere the night before. She carefully snuck through a propped open back door. The cleaning staff in the main lounge emptied the kitchen garbage pails and sprayed air freshener.

A red-haired older woman left the room and walked toward the bathrooms, leaving her keys on the countertop. Amalia ran into the kitchen area, grabbed the master key, and quickly opened her door. She unlocked it from the inside, then dashed back across the hall and threw the keys onto the floor near the kitchen counters. Hopefully, the cleaning lady would think they'd fallen to the ground.

When Amalia returned to her dormitory room and truly looked inside, the pit in her stomach grew even larger. Half the entire room had been emptied except for a single bed frame, mattress, dresser, and small corner desk. Rachel had moved out in the last twelve hours, leaving behind only a brief note.

*The school kicked me out for non-payment. I also had to get away from the baby's father. He definitely won't be able to support me. Be careful. I'll try to write to you when I know*

*what I'm doing about the pregnancy. The clinic told me that
I must decide by tomorrow. - Rachel*

Amalia's only other friend was now gone, leaving her crushed and confused and with no one to talk to about what Riley had done to her. The room faded as cold as the insides of her wearied body. She hid behind her door, listening to the noises in the hallway for twenty minutes until confident the campus staff had finished cleaning the floor and moved elsewhere in the building. Amalia grabbed her shower caddy and dashed to the bathroom. After catching her reflection in the large mirror above the sinks, she began to cry—not a flood of tears or even a pool floating around the whites of her eyes—just two single tears slowly streaming down her cheeks. Her mother had always told her she'd find misfortune. It devastated her to know the woman had been right. Not that Amalia had done anything wrong, but trouble always found her even when she behaved.

As she turned on the water in the shower, Amalia considered her decision to wash away any evidence of Riley's attack. Though he deserved to go to prison for what he'd done, reliving those moments by telling a police officer, a lawyer, or a courtroom seemed impossible. In her ethics course that semester, they'd learned a few basics about the law and reporting crimes. It was never easy on the victim. Being a victim was not who she wanted to be anymore. If Riley was potentially Rachel's ex-boyfriend, Amalia needed to forget what'd happened on every level and escape as soon as possible.

Amalia had long suffered from each of her mother's treacherous insults and abuses. She'd endured the malicious words the girls in Brant slurred at her every week. Carter pressured her to do whatever he wanted her to do. Riley attacked her in a way no one ever had before. She wouldn't agonize anymore about what people had done to her in the past. It was time to move on and get away from every negative part of her life.

After brutally scraping and scrubbing her skin raw to eliminate any trace of him, Amalia dropped to the cold tile floor. Her fingers viciously ripped open a couple of cuts, barely noticing the steady stream of blood swirling around the shower drain. Physical pain meant nothing to her in those moments. She squeezed into a tiny ball for what mimicked an eternity until finally pushing herself to tend to the scratches left behind. Amalia applied antibiotic cream to her wounds, then wrapped herself in a clean white towel and curled up on her bed, staring at the ceiling. An hour passed when her mind slowly built walls around the memories, and her stomach churned to the point of vomiting. Breathing in the damp basement air, or screaming, had parched her throat raw. It could have been either one, nor did it matter at that point. She climbed down the ladder and noticed the light on the answering machine furiously blinking at her. Seven messages.

Amalia replayed each one, all from Jonah, who'd been worried when she never showed up at his place. The last from just an hour ago indicating he would call the police if she didn't show up by noon. Upon noticing there were only a few minutes to spare, Amalia picked up the phone and swallowed hard to prepare herself for the conversation.

She wanted to tell him what'd happened but couldn't bring herself to do it. Jonah knew she'd slept with Carter and then with him. If he thought she'd also been with Riley, he'd call her the same nasty names her mother had always viciously tossed at her feet. Amalia wasn't a whore. It didn't matter that she didn't want Riley. That she didn't ask him to touch her. That she didn't invite it. That he took something from her. The only thought passing through her mind at that moment was how Jonah would handle what'd happened to her after she left his house yesterday.

The phone rang only once before Jonah spoke. "Hello."

"It's Amalia."

"Amalia, my love, are you okay? What happened?" His voice had a far more desperate tone than she'd imagined. It cracked. It held no confidence. It was as weak as hers.

"I'm fine. I fell and hurt my shoulder. I'm so sorry."

"Do you need help? I can come over."

"No," she cried, scanning the room and frowning at the torn dress on the floor. The bloody sheet tossed on Rachel's naked mattress. The remnants of her confidence shattered in the shower drain, washed away forever. "I went to the campus clinic, but they were already closed. I need to get a few ice packs and something to wrap my shoulder with."

"I have those things here. Why don't you come over? It's only a few minutes' walk. Or do you want me to pick you up?"

"No, I'll come by. It's hard to sit with the pain." Amalia couldn't let him see the room, but also needed to find someone who could help her with the injury. She agreed to meet him within the hour.

Amalia hung up the phone, uncertain if she would tell him what'd happened with Riley. If she'd truly planned to leave campus, she owed Jonah a goodbye and an explanation. He'd been so kind to her.

Between the shower, Tylenol, and pain relief cream she'd rubbed over her shoulder, Amalia found the strength to meet him. As she approached his front door, Jonah swung it open and looked at her with caring eyes and a comforting smile, then noticed a few marks and scratches on her face. "I'm so sorry." He leaned in to hug her, but she pushed him away.

"Please don't. I'm very sore." Amalia lifted her head, unable to look at him directly. She feared he would see right through her and know what'd happened. Or judge her. Even the kindest of men like Jonah couldn't help but hold doubt under these circumstances. She couldn't bear him knowing so soon after Riley had raped her.

"Where did all those bruises come from?" Jonah tried to caress her face, then covered his mouth in concern.

"From the fall." Amalia flinched and stepped backward, worrying he wouldn't believe her story. "I guess I rolled over a few times and banged into the lamppost and tree. It all happened so fast." She'd worn a high-collared shirt to cover most of her neck so the red marks from where Riley had gripped her throat weren't visible.

He reached for her hand, which she accepted. He was gentle, and it relaxed her. Despite a sudden fear of physical contact, she desperately wanted to believe there was some good left in the world. Amalia followed him into the living room and took in the surroundings. She'd remembered the room from her last visit. It was sparsely furnished—no paintings or photos on the wall. No figurines or piles of personal things. Just books and magazines. Almost empty of a personality. The Tylenol had dissipated in her bloodstream, letting her weakened body relax into the cushions of the covered armchair.

"How did you fall?" Jonah sat next to her, his hand not leaving hers. Nimble fingers lightly brushed her skin. At first, she wanted to throw his hand away, but the feeling soon distracted her enough to focus on remaining firm in her choice of words. "I wasn't paying attention on my way over to you and tripped on the edging of the flowerbeds. It was stupid." Amalia's mind flashed to the first time she fell against her shoulder. And then the second with Riley towering over her in the basement. Amalia cringed as her neck tensed up.

Jonah reached for her shoulder with his free hand and began rubbing the back of her neck. "Does this help?"

She gently shoved him away. "Please. It'll be fine, just don't do that right now." Amalia noticed the small scar on his neck. She'd been kissing that spot only twenty-four hours earlier.

"I have some prescription painkillers upstairs if you think they'll help. I had a muscle spasm from sitting at my desk for too long, and the doctor gave me these to help whenever it acted up. I don't need them anymore." He stood from the settee and strode toward the stairs.

Amalia needed time alone. It was too difficult being around him, around anyone. "Yes, maybe that will help."

Jonah navigated the stairs while Amalia hobbled around the room in circles, debating what to tell him about leaving Woodland. If she told him the truth, he'd insist on getting the police and college involved. If she told him her mother needed help in Brant, he'd let her go. Amalia had explained the tenuous relationship with Janet, but not all the sordid details of the past.

Amalia stopped near the beaten-up recliner in the corner, running her fingers across the smooth leather material. She startled as the front door opened, but it wasn't in her direct line of sight, and she couldn't tell who entered the foyer. Amalia worried every little noise would frighten her from that point forward. Questions would always plague her mind as to who lurked behind every wall and if she could ever trust a man again.

Suddenly someone came into view. At first, Amalia thought she was still on the floor in the basement, trapped in a nightmare. Maybe it wasn't over, and she couldn't break free. She focused on his unshaven face. His baseball cap set backward on his head with several locks of greasy hair pushing through the hole onto his forehead. And then on the wrinkled clothes stuck to his body. The same jeans and sweatshirt he'd worn the night before. Riley was in Jonah's house.

Amalia wanted to scream, but a paralyzing fear had taken over her body. She couldn't move from her spot, her feet firmly planted on the floor as if stuck in cement. Her head trembled, then a rough chatter appeared as her teeth banged together with ferocity. It couldn't be. She was hallucinating from her fears. But then he spoke to her.

"I knew you'd come running here."

"Riley."

"Good. I said you wouldn't forget me."

"You can't be here."

"Where? In Jonah's house?"

Amalia nodded as he stalked closer to her. When he was within a few feet, she fell back against the wall next to the recliner.

"Why are you following me?" she whispered, the only volume found within her desperate and nervous throat.

"Following you? No, you don't understand."

Amalia shook her head back and forth, willing herself to wake up or run from whichever reality continued to hold her captive. "Jonah's upstairs. I'll tell him what you did. You better leave."

"Oh, Amalia, my dear sweet, beautiful girl. I belong here." Riley stepped closer, his hands reaching for her body as each slimy word poured from his lips.

"No, you don't." Amalia shoved his hand away from her deteriorated frame.

Riley let her step away. When she balanced herself against the corner hutch, he pursed his lips together as if to kiss her. "I picked you out from all the rest, Amalia."

"What do you mean?" The room closed in on her, filling her with uncertainty over why he'd been in Jonah's house. "Who are you?"

"Rachel was just another way for me to get closer to you. I never cared about her. When I found you that day on campus, you were such a pretty little thing. But I scared you. You were so afraid of the big, bad Riley. I watched you run to him."

"To Jonah?" she mumbled, trying to make sense of the conversation.

"Yeah, away from me and to Jonah. I remember how he flirted with you. You enjoyed it. You were disgusted by me, but you were excited when he touched you." Riley reached his hand toward Amalia.

She smelled his stale body odor from the night before. He hadn't even showered since raping her. "Jonah was kind to me."

"He's always kind to his students. But never to his own son."

All the air disappeared from the surrounding room, as if a giant vacuum pulled the universe into space and left her alone in the void. All she heard was the word *son*. Amalia held herself up against the hutch when the room began spinning. "Jonah is your..."

Riley nodded with his lips set in a full smirk. "Yeah, he abandoned me with my whore of a mother. You're just like her, you know." He dangled Amalia's necklace in the air between them. "Quite a father figure, huh?"

"No, no." Amalia trembled uncontrollably. Her hands went to her neck, remembering when he'd taken it from her the night before. She'd forgotten about it, her mind focused only on what Riley had done *to* her.

"Yes, yes. It's yours. I'm gonna keep it. When I saw what a little tart my father had fallen for, I knew I had to have you myself. He couldn't be the only one to taste you." He swung the necklace back and forth before her as if he wanted to mesmerize her into a trance. Then he licked the pendant that hung from the chain.

"Give it back," she cried, reaching for it. Disgusted by his wagging tongue, Amalia lunged after him to retrieve the only remaining piece of her father back in her hands. She stumbled and fell against his chest.

"I knew you'd come back for more." His words burned against the soft flesh on her cheeks as he whispered to her. He licked the inner shell of her ear with his tongue. "So sweet."

Jonah's voice boomed loudly from the top of the stairs. "Amalia, I found the pills. I'll be right down."

As he descended, Riley pulled away from Amalia. She leaped around him and move toward the front door, shouting, "Jonah!"

Jonah reached the bottom step and looked at Riley, then over at Amalia. "Oh, you've met my son, Riley. I didn't realize he'd come by this morning."

Amalia was unprepared for the words Jonah delivered, assuming Riley had been lying. Memories of being in Jonah's arms as he made love to her traveled the perimeter of her conscious, followed by nightmares of Riley ripping her dress and kissing her lips. "No, he can't be your son."

Riley nodded. "Why yes, don't you remember? I told you he was my father the other day when you nearly knocked me down on campus."

Jonah looked at his son with confusion in his eyes. "Do you two know each other?"

Amalia's heart raced. She'd no breath left in her body and hyperventilated. Her chest heaved up and down as an alarming moan emanated from deep inside her. "No. Can't be. No."

Jonah raced over, pulled Amalia closer, and attempted to rub her back. "What's wrong, Amalia? Do you need water?"

She threw his hands away and nodded at him. She couldn't speak. Amalia wanted to tell him not to leave her alone, but breathing was her priority. The room grew darker once he ran to the kitchen. The cloud over Riley consumed her. She focused on controlling the spasms inside her chest, willing them to release her from their contemptuous grasp.

Riley's hands gripped her neck, squeezing tight enough to darken her skin an unnatural shade of red. "If you even think about telling him or anyone else what happened, I'll kill both of you. I'll kill your Jonah." Jonah with the drawled-out name, the last thing Riley said before he violated her the previous night. "I made Rachel run for her life. It might be time for you to disappear, too."

Riley pushed her forward and then released his hold. He stepped back as Jonah came running in the room with a glass of water he handed to Amalia.

"Drink it slow. Don't swallow too much, focus on breathing." Jonah lifted the glass to her lips as she tried not to gulp it down.

Within a minute, Amalia found her breath and quelled the immediate panic controlling her body. "Thaaannnkkk you." She moved toward the front door, unable to stomach being near Riley any longer. "I need to go."

Amalia couldn't tell Jonah what happened, even if Riley hadn't threatened to kill either of them. Riley was Jonah's son. Jonah would never believe her. He would take his own son's side. She reached for the door handle but had misjudged her loose grip. As she fell to the floor, an instant shock wave of pain permeated her entire body as though a semi-truck plowed into her.

Riley sniggered like a child while Jonah ran to her. Jonah struggled to pick her up, but Amalia shoved him away. "Don't touch me." Her voice carried the beginnings of a wail, but she kept it buried behind a stalwart shield, knowing she wasn't ready to release her pain in front of him. She grasped the door handle and rushed out of the house and down the path. Amalia swore Jonah had been following her, but she was too quick to catch. All the pain had turned to adrenaline, guiding her through every block beyond Jonah's house. All the way to where it happened. She ran to the back door and rushed inside to the basement, passing the cleaning crew who'd been polishing the first floor's marble hallways.

When Amalia arrived near the pile of rags, she searched for any remaining piece of evidence, throwing it in a trash bag. She wiped the spot of blood from the cement floor with the cleaner staring back at her on the metal shelving unit she'd almost knocked over earlier that morning. She rubbed the stain until it was gone. Disappeared from her view. From anyone else's view. From her life. When she finished, Amalia ran up the stairs and tossed the bag in the cleaning crew's large rubber pail.

An older woman stared at her. "Is there a problem, honey?"

"Not anymore." Amalia dashed out the door to her dorm room where she packed her suitcases with clothes, toiletries, her journal, and a few books. Less than an hour after leaving Jonah's house, she bought a ticket at the bus station back to Brant. Desperate to get away from Woodland, from Riley, Jonah, Carter, and the entire life she'd once hoped would provide her an escape, but now accepted was even more horrific than home. The only place Amalia could think of going was to her former prison, Brant, where she could be near her dead father.

## Chapter 26

# Brianna, September 2004

Brianna awoke the next morning with a desperate need for comfort, yet a desire not to be near anyone else. She ignored dozens of missed calls from her mother and Professor Villing, or Carter, as she now knew. She deleted all the voicemails without listening to them, then read a text message from Shanelle, who would arrive home in twenty minutes from brunch with her father.

After leaving the apartment the previous night, Brianna had gone to the athletic building to run the track and work out her frustrations. Her skin wouldn't stop crawling as her mother's revelations, and the fact she may have slept with her father, exploded inside her—if Carter was her father. Curiosity over how to explain such a screwed-up story to him crossed her mind the entire time Brianna circled the track. When they closed the building at eleven o'clock, she'd no choice but to return home, hoping her mother had left. All that'd remained behind was a note from Molly.

*Brianna,*

*I've rented a cabin just outside of town for the weekend. I'll give you some time tonight, but I'll be back tomorrow morning. We need to figure out how to move forward. There's more to the story. I'm so sorry. I love you.*

*Mom*

Brianna crumpled the note into a tiny ball and threw it in the trash, the only place her mother's words belonged. It's where they began—making perfect sense why it should be where they also would end. She quickly showered and waited by the curb for Shanelle to arrive. Brianna hugged Shanelle more tightly than she ever had before after jumping into the car. The moment their bodies connected, Brianna's anxiety level diminished. She needed Shanelle more than she'd realized. "I missed you."

Shanelle pulled away. "What's wrong?"

Brianna explained that Molly had slept with someone else besides Jonah and Carter, that Carter was Professor Villing, and that Molly had shown up sooner than expected. Brianna couldn't bring herself to reveal she'd slept with Carter, afraid of losing the one person who could help her deal with everything that'd unraveled in the last twenty-four hours.

"What a messed-up soap opera! You knew Molly was holding back, but I didn't expect this. Where's the journal? Maybe you can read more before she gets here."

"My mother stole the journal last night. Let's leave now. We're going to the dean's office. If my mother won't tell me the truth, I'll find out myself."

"Whoa, slow down. It's her journal. Technically, you found it, and she just took it back. No one stole anything." Shanelle rested her hand on Brianna's leg as they drove to the administration building. "Isn't Malachi supposed to arrive tomorrow to go with you to the dean?"

"Yes, he is, but I don't care anymore about him or the journal. I just want answers on what happened to Jonah. He needs to be my father." Brianna hunched over against the dashboard, determined to escape all the drama in her life once she got her answers. They arrived twelve minutes later and parked the car in a lot near the building.

"Do you want me to wait outside?" said Shanelle.

"No, I need you. We're finding out the truth today." Brianna looped arms with Shanelle before entering the main building. Dean Clayrent's office was on the second floor. When they showed up, his door was open, and a student was leaving.

Shanelle pushed Brianna into the room, offering the final motivation to get the answers she desperately sought. It was a small office; the walls covered in pictures of former graduating classes and the campus before its recent expansion and renovation.

"Dean Clayrent." Brianna's fingers tapped the doorframe. "Do you have a minute?"

A man in his sixties with thick glasses lifted his eyes from the desk, a surprised expression plastered across his face. "I'm sorry, did we have an appointment?"

Brianna shook her head. "No, but I..." She'd suddenly remembered the lack of a cover story and was uncertain how to begin. His neck craned forward, waiting for her to finish speaking.

"We're here to ask you a few questions about Dr. West. My friend and I wanted to take his class next semester, but we couldn't find him on the registrar's list," Shanelle interrupted, smiling at Brianna, then pushed her closer to the desk. "We took a chance coming by to ask if you might know what classes he's teaching. It's so nice of you to stay on campus over the weekend for students."

Dean Clayrent offered his hand to them. "Certainly, please do come in, ladies."

Both girls took seats. Shanelle spoke. "Thank you, we are very grateful you're making time for us."

Dean Clayrent nodded. "Unfortunately, I must apologize for the news I'm about to share. Dr. West is no longer on staff here." A wistful concern rose as he settled back into the chair. "He died earlier this year. How did you learn about his classes?"

Shanelle threw her hand to her chest. "Oh, that's awful. What happened?"

Brianna crossed her legs to stop them from shaking on the wooden floor.

"There was a car accident. I'm afraid he didn't survive." He paused, letting the news sink in. "What class was it you—"

"Was it only him in the car, Dean Clayrent? Such a sad event." Shanelle leaned toward him to emphasize how much she cared to hear more of the story.

Brianna caught on to Shanelle's intended path to keep the dean from changing the subject to the courses. "Very sad. I heard good things about him. His poor family." Visions of the accident began appearing inside her head. She needed to know who else was in the car that day.

The dean reclined back in his chair. "He was not alone when the accident happened. I never quite understood what... well, it was all rather odd."

"Life is so short, Dean Clayrent. That must have been horrible for you to lose a friend." Shanelle placed her hands on the desk. "I'll say a prayer for his family at church later."

Brianna settled into the chair as Shanelle manipulated the conversation. She admired her friend's energy and tenacity to get the answers. "Yes, we will. Poor family."

"It was his son in the car with him. Very tragic news." Dean Clayrent nodded at Shanelle.

Brianna gasped, then tried to control the thought of learning she might have a brother if Dr. Jonah West were her father. "Was his son hurt, too?"

Shanelle leaned back and grabbed Brianna's hand. "Oh, that would be awful."

"No. By some miracle, he survived the accident."

Brianna couldn't help herself. "Where is he now?" She wanted to meet him, to learn what he knew about her mother and if he had any siblings.

Dean Clayrent redirected the conversation. "Tell me, ladies, surely you didn't come to my office to talk about Dr. West. It was certainly tragic. You had some questions about his classes. How can I help?"

Shanelle coughed, then asked for some water. Dean Clayrent reached under his desk to the refrigerator and retrieved a small bottle. "Take this one, please."

Shanelle swallowed a few gulps, then re-capped the bottle. "The poor son. I'm sure he's terribly upset and having a challenging time handling it all." She shook her head. "Oh, the classes, right. Sorry, we are digressing."

"Yes, his son, Riley, had a troublesome time. He was in a coma for a couple of weeks, but then he moved into a recovery facility. I heard recently he was ready to be released. I'm not certain." He reached for a folder on his desk. "Which class was it you wanted to know about?"

"Business Course 200, Management Theories." Brianna shrugged at Shanelle, who'd thrown her a funny glance and then rolled her eyes.

"Poor Riley. I can't imagine still being in the hospital," Shanelle interrupted by kicking Brianna under the chair.

"Yes, Dr. Norikon has taken over those classes." He handed a sheet with the days and times to Shanelle. "No, it's not a hospital. They moved Riley to the Woodland Institution to recover from his wounds and subsequent depression. He's still in a bit of shock."

Shanelle replied, "Thank you so much. We've taken up too much of your time. We should be going."

"Did you want me to enroll you in the course or connect you with Dr. Norikon? She's a brilliant professor."

"No, that's unnecessary, you're such a busy man. We can take care of it. Thanks again." Shanelle looked to Brianna, who still remained in her chair. "Bree, are you coming?"

But all Brianna could think about was who had been driving the car and staring at her that day. Jonah or Riley?

\* \* \*

Thirty minutes later, the girls arrived at the Woodland Institution. When they stepped out of the car, Brianna's phone beeped. "It's my mom. Why don't you go inside to assess our options?"

"We make an excellent team, don't we?" Shanelle kissed Brianna's lips, then hesitantly pulled away with a glow on her face. "Mmm, maybe there will be more of that later."

As Shanelle rushed inside, Brianna picked up her phone. "Hi. How are you?" It wasn't her mother. It was Carter.

"I've been trying to reach you."

"I know. I had to talk to my mother."

"I have to admit it was a bit of a shock to see her again after all these years. I had no idea you were the daughter of Amalia Graeme."

"Neither did I." Sarcasm emanated from Brianna's lips while she kicked at the curb.

"What do you mean you didn't know?" Carter gurgled at her response.

"Nothing, it doesn't matter." Brianna had no idea who her mother was anymore. Molly had become someone vastly different from who she was twenty years ago when she'd known Carter Villing and Dr. Jonah West.

"I would like to talk with you again. I can explain how I knew your mother."

"That's probably a helpful idea, but I can't right now. Can we meet later or tomorrow? I'll text you when I get done here." Brianna desperately wanted to hang up to first discover any information she could about Jonah and Riley West before having to deliver the news that Carter might be her father.

"Where are you?"

"At the Woodland Institution. I had to stop by to visit someone."

"That's an unusual place to know someone," replied Carter.

"What do you mean?"

"I've been there a few times. I have a friend who is a patient. It's usually for people either in a coma or recovering from depression." His voice grew hesitant as he delivered each word. "And you?"

"I'm checking on something for a paper I'm writing. I gotta go. Call you soon. Bye." Brianna hung up her phone, then noticed her mother had texted.

**Molly**: *Where are you? I'm at your apartment.*

**Brianna**: *Did you know Jonah West was dead?*

Silence for a minute. A few '…' appeared on Brianna's phone, but no words.

> **Brianna**: *Why are you keeping the truth about my father from me?*
>
> **Molly**: *No, that's awful to hear he died. But I haven't talked to Jonah in twenty years.*
>
> **Brianna**: *I don't believe you.*
>
> **Molly**: *Please stop ignoring my calls. Pick up.*
>
> **Brianna**: *I'm at the Woodland Institution trying to find my father. You've been no help.*
>
> **Molly**: *Why are you going there?*
>
> **Brianna**: *To speak with Jonah's son, Riley.*
>
> **Molly**: *NO. STOP. COME HOME FIRST. TALK TO ME NOW, PLEASE.*

Brianna ignored the incoming calls from her mother. She needed to get to the bottom of the past before her mother fabricated any other lies or avoided the truth. She turned her phone off and shuffled toward the entrance of the building.

Shanelle met her in the lobby. "He's on the second floor. Room 212. You need to sign in. I told them you were a family friend who was in town for just a few hours."

"Did they believe you?"

"Were you not impressed by the way I worked Dean Clayrent until we got the answers we needed? I'm good. Too good."

Brianna nodded and leaned in to hug Shanelle. Placing her hands around her waist, pulling her closer. "Yeah, you definitely know how to work things. Thank you."

"You're welcome. I had to contact my father. Doctor privileges to the rescue. He called in a favor and got an approval for you to visit Riley. Riley has been fully recovered for weeks, just not speaking much."

"What did you tell your father?"

"That this was important to me. He knows how much I care about you."

"I'm not sure what I'd do without you."

"We can talk about that later. Go get your answers. Riley's in the corner room. I checked the map."

Brianna paraded down the hallway while smiling at Shanelle's words. A few moments later, she found the nurse's desk outside his room.

A slender woman parked behind a computer workstation stopped typing on the keyboard. "May I help you?"

"Yes, I'd like to visit a patient, Riley West. The front desk called up to mention me. I'm Brianna Porter."

"Oh, yes. Dr. Trudeau notified us that I could let you in. Riley is awake. I'll show you to his room." The nurse locked her workstation and walked around the counter.

"Thank you so much. I've been out of town and just learned about the accident. I feel so awful he was in a coma."

"Yes, but he's mostly healed now. With no family claiming him initially, or anyone available to make decisions, we couldn't do much but keep him comfortable until his insurance ran out. He had one friend stop in a few times, but no one else. Poor guy. I'm sure he'll be relieved to see you." When they reached the room, the nurse led Brianna inside. "Don't push him too much if he doesn't talk. He's easily agitated. We're waiting for the doctor's latest report before he can check out."

Brianna paused for the nurse to leave the room, then rounded the corner toward the bed. She glanced at Riley from the side before he knew she was near him. He was frail and weak. Very fair skin. As if he'd been sleeping for years. She searched for any resemblance, hoping he might have a similar facial structure or eye color, suggesting he was her brother. It was difficult to tell with no lights and the icy temperature in the room. A few chills crept throughout her body when she recognized him as the driver of the car.

Brianna nudged toward the end of his bed until he noticed her. Riley's head rested against a small white pillow, and his arms lay at his side with a tube sticking out of them connected to several machines beeping in the background. He scrutinized her every move, then blanched as white as a ghost when her face came into view.

Brianna stepped forward until her hands rested on the metal rod at the end of his bed. "Hi. How are you?"

His eyes opened wider, and he shifted in the bed, pulling himself into a more upright position. He opened his mouth, but nothing came out.

"Don't be nervous. I know you've been in an accident, Riley."

A harsh cough emerged from his lips. "Can't be."

"Don't worry. It's okay. Take your time. My name is—" She noticed his agitation increasing, then grew uncertain about remaining in the room.

"You were there." He started grunting and shaking his head.

"Shhh… Hold on. I'll get the nurse."

"No." His voice was deep. Gravelly. He reached for her, determined to keep her in the room.

Brianna nodded. "Okay. Do you need something?"

"Amalia. You were there. On the street."

Brianna's heart stopped at the revelation hidden in his words. He thought she was her mother when he'd seen her on the street. Brianna suddenly realized why Riley had been staring at her when driving the car months ago. She panicked at thinking she really had been the reason he drove the car into the building, killing his father. Was she truly to blame for the accident? The urge to comfort and connect with Riley brewed inside her jumbled mind. Was he the family she'd been looking for all along?

When Brianna brushed the top of his hand, Riley screamed and pulled back. Brianna listened to Riley repeat her mother's name as she tried to organize all the information learned the last few days. Riley freaked out, rattling the mattress on the hospital bed and pulling the tube from his arm.

The nurse who'd escorted her from the main desk came running into the room. "What happened?"

"I… I don't know… He started calling out a woman's name. I'll wait outside." Brianna rushed through the door and into the hallway. When the elevator popped open, and a doctor exited onto the floor, she jumped inside and rode it back to the main lobby.

Shanelle waited in the corner chair, texting on her phone. "What's the rush?"

Brianna shook her head. "He called me Amalia. He thinks I'm my mother." She bobbed her head as if it would shake the confusion loose. "That's why he crashed the car. He was shocked to see me that day on campus and just lost control of everything."

"You do resemble her, but Molly's blonde and pale. You've got darker hair and a different body type. I guess from a distance you might look identical." Shanelle pulled Brianna against her chest, rubbing her back in soft circles. "I'm so sorry you're going through such a disaster."

"He flipped out and tried to get out of the bed. I don't know what he wanted. What if he's my brother?" Brianna pushed her hair away from her eyes and focused on a painting on the wall in the opposite side. A watercolor of flowers in a countryside setting. Peaceful. Quiet. That's all she'd hoped for when she chose Woodland. To escape the craziness of New York City. To have an opportunity to meet new people and figure out what she wanted from life. She never expected to be in a place of far greater devastation.

After stumbling upon the journal, the quest to find her father had grown stronger until Brianna couldn't think of anything else but those answers. Her life had spun out of control the last few weeks since leaving home. She was tired of the lies and missing information, reluctant to believe anyone at this point. Everyone had it easier than she did. Why was she being punished?

"Chill, Bree. Look, let's go back upstairs. Maybe he's calmed down and will talk to you. If not, we'll figure out a new plan. You can still push your mom to explain more about the past." Shanelle had always known how to bring a situation from a full boil to a simmer.

Brianna wanted to tell Shanelle she'd slept with Carter, regardless of whether he turned out to be her father. She couldn't keep it a secret from the one person who'd been nothing but honest with her. "Shanelle, I need to tell you something."

Shanelle was distracted by a woman standing in the elevator as the doors pulled shut. "Your mother."

Brianna tilted her head, confused by Shanelle's reaction. "No, not about my mother. I need to tell you something I did. Something foolish."

Shanelle turned around. "No, I think that was your mother hiding behind someone just now. The journal was sticking out of her purse. I think Molly took it from the apartment. I only got a quick glimpse of her face as she walked into the elevator."

"I can't believe my mother has the journal again. We need that to get more answers." Brianna held in an urge to scream and rush over to the elevator. "It can't be. Why would she be here?"

"You said Riley recognized you. He called you Amalia. They must know each other."

Brianna grabbed Shanelle's hand, less interested in explaining what'd happened with Carter, but curious if it were her mother on her way to Riley's room. They trudged the path to the back corner and took the stairs, hoping to beat the elevator if they ran quickly enough.

"I'm gonna confront them both. This ends today," replied Brianna with a determined force ready to throttle anyone standing in the way of her getting the answers she'd been searching for.

# Chapter 27

# Amalia, April 1985

"You got a call from school earlier today, girl. If you don't return by Friday, they'll revoke your scholarship and throw you out!" Janet swished a giant slurp of tea while pointing her bony finger across the room as if she could force her demands on Amalia.

"Okay, Momma."

"Three weeks is long enough to mope around this house over a silly little pain in your shoulder. You don't know pain 'til you've had diabetes." Janet's hand slapped the table, disturbing both the contents of their bowls of oatmeal and the remnants of their brokered silence.

Amalia had returned home by bus two days after Riley attacked her on the Woodland campus. She'd been unable to think about anything but visiting her father's grave, hoping it would bring some solace to her riddled nerves. With no strength to argue, Amalia let her mother shout at her for hours until finally parts of what'd transpired at Woodland leaked from her lips to squelch the woman's acid tone. But Amalia would never tell her mother about the attack, fearful of what the woman would say or do while also impugning her. *Carter had left her after deciding to move to Europe with his mother when he graduated.* It was a lie, but it made the story of his absence easier to accept. Janet viciously blamed Amalia for losing the only opportunity to rebuild the store, highlighting her daughter's foolish notions of love and courtship.

Amalia's shoulder began to heal by the end of the first week, though most of the recovery kept her resting still in bed for hours at a time. She'd gone to the doctor, who prescribed a few painkillers and an antibiotic for the wounds on the back of her head and inner thigh. She hadn't told him what'd happened, instead choosing to attribute the damage to her fall in the flower bed onto a broken statue. The doctor asked a lot of questions, concerned that the wounds didn't match those that would come from such a tumble, but Amalia quickly grabbed her medication and never returned to his office.

By the end of the third week, Amalia processed what'd happened to her at Woodland. Unable to talk to anyone, especially her mother, she spent many days walking back and forth to the lake in search of answers and comfort. The physical scars and pain healed, but every glance in the mirror caused her to twitch and gag over the memories. Even when her mother had slapped her or hit her with the frying pan months earlier, there was a reason. Amalia had talked back when she shouldn't have or failed to clean something to suitable standards. There was some explanation for the punishment. But there was no explanation for what Riley had done to her.

No one could ever know that she'd been so careless and dirty, that she'd become a whore. Was Amalia too flirtatious? Did she not cover up her body properly? Had her desires for Jonah caused her to forget how to hold tightly onto her innocence? Had the rape been a punishment because she'd cheated on her boyfriend? She entertained every theory but could never quite settle on the right one.

Amalia contemplated what to do next with her life now that everything had changed. She returned to Brant only because there'd been no other place to go. She couldn't remain in Woodland for fear of seeing Jonah or Riley again. Or even Carter, who called a few days after she'd gotten home, hinting at coming by for a visit if she was interested in patching things. Amalia had picked up the phone expecting it to be the contractor requesting money for the next round of construction on the store. When Carter spoke, her voice went rigid and silent. She'd wanted to talk to him, but the words wouldn't appear. He kept asking if she was okay and why she hadn't been in school. When Amalia never responded, he told her he was through trying to repair things with her and that she should crawl back to Jonah if that's what she truly wanted.

Jonah was whom Amalia wanted at one time, but not anymore. As much as Jonah could have been her future, yet another man had been stolen from her life without any ability to prevent it. First, Amalia's chance with Bryan was ripped away when her mother intervened. Then the fire stole her father as punishment for what she'd done on the couch with Carter. Riley pilfered any hope for her future when he forced himself on her. The universe had a mind of its own when it told her she'd never be worth enough for anyone to love.

Amalia collected her dishes and clumped to the kitchen. Rain was in the forecast that day, meaning no walk to the lake. The Dodge was still not working. She was trapped inside the house with her mother.

Janet gulped the last of her oatmeal and dropped the spoon into the ceramic bowl. It resonated throughout the room, piercing Amalia's ears with the rattle of a thousand spoons. "Take my bowl, too. Don't be lazy."

Amalia ignored her mother's commands, dropping only her dishes in the sink. "I'll wash those later when I'm good and ready." She rounded the corner and headed up the stairs to her bedroom.

After pushing the door closed, Amalia grabbed her journal and began another entry.

*Dear Diary,*

*I stare at things all the time lately. I can't focus. I watch bugs crawl up the wall and wait for them to drop to the ground and die. I see Momma shuffle across the floor and hope she might fall. Her blackened toes are withering away from not taking care of herself anymore. I almost smell the rancid flesh. But I can't find the energy or desire to do anything that might help her.*

*I hate when the sun sets in the evening. I will it with all my energy to rise as soon as possible, but it never happens. I'm afraid of the dark these days. I sleep with the lights on, but I really don't sleep anymore. Something always chases me when I close my eyes.*

*When I visit the lake, I think of Jonah. And how he cared for me. He reminded me so much of Daddy. Not just in maturity, but in who he is deep down. Honest. Loving. Thoughtful. We could have had something.*

*Not like with Carter. Carter is too young and immature. He only wants to take me to bed. He longs for things he could never have here in Brant. He would have left here just as soon as he arrived. I know he wouldn't have been happy running a hardware store. Pushing him away is the only answer. I didn't mean to hurt him by being with Jonah.*

*I don't know where to go next. Momma understands we will lose the store. We can't run it. She won't run it. And I'm not strong enough. I need to leave Brant, but I have nowhere else to go. I only came home to recover, to feel close to my father. Old Spice is no longer a comfort. It stings as brutal as a piece of glass cutting open raw skin.*

*What Riley did will always torment me. I can't let myself think about him. My body shakes whenever I remember that sound of my dress ripping and him pulling me toward the floor.*

*I'm so tired. I need to...*

Amalia awoke the next morning to rain pelting the window across the room. She stirred in the comfort of her bed with gratitude for finally catching a few hours of rest, even if it'd occurred in erratic spurts. No one chased her this time. There were no happy dreams, but at least no nightmares.

Amalia rolled her body onto its side, landing on the pen which had slipped underneath while she slept. She rustled her hands atop the comforter, searching for the journal, but it wasn't anywhere she checked. Amalia swung her legs over the side of the bed, assuming it'd fallen to the floor.

When she stood from the bed, tossing the pillows aside and ripping off the comforter, fear crept about her skin. The fine hairs on her arm stood tall. Amalia dropped to her knees and extended her arms underneath the bed. But the journal was nowhere to be found. Panic set in.

Amalia rushed down the stairs only to find her mother sitting on the couch, devouring a piece of freshly made apple pie. "Momma, did you take anything from my room?" Her back tensed as she darted around in search of the only thing she had left from her father. The place was dirtier than usual. No one had cleaned in weeks. A half-empty carton of sour milk sat on the coffee table and its stench overtook the air.

"This pie is one of my best, girl. What a shame it's almost gone. I assumed you wouldn't want any." Janet shoveled another forkful into her sweaty, quivering lips. She growled with wild fury, a beast who knew it had the upper hand.

Amalia ran to the dining room, then the kitchen. Dirty bowls and dishes filled the sink high above the arm of the faucet. Crumbs covered the countertops. Flour and sugar were strewn across the floor. But no journal.

"It's a mess in here, Momma." Amalia leaned against the refrigerator door, compelling herself to remember where she might have left the journal. Certain she had it before falling asleep, nothing made any sense.

"Yeah, clean those up, girl. I'm in the middle of a fascinating book I stumbled upon."

Amalia's heart plummeted deep inside her weight-laden chest. "No, that's mine. Give it back." Her legs kicked up dust as she ran to the living room to protect her secrets.

Janet sat on the couch, retrieving the journal from underneath a pillow nestled at her side. She listened to the diary's pages slap against one another while fanning them near her ear. "Is the temperature getting hot in here, child? Or is it just these steamy words you've been writing?"

Amalia rushed to snatch the journal from her mother's shaky hands but fell into the cushions and buried her face in the couch, screaming. "It belongs to me. You're an awful woman." Anger flooded her entire body with rage at everyone who took things from her without ever asking permission. Always what other people wanted, never what she wanted. She squinted at her mother, lasering in for attack.

Janet flung her free arm toward Amalia, landing an open slap against her daughter's flushed face. "You apparently know how to keep those boys interested by turning into everything I ever said you'd become."

The intensity of being powerless thrashed Amalia. She sank into the couch, caressing her cheek from the sharp pain. She needed a moment to consider how best to retrieve the only item she'd trusted to keep her thoughts. "Please, Momma, just give it to me."

"When I'm done reading it, you can have it again. I'm not that cruel." Janet's eyes lit up as though she enjoyed torturing her daughter. "I see how you need a place to keep secrets. Since you got so many of them, you little hussy."

Amalia stifled the need to bash her mother with anything in reach. She pushed forward on the couch until her legs landed on the floor and pulled herself to a seated position. Janet's sickening Vicks VapoRub odor and the glossy shine around her mother's greasy neck saturated the room, now overpowering the sour milk. "Shut up, Momma." Amalia shrieked loudly. At the world. At God. At anyone who would listen to her.

"I should have started with the first page, but I didn't know what I was reading. You must have been writing up there in that dirty bed of yours. You've been fibbing to me about Carter." Janet popped a hard candy from the bowl on the coffee table into her salivating mouth.

The crunch of plastic unwrapping sent frenetic convulsions throughout Amalia's body, reminding her of all the times in the past when her mother slurred insults at her. She shook back and forth, grinding her teeth against one another. "I had to lie about it."

"I see. It also sounds to me like you let all those boys touch you, get inside you." Janet flipped open the journal to an earlier entry and read from it.

> "*And Jonah was so loving when he took me in his arms in the bed where I dreamed about our future. I felt genuine love from a man for the first time. I wanted his hands on my body as eruptions of lust poured from...*"

"Stop reading." Amalia covered her ears with both hands, humming tunes inside her throat to keep the anger from growing. As she throttled back and forth, images of Riley carrying her down the basement stairs pounded inside her head.

"It's a good thing I told that Bryan boy to stop sniffing around you when he came back to visit after your father died." Janet clicked the candy between her teeth and glared directly at her daughter. "What are you shaking like a baby for over there, child? You're a grown woman from what I read about your little activities back at school."

The words burst from her mother's mouth as circuits would blow during a lightning storm. Amalia's body tensed, reaching a rhythmic pulse while bouncing on the edge of the couch. "What do you mean Bryan came back here?"

"He stopped by after you returned to school... I think he wanted to pay his respects for your daddy passing on. Maybe check on you. Bryan told me he'd takin' a liking to you and thought maybe you two might get together in the future." Janet's index finger scratched bits of candy from the remaining teeth she still had in her mouth.

Amalia's head twisted away from the floor and back to her mother. "What did you tell him about me?"

"Oh, not very much. I just said you'd planned to marry that Carter boy and settle down real soon." Janet's finger slid from her lips, a piece of moistened apple pie crust stuck to her fingernail. She looked down at it as though it were her last meal and nibbled away.

The sucking noise from her mother's dirty lips sent shivers through Amalia, prompting her to stand tall and stiff. She was unable to handle any more venom from the woman. "You are the devil. You ain't no mother. You are nothing but a nasty, bitter old woman who should've died years ago."

Janet popped another hard candy in her mouth and flipped pages in the journal. "I'm a little confused. First, you lust after Bryan. Then you want Carter. What about this professor, Jonah?" She extended the latter part of Jonah's name. "I think little whores like you are the veritable devils, child."

Amalia thought of nothing else but Riley at that moment. She lunged toward her mother. Every foul insult channeled its way through her memory until Amalia wrestled her mother to the ground. She'd never been a violent girl, but the rage inside her had grown so volatile nothing could control it.

While rolling around on the floor, they knocked over the coffee table. The bowl of candies slid across the room, and the journal fell from Janet's hands. A puddle of sour milk dripped around them on the floor, pooling closer to the open pages.

"I never wanted you anyway, Amalia. You were an accident I prayed went away. I got this damned sickness because of you."

Amalia rolled on top of her mother to stop her from speaking. "I hate you."

Janet lay flat against the floor, one arm twisted behind her back, staring up at her daughter. Her breath grew winded, and her face reddened. She tried to speak but couldn't find any words. The candy slipped into the woman's throat and blocked her airway, causing her to choke and gasp for air. Janet's face turned blue as her greasy gullet swelled with fierce intensity. She coughed, then wheezed for breaths that no little interest in finding their way to her.

Amalia gripped harder and tighter, growing frightened as the room spun around her when she lost full control. She forcefully squeezed her mother's neck, banging Janet's head against the floor.

The phone rang in the background. Janet's free hand reached up and tried pushing her daughter away. After six rings, the machine picked up.

*Graeme residence. Leave a message.*

Her father's voice summoned a calm to counter Amalia's raging fury. Her arms weakened, and her hands pulled away from Janet's neck.

Janet threw herself forward with such force, the candy dislodged from her throat, flung out of her mouth, and landed on Amalia's cheek.

The machine recorded a message. "Hi. This is Dr. Jonah West. I'm calling about one of my students, Amalia Graeme. I would like to speak with her about her absence from campus. If you could have her call my office as soon as possible, it would be greatly appreciated. Thank you."

Amalia never even noticed the butterscotch hitting her skin, nor the message left on the answering machine. She pulled her slippery hands away from her mother's neck, the smell of the Vicks VapoRub dominating all her senses at that moment. Amalia had fallen into a trance, unaware of anything around her, as though she floated above the room watching it all happen.

Janet panted uncontrollably, throwing her hand against her chest. Her face had swelled and turned a deep bluish purple, as if she had an allergic reaction to something touching her skin. "Amaliaaa... Help me." Janet reached for a broken table leg and banged it against the couch to divert her daughter's attention.

Both the noise and her name being called released Amalia from her temporary distraction. She looked around for Riley but couldn't find him. He was never there. It was only her mother choking and clutching her chest. "What's wrong, Momma?" Amalia panicked and attended to Janet, grabbing her hand and forehead.

"Heart." Janet tried speaking but only got out a few words. "Attack." She heaved forward, sweating profusely as the lids of her eyes fluttered shut. "911."

Amalia took in the room's expanse as her body filled with indignation. She noticed her open journal tucked under the couch. Her feet sank into puddles of liquid and candy spilled on the floor. Upon remembering that Janet had read the intimate details of her days at Woodland, Amalia grabbed the broken table leg from her mother's hand, uncertain if she had the courage to do what she desperately yearned to do next. She raised it high into the air, mumbling under her breath about someone needing to pay for all the pain and hurt. Amalia slammed the table leg down in front of her with every drop of energy left in her body. She descended to the carpet in tears as blood dripped from the splintered wood and fell into the pool of soured milk.

"Oh, what have I done?" screamed Amalia until her voice went hoarse and her body limp.

Chapter 28

# Brianna, September 2004

Brianna and Shanelle huddled in a nearby corner while the front desk nurse took a bouquet of flowers from Molly. When the nurse approached the back of the reception area a few seconds later, Molly dashed toward Riley's room unnoticed. The journal stuck out of her handbag, bouncing feverishly as Molly rushed down the hallway.

Brianna wanted to run after her, but Shanelle held her back. "Wait. I've got a plan. Let me find out what your mother said to the nurse. Then you go to Riley's room while we're chatting."

"Brilliant."

Shanelle interrupted as the nurse returned to the front desk. "Hi. Could you tell me who delivered those flowers?"

The nurse's gaze darted back and forth behind Shanelle. "Oh, she's gone already? I don't know... she had a delivery, but I thought it needed my signature before she could leave. My pen ran out of ink. I went to the back to get a new one. The kook must have left while I turned away."

"Who were they for?" Shanelle always brought out the thoughtful and concerned citizen persona when she wanted to accomplish something important.

"A patient. I can't bring them in now, he's resting. We had to give him a mild sedative after he woke up in a panic. Can I help you with something?"

"No, thanks. I'm waiting for a friend to finish visiting someone. I'll just hang out over here in this sitting area."

While Shanelle distracted the nurse, Brianna snuck around the corner to the outside of Riley's room. Brianna impatiently leaned against the wall, casually checking her phone in case anyone questioned why she was lurking outside the doorway. Molly's voice was low, but loud enough for Brianna to hear the words.

"Good, you're awake. I wasn't sure what I'd walk into... a man on his deathbed or a slimy asshole who always gets away with things. Although I never wanted to think about you again, I've been forced too many times over the last few years. Whenever the news or other victims commented on the nasty things men do to women in the name of love, I thought of tracking you down to get my revenge. I'd finally started to let it go, at least until my daughter went looking for you, you son of a bitch," said Molly.

Brianna listened to his silence and contemplated what was behind her mother's angry tone and accusatory words.

Riley's voice was groggy, yet clear enough to reach the hallway. "It really is you. I thought I was hallucinating earlier when you were in my room."

"I just got here now, but it's definitely me. Tell me, Riley. Did it empower you to hurt me? To attack me that night on campus nearly twenty years ago? To rape me?"

Brianna thrust her hand over her mouth, gasping when she learned what Molly had been hiding all along. Brianna had never known how difficult things had been for her mother.

"You're wrong. You wanted me. I know you did," said Riley.

"I didn't want your disgusting hands all over me. I ran away from you all those times before. You wouldn't leave me alone. To think you could be Jonah's son. You're a perverse fate we've all had to suffer—"

"That's not how I remember it. Sure, I was a little rough, but that's how you and Rachel liked it."

"Shut up, Riley. I don't want to hear your lies. You raped me nineteen years ago. You attacked Rachel, too. Then you demanded she get an abortion like it was a trivial decision a girl could make with only a moment's consideration. It's sickening to think of the fracture you've—"

"Rachel was just a means to get to you. I never cared about her. She gave up your secrets quite easily."

"She told me years ago about the betrayal and what you'd wanted all along. Rachel may be the reason this all happened, but you're the callous monster who haunted me for years. Not her." Molly grunted and rattled the bed frame. "It's a good thing you never got your hands on that baby girl. I can't imagine what kind of father you'd have been."

"What the hell are you talking about? Whose baby?"

"Nothing. I don't know what I was saying," mumbled Molly.

"What baby girl?" His voice rose.

"Forget it, asshole. I think it's time you paid for everything you did."

"I did nothing. You should be the one to suffer. I noticed you on the street before I had the accident. This was all your fault."

"What are you talking about?" said Molly.

"Months ago. You were walking with some black girl at Woodland College. I was driving my father back to his office to pick up his briefcase. I couldn't believe you'd come back after all these years."

"It wasn't me, Riley. That was my daughter and her friend, Shanelle."

A few seconds of silence passed. Brianna struggled to breathe as the walls closed in on her. Everything had become too clear in too brief of a time.

"Your daughter? She looks so much like you."

"Stay away from her. If you touch a hair on her head, I'll return the favor, twentyfold. Beat you until you bleed. Drag you to a dark, damp, cold basement. Torture every part of your body until you beg me to save you. But I wouldn't save you. I'd destroy you for going anywhere near my daughter. I'd watch you die before my very eyes. Ever since I met you, I've been well acquainted with the thought of killing someone. It's not easy to shed that desperate need for revenge. Is it?"

All the energy drained from Brianna while listening to the account of what'd happened. This woman was not the same mother she'd known all her life. How could she have hidden so much pain and suffering? Distracted by images of Riley attacking her mother, Brianna dropped her phone to the ground.

The nurse came running. "What's going on?"

"Who's there?" said Molly while still hovering in the room.

Molly's footsteps echoed in the outside hallway on their walk toward the door. Brianna took off around the corner and grabbed Shanelle's arm, leading her down the stairs. They stopped midway between floors to catch their breath.

Brianna clutched the handrail with whitened knuckles as drops of perspiration fell from her forehead. "It can't be him."

"What happened? Talk to me." Shanelle repeated herself several times until Brianna stopped ignoring the plea to snap out of her daze.

"My father. My father might be Riley. He raped her."

"Oh my God!"

Brianna suddenly realized why her mother had kept the identity of her father a secret for all those years. "She doesn't know who my father is because she didn't want to know, Shanelle."

"I don't blame her if you're the result of him attacking her."

"Oh, no, what a nightmare!" Brianna's voice grew hollow and distant as she slid down the wall to the steps. "If it's Jonah, I'll never get to know my father. If it's Riley, he's a rapist. If it's Carter, then I slept with my father." The words escaped her lips without her even realizing she'd blurted her confession.

"Wait, what did you say?" Shanelle jostled Brianna's body until they were face to face. "*Slept* with him?"

Brianna curled into a ball. "I slept with Carter yesterday. I wanted to prove to myself how I truly felt about you. I wanted to know I could freely choose you with no worry or hesitation."

Shanelle pushed Brianna's hands away. "I gave you the chance to come to a bar with me where you could experiment around other women. I understood if you needed to go on a few dates with a guy before deciding your future. To experience a few steps down each path so we could analyze it and talk about what it meant. Not for you to sleep with him. How could you do that and not tell me what happened until just now?" Shanelle raced down the remaining stairs, then turned back to look at her friend. Her crushed eyes narrowed on Brianna while waiting for a response.

"I didn't want to tell you this way. After the impact of what my mother said to Riley, my words came out the wrong way. I'm so sorry. Don't leave me right now, Shanelle. Please."

"No, you can't throw me aside when you don't need me and yank me back when you do. I know you're hurting right now, but who you need is your mother. Not me. I'm out of here until you grow up." Shanelle busted through the door and exited the hallway. It slammed shut, reverberated in the stairwell, and pounded inside Brianna's head.

For the first time, Brianna had truly seen Shanelle crying. And it was all her fault. She pulled her knees tightly to her chest and began sobbing. "All I wanted was to find my father and to decide if I loved you, Shanelle. How did it come to this?"

She sat against the cold tiles for thirty minutes, fixated on the wall in front of her. The whole space was gray. No color. Nothing with any personality or feeling. Just two sets of staircases, one going up and one going down. It matched the choices unfolding in front of her. She could comfort her mother. Or she could chase after Shanelle. There were always two paths in front of her, and she never knew which to take.

Brianna's experience with Carter forced her to recognize she wasn't physically or sexually attracted to men. She was scared to let go of being with a man, assuming that meant she was also foregoing the search for her father. But that search would always remain in her heart until Brianna found him. It was separate. A different part of her. She'd merely confused her fear of abandonment with the inability to accept the truth about what she really desired. Inside, Brianna was searching for a woman to love as a partner. Shanelle. Shanelle had been there for the last two years. Through every lost soccer game, fight with friends, or disappointment at the curve balls life had thrown in the way. Shanelle supported her during the search to find her father. Shanelle never let her down. Shanelle was who she loved.

Brianna knew her emotional state was too fragile to chase after Shanelle and deal with the repercussions of hurting someone she loved. Her experience with Carter had taught her to trust her instincts. Finding her father was important because it would tell her where she came from, but not where she would go in the future. Brianna no longer needed to justify her sexuality to anyone else, or to herself, because she had already known the truth—and she accepted it. Once she understood that her tunnel vision had been blocking the obvious facts surrounding her, the true path became crystal clear. Piece by piece she would get her answers and correct everything that had gone wrong.

Brianna was afraid the nurse would catch her if she tried to sneak back into Riley's room to find her mother. Instead, she called Molly's cell, knowing it was time to have a heart-to-heart conversation.

Molly answered on the first ring. "Honey, I've been trying to find you all day. What happened?"

"I'm so sorry, Mom. I think it's time we talked."

"It's been too long. There are things I haven't wanted to tell you because I couldn't handle reliving my past. It's not easy, Brianna."

"Where are you now?"

"I'm on my way back to the cabin I rented for the weekend. How about you?"

"Still at the institution." Brianna paused, hoping her mother would confess she'd been there, too. She wanted the games to end and the conversation to be open.

Molly replied, "Okay. Why don't we meet up at your apartment? I'll drive over right now."

Brianna knew Shanelle had gone back to their apartment to recover. As much as Brianna wanted to repair the damage she'd caused, it wasn't the right time. "No, I'll come to the cabin. Shanelle and I had a fight. It's better if I stay away."

"I know what's going on between you and her. I know you've had some secrets, too."

The strings of Brianna's heart snapped loose. It was time to come out to her mother, but not on the phone. "I know, Mom. I should have told you sooner. I was scared and confused." Her eyes welled.

"The Crestwood Resort and Lodge is just off Exit 33 on the main highway. Get here quickly. Safely. I love you, Brianna."

"Got it. On my way. I love you, too, Mom."

As Brianna hung up the phone, the door slammed shut at the top of the stairs. She turned to check who was there, but no one was in the alcove. She raced up the steps to discover who might have been hiding in the hallway, but she was distracted by her ringing phone. "Yeah?"

"Brianna, it's Malachi. Do you have a minute?"

"Sure. Are you back up north?"

"I'm on the plane in Mississippi waiting for the tower to clear our flight. I have more news for you."

"It can't be any worse than what I just learned."

"Are you sure you're ready to know?"

Brianna replied with apprehension, "Hit me with it."

"I found a local news article that talked about when Molly's mother died. There were a few rumors that it wasn't from natural causes."

"Are you saying someone might have murdered my grandmother?"

"Not just anyone, Brianna. My contact suggested Molly may have been the one to kill her."

Brianna shook her head. "No… no… no… this can't be happening. Who said that?"

"Listen, the plane's about to take off. I gotta shut down. I'm flying back to New York, and then I'll drive to Woodland tomorrow. We need to figure out how to approach your mother together with this information."

Brianna listened as the phone connection went dead. She couldn't believe it was true. Her mother had always been a gentle and kind woman. She wouldn't even squish the occasional spider or mosquito. And when they had a rat in the apartment, Molly had insisted it not be killed. Malachi had incorrect information, or someone in Brant was just being a nasty gossip. Brianna wouldn't accept any other answer.

She texted Shanelle to work through all the remaining items on her checklist.

> **Brianna**: *I'm a fool. Please forgive me.*
>
> **Shanelle**: *I can't talk about this right now.*
>
> **Brianna**: *I'm going to tell my mother the truth about us.*
>
> **Shanelle**: *What is the truth this time, Bree?*
>
> **Brianna**: *Never been more positive about what I want.*
>
> **Shanelle**: *That's good to know.*
>
> **Brianna**: *I'm going to meet her at a Crestwood cabin. You need to be there when I tell her.*
>
> **Shanelle**: *I need to take care of something first. I'll come by tomorrow when I've cooled off.*
>
> **Brianna**: *Thank you. I'll call you later with the directions. I promise I'll make things better.*

No response, but Brianna needed to stop the quicksand from swirling around her. She dialed Carter's number to deal with the next issue on her checklist.

"Hello." His voice was distant, cold.

"It's Brianna. I need to talk to you. It's important."

"I've been thinking about everything that's happened since I ran into your mother. I need to ask you a question."

"Sure, go ahead." Queasiness settled in Brianna's stomach, and she swallowed hard.

"When's your birthday?"

"Why do you want to know?" Her hand instinctively pressed down on her chest, hoping to keep viscous bile from rising any further.

"You're eighteen years old, right?"

Brianna hung her head and breathed in quick gulps of air. He'd come to the same conclusion she had. "Yes, I am."

"I can't believe I'm going to ask this next question."

"Then don't. We should talk about this in person with my mother. Can you meet me in the main lobby of the Crestwood Resort and Lodge in thirty minutes?"

# Chapter 29

# Amalia, May 1985

Amalia sat on the swinging bench on the front porch of the Graeme household, mindlessly pushing backward and forward with her feet, hoping the warm spring breeze would carry her away. Ever since she'd gotten home from her appointment that morning, Amalia had known with full certainty that luck would never be on her side. She would always be the one left behind to suffer in misery.

Three weeks had passed since Amalia buried her mother in the cemetery plot next to her father, against better judgment and bitter instinct. Janet had done little for her or Amalia's father during either lifetime, and there was no reason the woman should be buried in permanence next to the kind and loving Peter Graeme. Except Amalia had no other options, money, or solutions at the time.

It had all happened so fast that fateful day her mother had a heart attack. Once the local medic had arrived at the Graeme household, he pronounced Janet Graeme DOA. Dead on Arrival. Those were unfamiliar words for Amalia, but ones that mirrored how she interpreted her own life. The medic tried to revive Janet even though he'd already known there was little chance of the woman surviving a massive coronary event. Janet hadn't been to the doctor very often and was unwilling to listen to any physician who insisted she cut out all the sugar and bread from her diet. It was bound to happen, eventually. Little, if any, guilt plagued Amalia over their final argument, the probable inciting factor for her mother's death.

Part of her had wanted to let her mother die on the floor in front of her. Amalia kept at bay a temporary desire to beat her mother with the table leg as punishment for years of abuse. But she knew gasping for a few last breaths with your daughter standing before you, unwilling to help while she brandished a bloody weapon, was a cruel death even for someone like Janet Graeme. Amalia had a moment where she stared into her mother's cold and lifeless eyes as the woman struggled to speak.

Amalia couldn't be certain if it were the lack of oxygen traveling to her mother's brain or a willful need to withhold a true maternal connection even in moments before her death. But she couldn't hurt the woman. It would make her no better than her mother. After she'd picked up the table leg while her mother closed her eyes for the last time, Amalia swung hard and beat the table in frustration. As soon as it was obvious Janet hadn't been faking the heart attack, Amalia dialed 911 and begged for an ambulance to come quickly. While waiting for the nearest vehicle rushing from twenty minutes away, Amalia pulled splinters of wood from her fingers, cleaned the blood dripping on her palm, and bandaged the scratches on her arm from when they'd tumbled on the floor. She mopped up the spilled milk, and she moved the table out of the way, so the rescue team could more easily attend to Janet.

When the medics removed her mother's corpse, and Amalia was alone in the Graeme family home for the first time, a sudden sharp twinge of sadness overtook her body. It had always been easy to cast her mother as the evil woman who'd caused the downfall of the entire family. It soon became clear to Amalia that it wasn't just Janet's fault. Janet had been the only honest one in the family. She told it as she saw it even if her words were misguided and cruel. She spewed her venom no matter what the impact or reaction would be from those around her.

Though Amalia loved her father more than anyone else, he'd contributed to the problems in their family through lies of omission and his failure to do anything about the abuse. He couldn't have been so blind never to notice the bruises or his daughter's withdrawal from everyone around her. Peter could have better protected Amalia, and maybe she would have been stronger rather than simply accept her fate as an abused young girl. Although Amalia had fought back occasionally, she allowed herself to be a victim in Brant, which made her accept that she'd allowed herself to be a victim at Woodland. Years would pass before she felt any different or found strength to trust others or in herself.

After the funeral service, the bank officer and the attorney left Amalia alone for a few days, allowing her time to grieve and consider the decisions she had to make. Construction stopped at the hardware store while the bank personnel partnered with the local real estate agency to put the place up for sale. Amalia wouldn't give them an answer on what to do about the future of the Graeme family home.

Although a sad and heavy cloud hung over Amalia's head ever since her father and brother died, she now truly understood what it meant to be an orphan. Despite the caustic relationship she shared with Janet, there had always been the slightest pull between them, as if one day they might repair the fractured link. A chance to find common ground perhaps when Amalia settled down with her own husband and family. A reason to forget the past and focus on a better future. Deep down she knew it was futile. Friction defined them. Pride stopped them. Reality trapped them.

Amalia had learned a lot about life in the five months that passed since her father's horrific death in the fire. Nothing was constant. Everything changed. Even if you tightly grasped that which you held dear, it's never meant to stay with you for very long. At least not for someone like her. Greg had been lucky for a few years by escaping the quicksand that was Brant. But even their desperate and clingy town wouldn't release him forever and called him back to perish in a fire as a punishment for ever wanting or trying to have a better life. Brant was not an ideal home to raise a family if you had hopes for a happy future. There were those residents who only wanted you to fail so they could eagerly claim they'd made it a step further or a day longer than you. Then there was the belief from the long-standing citizens who considered it a parent's right to discipline their child any way they chose.

For Amalia, the thought of how to treat one's children haunted her in new and unexpected ways. She initially suspected her body was in shock after missing her regular bleed the first month. Assuming something had been damaged during Riley's attack or that her body was protecting itself, she gave no thought to anything more serious than a delayed period. It was a welcome change, the monthly cycle never being a part of a woman's life that she wanted to deal with. After her first few experiences with sexual intercourse, everything in that general vicinity operated differently, as though she'd passed to a different level of womanhood with no real instructions.

Amalia wanted to talk to someone about it, but she never had the confidence or ability to discuss the attack with anyone in Brant. The ladies at church would have been appalled at knowing she'd slept with not only one boy, but multiple, before getting married. When she tried to solicit their help and affection after Janet died, elderly Mrs. Newton even suggested Amalia was the reason Janet died of the heart attack. They wanted the Graeme family gone from their peaceful town, and she was the last to go. The girls from Amalia's softball team either moved on from Brant, ran away to college, or turned their backs on her long ago.

When Amalia missed her second monthly bleed, she feared something serious had been wrong with her. Still having no access to a computer or any sort of book that helped her sort it all out, she was stuck with a choice—visit the physician or buy a home pregnancy test. She first chose the home pregnancy test but had to make the four-mile excursion to the next town over where she bought it without being recognized. Amalia thought of Rachel during the entire walk, worried that she'd never heard from her roommate after the last note left on campus saying she'd been kicked out of Woodland.

Urinating on a stick didn't seem like a normal thing to do, but Amalia had no choice in the matter. When the required number of minutes passed by, painful ones heroically carrying every known fear on their back, Amalia opened her eyes to a distressing confirmation she'd already accepted in her heart. She made an appointment and patiently waited a few days before the doctor ran the proper tests.

It had all concluded earlier that morning. She'd been swinging in the porch chair ever since returning from his cold and judgmental office earlier that day. No matter how hard she tried to understand why the very thing she'd always been afraid of came true, Amalia couldn't find a reason—except punishment for the choices she made in not listening to her mother all those years when the woman had predicted her daughter's fate. Amalia assumed it meant her mother had always been right about the way her daughter behaved around boys.

Amalia gazed into the distance across from the house for hours until the hunger pains grew too strong to ignore. She wandered to the kitchen and made herself a tuna sandwich, unsure if it were even something that could harm the baby. The doctor had suggested she buy prenatal vitamins and had given her a list of things to avoid. It didn't matter to her at that moment. She would read it all later, once there was a chance to decide her next steps.

Curled up in her father's chair later that afternoon, Amalia called Jonah's office, hoping to hear his voice on the answering machine. When he picked up, she became frightened and concerned Riley would follow through on his threats to kill them both if she ever revealed what'd happened between them. She kept telling herself it didn't happen *between* them. It happened *to* her. He did something awful to her.

Now Amalia didn't have only her life to protect, but the baby's life growing inside her body. Ending the pregnancy like Rachel had probably chosen to do wasn't an option—that had been one opinion Amalia and her mother shared. It wasn't about whether a baby was a gift from God, or if aborting it was considered murder—those being Janet's thoughts. It was about holding on to someone she'd already loved the moment the doctor confirmed the pregnancy—those being Amalia's thoughts. Her father was gone. Her mother. Her brother. Even the potential fathers of the baby were no longer in her life.

Amalia reached for her journal, feeling grateful she could keep it out in the open without the terror of who might read it. There wasn't anyone to fear anymore as long as she never went back to Woodland. She was alone and would be for an exceptionally long time. Amalia accepted her fate to remain in Brant.

*Dear Diary,*

*I found out today I'm going to have a baby. I already figured it out myself a few weeks ago, but I didn't know what to do. I'm alone now. It'll just be the baby and me. Probably forever. I don't expect to ever fall in love again. I don't think I can trust someone to treat me fairly. It isn't always their fault. I'm a hard girl to love. I know this to be true, and not because it's what Momma always told me. Even I have trouble loving myself.*

*I don't know whom the father is. And that's scary. It could be a good man, but it could also be a terrible man. Carter promised me he wouldn't get me pregnant the first time, but he didn't use any protection. I should have insisted on it. I only blame myself. If he is the father, then I welcome this baby with open arms.*

*I called Jonah today. I hung up when his voice beckoned on the phone. I miss him more than ever, but I know I can't see him again. It will cause too much damage. I never worried when he told me the condom broke after we'd been intimate. I'm not sure I understood what that meant at the time. I hope the baby is his. Maybe someday we will find our way back to one another. Time needs to pass before I risk either my life or my baby's life. Or even Jonah's.*

*I'm scared it could be Riley's baby. I'm afraid of what kind of little monster could be growing inside me. Someone who could attack others as its father attacked me that night in the basement on campus. I should have called security, but I wasn't myself. I didn't know any better. I didn't know a lot of things I know now.*

*Like everything you do has a consequence. That fate is never your friend. Sometimes it teases you with a tempting desire, then rips it away. I want to think of my baby as an unexpected impact of destiny calling the shots. As someone who can love me. Someone I can love who will never go away.*

*I must decide about the future. I need a fresh start. It's a beautiful day out, and getting outdoors might help me think better. Perhaps I'll take a stroll to Lake Newton. It's been forever since I saw the flowers bloom or took a canoe ride across the calm water.*

*Love,*

*Amalia*

When she arrived at the lake, Amalia's breath drew in the sweet scent of jasmine lining the pathway to the dock. As her feet landed on the old wooden planks, a comfort settled inside her and pushed her to remove her shoes and socks to dip her feet in the water.

The water was still a bit cool, but it refreshed her body and her spirit as if there might exist a chance to survive everything she'd been through that year. The sun rose high that afternoon, beating down against her skin like little bundles of warm kisses. Lost in the pleasures of birds chirping and waves gently lapping against the wooden poles, Amalia's mind relaxed into the surroundings and allowed her to forget who she was. Until a voice calling her name startled her back to reality.

"Amalia Graeme?"

She raised her head from her self-induced daydream and craned toward the noise's origin.

"Amalia, is that you on the lake?"

Amalia lifted her feet from the water and pushed herself off the dock into a standing position. As she turned around to see who was shouting her name and blocked out the sun's glare with her hand, an enormous smile overtook the permanent gloom on her face. "Bryan?" The chill in her feet from the cool water disappeared and was replaced by a warmth generating in her legs and slowly working its way up her body until it landed deep inside her chest. Amalia did nothing but stare as he promenaded down the dock toward her.

"I can't believe I found you here." Bryan still resembled the adorable guy she thought had been flirting with her the summer before, except his hair was buzzed so short his scalp shined through.

"Oh, Bryan." Amalia lifted her arms as he reached her and fell against his body in a bear hug she desperately needed. "I've missed you so much."

"I've missed you, too." Bryan quietly released her from his grip and gave her the once-over. "I'm so sorry about your mother. I just got back from New York City a few hours ago."

"How did you find me?"

"I went to the house, but you weren't home. I thought maybe I'd take a quick stroll around the lake, never expecting to meet you here."

Amalia summoned her courage to the surface and pushed the words from her sorrowful lips. "It's been an awful time the last few months. It must get better somehow, right?"

Bryan nodded. "I'm sure that guy you've been dating helped you through it all. Your momma told me he was about to ask you to marry him the last time I was home, right after your daddy's funeral." His eyes blinked a few times, waiting for her to respond. "I'm really sorry about him and your brother. It's been a hell of a year for you, Amalia Graeme."

A sudden rush of anger streamed throughout Amalia's blood. Even in death, Janet would destroy her daughter's chance of happiness. "No, I'm not engaged. He's... he's not around anymore." She began crying despite being clueless why Bryan so easily stirred her emotions.

Bryan pulled her close and rubbed her back. "It's okay. Shhh, we don't have to talk about it. I'm here for you."

Amalia needed a friend. Someone who listened to her but didn't judge her. She wanted to tell him the whole story of what'd happened since she was last with him. She collected her socks and shoes and grabbed his arm, comforted around another man for the first time since Riley had attacked her. "Let's take a walk to that old magnolia tree where I was supposed to meet you."

Their walk lasted over two hours, and Amalia told him everything that'd happened. From her interest in Carter the previous summer when Bryan left for New York City, to getting caught by her father on the couch. From meeting her temporary savior, Jonah, to losing her friend, Rachel, when she abandoned Woodland without any good-bye. From living with the knowledge she'd been estranged from her father when he died in the fire, to the details of the night Riley took advantage of her innocence in the basement.

Bryan listened the entire time, even stopping to let her cry on his shoulder when it became too much for her to handle. He held back her hair when Amalia suddenly became ill and suffered through morning sickness. Bryan had been very understanding about her pregnancy, insisting she'd done nothing wrong.

"Amalia, I would love to help you through this, but there are a few problems that might stand in the way." He stood squarely against her, his arms reaching for her hands. "Is it okay if I hold your hand?"

"I don't usually like to be touched by anyone since Riley attacked me, but I know this is safe. That you're safe. I trust you to show kindness to me. You are my friend." Amalia couldn't be certain that Bryan would always be gentle, but she needed to believe the world harbored more than just evil men. She forced herself to take small chances as part of her approach to recovery and not to allow the doubt to color her entire future. Trust needed to be earned, not just given out like candy at Halloween. Bryan's soothing manner suggested he was worthy of her trust.

As Bryan smiled, Amalia understood for the first time what it meant to have a friend who genuinely cared about you and your wellbeing. He'd no ulterior motives. He realized she was in no place to think about developing feelings for anyone. He knew what was best for her at that time.

Bryan pulled Amalia down to the large rock along the pathway. "Sit with me. Let me tell you a bit about what I've been going through. Is that okay?"

She nodded. "I'd rather hear about your life right now rather than think of myself." Her blistery eyes poured like a streaming faucet, but it was still one of the first times she'd experienced happiness in the last few months despite the tears clinging to her skin.

Bryan released her hands and placed them on his knees. "When you didn't show up last year, I took it seriously, but don't think I was upset with you. I figured I was too forward with you. I've never been particularly good with girls." He shrugged and dipped his head lower.

Amalia wiped the tears from her cheeks. "You're better than you think, B-Balls."

"A lot has changed for me, too. My uncle ran a warehouse in New York City by the shipping yards. He needed some help and offered to put me up for a few weeks until I decided what I wanted to do with my life. I figured you weren't interested, and there was nothing left for me in Brant. I left that weekend on the bus."

"I'm so sorry I couldn't meet you. I wish I'd known you'd been considering leaving."

"It's okay. Let's keep the past in the past right now." He paused to ensure Amalia was comfortable with everything he'd shared. "After a few months, my uncle gave me a bunch of cash and told me to buy myself an apartment in a building he was planning to live in, eventually. I wasn't sure where he'd gotten the money, but I'd known he was hiding something from me. He helped me get established, and now I own a small two-bedroom apartment on the Lower East Side of Manhattan."

"Not bad for a scrappy kid from Brant, Mississippi, huh?" Amalia enjoyed whenever she made him grin.

"It was rough for a little while. My uncle angered a few people at the dock and had to disappear. That's why he gave me the money. He finally returned to New York last month after changing his last name and opened a jazz club in the basement of the apartment building. He just bought the rest of the apartments in the place and is renting them out."

She moved her hand back to his when it fell from her lap. "I'm glad you're okay. That could have been scary."

"After a few more months when I'd learned about your father's tragic death, I came back here to visit you. Your mother told me that you moved on with a new boyfriend, so I enlisted in the Air Force to make a fresh start. They accepted me, and I went through basic training for several months this year. I'm home on leave for three days to take care of some business back here in Brant, but then I need to visit New York City to close up my apartment."

Amalia's stomach trembled as he spoke. She'd finally gotten Bryan back, even as a friend, but he would leave her very soon. "I don't want you to go."

"I know, but this is something important to me. There's a disconnect between me and what I want for my future. The Air Force will give me an education, discipline, and a career. Someday, I can protect our great country and possibly settle down with a family."

Amalia tried to understand his words and prevent her own emotions from stealing the spotlight. "That would be good for you."

"I have an idea... since you need to leave Brant, and I don't have anyone to watch over my place in New York City. Uncle Lenny would, but I'm not sure I trust him not to destroy the place." His roar made her smile, as if everything painful had temporarily abandoned her body. "You should move into my apartment."

When the words left his mouth, Amalia knew someone had been finally protecting her despite everything that'd happened. "I think that could work."

As he continued telling her the rest of his plan, little by little the fears and concerns of the past, and the darkness and the loneliness of the present, dissipated inside Amalia. Though she had many feelings to explore, trust in people to build, and confidence to find within herself, she'd accepted that things could finally fall into place for her. An opportunity to change the future to the one Amalia had always wanted but could never quite hold on to.

Chapter 30

# Brianna, September 2004

After the taxi dropped her off, Brianna verified with Crestwood's front desk that Molly had returned to cabin fifteen, the last one on the northern trail. She asked the clerk to hold off on calling her mother as she had a few things to address before meeting Molly. She took a seat on the closest sofa, debating whether to tell her mother she'd invited Carter over to the cabin to talk to them. Brianna wanted time alone to analyze his facial expressions and understand what he thought as she told him all she'd learned. She also wanted to study his physical features to determine if they shared anything in common, curious if now that she knew he could be her father, it would appear obvious.

Brianna tried to relax, but her legs had a mind of their own kicking and shifting as she changed positions on the sofa. The clerk stopped by to ask if she'd wanted anything to drink, but Brianna waved her away. After Brianna left her best friend instructions on how to find the cabin, Shanelle still hadn't called back to confirm she would be there when Brianna talked to her mother. It'd been over an hour since the call went to voicemail after many torturous rings. She texted a few messages, no response. Shanelle's phone never left her hands—it was usually attached as though it were another appendage.

When they'd first met, the girls would text each other all night in bed from their different homes—a way to connect, to know they were always at each other's side. Even as they grew closer to graduation,

Brianna couldn't fall asleep at night until she got the official sign-off, *ShanOUT*, returning with her own *BreeOUT*. She tried again, but this time it transferred to an immediate voicemail. Either Shanelle had turned the phone off or suddenly blocked her.

Carter lumbered across the parking circle in the front of the building. As he took each step, Brianna searched for any similarities in the shape of their noses or the way his body moved. Nothing was obvious, though he, too, had high cheekbones. She'd hated hers as a child, only learning to love them in the latter years. She considered them too defined, too structured, and always standing out when she smiled. Now she thought they strengthened her. While hers were more prominent, Carter's rounded down his cheeks to a squared chin. Not an exact match.

As soon as he passed through the revolving door, he turned left into the main lobby. "I'm sorry. Traffic."

"No worries. Sit, please." Brianna extended her hand to the chair opposite of her. "I'm sorry to be so vague on the phone. This is awkward."

"Yeah, I agree." The veins in his forearm twitched every few seconds as he settled into the seat. He leaned forward while studying every feature on her face. "You resemble your mother. I think that's why I found myself so interested in you when we first met. I just didn't know it right away."

"You looked familiar when I first met you, too. But I can't really figure out why. Maybe it was just fate playing games with us, so you'd connect with her again."

"Where is your mother?" Carter lifted his head.

"Up the hill at the last cabin. I should call her before we talk." Brianna had no logical approach to handle the situation, unsure whether to ask questions or have him tell her all he knew.

"I'm confused. Maybe you could clue me in on what I've missed before meeting Amalia again." Carter couldn't sit in one position for more than a few words and kept uncrossing and re-crossing his legs. "We didn't exactly end things on a friendly note all those years ago."

"Why don't you start by telling me how it ended?"

"Wait, can I ask my question first? I need to know if something twisted has happened here." A few worry lines had developed on Carter's face since the last time they were together. It hadn't aged him but just emphasized the extent of the anxiety in his voice earlier on the phone.

"I know what you want to ask me, but I don't have the answers." She stared directly at him, unable to peel her focus away from the man who might be her father. Though paralytic fear and a repulsive knot had settled in her stomach, she needed to temporarily lock away the intimate experience with Carter somewhere deep inside her psyche to avoid vomiting. Brianna turned away in the hopes she could salvage her strength to continue. "Go ahead. Maybe it will be different if you say the words."

Without hesitation, he asked, "Are you positive that I'm your father?"

Brianna fixated on a stain in the ceiling's corner. She was incapable of choosing the words to continue the conversation. When the silence became too much to handle, she swallowed hard and blurted the answer despite the pain blasting her upon hearing any acknowledgment aloud. "I'm uncertain, but it's highly possible. I've never met the man before... my mother's never been able to tell me the truth."

Carter dropped his head and waited for a large group of people to exit the lobby. "Shit." He ambled toward the front window a few feet from where they sat. "It was only one time we slept together. We could do the math to check if the timing lines up." His shoulders tensed with his back facing Brianna while shoving both hands in his jean pockets.

She huffed in disgust at his ignorance over what'd really happened in the past. "I'm not sure that will solve the problem. May I ask you a few questions now?"

"Do I have a choice?"

Brianna clasped her hands together with her fingers, interlocking and rubbing one another. She focused on a young boy holding his parents' hands as they skipped through the doors and up to the reception desk. They seemed so happy. Everyone had two perfect and normal parents except her. "Not really."

Carter turned around. His discontented countenance resembled a man who'd lost something important and was desperate to reclaim what once belonged to him. When he spoke, vicious anger fueled his words. "Stop playing games and ask me whatever you need to know about me. Damn it, this is a fucking mess."

"Don't get pissy with me. I have no clue what happened back then. I just know I have no idea who my father is." Brianna's lips stretched tightly against one another, struggling to hold in the venom she wanted to spew but knew wouldn't help the situation.

"You need to understand this isn't a simple conversation. I'm not sure how much you know about your mother and me."

"Then tell me."

Carter nodded in exaggerated slow-motion while gritting his teeth. "Fine, we'll play this your way for a bit. Amalia and I had a big fight after she did something foolish. We'd been dating for about seven or eight months. Went through some rough stuff after her father and brother died. I thought we'd make it through the pain."

"My mother had a brother?" Brianna's head threatened to explode. The woman had been keeping way more secrets than she'd even thought possible.

"You know nothing about her past, do you?"

Brianna shook her head. "Apparently not."

Carter reached a hand to her knee, hesitating at first. "Yeah. Greg was my best friend at Woodland. I visited their family in Brant, Mississippi for a few weeks. Almost moved there to be with your mother. Is that what you want me to talk about?"

Brianna processed his words, searching for the right way to move forward. She needed to know about Riley more than her mother's childhood in a place she'd never heard of until about a week earlier. Malachi could tell her about Brant. Of everything at her feet, learning more about her father was the priority. "No, there's something else more important. Do you know someone named Riley West?"

Carter's sullen gaze shifted from side to side. He idled at the window in contemplation of how to respond to the question. He circled back and sat on the arm of the chair. "Yes, but what does *he* have to do with this?"

"Were you friends with Riley when he knew my mother?" Brianna thought she understood the real Carter during the few times they'd hung out, but she had little confidence in her instincts anymore. Could he have been covering up what'd happened to her mother? The incident with Doug and the news she'd overheard when her mother revealed Riley's attack kept flashing in her head. *Were all men assholes?* Brianna was unwilling to let go of her quest until she understood all the information Carter had.

"To be honest, I wasn't aware they'd known each other." His head leaned in further toward her as he studied Brianna's face. "I only became friends with Riley after your mother left Woodland."

"Please, just tell me everything you know about him."

Carter rolled his eyes. "Okay, but I'm not sure why he's important. I'd been angry and moping around campus during those first few days after Amalia left me. Riley and I ran into one another and soon discovered we had a lot in common. He'd grown up without a father, and so did I. He and his mother had traveled around a lot, as did my mom and me. Riley and I had a kinship from similar experiences in life and hung out that summer."

"But you were never around him at the same time as my mother?"

"No, I don't think they ever met. Why do you keep asking me?"

"I'm sorry to dredge this all up. I'm just trying to figure out what happened after she broke up with you. How long did you hang out with Riley?"

"Not long. He obsessed over some girl he'd just met in Pittsburgh and tried to get me to find information about her. I had started getting serious with another girl on campus, and it became weird to hang out with Riley. His father even suggested I should stay away."

"Did you listen?" Brianna believed his responses but wasn't ready to tell him why she'd been asking questions about Riley.

"Yeah, and by the end of the summer, I moved to another part of Pennsylvania and eventually got married. I told you some of that already… when we were at Kirklands. I guess that's about when I stopped talking to Riley and hadn't thought about him for years until I moved."

"Back to Woodland?" Brianna continued pushing for answers to see if she could fit the remaining pieces of the puzzle together.

Carter puffed his chest in frustration. "Sort of. When the marriage ended with my ex-wife, I went back to school, got a few degrees and started teaching at different colleges all over the state. Woodland offered me a new position about two years ago. I had good memories of the place and decided to give it a chance."

"Okay. Just a few more questions. Did you ever pick up with Riley again when you came back to Woodland?"

"No. I'd seen him in town a few times, just floundering around on his own. I don't believe he ever left Woodland. Must have moved in with his father, Jonah, at some point." Carter's face grew redder as he spoke. "Is there a reason you're asking so many questions about Riley?"

"Yes, there is, but I'll explain in a minute. You never talked to him again, right?" Brianna wanted to believe Carter truly knew nothing about Riley's attack before bringing up the history. She needed to verify she could trust his reaction to the news that Riley might be her father.

"Well, no, I sort of did. After I heard about his recovery from the accident a few weeks ago, I visited him at the institution."

"Why would you do that?" Brianna's blood pressure rose at the thought of someone caring about Riley other than her. *What if he wasn't a monster?*

"Even though we weren't friends anymore, I knew no one else would check on him. Riley had always been rude and difficult. I'd heard he was arrested a few times for aggravated assault and public intoxication. Rumors from other staff at Woodland were fairly persistent. Jonah kept trying to help Riley, but he could never get through to his son. Riley was poisoned years ago by whatever had happened with his mother, and he just treated people like crap ever since then. I thought going to see him at the hospital was the right thing to do at the time. He wasn't very alert and barely spoke to me."

"He's talking now." Brianna struggled to make sense of the situation, waffling between casting Riley as a vicious rapist or a misunderstood and lonely man. Was it possible for someone to repent after nearly twenty years? "I'm going to tell you something, but I still don't know what it all means. It's really not even my story to tell you, but I just need answers."

Carter's eyes opened wide, and he fell back in the chair. "Okay, go ahead."

"I overheard my mother talking to Riley at the Woodland Institution earlier today. She accused him of... of raping her." Brianna's heart clenched as the pain her mother had gone through ravaged her thoughts and composure.

Carter's jaw dropped a few inches. His focus turned inward as he processed Brianna's revelation. His expression churned from confusion to anger, his pupils enlarged, and his breath quickened. "I don't know what to say. He often obsessed over girls, but I didn't think Amalia and Riley had ever met. Maybe through his father. She was awfully close with Jonah."

"I'm aware of that. It doesn't explain the order of how things happened in the past."

"Yeah, well, now I don't know what to think anymore. Give me a minute to process it all."

Brianna considered calling her mother as they idled in silence. Carter tapped his foot on the floor in a mechanical pattern. It reminded her of Poe's short story, *The Tell-Tale Heart.* A nonstop tapping, rapping at her door. He grew nervous and more furious with each beat.

Carter lifted his head, and a shocked expression overtook his face. "Riley had Amalia's locket. The one her father had given her before he died."

"What do you mean?"

"A few weeks after we'd begun hanging out, I found the locket on the floor of Riley's car. When I picked it up and read the inscription, I recognized it. Asked him about it."

"What did he say?" Brianna's heart thumped as loud as his foot's tapping.

"He claimed his father must have dropped it one day."

"Did you ever find out from Jonah?"

Carter became withdrawn. "I don't think we should talk about all this old history without Amalia. Let's walk to the cabin to see if she can fill in the blanks."

"Please. I'm trying to understand when Riley attacked my mother. I can't ask her that question until I know everything you know."

"Fine, but surely you can understand why Jonah and I were never close. I couldn't confront him without appearing like a fool."

"But you must have gotten over it. Did you ever visit with Riley and Jonah together?"

"No. I didn't even know Jonah was Riley's father until Riley brought me back to Jonah's house one day. That's when I started thinking something was odd about Riley. He was always vague about how he and Jonah got along. Then I caught Riley smoking crack a few times. He wasn't quite right in the head, if you know what I mean." His voice etched louder with each explanation of everyone's past behaviors.

"Yeah, I'm getting that picture. I guess it must have been awkward to see Jonah after what happened with my mother." Brianna knew she was treading on thin ice, but she also needed answers.

"Yes, at first, I was angry when Amalia fell in love with Jonah. I thought she was just caught up in a fleeting moment of admiration. I loved your mother and wanted her back. She was always such a sweet girl before things blew up that weekend. But she wouldn't take my phone calls." Carter's attention disappeared as he finished telling Brianna about his relationship with her mother.

"Did my mother ever tell you she was afraid of someone?"

Carter gave the question a few seconds of deep thought. "Son of a bitch. Amalia once told me someone had been following her a few times."

"You didn't believe her?"

"I did, but she handled it. She promised to tell me if the lunatic ever approached her again. I wonder if it was Riley."

"Do you believe he could have attacked her?"

"It's possible. And I'm gonna find out."

"What do you mean?" Brianna was shocked at his response and increasing irritation.

"I'll kill that bastard if he hurt your mother." Carter jumped up, ready to leave while gritting his teeth and clenching his fists. "I never got over—"

"Wait, what about talking to my mother so we can make sense of this all?"

"I'll come back. Right now, I need to find out if Riley did anything to her. If he's part of the reason she left town, and that's why I lost her..." Carter rushed out the door with vengeance in his eyes.

Exasperation ripped at Brianna's core over provoking Carter's fury, but she had more pressing matters. She left the main building and strolled the long path up the hill to cabin fifteen. It was time to get Molly's explanation of everything that'd happened that day on campus nineteen years ago. As she started the climb, her phone rang.

"Shanelle, is that you?" Brianna gripped the phone so tightly it almost slipped from her fingers.

"Yes. I'm sorry I've been AWOL. I'm angry with you, but I can't dwell on that right now. I need to update you about something."

"Where are you?" Brianna stopped halfway up the hill, pausing to collect her thoughts and breath.

"I'm with my father, running some tests for you."

"I don't understand." When Brianna reached the final peak on the precipice, a prominent and breathtaking view and cavernous backdrop of thick evergreen trees and mountainous terrain astonished her. She wanted to soak in its beauty, but the elusive answers were too close to waste precious time.

"The only way you'll know your father's identity for certain would be by running a DNA test. I've been studying it in one of my classes and asked my father to help."

"A DNA test, but how?" Brianna was curious to know what it all meant.

"I'll explain it when I can get to the cabin tomorrow. My father has a few more things to do at the lab before they finish all the tests."

Brianna closed her eyes. "Thank you, I'm so sorry." Static blasted through the phone and cut off the call. "Are you there, Shanelle? Shanelle?" They'd gone too far into the mountains, and her phone had disconnected by the time she'd reached the top.

Brianna arrived at a charming two-story cedar building nestled in the woods and jutting off the mountain cliff. Surrounding the front entrance were large pine trees and a well-landscaped yard, but the land behind the cabin dropped at least fifty feet into a generous ravine. As she stumbled around the side, navigating the downward-graded slope, it became arduous and dizzying. Tall, thick cast-iron spires surrounded a manmade fire pit near the back entrance where Brianna assumed guests toasted s'mores and told ghost stories—it was a magical view they could enjoy once she had all her answers. When she traversed the final section of the path, she lifted her gaze, impressed by a gorgeous picture window on the cabin's second story that overlooked the sweeping valley. When staring at the distance between the cabin and the sharp decline to the ground far below made her nauseous, she slowly stepped away.

Brianna shuffled back to the front yard and raised her hand to knock on the door, but it swung open before her knuckles hit the barrier.

"I knew you'd be there," said Molly.

"How?"

"A mother always knows."

"Are you alone? Or did Malachi arrive yet?"

"He'll be here tomorrow. He's coming back from some out-of-town case he was working on." Molly stepped forward and hugged her daughter. "Come in, let's talk."

It was a different type of hug than they'd shared the last few years. One that brought Brianna back to her childhood when her mother's embrace made all the problems of the world go away. Back then, the problems had only been a skinned knee or a nightmare about being lost in the woods. Now it became finding out if you'd slept with your father, if he'd died in an accident caused by his rapist son, or if that rapist son is your real father. But also, finally revealing to your mother you are gay. "I'd prefer to go first, Mom."

They huddled close together under a plush, white blanket on the sofa. Brianna's head lay against her mother's shoulder while Molly rubbed her daughter's arm. "Where's Shanelle?"

Brianna swallowed hard, pushing her toes against the softness of the shag rug. "I told her what happened between Carter and me."

"I'm sorry, honey. Shanelle's your best friend. She'll come back."

"She's more than my best friend." Brianna replayed the conversation in her head, knowing the words wouldn't come out the way she'd once planned. "I feel things for her that I never felt with Doug or other guys."

"I know. I've always known." Molly pulled her daughter in closer.

"But how? Why didn't you ever say anything?"

"It's not something I understood. It wasn't obvious. I just knew how you looked at Shanelle. The tenderness in how you spoke about her was genuine and heartwarming."

"I always felt different from everyone else. Like I couldn't fit in." Brianna's upper lip trembled while trying to hold back the tears. She'd needed to talk about this forever, and it was finally coming to fruition.

"You are different. You're smarter and have a deeper connection to your emotions than most other people. Some people spend their entire life unable to recognize what they want or need, but you've fought for it as far back as I can remember, Brianna."

"Are you okay with this?" Brianna wanted her mother to accept her but could never be certain how Molly would react, especially after everything that'd happened in the last few weeks. Their relationship had always been strong. The two of them were against the world together, even when Brianna yearned for more. Ever since Brianna feverishly pushed to get information on her father, there was a growing disconnect between them—a gap filled with silence, fear, and remorse.

Molly sighed. "I never told you anything about my parents, did I?"

Brianna shook her head, perplexed at where her mother's words would lead them. She worried if this were when Molly might reveal she'd killed her mother. She still feared what Malachi had yet to disclose from his trip to Brant.

"My mother was the daughter of a Baptist preacher. I never knew a lot about her childhood, but her father wasn't particularly good to her. I think he abused her when she was a little girl. Something had to turn her into the monster she'd become by the time I was born."

"What does that have to do with me being gay?" Brianna feared her mother was about to go off on some weird religious rant, despite neither of them having gone to any sort of church service during her lifetime.

"I never admitted it, but I hated my mother. I hated everything Janet Graeme stood for. That woman tortured me for years. She toyed with my father, too. She always had to have control. I used to listen to her preach how she was a good and faithful woman and how the Lord would provide for her. I never had much use for religion back then, not sure I even do now. I know the Lord didn't create that woman or intend for my mother to do the things she did. He didn't teach her to become such a vile creature." There was a calmness about Molly's voice, as though she'd processed everything that'd happened to her over the years, no longer the same little girl she once was.

"I didn't know you had such a horrid childhood."

"It wasn't always bad. My father and I had a close relationship. I miss him every day since I got the awful news. He died in a fire at Christmas time while I was away at Woodland. I had a brother, too. They'd been trapped in the basement and suffocated to death."

"That must have been horrible. I'm glad you're finally telling me about it." Guilt crept into Brianna's body for pushing her mother to explain the past, never knowing how painful it'd truly been for Molly.

"To answer your question, I never want to be that kind of mother—judgmental and domineering. She was disgusting and ruthless. I had no support from her, but you will always have my support. No matter what you do or who you are."

"Would you accept it if I told you I want to be with Shanelle?" Brianna thought about all the times she pushed her friend away, asking for more space and freedom to make her own decision. Shanelle had always listened and waited patiently. She may have been direct and forceful with her advice, but she'd always let Brianna make her own choices. Shanelle might be her perfect soulmate.

"Yes." The answer came quickly, no hesitation or doubt. "I've noticed how you behave around her. You're passionate about life and invested in everything you do together. I was afraid she'd take you away from me. I was alone once a long time ago before you came along." There was a melancholic tone to Molly's voice when she spoke. A remembrance of a past that once had the opportunity to develop into a wonderful future but had been abandoned for reasons no one understood.

"Is that when you met Carter?" Brianna let out a deep breath and blinked her eyes. "I need to know more about you and what happened at Woodland."

"Carter was my brother, Greg's, best friend. He stayed with us the summer Greg graduated from college. At first, I thought he was just a mean boy who'd caused someone I cared a lot about to leave town. But I fell hard for Carter that fall. He represented my escape from Brant from a life that made me incredibly sad."

"Did you love him?"

"I think I loved him as much as a girl could love someone when she never knew what love was. He was a decent boyfriend. I didn't know it at the time, but he was no different than all the other guys who were still trying to grow up and become men."

"Men act pretty immature, don't they?" Brianna giggled for the first time in days, suddenly wanting to say what'd been brewing inside her for years. "They're just walking assholes."

"Yeah, they certainly can be... walking assholes. I like that." Molly took a sip of water and laughed. She explained how she'd known little about sex or her own body when she was a teenager. She told Brianna about the family hardware store where her father and brother died, even showing her a picture of her and Greg from the year Greg had graduated.

Brianna's lips crinkled when she noticed Carter in the background behind Greg. "That's probably why Carter looked familiar. I saw this photo in your nightstand drawer once before. It's a little blurry, and he looks different, but now I can see the resemblance."

"I forgot the photo was saved in there until I saw it this summer after you left."

"Tell me how you met Jonah." Brianna wanted every part of her mother's life unveiled while Molly was being open and sharing things like they hadn't ever before.

"Jonah was there for me when my father died. I didn't love Carter, but my mother wanted me to marry him to save her from a future she was scared to live without someone to support her. She was a bitter old woman who couldn't do anything to take care of herself."

"I'm glad I never met her. She was the grandmother from hell."

"That's probably where she came from." Molly's chuckle wavered when she explained the significance of her mother's obstinance. "I say that now, but back then, I listened to everything she said to me until she began disparaging my father. It made me miss him even more. I found myself spending more time with Jonah. Some days, he was a replacement for the love I'd lost when my father died in the fire. Other days, I found myself attracted to him and his comforting arms and brilliant mind. He was an amazing man. I was terribly upset when you told me he died in a car accident earlier this year."

Choosing between comforting her mother over the loss of Jonah and thirsting for the entire story of the past ripped through Brianna with a vicious power. "Did you love Jonah more than Carter?"

"I loved Jonah. He could have been my future. I was just too young, and he had too much guilt over neglecting his son, Riley, when he'd been a child."

"I overheard you talking to Riley, Mom. I know what he did to you." Brianna rested her hand on her mother's leg, then looked up at her eyes. "You were brave."

They cried together when Molly revealed the story of Riley's attack. Molly shared some ways she tried to motivate herself to survive the ordeal. "It was a different time. Society still some blamed women for men's behavior. Hell, they even do it today sometimes. I couldn't handle telling anyone else, especially not once I went back home to Brant to live with my mother."

"What happened when you told her?"

"I never told her about it. I didn't have the chance to."

"What do you mean? Even someone like her would have supported her daughter if something that bad had happened."

"No, my mother wasn't very loving." Molly paused and drew in a deep breath. "That's why I was so upset when you told me you had the journal I'd written. She'd found it, too."

Brianna suddenly felt as small as a speck of sand on the beach. She'd been wrong to invade her mother's privacy, but now she was just as bad as her wicked grandmother. Brianna began to understand why her mother had kept so many secrets. "I'm sorry I did the same thing. Can you forgive me?"

"Of course. You were only trying to understand more about yourself. My mother didn't care about me. She wanted to torture me with my secret diary entries to entertain herself with stories of her daughter's pain and sadness."

"I can't believe how awful she could be. I know you took the journal from my apartment, but I understand it belongs to you. I'm glad you have it back again."

"I thought I'd thrown it out years ago until you stumbled upon it in the duffel bag. I planned to get rid of it permanently once you found it again, but I don't have it anymore. I thought you did." Molly leaned forward and tilted her head in puzzlement. "Don't you?"

Brianna scrunched her eyes together and shook her head. "No, I haven't seen it since you arrived at my apartment."

"I had it with me in my purse when I went to the institution, but when I got back to the cabin, it wasn't in my bag. I guess I just assumed you took it somehow." Molly sighed heavily. "I suppose it's good that it's gone."

"Maybe Shanelle found it."

"It doesn't matter anymore. I lost everything important my father had ever given me. It just wasn't meant to be," replied Molly. The sadness in her voice grew more prominent with each crack between the delivery of her words.

"What happened when your mother read it years ago?" Brianna rubbed her mother's hand.

"We had a huge fight. She told me I was a whore who deserved all the trouble I'd found, and if Carter and Jonah were both smart, they'd never speak to me again. She'd read everything about them from my diary entries."

"Is that when your mother died?" Brianna remembered that she'd called her mother a whore back in the campus apartment. She threw her hands to her eyes and silently prayed her mother knew it was just angry words that had no truth.

"Sort of. She'd been sick. Diabetes. Heart Disease. She blamed my birth as the reason she'd gotten so sick and hated me all my life."

"That's terrible." Brianna braced to learn what Molly had done to her mother. It was time to hear the truth.

"We had a moment where she lay on the floor looking up, knowing that I would watch her die in front of me. Even in death, her empty and soulless eyes wouldn't beg forgiveness for all she'd ever done to hurt me. Janet Graeme would never admit her faults. I'd always be the one to blame, yet I forgave her not because it was the right thing to do, but because I knew the embarrassment and shame would force her to leave the world more quickly and to allow me a chance to truly live."

"No daughter should ever experience that kind of pain from her mother. You must have wanted to hurt her," said Brianna. Her legs shook with fear as she waited to find out if her mother was a murderer.

"I admit there was a part of me that wanted vengeance for it all. It took me a long time to forgive myself for hating her. But she died from the heart attack, and there wasn't anything I could do to save her. I had an opportunity to hurt her, but I couldn't be as villainous as her." Molly looked up to the ceiling and shook her head as memories flooded through her mind.

"I'm so sorry. I can't believe you've sheltered me from all this over the years. What happened after she died? Did you ever spend time with Carter or Jonah again?" Brianna knew she was pushing hard, but the implications of sleeping with Carter kept scraping at her insides, stirring up grave humiliation and channeling a sense of disgust. She'd been in a constant state of nausea ever since recognizing the potential truth it would bring to her world.

Molly explained that she never went back to Woodland after leaving campus, especially once she'd learned about her pregnancy. "Even the others in Brant couldn't help me. The people at my mother's church once accused me of hurting my mother... of causing her death. They never really knew how mean and hurtful Janet could be. Once I knew I was truly alone, I had to start over. I had no mother or father. There was no husband to help me care for you. I was afraid Riley might have killed me if I told anyone."

Brianna understood the pain her mother went through nearly twenty years ago, feeling just as isolated as she felt herself today. Her mother wasn't just her mother. She was a victim, a girl learning how to fall in love and trust others around her. She fell for two men, yet had never been taught how to handle the emotions or the balance of exploring differing attractions. "I think you were very strong to do this all on your own."

"I wasn't strong back then. When I realized Carter and Jonah were just a way to escape the burdens life had given me, I thought I wasn't meant to find someone special. I didn't think I was worthy of love."

"Is that why you never allowed yourself to date again?" It all fell into place for Brianna as she suddenly thought of Molly as a woman with needs, desires, and fears—not just her mother. Brianna was just like Molly in every important way.

"I couldn't bring myself to ever trust in love again," replied Molly. "It wasn't part of my destiny. It wasn't about escaping Brant or Woodland. It was about escaping a life that was disappearing deeper into a vacuum in a way I'd never be able to recover again."

"It's almost as if I'm repeating the same steps you did. You chose Carter to get out of Brant, just like I tried to cling to him to avoid accepting I was gay." Brianna sipped her glass of water, swallowing each drop as though it offered a way to temporarily forget the horrors of everything her mother had lived through.

"Life is too short not to be yourself or accept the person you love. I wish I'd known years ago. I would have saved myself a lot of trouble even though I don't think it would have changed anything."

"How can you say that after all you've been through?"

"Because I have you. If things didn't happen the way they did, I might never have given birth to the most beautiful and amazing daughter I have now."

"Stop it. You're being too sentimental. I can't deal with it."

"I know, but it's true. You need to be proud of who you are. If you want to be with Shanelle, I'll support you one hundred percent. I don't want you to ignore the chance for love like I did for most of my life."

"Why did you never let yourself find love, even after I was born? It's been almost twenty years." Brianna never understood why her mother hadn't dated the entire time she'd been living in New York. It was as though Molly wanted to remain single and unattached for the rest of her life.

"That's a whole different story, perhaps another day. I've revealed enough for now. Be honest with me. After all this... do you truly need to find out whom your father is?"

Brianna trembled. "I have to know. Maybe if I'd never met Riley, or slept with Carter, I could have let it go. But I'm so close now, even though I've made a mess of things, Mom."

"No, honey." Molly placed her fingers on the edge of Brianna's chin and pulled her daughter's face toward her. "I made the mess. I chose not to find out his identity. All you did was sleep with someone to figure out yours. It's all my fault."

"What happens if Carter is my father? How do I live knowing we had sex? It's some white trash story you hear about but never believe could happen to you. Of all the men in the entire world, I sleep with the one guy who turns out could be my father. I don't understand what I was thinking. I'm so stupid."

"Brianna, you can't rationalize it that way. It took me years to stop believing I was at fault for what Riley did to me. I wasn't. It was always him. He had problems. Not me. We can't blame ourselves for things that are out of our control."

"I know, but you thought Riley was buried in the past. Then I brought him back. What if he's my father?" Brianna cringed at the thought of being born from a monster like him.

"I pray that he isn't. He knows I have a daughter, but maybe he won't figure out that he could be your father."

"I can't imagine being the product of rape. How could I ever have a relationship with him?"

"If we find out he is your father and you don't want him to know, we can hide it again. Just like Rachel did with her baby. It'll be your decision."

"I wondered what Rachel had to do with everything. I thought at one point she might have been my actual mother."

Molly cracked a wide smile. "No, I'm definitely your mother. I'm not exactly sure what happened to Rachel after she had the baby."

"You found the scrap of paper with her address in my room, didn't you?"

Molly nodded. "I did. As angry as I am with her for what she did to me, I never wanted Riley to find her."

"Wait, why were you upset at Rachel? What happened?"

Molly pressed her fingers deep into her eyes to relieve the tension. Every piece of the past she'd worked hard to get rid of had come back full circle. "Rachel was my college roommate…"

## Chapter 31

# Amalia, June 1985

Bryan had only returned to Brant for a few days before needing to check on the New York City apartment and ship out for his first call of duty. They hadn't told him where he would go after his basic training program completed, but he'd find out soon enough. While staying in Brant, he and Amalia built a plan for the sale of both properties and subsequent move to New York City. They first met with the bank addressing all the open mortgage and tax issues and cleared the house for sale to one neighbor who'd always wanted the additional land. Then, Bryan met with the owner of the building that housed Graeme Hardware Store to convince him to purchase the equity Peter had with his shares for a reasonable price, especially given it was in the middle of construction repairs from the fire.

While Bryan was in town handling the transaction, Amalia prepared for the move at home. As she was packing her address book, a small piece of paper fell from it. Rachel's phone number beckoned Amalia to try one final time to reach her friend before leaving Brant. Amalia had always wanted to know what'd happened to Rachel after she took off in the middle of the night with little explanation. She dialed the number and was surprised when her former roommate answered on the first ring.

"This is Rachel."

"It's Amalia Graeme. I found your number again and wanted to check on you. I never got to say goodbye."

Rachel hesitated on the phone, then responded. "Hi, Amalia. I'm so sorry that I left without ever calling you back."

"That's okay. I've been wondering what happened to you and the baby."

"I'm due next month. She's going to be adopted by a couple from California. I couldn't go through with an abortion, but I also know I can't take care of her. She would remind me too much of what happened with her father."

"Can I ask you a question?"

"Sure."

"Was Carter the baby's father?"

Rachel snuffled. "No, that would have been so much easier. Carter and I were never together. We were just friends because of my sister."

"Oh, I guess that makes sense. I always worried you two had been seeing each other on the side."

"No, Carter wasn't my type," Rachel replied with indifference at first, but quickly grew serious. "You should have been more afraid of my sister going after him. I'm so sorry you and Carter broke up."

"How do you know about that?" Amalia tried to determine how Rachel would have known if she'd escaped the campus prior to Amalia.

"My sister and Carter have been dating each other the last few months. I think she tried to get him to dump you a few times, even went to his room one day to tease him. She thinks he's going to propose to her this summer."

Amalia sighed, partially relieved, but also recognized it no longer had any reflection on her current situation or life. She was glad he moved on and didn't want to think about him being her baby's father. "I see. I just thought you'd been keeping a secret from me about him. He always acted nervous when I brought your name up."

"I think he was worried I might say something to you about him and my sister. They hooked up a few times, even while you two were dating. She went with him to Europe over the Christmas holiday. I probably should have warned you, but she's my sister and was helping me with the baby."

"I'd always known not to trust him, but my mother pressured me to keep him around. I miss how close we were during Thanksgiving break, Rachel."

"I was scared that weekend and needed a friend once I discovered I was pregnant. I'm grateful you were there. I should tell you the truth about the baby's father."

Amalia swallowed—ignoring the pit in her stomach—and responded. "I think I know who it is."

"The baby's father's name is Riley. He isn't a very nice guy and tried to push me to get an abortion. I led him to believe that I ended the pregnancy, but that's when I asked my sister to help me get away."

"I'm glad she helped you. I know how confused you were." Amalia's shoulders tensed at hearing Riley's name again. She prayed he wasn't her baby's father, too. "And I know how horrible he can be."

"I told my sister everything Riley had said and done to me. At first, he was kind, but then he just turned into a creep. The adoption was all her idea, she helped find the couple."

"I'm so sorry. I hope everything turns out okay."

"It did, thanks." Rachel hesitated before responding. "By the way, there's something I should have warned you about before I left. I was just too scared and rushing to escape."

"What is it?" Amalia's legs jiggled nervously at the kitchen table, prompting her to wish Bryan was home with her. She'd grown dependent on him the last few days and knew he'd keep her calm.

"You need to be careful at Woodland. Riley asked a lot of questions about you at the beginning of the semester. I thought he was just being friendly. He wanted to know about your class schedule and your relationship with Dr. West."

"Oh no, you told him about Jonah?"

"Yes, I'm so sorry. I needed to get away and offered him something in return. I let him read a few pages in your journal one day."

"What? You weren't supposed to tell anyone. It was a secret." Amalia's anger and frustration intensified at the thought of Rachel's betrayal. "How could you?"

"I'm a horrible friend. He threatened me after I got pregnant. I just started telling him things. I didn't realize how dangerous he could be, but then I tried to protect myself when he got obsessed with you. I thought it would give me an opportunity to get away, and he'd eventually leave you alone."

"Why didn't you tell me? We could have asked for help." Amalia wanted to scream at everything occurring around her that she'd never known about. She considered telling Rachel what happened with Riley, and about her own pregnancy, but she couldn't trust her former roommate and friend anymore.

"I know. I should have told you, especially after I realized Riley was Dr. West's son. I was a terrible friend. I... I should have." Rachel became silent.

"I trusted you. I never had a friend before, and then you came along. I thought something was wrong with me. That I was unlovable." Amalia began sobbing as she spoke. Her words were broken and nearly inaudible. "I knew... you had secrets... and Riley kept... stalking me. He's a monster." Amalia held back a need to vomit and screamed inside her head.

"I told him to leave you alone. He promised, once I lied and told him I had an abortion. I'm so sorry."

"This is all your fault. He never would have..." Amalia stopped herself and pounded on the wall beside her. "I don't know what to say... don't ever call me again. You're just as bad as he is." She hung up the phone, exasperated and unable to handle the truth about everyone who'd manipulated her in the past. Rachel was to blame for Riley attacking her in the basement. If she'd given her any hint about how dangerous Riley was, Amalia could have told Jonah or campus security—he wouldn't have raped her.

Amalia mindlessly tossed the scrap of paper into the fold of the address book on the table and rushed outside to let the cool breeze brush against her face. Rachel's mistakes had led to all of Amalia's problems. She screamed and kicked at a pile of dirt in the flower garden, falling to the ground in tears. It was as if everything had come flooding back at her during those few moments. She laid on the grass until the strength to move forward nudged her as quietly as possible to climb out of the depression.

When she ran back inside the house, Amalia swept all the items off the table with fury into the last remaining box yet to be packed. As she sealed it with tape, she told herself everything needed to stay in the past. She had to forget everything before her future life in New York City began. It was the only way to give her a last chance at successfully moving forward with Bryan. She couldn't let everyone who'd hurt her distract her from being happy again. Enough punishment had found its way to her life for unknown reasons, but it was finally time for her to escape and start fresh. She focused on packing, knowing it would only be another hour until Bryan returned.

Amalia was willing to part with most of the furniture in the house knowing none of it was in decent shape nor did it hold many good memories. The only memento compelling her to keep was the lace curtains once promised to her brother. She saved the journal her father had given her, and that was all she needed from him ever since Riley had stolen the locket from her. When he returned, Amalia and Bryan finished putting everything in order but also discussing how she needed to focus on her recovery. Later that evening, Bryan took her to dinner in one of the neighboring towns where they ate a wonderful meal under a beautiful old chandelier lit by candlelight.

"I don't know how to help you recover from being attacked, but you can't do it alone. You need to have support, someone to help you through the nightmares and the fear over what he did to you." Bryan wrapped his arm around her shoulder checking it was okay before doing so. "Tons of counselors work in New York City. Stuff like this happens way more than you think it does."

"I know, and I will. I'm hoping when I locate a clinic in New York, my doctor might help me find someone to talk to." Amalia no longer worried when Bryan touched her. He'd known to use caution, to check first, sometimes even wait until she reached for his arm or his hand first.

"I won't be there when you arrive in a couple of weeks, but you have the key to get in. New York City's gonna be much different than either Brant or Woodland. It's a fairly safe area, but it's quite crowded. They're trying to clear off the drug pushers from the streets." He scooped a few noodles onto his fork and took a bite.

"I'm not nervous. I'm looking forward to the change. To the real world. I'm tired of the blinders I've had on my whole life." Amalia chortled as he dropped sauce on his napkin, remembering their childhood dinners where she was always the silly one. "This could be exactly what needed to happen for me."

"I'll write to you while I'm away. I should have some downtime while I'm on the base. It can't all be work, right?"

"I certainly hope it won't be. You need a break. I'll write to you, too. Every week. I can tell you all about the baby's growth and my life getting familiar with New York City." Amalia took a drink from her water glass, swishing it around between her teeth. "I bet even the water tastes better there."

They laughed and finished eating their dinner. He ordered tiramisu for them to split as a dessert, then drove them home and tucked her into bed. She set up her brother's old bedroom as a place for Bryan to sleep for the night, telling him she'd set an alarm and wake him up in the morning to start his trip to New York and the Air Force base.

As she lay in bed that night, Amalia pulled out her journal to write another entry.

*Dear Diary,*

*It's been a while since I told you last time I was pregnant. I think it's a baby girl. At least I hope it is. I don't think I could raise a son on my own. I wouldn't know what to teach him about life. I know what it's like to have a parent not teach you the things you're supposed to know.*

*Bryan came home. He surprised me at Lake Newton a few days ago. I didn't realize how much I missed him until I turned around, and his handsome face stared back at me. He wants me to move to New York City with him. To sell the house in Brant and forget about this place.*

*Well, he didn't ask me to move in with him, just to stay in his apartment. Bryan's shipping off to an Air Force base somewhere else in the world. How exciting for him. I'm going to take care of his apartment while he's away. It works out for the both of us. I can figure out what to do next, and he has someone to keep everything safe.*

*He's been caring and helpful ever since returning to Brant. He'll be away for a few months, but he's promised to write to me every chance he gets. And when he returns, maybe he'll want to help me raise this baby. Bryan's already told me he wants to remain a part of my life.*

*When I think about all the things I loved about Daddy, and about Carter and Jonah, they all add up to Bryan. He's exactly what I needed, but I didn't know it all along. It's funny how life works. Dangles things in front of you, then takes them away just as quick. I would never have thought this is where I'd be when he and I met in town last year. Him shipping off. Me with a baby on the way.*

*I've decided not to figure out the identity of the baby's father. I don't want to revisit the past. Even Bryan thinks it should stay in the past. No good can come out of it. I don't want it to be Riley. Jonah won't be able to protect me if I try to find him again. Carter won't speak to me anymore, and he's moved on with Rachel's sister. I've done him wrong, just like he's done me wrong. He deserves happiness, but Carter's also partially to blame for being too pushy about sleeping with me in the first place.*

*I'm hoping New York City will give me a fresh approach to the future. I can put everything that happened at Woodland behind me. I know I must if I want to survive.*

*I'll write again soon. I need to get some sleep before Bryan leaves in the morning.*

*Love,*

*Amalia*

Amalia awoke the next morning to pots clanging and drawers slamming shut in the kitchen. She threw on a robe and trotted downstairs. Bryan flipped pancakes on the griddle while coffee percolated in the pot.

"It smells delicious." Amalia rubbed her eyes until they were fully awake enough to absorb her surroundings. "No one ever cooks for me. Well, once, but it wasn't very—"

Bryan lifted and kissed her hand. "You deserve a home cooked meal before I get on the road. It's my way of saying thank you for letting me stay here the last few days."

Amalia rolled her eyes. "You're thanking me? I should thank you for all you're doing for me."

He plated the food, and they ate breakfast together. When it came time to leave, Amalia followed him to the front porch and held the door while he carried out his bags. Bryan dropped them in the back seat of the rental car and ambled back up the path. "I'm all ready to go. You've got the key and the directions I gave you once you arrive in New York City?"

Amalia gave a thumbs-up gesture. "I'll be all right. I promise." She was comforted by the warmth he offered her when no one else could or even cared to try.

Bryan inched toward her until he stood by her side. "Is it okay if I give you a proper kiss goodbye, Amalia Graeme?"

She smiled. "Yes." Because it was okay. She wanted him to kiss her. Amalia wanted emotions inside her other than fear and emptiness.

When her lips met his, the innocence of their first conversation from the previous summer flooded her mind with the possibilities of a future where she might have a husband and a family to cherish.

Bryan pulled away. "I'll be home very soon. I left you a letter on the dresser to read. Wait 'til I'm gone, and you need to connect with me."

Amalia waved at him, her emotions brimming on the surface. She contained them, knowing it was the only fair thing to do. She wanted Bryan to depart, knowing she'd grown strong because of everything he'd done for her in three short days—things no one else had been able to do for her in years.

As soon as his car was far enough away, so all that remained was a faint bit of dust kicking up from the road, she wiped the tears away. It was time to move on. Amalia slipped a dress over her head, enjoying as it fit snugly against each of the new curves forming around her belly. She'd soon no longer be able to wear her current clothes, especially after putting on weight and passing the three-month mark in her pregnancy.

Gaining weight had been fine with her. Amalia didn't mind being able to eat as much as she wanted to without a care about her looks. She could always blame it on the baby and worry about losing the pounds later. It was time to sign the final papers to close the bank account and sale of the house. Once completed, it would leave her with a small amount of money to begin her new life in New York City.

Standing in the bedroom and staring at her reflection in the mirror, Amalia recalled the conversation with Bryan the day he'd found her at Lake Newton. Once he'd fully explained his idea, she was quick to accept the opportunity that'd been thrown in her lap. She'd wanted to leave Brant for as long as she remembered and was now confident something good had finally happened to her for the first time in her whole life.

Amalia left her bedroom and stepped down the staircase. Her fingers brushed the walls where a few pictures of her family once hung. She recollected all the times she'd run up and down the stairs, crashing into her father or brother, nearly knocking the frames off the walls.

How her father would comfort her from all the arguments with her mother. The stains on the wall from years of grit gawked back at her with jealousy that she'd found a way to leave.

When she reached the bottom of the stairs, Amalia looked across the living room at the spot on the floor where her mother had died from the heart attack. She'd never have to see it again. Everything that happened in the house had occurred for a reason. She may not have known, but it had all navigated her to this day. To her freedom.

Though saddened this path meant Amalia had lost her father, it was something she'd never had control over. The choices people made dictated whether they stayed or remained in every situation. Whether they could be happy or sad. Lived or died. In a different world, her parents had divorced, and she lived with her father in a better place. In a different world, Riley had never been born, and she had Jonah all to herself. In a different world, Carter never came to Brant with Greg but married some girl like Rachel's sister. In a different world, she and Bryan fell in love that first summer and left Brant to build their future together. The options were endless, but the visibility into such a world hadn't existed until now.

Amalia shuffled to the kitchen picturing all the meals she'd cooked—some good, some bad—depending on how much tension poisoned the air between her mother and her that day. Watching out the window at the netted hoop nailed to the garage wall, she recounted the days fighting over the basketball with her brother, never actually beating him at any games.

Everything in her past would remain at that house. Memories were sometimes meant to stay behind, to allow her to run toward a future that might finally allow her freedom from the world that kept her captive for so long. For such a young girl, she'd already been through too many tragic situations. It was her time to succeed, to win. It was her time to find happiness and climb from the hole that'd nearly swallowed her up.

Amalia walked into town, met the lawyer at the bank, and signed away all the history from her life. She accepted their check—enough money to take a few classes at a business school and buy all the things she needed for the baby. As the attorney drove her to the bus station a few town's away, Amalia closed the book on her life in Brant, confident she'd never need to return to the traumas of her childhood or the tragedies in Woodland. It was time to begin her new life in New York City and focus on raising a baby and building something with Bryan.

Amalia napped for the first part of the journey but was awoken when it stopped in Pittsburgh for the final passenger pick up. A few people shuffled into the seat across from her as she realized they weren't all that far from Woodland College. As she settled back into her seat on the bus, Amalia remembered the letter Bryan had told her he'd left behind. She searched through her bag until finding, unfolding, and flattening the paper out on her lap. When the bus pulled onto the highway for the beginning of her two-day journey, Amalia began to read.

*My dearest Amalia,*

*I never thought we'd meet again after you didn't show up at the magnolia tree. I always thought I'd done something wrong. But that wasn't the case. It was just a case of bad timing. I had too many questions in my mind about my future. Too many things I wanted to understand and experience.*

*Leaving Brant and going to New York City was the best decision I ever made. I remember giving you a tough time last year when you said all you wanted to do was leave our hometown. But you were right. It needed to happen.*

*Just like it needs to now happen for you. I'm glad we will have this distance between us while you get settled and I head off to my first real Air Force base. It's a chance for us to determine if we're strong enough to stay together while apart.*

*I suspect if we'd have gotten together last summer, you might have never left Brant. I would have stayed with you and run the hardware store with your father. We'd have a couple of kids and grow old together like our parents did. Never fully happy. Never knowing that wasn't the only way to live a life.*

*There's nothing wrong with it. But that's not who we are. We both have hopes and dreams to experience the world. We know bigger things exist out there for us besides what our little hometown offered.*

*I think we have a chance now. Unlike before. I'll miss you every day while I'm gone. I know you will miss me. Not a day will go by I don't wonder what kind of future we are going to have together.*

*Because that's what I want. A future together with you. If you're ready to have me, I want to help you raise this baby as my own. We can forget the past ever happened and build our own life together. Just you and me, and the little girl you're so certain is growing inside you.*

*I thought about something you said while I was home, how you wanted a new identity. A new name. Maybe you should stop going by your birth name, Amalia. I've always thought you looked like a Molly with those beautiful blonde curls around your face.*

*I can't wait to talk again. As soon as I arrive, I'll send you another letter with the address where you can reach me.*

*With all my love,*

*Bryan*

Amalia cradled the letter against her chest and breathed in deeply. The past disconnected from her in the way it was supposed to, but a voice across the aisle soon interrupted the transition.

"Are you okay, Miss?"

Amalia wiped her cheek with the sleeve of her blouse. "Yes, I am now."

"Good. We're on this bus for a long time, all the way to New York City. I don't want to worry about a pretty young girl crying the entire way through. I'm Dr. William Trudeau but call me Bill. This here's my wife, Maria. We're on our way back home after visiting family in the area. What's your name?"

A smile brightened across her face as she looked into his eyes, thinking he was a kind man. She then noticed his wife's round belly. "My name is Molly. It's a pleasure to meet you. You too, Maria. How far along, may I ask?"

Maria shifted on the seat and leaned against her husband. "Seven months. It's a girl. I can't wait. She's a kicker."

The glow on Molly's face shined brighter than a sunrise. "I'm three months along and moving to New York City. Have you chosen any baby names?"

"Congratulations. We live in New York, too. We're gonna call this little one, Shanelle."

"Oh, how sweet. Maybe our daughters will grow up and be friends someday."

# Chapter 32

# Brianna, September 2004

After Molly explained what'd happened with Rachel, Brianna theorized she might have another family member to connect with should Riley or Jonah be her father. The daughter Rachel gave up for adoption would be her half-sister or niece. The only potentially positive news to come out of the situation—someone who shared a connection that no one else in the world shared with her.

They spent the rest of the evening curled up on the sofa together, watching the movie *Gone with the Wind*. Molly had wanted to watch it ever since Jonah suggested the flick, but she couldn't stomach the idea of revisiting her past. She never got over losing Jonah, only packaged him in a box hidden deep within the recesses of her mind. When Brianna stumbled upon the movie through the cable movie listings, they both settled in for the night to live in someone else's world and give themselves a break while Shanelle completed the DNA testing with her father.

While dawn broke the next morning, Molly showered and dressed. A knock at the door startled Brianna, given how early it still was. She flipped on the living room lights and peered through the door's peephole. Carter stood outside in the same clothes she'd seen him in the prior day, just more haggard and disheveled.

She opened the door a few inches and peered outside. "I've been try-ing to reach you all night. Why didn't you pick up?" Brianna stepped back and ushered him into the cabin.

"I'm sorry. I had a lot to process. I freaked out about a few things." He entered the entryway, remarking at the lofty ceilings and huge second-story picture window. "That's beautiful. Great craftsmanship built into the stained glass and molding. I've always had a thing for architecture and design."

"It's gorgeous. You should view the landscape from the library win-dow in the back. It looks out over the entire valley." She smelled beer and tequila on his clothes and assumed he was still drunk. "Where have you been? Do you need coffee?"

"That'd be great, thanks." He fell into one of the kitchen chairs and slumped against the back as if it were his only comfort in life anymore. "I want to speak with your mother right now."

Brianna closed her eyes, unsure which was worse—knowing she may have slept with her own father, or that both she and her mother slept with the same man. Neither was something she thought long about, feeling grateful there wasn't any food in her stomach. It would have come barreling up at that point. "She's in the shower. You never told me why you didn't show up last night."

"I'm sorry about all this. I had no idea you were her daughter." His hands covered two days of stubble on a tired face. "I think that's maybe why I was attracted to you."

"I don't understand." Brianna handed him a cup of dark roast coffee. "There's no milk, sorry."

"Thanks. This is fine." He drank a large gulp before sharing the con-tents of his broken heart. "I never got over her. Even after I got married and divorced, I always came back to Amalia Graeme breaking me all those years ago."

"You loved her."

"Maybe I still do." He stared back at Brianna, his expression serving as the only remorse behind his words. His body shook with fury over what'd happened in the past, how cheating on her had partially caused their breakup.

"I can't talk about this. I just need to find out if you're my father. Then I can decide how far I am on the white trash scale." Brianna turned away, fumbling with the spoon on the countertop.

"We didn't know. You can't blame yourself." Carter shuffled toward Brianna, reaching his hands toward her shoulder.

When she turned around, she pushed his arm away. "Is that a fatherly hug you were about to give me? Or a reminder of that time we had sex the other day, Dad?"

"Stop it. We need to talk with Amalia. We don't know that you're my daughter."

"She prefers to be called Molly now." Brianna pushed by him down the stairs to fetch her mother. "Answer my question. Where were you last night?"

Carter leaned against the side wall between the kitchen and the hall, rubbing the bridge of his nose. "I told you I went to visit Riley, but the place was closed. I had a few too many drinks at a nearby bar, then tried to see him this morning." His sweaty forehead peeled from the cedar plank, and he glanced at her with slanted eyes ready to jump from their sockets. "What's with the inquisition?"

"You showed up here at the crack of dawn. Seriously?" Brianna grunted and cracked her knuckles in frustration. "Did he admit that he's a masochistic son-of-a-bitch who hurt my mother? Or are you gonna cover for him, too?"

Carter reached for her arm and held her back, his face twisted in anger and spewing words at her like an automatic rifle. "Listen to me for a minute. This is important. This was my life, too. You're not the only victim in all this. We've all been damaged as a result of poor decisions."

Brianna shook his hand from her arm, infuriated over his attitude. Only days ago, he was sexy. Now he just made her ill. "Stop playing games with me. It's like a sick round of Russian Roulette. Carter, Riley, or Jonah. Who got my mother pregnant? Let's spin the wheel to pick the most fucked-up disaster!"

Carter rubbed his temples with both hands. "She never slept with Jonah. You're confused." Carter paused as all color drained from his face. "Amalia just thought she'd fallen in love with him, but it was a mistake."

"Umm, wait. You didn't know they had sex?" Brianna turned back to try to make sense of Carter's words.

He slammed his fist against the wall. A rage built in Carter's eyes, and a grim expression formed on his lips. "I didn't. How could she do that to me?"

Brianna threw her hand in the air to stop Carter. "Stop! This isn't about you. It's about whether you, Riley, or Jonah is my father."

"Oh, that's right, you wouldn't know." Carter's head shook back and forth, and his voice hissed with contempt. "I probably should share some news with you."

Brianna pulled her hand away from the stair railing, wishing she could find her mother but knowing Carter must have something of value to add to their conversation. "Just tell me. Cut the drama."

"Jonah can't be your father."

"That makes little sense. They slept together." Every time she said the words, the disgust inside her intensified tenfold.

"Don't remind me! The shock at hearing you the first time is... well, it's just making me want to hurt her as much as she hurt me." Carter cursed and threw his keys across the room. "Jonah couldn't have any other children."

Brianna didn't know what to feel at that moment. She'd little energy left to handle any more devastating news. "Are you certain? How would you know?"

"He had a vasectomy. They're usually permanent, although sometimes it fails. It's highly unlikely."

"Why would he tell you about it?"

"Jonah overheard Riley and me bragging about sleeping with a bunch of girls that afternoon I went to his house. He told us to be careful and not to make any mistakes, that he'd already done something to prevent any future accidents."

"Are you serious?"

"We were a bunch of guys shooting the shit. This was before I knew Riley was that crazy." Carter cast his eyes downward toward the floor and tapped his shoe against the baseboard molding. "Riley was furious that his father might have been calling his birth a mistake, yelling at Jonah about not being around when he was a child. When Riley stormed out, Jonah mentioned he had a vasectomy several years after his son was born to prevent himself from having another child. Jonah never got over the guilt of abandoning Riley."

"That's ridiculous. So, Jonah can't be my father?" Brianna's heart and hopes spilled to the floor of the room in a way they might never be picked up again.

"Not if what he told me was true. And there was no reason to lie to me."

"I can't make assumptions. I need to know for certain." Brianna's face flushed upon realizing she'd made the entire situation even worse. "I'm sorry I told you she slept with Jonah. I thought you knew."

"Not until now." Carter paced the floor and cracked his knuckles in anger over Amalia's betrayal from years ago. As he was about to speak, a car pulled into the driveway.

Brianna pushed the news about Jonah out of her mind, left Carter in the house, and ran outside to greet Shanelle. "I'm so sorry. I've missed you so much. We have to fix us, but there's too much going on, and it's all out of my control right now."

"Sleeping with that bastard was within your control, Brianna." She pointed at Carter, who'd made his way to the front door.

He threw his hands up in the air with palpable force. "What's with the attitude toward me?"

Shanelle stomped up to Carter, her face an inch from his. "Listen to me carefully. You've messed with the wrong group of women, asshole. Stay away from Brianna. And Molly. And me." She punched his chest with enough force to drive his entire body into the doorframe.

He stepped backward into the cabin. "I'm not trying to start any-thing. Just figuring this all out. So, settle down, will you?"

Shanelle sneered. "I will if you do."

"Fine." Carter scowled, but before he could continue speaking, a voice behind interrupted them.

"Enough. This is my life you're all talking about. I'll be the one to decide how this goes forward." Molly released years of pent-up anger when she wandered into the hallway and raucous commotion. Her hair dripped on the floor. No makeup had been applied after her shower. "Do you understand?"

Everyone nodded. Brianna grabbed Shanelle's hand, needing com-fort as her mind absorbed everything coming together around them. "Tell me how this whole DNA testing stuff works."

Shanelle explained her father had connections from previously working at a Pittsburgh DNA testing facility before moving to New York. He'd called in a few favors and was able to get them to agree to rush the analysis if we got all the samples to the facility as soon as possible.

"Is that why you didn't pick up my calls?" Brianna had grown con-cerned at someone keeping another secret from her.

"I didn't want to lie to you, but I had only good intentions. It's wrong to hold information from someone you love, especially if we were talk-ing on the phone and had an opportunity to discuss it. I figured if I did everything myself behind the scenes, then we'd move this whole situation along more quickly."

Brianna knew that was Shanelle's way of chastising her for what'd happened with Carter. For sleeping with him and not discussing it beforehand.

"I don't understand." Molly's eyes opened wide with curiosity.

"DNA testing is done on someone's hair follicles to prove paternity. I took a few from Brianna's brush." Shanelle smiled while draping her hand around Brianna's waist.

"Don't you need samples from Riley, Jonah, and Carter to complete the testing?" Molly's hollow eyes had weakened into dark bags that swallowed her energy. She couldn't take the embarrassment of every-one knowing a secret she'd worked so hard to hide for almost twenty years.

"I took a sample of Riley's hair while he was sleeping yesterday. After you both left, I went back to the institution to check on him. He'd been knocked out from the sedative the nurse gave him and didn't even know I was there." Shanelle lifted her eyes to check if Brianna was pleased or upset at her actions.

"Was that you at the door in the stairwell yesterday? I thought someone was listening to me," replied Brianna.

"No, I went through the back way, so the nurse wouldn't stop me, or I didn't run into you again. I don't know who you saw."

"Don't you need a sample of my DNA, too?" Carter pulled his hands back and stuck both in his pockets while looking around the cabin, uncertain of what unfolded before him.

Shanelle shook her head. "I found a few on Brianna's pillow. You're the only one with straight blond hair. I'm certain they came from your head since no other man was ever in her bedroom until you showed up." She paused for a few seconds to let the extent of her words sink in. "I also had some of yours, Molly, from a jacket you'd left behind. I took it from your rental car while you were at the Woodland Institu-tion talking to Riley. By process of elimination, if neither Carter's nor Riley's match Brianna's, then Jonah must be her father."

"You really are like Hercule Poirot," announced Brianna to Shanelle before pushing Carter to explain what he knew about Jonah's vasec-tomy. When he said it out loud for the second time, Brianna truly un-derstood what his explanation meant regarding who her father might be. "Oh, God, no!" A rapist or sleeping with her father were the only two remaining options—both disgusting and vile.

"I know what you're thinking, honey. If it's not Jonah, then we will deal with the repercussions." Molly cradled her daughter, ignoring her own fears. "Shanelle, how long does it take to find out the results?"

"They usually need forty-eight to seventy-two hours to complete testing, but my father got them to make it their top priority." She checked her watch to verify the current time. "Based on how long they've had the samples, it should be ready in an hour. Even then, there's a slight chance it's inconclusive, but we can run more tests. Maybe this will make everyone a little calmer." Shanelle reached her hand toward Brianna, who'd started to quietly weep. "I just stopped by here first to tell you it would all be over soon. I wanted to give you some sort of giant leap forward to figure everything out."

"I don't know how to thank you." Brianna rested her head on Shanelle's shoulder. Her world stood still for the briefest of moments, allowing a small amount of relief to her pain.

"I'm going to wait in the main lobby. The DNA facility will send a messenger over there as soon as the results are ready." Shanelle stepped away and kissed Brianna's forehead. "We can talk about us after you get these answers. Do you want to wait with me?"

Brianna turned to her mother as more guilt crept inside her for leaving Molly alone. "I think I should wait here with my mom. We haven't finished talking."

Shanelle squeezed Brianna's shoulder. "I'll come back to the cabin as soon as I have the results in my hands." As she walked out the cabin's front door, Malachi jogged up the path carrying a large box.

"Everything okay here?" he asked. "I brought breakfast."

Molly introduced Carter and Malachi. "Could you guys wait in the upstairs library for a few minutes? I'd like to talk to my daughter alone downstairs."

Carter and Malachi shuffled toward the back of the house. "There's a magnificent view of the entire valley from up there. Let's go look."

Molly patted the cushion next to her on the sofa. "Come, sit. How are you feeling?"

Brianna pondered the question. No matter the answer, the results would bring some amount of destruction to their lives. Part of her wished she'd stopped the search when it first started getting so complicated, but now it was too late. "I've fallen down a well, and no one knows where it is."

"I should have found you sooner. I'm sorry this has happened."

Brianna knew she couldn't blame her mother, especially after learning the entire story from Molly and Carter. "I appreciate that, Mom. But now that we're at *this* place, we can never let it happen again."

"We won't. No more secrets. The past is about to come full circle, and you will know everything soon. Whatever happens, we'll address it together."

"I never asked you if you were okay. I mean, you just learned Jonah died. I watched it happen." Brianna shivered upon remembering she'd both caused and witnessed the accident.

"I thought I said goodbye long ago to Jonah. I'll have time to deal with my regrets when this is all over."

Brianna laid against her mother's arms, comforted by the reminders of her childhood before everything had gotten so complicated. She longed for the days when it was only about what cartoons to watch, making pancakes together on Sunday mornings, and racing to reach the mailbox first. Molly always let her daughter win. She'd learned the parenting trick from her father.

"It's getting a little chilly in here. Maybe we should start a fire while we wait," said Brianna.

"I'll get some wood from outside." Molly attempted to leave, but Brianna grabbed her mother's arm.

"No, you go talk with Carter. We've left him up there alone with Malachi for too long. I'll get the wood."

"Okay. Thank you, honey." Molly walked to the library to check on the two men.

Brianna pulled on a sweater, slipped into her shoes, and walked out the back door to collect firewood from behind the house. She jumped when the door banged shut behind her. Her nerves were on the edge of a full breakdown. She searched for a few dry pieces from the bottom of the pile under the covered awning.

After filling a basket, Brianna sat against a stone wall worrying over the results of the DNA test. She couldn't imagine having to live the rest of her life knowing she'd slept with Carter if he turned out to be her father. That kind of damage would be permanent, but if she'd been a product of a rape, there would be no reason to get to know Riley. Either way, there wouldn't be a chance for her father to walk her down the aisle or reminisce about what they'd missed over the years. She'd never want to see either of them again. Then Brianna realized she and her mom had slept with the same man, propelling her to kick the pile of logs to vent the pain.

After a few minutes, her fog lifted, and she rolled the wagon full of wood to the back door and pulled it inside. Brianna grabbed two logs and pounded up the first set of stairs to the main entrance. When she entered the hallway, a loud noise from the second story echoed inside the cabin. She rushed up the stairs and glimpsed someone being thrashed back and forth near the large picture window.

Brianna dropped the wood and ran up the stairs to the top landing. Carter, Malachi, and Molly stood on the far side of the room across from where Riley held a knife to Shanelle's throat.

"Tell me where to find my daughter, bitch," Riley screamed as sweat poured down his cheeks.

Brianna could only see a small part of what was going on. She inched her way to the library and focused on her mother.

Molly tried to calm Riley. "What are you talking about? Let her go, and we can talk about this."

Riley pushed the blade of the knife further into Shanelle's neck. A drop of blood seeped through her skin. "If you won't tell me where my daughter is, we'll all wait right here until someone finally confesses."

Malachi approached from the left side. "Riley, this isn't helping your cause. Put the knife down and let's talk calmly."

"Don't move another inch. I'll gut her," threatened Riley.

"Stop." Shanelle tried to release herself from his grip, but his hands were too strong and tight around her.

Riley's eyes grew wider. "She needs to pay for causing my accident. If I hadn't run into her that day on campus, my father would *not* have died. I wouldn't have ended up in the institution for months. I wouldn't be alone right now. If I have a daughter out there, I deserve to meet her."

Taking Malachi's lead, Carter tried to approach from the right side. "Let her go, Riley. Listen, man. I came by to talk to you earlier this morning, but you'd checked yourself out of the institution. What's going on?" When Carter approached too closely, Riley jabbed the knife in his direction, then toward Malachi to keep them both at bay. Both stepped back to join Molly.

Brianna listened in struggling to get in the room without being noticed. She signaled to catch Malachi's attention, but he didn't want Riley to know she was there until he produced a plan to get control of the situation.

"The nurse had given me some sedatives after Amalia visited yesterday afternoon. I laid in the bed pretending to swallow them and fall asleep. Once she left, I spit them out. Then my little friend here showed up and grabbed a strand of my hair. I knew something funny was going on ever since you all showed up on campus and then again in the institution."

"No, Riley. You're just confused. Let Shanelle go. She hasn't done anything," cried Molly.

"Yeah, right. After she left, I was pacing back and forth in my room thinking about how I could get out of that place. That's when I found something underneath my bed. It was some sort of diary."

Molly gasped upon discovering where she'd lost it. It'd fallen from her purse when she rushed out of the room to avoid being caught by the nurse. "No, you stole it from me."

"I didn't steal anything. Someone left it there, but imagine my surprise when I found it again after all this time. It was your diary, Amalia. I remember seeing it in your dorm room years ago. I flipped it open and read a few pages again." He snorted to prevent more snot from driveling out of his nose. "That's when I read about Rachel giving birth to my child and never telling me. She was supposed to end that pregnancy. Is that what's in the envelope? Answers about where my daughter is?"

Shanelle shook her head. "No. It's not what you think. Just let me go, and we can talk about it."

Riley traced the knife from the side of her neck up to her cheek. "Where are you hiding my daughter?"

Brianna realized that Riley thought the envelope contained information about Rachel's baby. He'd no idea that Shanelle had processed a DNA test to determine whether Brianna might be his daughter.

"Did you read the whole journal?" asked Molly while clinging to Malachi's arm.

Riley shook his head and gripped Shanelle tighter. "Nah. Just a few pages, and that's when I decided to get the truth directly from you."

"I don't understand. How did you find this place?" asked Carter.

"I thought about my options overnight, then I snuck downstairs this morning. I was just about to get in a taxi when you showed up. I watched you go inside, then come back out a few minutes later. I had the taxi follow you after you left the institution. I hid outside deciding what to do, and that's when she came walking back from the main lobby over to this cabin with an envelope in her hand." Riley had followed Shanelle up the stairs, finally catching her at the top before she entered the library. He pulled out a knife and grabbed her, thinking he could make a trade. Her safety for the information he wanted. He'd guided her to the back of the room near the picture window. "I just didn't know you were all here until now. Where is it?" Sweat poured down Riley's face and dripped onto Shanelle as he squeezed his arm around her and flicked the blade against her stomach. "Answer me."

Brianna knew she had only one chance to prevent a disaster. She stepped into the room and held onto the back of the sofa to balance herself. Her legs were too weak, and her mind was uncertain what to do. "Riley, stop! You're hurting her."

"Ah, the other little troublemaker appears!" said Riley with eyes bulging wildly.

Shanelle pulled her lip into her mouth before stomping on Riley's foot. The disruption caused Riley to loosen his grip, but not enough for her to separate from him.

As Brianna ran toward them, Riley whipped Shanelle back in his direction. "You can't keep any more secrets from me."

Molly and Carter stopped running when Riley feverishly thrashed the knife like a maniac. On his final jab, he sliced open Shanelle's forearm. She screamed out in pain and tried to cover the wound, but Riley wouldn't let her.

"Please don't," yelled Brianna as she rushed toward them.

"One more move, and she's dead." Riley pulled Shanelle backward. "Where are you hiding my daughter? She's all I have left now."

Brianna landed a few feet away, but not close enough to reach either of them. Shanelle shrieked and tried to dislodge Riley's grip on her, but they tripped over the ottoman. They both fell toward the large picture window and blasted into the panes of glass. The loud shattering of the entire structure startled everyone, and they screamed in panic as both Shanelle and Riley teetered on the edge.

Brianna crawled forward a few feet and tried to reach for Shanelle's ankle, but she wasn't close enough to catch her before she plunged to the ground. Though she'd missed grabbing hold of Shanelle, Brianna's hands snagged Riley's foot as he tumbled downward. When Riley dangled from the window ledge, his expression turned from a menacing simper to pure terror at the thought of plummeting several stories below. Brianna's grasp was the only thing keeping him from dropping out the window just as Shanelle did.

Malachi found his phone to call 911 in the commotion. Carter and Molly ran toward the window, shouting and trying to help Brianna hold Riley, but it was too late. His weight was too much for her to lift. Riley's dirty sneaker slipped from her newly open clench. Brianna shook with primal fear. Did she choose to let him fall or had the entire situation just been too much for her to handle? It'd all happened too fast. She listened as two voices screeched, then heard the thump of a body as it crashed into the wrought-iron spires surrounding the fire pit. Brianna couldn't bear to look out the window and took off running down the stairs and around the side of the cabin. Malachi, Carter, and Molly rushed in pursuit after her.

Brianna panicked upon stumbling on an unconscious Shanelle lying on a pile of burnt wood to the side of the fire pit. Blood dripped across her face, and her body trembled. The sheer speed at which she went through the window caused enough trajectory that she narrowly missed colliding with the wrought-iron spires, but Riley's slow and steady drop to the ground forced him directly in the object's path. Two thick rods protruded through his abdomen, surrounding him in a pool of blood. Blood that'd spurted from his body toward Shanelle's face, into the pile of wood, and across the ashes beneath them.

Riley moaned in agony, repeating, '*Where are you hiding my daughter?*' He extended a hand out to Brianna begging for someone to help. She stood there, empty and incapable of doing the right thing, paralyzed from moving in any direction. Shanelle laid on the ground to her left. Riley to the right.

Shanelle was her best friend. The girl she now knew she loved. The only person who sacrificed herself to help Brianna find her father.

Riley had raped her mother. He'd attacked Shanelle. He was a monster. But he might be her father. The father she'd wanted to meet ever since she was a little girl.

There'd always be two decisions haunting her, and she'd never known how to choose.

Brianna cried relentlessly, unable to grab hold of his hand. She rushed to Shanelle's side. The police soon arrived and immediately made sense of the situation. The ambulance attended to Riley, who was barely breathing by that point. He kept whispering, '*Where are you hiding my daughter?*' to an officer who appeared to be in charge.

Molly cradled Brianna as she broke down in tears at everything happening around her. There was a slow-motion tornado destroying everything in its path. Carter bent down on one knee nearby and scratched at something in the ashes. Brianna glanced over at him, uncertain what he'd found. As she was about to ask, the medical workers pushed her and Molly out of the way to get to Shanelle. Malachi helped the medic lift Shanelle onto a stretcher, taking extreme caution not to shift any part of her body.

Brianna tried to board the ambulance, but they wouldn't let her given she wasn't family. She tried to rush to Shanelle's car, but Detective Benton stopped her, insistent she give a full statement before leaving the scene of the crime. Brianna explained everything she knew, worrying the entire time about Shanelle's injuries. The police officer cared little about her concerns, only collecting as much information as he could for his report. He was persistent and asked her to repeat the story several times before Malachi stepped in to convince the police officer to permit Brianna to wait at the hospital until there was more news on Shanelle.

After taking their statements, one of the cops escorted Carter, Malachi, Molly, and Brianna to the hospital waiting room. Malachi used his clout and experience as a former police officer to provide Detective Benton with a full picture of what he'd witnessed. Carter and Brianna sat in the hospital waiting room with two officers standing by. No one was permitted to leave, given the detective hadn't been certain what transpired in the preceding hours. They would all remain under close supervision until Shanelle woke up and could tell her version of the story.

Molly called Shanelle's father to let him know his daughter had been hurt. Dr. Trudeau responded that he was leaving the DNA laboratory to visit his daughter. Molly hung up and approached Brianna. "How are you holding up, honey?"

Brianna couldn't focus at first. She worried about Shanelle being unconscious for far too long. She agonized over what'd happened to Riley, knowing he looked near death when she left the cabin. She still worried he had fallen because she didn't have the courage to save him. As Brianna's body trembled in shock, confusion set in over some missing information in her mother's story that didn't add up about her father. "There's still something I don't understand, Mom." Brianna wiped her face with her sleeve and blinked in desperation. "Why did you tell me my father was in the Air Force? And how did you end up in New York City? It's not making any sense."

"I suppose I need to tell you a bit about Bryan Porter."

Chapter 33

# Amalia, December 1985

Arriving in New York City as an eighteen-year-old on your own doesn't resemble a kid in a candy store for the first time. It's also not as scary as one might expect it to be, despite the overwhelming number of half-naked women parading up and down 42$^{nd}$ Street. People weren't unfriendly, but they didn't extend a welcome mat. Not that she expected one after all she'd been through in her life, nor based on what Bryan had told her when he'd given her survival pointers.

Getting from the Port Authority bus station to the Lower East Side was easy, at least once she'd found the signs for the exit onto 8$^{th}$ Avenue. Amalia waited on the corner, waving her hand while a middle-aged man in a suit stopped in front of her and caught a taxi. At first, she thought he was hailing the cab for her until realizing he had been much more selfish. He jumped in, pulled the door shut, and rolled down the window. "This is New York City. You gotta move faster than that, kiddo." At that moment, Amalia knew a thicker skin and tougher attitude was necessary to survive in a big city.

When she finally caught a cab, the speed at which it switched lanes made her dizzy and more nauseous. Afraid to ask him to pull over, Amalia held her breath and stomach, silently praying not to get sick before he'd brought her home. Home was New York City. It hadn't quite sunk in yet. Still frightened over the decision, she tore out of the cab, handed the driver a bunch of cash—an amount Bryan told her should be enough—and trudged up to the front of the building.

Amalia searched for the key and bounded the concrete stairs. The hallways were narrow, and there was barely enough room to drag the luggage behind her. She brought one up at a time, unsure whether it was safe to leave them in the small lobby. Once she made it to the first platform and caught her breath, a portly man yelled at her to move the luggage. Amalia rushed back down the stairs, apologizing for being in his way.

"Don't worry about it, sugar. Who you lookin' for?" His slicked-back hair and open-collared shirt didn't help her burgeoning desire to vomit. But that wouldn't have made for a good impression, as she'd known he was Bryan's uncle and the owner of the jazz club in the basement. Bryan's description was dead-on accurate.

"You must be Uncle Lenny. I'm Bryan's… friend. I'll be staying in 3A for a while. Call me, Molly." She extended a hand, hoping her gesture hadn't been too friendly. She was grateful for the well-lit entranceway and the double locks on the front door. It'd looked too sketchy outside.

"He said you were young, but I didn't expect a child. I ain't gonna be no babysitter." He faked a quick handshake, then palmed the side of his head to flatten out his hair. "You eighteen yet, sugar?"

Molly nodded and pulled her hand back. "Yes, I am. Bryan told me you'd be willing to help me get set up here. I just arrived from Brant."

"I grew up in one of them hokey towns, but it's been a while. Ain't never goin' back." He threw his arm toward the stair landing. "Go on, take your bag. I'll carry this one for you, just this once. Don't make it a habit of relying on Lenny too much now."

Molly had been more cautious around people after everything she'd been through at Woodland, but Lenny had a gentle approach to him, almost brotherly. "Thank you. I won't ask for much, just to figure out which way is north and which way is south." She grinned and stumbled up the steps.

"Well, here's your first tip, Molly." He paused at the landing and breathed in deeply. A small wheeze emanated from his throat as he patted his forehead dry with a dark-colored handkerchief. "Ain't no north and south in New York City. It's uptown and downtown. My nephew didn't teach you the basics. I'll have to put myself out more than I expected for you."

Molly fumbled for the right words. "Thank you. I don't mean to burden you."

A sly smirk formed on his face before he let out a boisterous guffaw that filled the small hallway. "Second tip. Lenny likes to tease pretty young girls. Don't worry about being a burden to me. Bryan Porter's good people. I'm glad to be of service. I'll tell ya when you're askin' too much."

Lenny showed Molly to Bryan's apartment and helped bring in the luggage. After a quick tour, he excused himself to open his place for the night's first music act. He'd rented out the first floor of the building for his jazz club while a small studio on the second floor right above Bryan's club served as his apartment.

After he left, Molly quickly absorbed her new surroundings. She found a concise list of instructions on the kitchen counter. Bryan had been thoughtful enough to give her the do's and don'ts in the building, which neighbors to ignore, and which ones to ask for help. Lenny and Mrs. Pollardo were on the top of the list. Mr. Pollardo was not on the good list. As the weeks went by, Molly and Lenny developed a solid friendship, and she'd come to treat him as the brother she'd lost when Greg died.

In the first month, Molly secured a job as a hostess at a restaurant a few blocks away. A small Italian place that hadn't needed anyone but thought a buxom girl in the front window would attract more customers. And it did until she'd showed from the pregnancy. Then they'd fired her since she couldn't dress the way they'd wanted without looking tragic.

Soon, Molly found a job doing inventory in a few small businesses around the neighborhood. It was long hours, but she had little to do other than explore the city and adjust to the changes in her life. Preparing for a baby was completely disconcerting for Molly, who'd never been close to her mother to know what it was supposed to be like.

Molly considered reaching out to the couple she'd met on the train but could never remember their names. She'd been too distracted by reading Bryan's letter at the time and only remembered their faces and how kind the man's eyes were. Molly couldn't ask anyone for help without feeling the need to do something in return, yet she'd nothing to offer. Lenny's sister, who had a couple of her own kids, lived a few blocks away and helped connect Molly with a doctor to help her prepare for the baby's arrival.

Bryan mailed her letters often asking for regular updates on the baby and her experiences in the city. Those were her favorite moments—reading his words and feeling the comfort of his voice whenever he'd squeezed in a quick call to check on her. Their relationship blossomed over the summer and early fall as they grew closer, despite being physically separated.

Each night, she'd open her window and listen to the jazz ensembles wander through the alley, the saxophone's notes hugging the building's bricks and curling all about the atmosphere in her apartment. It comforted her to have such beautiful music surrounding her baby as she grew inside her womb. When the cooler autumn weather arrived, Molly began knitting a few blankets and clothes for the baby. Lenny stopped by one night asking Molly if she'd received any recent messages from Bryan.

"No, I'm not sure what's going on. I usually have a letter from him every week. It's the third week in a row with nothing." Molly rubbed her growing belly as fatigue settled once she hit her seventh month. Sleeping had become impossible, and the stairs were more than she could handle. She only left the apartment to go to work and spent less time exploring all the city had to offer.

"He'll call. Sometimes they get sent off base for a while and get no chance to update their loved ones back home. Don't get yourself upset. Think of the little girl you need to protect inside you, sugar."

Molly had been grateful for Lenny's support, especially when three weeks turned into four weeks and then into six weeks. Molly grew worried, having no other way to contact Bryan. A few days after Molly's eighth month passed, her doctor ordered complete bed rest. Exhaustion and fear took over and distressed the baby. Molly didn't mind being stuck home at first, as she preferred hibernation in the comforts of her own apartment rather than dealing with people on the streets or at the office.

She'd been fixing some breakfast one morning when the buzzer rang, indicating someone was at the downstairs door. Molly pressed a button and answered the call. "Can I help you?"

"Yes. I'm looking for Amalia Graeme." An authoritative male voice blasted through the speaker.

"That's me. Who are you?" Her stomach fluttered.

"I'm Sergeant Connolly from the US Air Force. May I come upstairs?"

Molly stepped into the living room and peered out the window. She'd only two windows in the entire apartment—one in the kitchen overlooking the courtyard behind them and one out the front of the building where she glanced at who stood on the street. She confirmed it was a man dressed in a military uniform. Molly hadn't been familiar with any of the military branch clothing—Bryan never had a chance to wear his around her—and was uncertain about ranks. She buzzed him in.

Excited to receive something from Bryan, she unchained the lock on the door, her hand holding firm on her belly as if to comfort her baby upon learning good news about her father. Molly cracked open the door as the two men ambled up the stairs. "Do you have a message from Bryan?"

But they did *not* have a message from Bryan in any way she'd expected. Bryan had disappeared weeks before while on a short mission to track down a lead they'd gotten from one of the forces on the ground. He'd been a co-pilot in a plane that'd landed but never took off again. All indications up to that point were that he'd either been captured by enemy forces or had somehow gotten lost in the desert. Bryan had listed her as his first point of contact. Recently changed, Sergeant Connolly pointed out.

Molly's heart raced while they spoke to her, nervous over what it all meant. She held out hope for weeks from Thanksgiving until Christmas, assuring her unborn daughter that Bryan would come home to them, so they could be a family. Bryan's command officers promised to update her with any information as soon as they'd found him. She cried herself to sleep for the entire month of December, begging for positive news and offering anything she had left to see Bryan one more time.

On New Year's Eve, Molly went into labor. It was mid-afternoon when the contractions had begun sending shooting pains throughout her body—ones she welcomed with open arms as it meant she'd no longer be alone. Around eleven thirty, the nurses told her it wouldn't be long before she'd give birth. Molly pushed when the nurses told her to push and held back when they told her to breathe. She'd grown unaware of how much time passed, focusing only on doing what the hospital staff told her to do.

The nurses spoke to her shortly before midnight. "You might have the first baby of the New Year, Molly. Are you ready, sweetheart?"

Molly smiled, suddenly remembering the nights she'd watched the ball drop with her father when she'd been a child. Every year but the last one. "It's the perfect way to start out the new year." A few minutes later, Molly gave birth to a healthy infant girl shortly after midnight passed. The ball had dropped on the TV in the background while her new baby daughter screamed during her arrival into a world that wasn't ready for her.

The nurse congratulated Molly and quickly began cleaning up the baby. "Have you selected a name?"

Molly shook her head. "No, I'm waiting to tell someone special he's a new father and ask what he thinks we should call her."

* * *

Two days passed before Molly was ready to leave the hospital. The nurses began pressuring her to provide a name for the baby, so the paperwork was easier, but Molly refused. As she packed her bag that afternoon, someone knocked on the door.

Molly turned around, keeping her gown closed with one hand, so she wasn't flashing the entire hallway. When she glanced up, it was the Sergeant who'd visited her the prior month. "Is Bryan okay?"

Molly had already known from the hopeless desolation in the man's eyes. Though they were trained to deliver the news without emotion, the lost countenance in the sergeant's soul as he processed that she'd just given birth revealed his true sentiments.

Bryan hadn't been found, but the base where he'd been stationed received several reports they deemed conclusive of his death. Rebels on the ground had captured and executed Bryan, his clothes and identification found in a bag with enough convincing information it'd been accepted as proof.

The sergeant left Molly with a card and a request to follow up with them in a couple of days after she'd settled back at home. Once they exited, she slipped into the bed and crawled under the covers. When Molly called for the nurse, she asked that they bring her daughter to her.

As the nurse handed the baby to Molly, she gently brushed the warm skin on her daughter's forehead. "I have a name for my baby girl. I want to call her Brianna. Brianna Porter. She's named after her father, the man who was going to raise her with me. He's gone now, but I want to honor him and remember him always." Molly broke down in a puddle of tears upon realizing her life had taken yet another devastating turn for the worse.

* * *

When Molly arrived home the next evening, Lenny helped her settle into Bryan's apartment. She spent the first few days worrying about everything, unsure if she was ready to be a mother or even raise a child on her own. Giving the baby away was never an option, but Molly had also known she'd no one to help her. Each time she smelled the pure innocence of Brianna, Molly grew confident she could address anything thrown at her. She'd already handled more in her brief existence than most other people throughout an entire lifetime.

A few days later, Molly called Sergeant Connolly to understand what they needed from her regarding Bryan's death. Although it would take some time to process Bryan's last will and testament, he'd named her as his beneficiary. Over the coming days, Molly learned Bryan had left some money and his apartment to her, ensuring she would be properly taken care of should anything happen to him while he was on tour. It hadn't been a tremendous amount, and there was still a small mortgage on the apartment, but she'd have enough to get started on her own in New York City.

The sergeant also gave Molly a large duffel bag Bryan had left behind at his base. When he left, Molly cradled the bag and sobbed over what could have been with Bryan. Everything had been stolen from her in the last year. Bryan was supposed to be her baby's father, a chance to correct all the pain of the past. A new beginning with a wonderful man who might become her husband one day, a father to help raise her baby daughter, and a hope that everything she'd been through at Woodland was just to shape her into the powerful woman she would eventually become.

None of it would happen anymore. The grief over losing her father just over a year earlier had only been the beginning of a series of events that would forever cast her future in the wrong direction. While sitting in her bedroom, Molly took out her journal to write a new entry but couldn't find the words to express her anger. When there was a knock at the door, she tossed the journal on the bed near one of Brianna's hospital baby blankets, walked to the front hallway, and grunted in frustration. "What do you want?"

"Molly, honey, it's Lenny. Can I come in?"

"If you have to. What do you need?" Molly opened the door, shuffled back to the bedroom, and swatted her journal to the floor.

Lenny followed behind her. "I don't need anything. I'm just checking on you. Gonna miss that nephew of mine, but I'll always be glad he brought you to me." Lenny placed a hand on her shoulder, noticed the duffel on the floor, and picked up the journal. "What you got here?"

Molly tried to hold back the tears, but they fell from her eyes like a waterfall. "It's a journal I used to keep important things in, but I don't want it anymore. You can throw it out."

"Oh, sugar." Lenny reached over to hug her, but when the baby cried, she pulled away and rushed to the nursery. While waiting for her, Lenny flipped through the journal and recognized how important her words might be in the future. Though she was too far away, he said, "Nah. You're gonna want this again one day. Memories are too precious just to forget, sugar." He picked up Bryan's duffel and opened the large pouch on the far side near the bottom. He wrapped the journal in Brianna's baby blanket, placed it inside the bag, zipped the pocket, and put the duffel inside the back corner of the closet.

"I'll leave you alone for now, Molly. Don't forget, I'll always be around if you need me." He trudged down the hallway when she waved goodbye. As he let himself out, the door scraped against the floor and got stuck on a piece of raised floorboard. "Humph. I've gotta fix this someday, Molly. Need to make sure you can open the door when it needs to be opened, and you can keep the door closed when it needs to stay closed. You've got precious cargo on board now."

\* \* \*

As time passed, Molly enrolled in nighttime courses to get her accounting degree. She'd always been skilled at managing Graeme Hardware Store's books, working with the inventory accounting specialists at the various local businesses, and helping Lenny with paying bills at his jazz club. She also found a sitter who would babysit Brianna once she was old enough to be left in the sitter's care, so Molly could continue working and go to school at nights. Eventually, she became every other young single New York City mother fighting to survive and raise her family amidst all the worries of being able to pay the bills and keep your loved ones safe.

Molly slowly shed her former self, forgetting about her parents and choosing to be the type of mother she'd always wanted to have when she'd been growing up. Choosing not to remember her time at Woodland and letting go of both Carter and Jonah, as though they'd only crossed her life for a brief time to help push her toward the future she was destined to live out. Burying all that Riley had done to her, locking it away in a box that had no key, had been the hardest part. Molly covered it up with positive memories of her escape. She pretended it never happened, believing it was only a bad dream she could ignore. She told herself it helped strengthen her to become someone capable of facing the realities of a cruel world. But it would never go away in its entirety. Every time someone bumped into her on the street or pronounced words the way Riley did, flashes of the academic building's basement haunted her.

Molly spent time in the public library researching how to survive the trauma of rape and volunteered at shelters to help battered women. She stood outside the entrance to a room where there was a rape counseling session she'd learned about from a bulletin board in her doctor's office. But she couldn't let herself go inside. She'd told no one what happened to her in constant fear of reliving the nightmare again. And she assumed if she never spoke about it, perhaps one day she might get over the pain and terror still left behind.

In the beginning, curiosity over the identity of Brianna's father crossed her mind, but whenever it persisted too deeply Molly remembered Bryan was her baby's father. Or at least he should have been, and that's all she needed to know for the future. She closed the door on everything that'd happened to her before she moved to New York City, convincing herself that Brianna was the true start of her life. There'd been no Brant. Or Woodland. Or Graeme family. No Carter. No Rachel. No Jonah. Definitely no Riley. Or anything else except she'd loved a man named Bryan Porter who disappeared one day and left her a young pregnant girl learning to survive on her own.

Molly wanted to raise her daughter as a strong, independent, and intelligent woman who needed only herself to survive. As part of her life strategy, she focused on getting her college degree to replace the one she'd never received the first time around. Molly joined a nearby business as a lead accountant where she helped the company grow and prosper, making up for the Graeme family business that perished in the fire. She convinced herself there wasn't ever a need to have a man at her side, as everyone she'd loved once before was stolen from her. Molly wanted her daughter to grow up protected and nurtured as though children only ever needed their mothers to make the world a better place. Molly never had the mother she needed as a child, which meant she had to ensure Brianna always had a mother to shield her from the harsh realities of life.

# Chapter 34

# Brianna, September 2004

When Dr. Trudeau arrived, Detective Benton informed him what they'd learned thus far. He rushed into the room to meet with the surgeon, not even stopping to greet Molly or Brianna.

The detective approached Molly as she cradled Brianna. "Ma'am?" he whispered.

"Yes, is there any news on Riley?" she asked.

Benton nodded. "I'm afraid he didn't survive. The medics couldn't do anything to save him."

Molly closed her eyes, feeling torn between knowing Riley had been punished with the loss of his life for all that he'd done to her in the past, and that he might be the father her daughter searched for. She pulled Brianna close and hugged her. "It's okay. We'll get through this."

When the detective sauntered away, Carter handed Brianna an envelope. "This was on the ground near the fire pit. I took it before the ambulance showed up. I think it's the results Shanelle had in her hand when she and Riley fell out the window."

Brianna thanked him and tucked her hands into Molly's warm grip. "Are you ready to find out who my father is?"

Molly rubbed her hands together, clenched her fists, and closed her eyes. "I'm ready if you are."

Brianna tore open the envelope and handed the contents to her mother. "We'll do this together."

Molly scanned the paper and spoke with an air of timidity. "When they compared your hair with Carter's hair, it was not a match. There is no chance he is your father."

Brianna sighed with heavy relief from deep inside her body. "Are you sure? Please, please, tell me it can't be him."

Molly nodded. "Assuming that was his hair, he can't be your father based on what the results reported."

Brianna closed her eyes. "What else does it say?"

The room was quiet for a few more seconds. Molly continued reading. "When they compared the sample Shanelle took from Riley with your hair, it was a strong match."

"Does that mean what I think it means?" A glimmer of hope accompanied Brianna's voice that Jonah could still be her father despite what she'd learned, but soon receded once her mother's distraught expression formed.

"Yes. They matched my DNA with Riley's and yours, and it helped them come to a positive conclusion. Based on the samples provided, Riley is your biological father."

"Oh, Mom," cried Brianna.

Molly crossed to the far side of the room to hide the shock destabilizing her core. She focused on the moments spent lying on a basement floor where the innocence of life was stolen from her with no second thought. When she was conscious enough to know the terror of one human violating another human purely for the sake of experiencing a few minutes of sexual gratification. When she disappeared into a nightmarish world of chaos and disorder only for her body to be at the same moment preparing for the creation of a new human being born from a devil.

Brianna's eyes filled with burning tears upon remembering that her grandfather died in a car accident she sneaked away from. She could have shared a moment with him in person, if only she'd not been so afraid and selfish. And now, at the pinnacle of her entire search, all she had left was to imagine what it would've been like to be his granddaughter. Not only had Brianna lost the opportunity to know her father, but she would never understand the warm embrace or generosity of a grandfather who could make her feel like the most special little girl in the entire world.

Her throat itched and throbbed as a flood of sounds and images poured into her soul. From holding Tippy the cat in her arms as she died, to lashing out at her mother and calling her a whore. Brianna let herself drown in the misery for another minute, but then forced herself to accept that she'd made many foolish mistakes in her life, and it was time to move forward and be a better daughter and woman. "Are you okay, Mom? I'll do anything I can to help you."

Molly stared out the window, unable to respond. In the darkest hour of her life, when a small part of her wished Riley had killed her after raping her, she'd forced herself to dream of a different world that must have forgotten she existed. Molly wanted Jonah to be Brianna's father. And when that wasn't possible, she pleaded with whoever controlled her destiny for it to be Carter. But neither would come true. She would forever have to accept it was Riley who'd traumatized what should have been the happiest moment of her life—the moment Molly became a mother.

"Mom?" Brianna shouted through the stagnant air. "Just tell me what you need and it's yours. Anything. I want to protect you the way you've protected me my whole life."

Molly turned back toward the center of the room after boxing up the last painful moments with Riley. It was no longer about what'd happened to her. It was now only about how to help her daughter deal with the truth. "Has anything changed now that you know your father's name?"

Brianna breathed in heavily, then exhaled warm sticky air. "It's changed, but not how I expected. I thought I'd meet him. Talk to him. Have a family to embrace me. But I watched him die, and I couldn't reach out to him in those last few seconds. I couldn't be strong like you."

"It's not your fault he died." Molly squeezed her daughter's shoulder and breathed in. "I've had years to think about everything that's happened. You'll find closure in time, honey."

"It was never that you're not enough, Mom. I don't need anyone besides you or Shanelle. I just wanted to have a connection to where I came from to learn if there were others like me out there or to know that I belonged."

"We can try to reach Rachel. Maybe she can get you in contact with the couple who adopted her daughter. I know little about her anymore, but she might be willing to help after learning more about you."

"I don't need to know today. I just need to know I can decide in the future, that it's not a mystery or that you're not hiding it from me anymore." Brianna drew her mother in for a warm embrace. "That there's someone else out there in case I ever lost you."

"You will not lose me anytime soon, Brianna." Molly brushed her daughter's hair away from her face and leaned her forehead on her shoulder.

"I know that now." Brianna squinted between tears, as Carter walked into the room.

Molly replied, "You wait here for Dr. Trudeau to come out with news on Shanelle. I should tell Carter what we learned."

Brianna fidgeted with her hair, threw herself into the corner seat, and rubbed the palms of her hands across her thighs as a distraction while her mother shuffled toward the exit.

Molly motioned for Carter to follow her, and they stepped outside. "You're off the hook."

"What do you mean?" Carter asked.

"Riley is her father."

"I guess that's the better of the two outcomes given the choices." As his shoulders relaxed, relief flooded his body.

Molly acquiesced. "I suppose it is."

"I'm sorry I wasn't someone you could count on back then." Carter's response had a sincerity Molly hadn't ever noticed before.

"I'm sorry I hurt you when I slept with Jonah. You and I weren't meant to be together. You were just supposed to help me get out of Brant. I would never have had Brianna if I hadn't met you."

"I'm not sure I understand."

"If I hadn't met you, my mother would never have forced me to go back to Woodland after my father died. I fell for Jonah because I needed someone to replace my father. An older man who made me learn to trust myself, to gain confidence, and to be all the things I needed to grow up—a father figure. Riley only attacked me because he wanted to hurt Jonah, the man he deemed the center of all his problems. In the end, it all led to me having Brianna, even if it was a result of something vicious and traumatic."

"She's an amazing girl. I know I messed things up for her right now, but I promise to stay away. I understand what she has with Shanelle. I was only an intruder."

"Life just happens sometimes. You can't predict it. You don't know where it will drop you off unexpectedly. You only get to pick up the pieces when it's all said and done." Molly sighed as she locked eyes with Carter. "Brianna will figure this out. I learned how to take care of myself all those years ago. She will, too."

"Something tells me you might be right this time."

Molly exhaled anxious breaths. "Who knows, but right now my daughter's happiness is the only thing I can worry about. I need to check on her and Shanelle. You should probably leave now that we know the truth."

"I understand." Carter assented and began walking away. Before he turned the corner, he leaned back and tipped his head at Molly. "By the way, I found something that belongs to you. I slipped it into your pocket when no one was paying attention."

Molly smiled. "Let's stay in contact, Carter. I just need a little time to guide Brianna through all this shock."

She ended the conversation with him and reached a hand into her sweater, a red one that reminded her of the blouse she'd fought over with her mother as a young girl. Molly pulled out a small velvet bag, untied the string, and emptied the contents on her lap.

The locket Riley had stolen the night he attacked her had come home to her. She pulled it to her lips and kissed the pendant, then read the inscription from her father. She finally had a piece of her heart back now that she held the locket in her hands. To Molly, it was a sign that she could freely share her love with someone else again in the future. Her father was telling her to trust people again.

On her lap also lay a brief note from Carter.

> *I found this in a drawer when I went to Riley's room this morning. I thought you'd want to have it again. When I met you in Brant, we were immature kids who had much of our lives to live before we were ready to truly understand what the world had to offer. Maybe now we can try to build a friendship after losing all these years together. I'm willing to let go of the past and look toward the future. How about you?*
>
> *P.S. Happy Birthday. You're still as beautiful as ever.*

Molly gasped upon realizing he'd remembered it was her birthday. In all the commotion, she'd forgotten about it that morning, but it was now front and center in her mind as the day ended. After nearly twenty-years, Riley paid for his sins with his life. It was horrendous that his death meant Brianna wouldn't know her father, but it was better never to let that type of monster into their lives. Molly held the locket in her hands and recalled memories of her father, feeling grateful to finally have a piece of him back after two decades. She could finally let go of the past and move forward in her future.

Malachi walked into the room and gave a thumbs-up gesture. "I think everything will be okay. The Woodland Police Department believes all our statements now that Shanelle confirmed everything we said. All our stories were the same. I told them the envelope was about

James J. Cudney

Rachel's baby and that's why Riley kept asking about his daughter. I don't think they'll ask any further questions about Brianna."

Molly hugged Malachi. "Thank you for being here."

"You're welcome. So… about that date I keep mentioning… any chance you'll consider going out with me now that I'm no longer on the case?"

In one week, Molly went from being single and almost losing her daughter to Woodland College, only to have Carter reappear in her life, and Malachi fall into her lap. And now they both wanted to spend time with her. *Why are there always two choices?*

\* \* \*

Dr. Trudeau stepped into the waiting room after his visit with Shanelle and the police officer. He approached Brianna. "She wants to see you. You're welcome to talk with her for a few minutes, but not too long. My daughter has a few sprains and a possible concussion, but no internal injuries or permanent damage."

"Thank you, Dr. Trudeau. I'm so sorry about everything."

"Why are you sorry? You did nothing wrong."

"Shanelle tried to help me. Riley only attacked her because he thought she had information on his daughter. But it was about me…"

Dr. Trudeau interrupted Brianna when he leaned in to hug her. "My daughter loves you with all her heart. She always has. I wouldn't have expected her to do anything else but try to help you. I understand what it's like to be in love."

Brianna swept some stray hair away from her eyes. "I told my mother about Shanelle today, and that I want to be with her."

"I'm glad you finally figured it out. I know it's been hard for you."

"You knew?"

"Yes, honey. Shanelle and I are close. She never gave me any specifics, but I know how important you are to her."

"She is my everything. I just didn't know it. The stupid search for my father was always in the way. And now I'll never get to know him."

Brianna hung her head, uncertain what to do with the devastating loss other than trudge through the anger and pain.

"I read the results before sending them with the messenger to Shanelle. I wanted to verify everything was done properly. I know you're disappointed to learn that Riley is your father. Shanelle told me he wasn't an honorable man."

"No. I should never have searched for him."

"Life is complex, Brianna. It's not always black and white, good or bad. There's a lot of gray in between. Sometimes we have to suffer through something difficult to find that solitary ray of hope."

"I just wanted to know where I came from. I didn't want to hurt anyone else."

"You've suffered a lot more than most people your age. I may not know all the details, but I know your mom has been through the wringer, too. She's a good woman."

"I realize that now. I just wanted to have both a mother and a father. I guess we don't always get what we want, do we?"

"No, but that doesn't mean things have to be any different. I've known you for a few years now. You've been at my house tons of times. It's like you're part of my family. I'll be here for you whenever you need anything."

"Thank you, Dr. Trudeau. It means a lot. Hopefully, Shanelle will forgive me."

"Why don't you go check on her?"

Brianna hugged him and braced herself for seeing Shanelle. When Brianna left the room, Dr. Trudeau walked over to Molly and tapped her on the shoulder—she'd been facing the opposite direction.

"You must be Brianna's mother. I'm Shanelle's father. I can't believe we've never been properly introduced—"

"I know you," said Molly while turning around.

Dr. Trudeau angled his head in confusion. "I'm sorry. Have we met before?"

"On a bus heading from Pittsburgh to New York City about twenty years ago. I was pregnant with Brianna." Molly chuckled in disbelief, remembering that sometimes positive things from the past popped up again in the future. It wasn't always just the bad memories. "I could never recall your name that day we met. I was so upset. But I always remembered your kind eyes."

A huge grin formed on Dr. Trudeau's face. "I thought Brianna looked familiar, but I could never place it. Isn't that a funny twist of fate?"

Molly hugged him, contemplating the relationship between their two daughters. "Please tell me... how is Shanelle really doing?"

"Oh, I have a feeling she's gonna be..."

\* \* \*

Brianna entered the room and stood next to the bed, holding back her tears. She rubbed Shanelle's palm as her best friend's eyelids fluttered open. "It's always been you."

Shanelle's whispered in a groggy voice, "Are you saying what I think you're saying? Maybe it's just the drugs confusing me."

"I'm so sorry for everything. I wish I could turn back the clock." Brianna squeezed Shanelle's hand.

"It wasn't your fault. Did you get the DNA results?"

Brianna reflected on how her name had been chosen and what having a biological father meant regarding her identity. It wasn't always about DNA. Was Bryan supposed to be the father she never had a chance to know? Or had Lenny been occupying the role whenever he picked her up after she'd tripped on the sidewalk or he checked on her when she stayed home sick from school? Or would it be Dr. Trudeau caring for her in the future when Brianna finally allowed herself to be in a relationship with Shanelle? "Yes, the tests determined that Riley is my father."

"My dad told me Riley didn't survive the fall. I'm so sorry how this all came together."

"Thank you, but I've learned it's okay not to have a father. I might have a sister. I have my mom. I have you. I have your family. That's truly enough for me." Maybe each of the possible fathers filled a hole in

Brianna's heart at various periods throughout her life. Perhaps multiple representatives watched over her as pseudo father figures who could be everything Brianna needed them to be for just that specific moment in time. "I guess I just never recognized it until now."

"I think you took the long route to come to that realization."

"I wasted so much energy deciding how to choose who I loved when I knew the answers all along. In those moments when I thought I'd lost you, I heard only your voice inside me. That's when you'd left an indelible mark on my soul with the imprint of our shared future."

"It was rather clever of me to show you how to figure it out, wasn't it?"

"What do you mean?" Brianna smiled while trying to understand Shanelle's words.

"All I had to do was crash through a window to convince you of our love. Now, we just need to glue ourselves back together piece by piece."

Brianna rested her head against Shanelle's cheek. "True, but next time, maybe you should be less dramatic, and I should be more open-minded. I think we both learned a lesson here."

Shanelle nodded. "Yes, that's an excellent compromise. Besides, didn't I tell you in the car on our way to Woodland... *it's your time to take the lead!*"

"Yes, you did... now move over. I'm getting in bed with you."

"This isn't exactly what I had in mind when I talked about you *climbing into my bed* for the first time."

"I know, but I can at least show you a preview of things to come." Brianna pressed her lips against Shanelle's and kissed her with years of built-up passion that was ready to be released. That's when the earth finally moved for her for the first time. It was like an earthquake, complete with thunder, lightning and all the effects she'd been hoping for. "I love you, Shanelle Trudeau. You're gonna regret saying it's my time to be in charge!"

# About the Author

James is my given name, but most folks call me Jay. I live in New York City, grew up on Long Island, and graduated from Moravian College with a degree in English literature. I spent fifteen years building a technology career in the retail, sports, media, and entertainment industries. I enjoyed my job, but a passion for books and stories had been missing for far too long. I'm a voracious reader in my favorite genres (thriller, suspense, contemporary, mystery, and historical fiction), as books transport me to a different world where I can immerse myself in so many fantastic cultures and places. I'm an avid genealogist who hopes to visit all the German, Scottish, Irish, and British villages my ancestors emigrated from in the 18th and 19th centuries. I write a daily blog and publish book reviews on everything I read at ThisIsMyTruthNow via WordPress.

Writing has been a part of my life as much as my heart, my mind, and my body. I decided to pursue my passion by dusting off the creativity inside my head and drafting outlines for several novels. I quickly realized I was back in my element growing happier and more excited with life each day. When I completed the first book, *Watching Glass Shatter*, I knew I'd stumbled upon my passion again, suddenly dreaming up characters, plots, and settings all day long. I chose my second novel, *Father Figure*, through a poll on my blog where I let everyone vote for their favorite plot and character summaries. My goal in writing is to connect with readers who want to be part of great stories and who enjoy interacting with authors. To get a strong picture of who

I am, check out my author website or my blog where the 365 Daily Challenge reveals something about my personality every day. It's full of humor and eccentricity, sharing connections with everyone I follow—all in the hope of building a network of friends across the world.

### List of Books & Blog
Watching Glass Shatter (2017)
Father Figure (2018)

### Websites & Blog
Website: https://jamesjcudney.com/
Blog: https://thisismytruthnow.com/
Next Chapter author page:
https://www.nextchapter.pub/authors/james-j-cudney

### Social Media Links
Amazon:
https://www.amazon.com/James-J.-Cudney/e/B076B6PB3M
Twitter: https://twitter.com/jamescudney4
Facebook: https://www.facebook.com/JamesJCudneyIVAuthor/
Pinterest: https://www.pinterest.com/jamescudney4/
Instagram: https://www.instagram.com/jamescudney4/
Goodreads: https://www.goodreads.com/jamescudney4
LinkedIn: https://www.linkedin.com/in/jamescudney4

Dear reader,

Thank you for taking time to read *Father Figure*. Word of mouth is an author's best friend and much appreciated. If you enjoyed it, please consider supporting this author:

- Leave a book review on Amazon US, Amazon (also your own country if different), Goodreads, BookBub, and any other book site you use to help market and promote this book

- Tell your friends, family, and colleagues all about this author and his books

- Share brief posts on your social media platforms and tag (#FatherFigure) the book or author (#JamesJCudney) on Twitter, Facebook, Instagram, Pinterest, LinkedIn, WordPress, and YouTube

- Suggest the book for book clubs, to book stores, or to any libraries you know

Father Figure
ISBN: 978-4-86750-015-6

Published by
Next Chapter
1-60-20 Minami-Otsuka
170-0005 Toshima-Ku, Tokyo
+818035793528
3rd June 2021

Lightning Source UK Ltd.
Milton Keynes UK
UKHW011829170621
385713UK00001B/117